D0252729

Viper Wine

Viper Wine

a novel

HERMIONE EYRE

HOGARTH
LONDON/NEW YORK

This is a work of fiction. Names, characters, places, and incidents either are the product of the author's imagination or are used fictitiously. Any resemblance to actual persons, living or dead, events, or locales is entirely coincidental.

Published in the United States by Hogarth, an imprint of the Crown Publishing Group, a division of Random House LLC, a Penguin Random House Company, New York.
www.crownpublishing.com

HOGARTH is a trademark of the Random House Group Limited, and the H colophon is a trademark of Random House LLC.

Originally published in Great Britain by Jonathan Cape, a division of Random House Group Limited, London, in 2014.

Library of Congress Cataloging-in-Publication Data
Eyre, Hermione.
Viper Wine : a novel / Hermione Eyre. — First American edition.
pages cm
1. Stanley, Venetia, –1633—Fiction. 2. Digby, Kenelm, 1603–1665—Fiction.
3. Courts and courtiers—Fiction. 4. Beauty, Personal—History—Fiction.
5. Great Britain—History—Charles I, 1625–1649—Fiction. I. Title.
PR6105.Y725V57 2015
823'.92—dc23
2014023045

ISBN 978-0-553-41935-1
eISBN 978-0-553-41936-8

Printed in the United States of America

Book design by Ellen Cipriano
Jacket design by Elena Giavaldi
Jacket photography: National Trust Photo Library/Art Resource, NY

10 9 8 7 6 5 4 3 2 1

First American Edition

Dedicated to Anne Clements Eyre
and Alex Burghart
with love and thanks

CONTENTS

Viper Wine

Venetia, Lady Digby, on her Deathbed
by Anthony Van Dyck, 1633

Prologue

From letters written by Sir Kenelm Digby, May–June 1633

When she had been dead almost two days I caused her face and hands to be moulded by an excellent Master, and cast in metal. Only wanness had defloured the sprightliness of her beauty but no sinking or smelling or contortion or falling of the lips appeared in her face to the very last.

We found her almost cold and stiffe; yet the blood was not so settled but that our rubbing of her face brought a little seeming colour into her pale cheeks, which Sir Anthony Van Dyck hath expressed excellently well in his picture . . . A rose lying upon the heme of the sheet, whose leaves being pulled from the stalk in the full beauty of it, and seeming to wither apace even whiles you look upon it, is a fit emblem to expresse the state her body then was in.

[This painting] is the onely constant companion I now have . . . It standeth all day over against my chaire and table, where I sit writing or reading or thinking, God knoweth, little to the purpose; and att night when I goe into my chamber I sett it close to my bed's side and methinks I see her dead indeed; for that maketh painted colours look more pale and ghastly than they doe by daylight. I see her, and I talke to her, until I see it is but vain shadows.

Nothing can be imagined subtiler than her hair was. I have often had a handful of it in my hand and have scarce perceived I touched anything. It was many degrees softer than the softest that I ever saw.

Her hands were such a shape, colour and beauty as one would scarce believe they were natural, but made of wax and brought to pass with long and tedious corrections.

Many times she received very hard measure from others, as is often the fortune of those women who exceed others in beauty and goodness.

I have a corrosive masse of sorrow lying att my hart, which will not be worn away until it have worne me out.

I can have no intermission, but continually my fever rageth. Even whiles I am writing this to you, the minute is fled, is flown away, never to be caught again.

In a word, shee was my dearest and excellent wife that loved me incomparably.

White Noise

. . . slknxsnaosihnfbbfcalslnjzalkn . . .
Please tune your receiver to the required frequency
"smaismrmilmepoetaleumibunenvgttaviras"—Cryptic anagram sent on 30 July 1610 by Galileo Galilei to his patron Johann Kepler.
Tuning in progress
"altis simum planetam tergeminum observavi"—the same anagram rendered into Latin.
Tuning complete
"I have observed that the most distant of planets has a triple form"—Galileo's anagram announces his discovery of the rings of Saturn.

SIR KENELM DIGBY and his young son were standing on a hillock, gulping at the stars. It was June, and the heavens were royal blue, humming and hung with silver moonfruit. The son, who had been hastily wakened, wore a nightshirt, and half-laced boots; the father's doublet was loosened, as he had dined well. He was lately home from a sea voyage that had kept him away a year, and the boy fancied he still smelled salty.

"Which one do you want, darling?"

The boy pointed to a speck below Saturn, between the Perseids and the lower Cassiopeia constellation. Sir Kenelm hoisted little Kenelm onto his shoulders easily. "Well, you have chosen wisely. You have chosen a moon of Saturn, which hangs about the big planet like you hang about my neck." Sir Kenelm grasped his son's ankles, making him squirm with pleasure. "Your planet is covered in a frozen crust, like the River Thames in winter, except it is mint-green coloured and striped with orange, like a tiger."

"Roaaaaar like an Araby tiger."

"Indeed. Under the ice on your planet, there is a sea which bursts up through the ice into great plumes, like the grandest fountains you see in palaces. The moon stays close to its father Saturn with a girdle of light and dust which keeps them in each other's thoughts. This moon is much smaller than Saturn; it is the same size as England, and would take only five days to ride across. It is a pleasant little planet, although a trifle cold, and I think you would not like it as much as you like your own bed." Sir Kenelm was stomping over the grass tussocks now, back to Gayhurst House.

"How old is my planet?" asked the boy, who was at that point in life when the concept of age is new and compelling. Sir Kenelm knew the earth to be about four thousand years old: he had found fish bones in the English hills, deposited there by the Flood. But this moon of Saturn?

"Oh, it is a young planet," said Sir Kenelm. "Of about one thousand years."

Sir Kenelm did not know that everything he had just said was true. Or at least, that it would be said again four hundred years later, when images and data from the Cassini monitor arrived on earth. Sometimes his mind was double-hinged, and could go forwards as well as back. He was often like a string that vibrated with strange frequencies, but most of the time he was the most obstinate fool imaginable.

He could not even remember if, thirty years ago, his father had also waked him and walked him out to look at the stars. His mother once said something of the sort. Kenelm tiptoed noisily past the sleeping nursemaid into the boys' room, which smelled of cloves and sweet vomit, and as he tucked young Kenelm in his cot, he seemed to remember being tucked in himself, like an obverse image, and a distant bell rang in his mind, which sounded like a revelation, until he realised it was the church bell up the lane at Olney marking the hour. Had he been taken out in his bedclothes to wish upon a falling star? It seemed unlikely, but it was hard to remember events before his father's Great Undoing.

Venetia's door was unlocked. Her candle had burned out and Sir Kenelm unlaced himself in the dark, with practised hand. He touched the fragment of the wand of Trismegistus which he wore round his neck as a talisman, said his alchemist's Amen three times, and slipped into bed next to Venetia, fitting his chest to the warmth of her back, breathing the stale perfume of her hair. He loved her so deeply when she was sleeping. Venetia, asleep, was Perfection. Awake she was Problematical. Since he came home Venetia had become more . . . anxious. More challenging. More troubled. These and other tactful verbal constructions, euphemisms and put-downs for women from the future crackled like static through Sir Kenelm's sleeping mind as it drifted up, up into the darkness above their curtained bed, up, above the brick gables of Gayhurst, up, above the darkened, gaping fields of Buckinghamshire and the badly drawn outline of the British coast, until he could go no further and simply bobbed, like a tethered balloon, while satellites in orbit sallied gently past his ears.

A Discourse Between Brothers

August 1632

SUNTANNED AND ALIEN, Sir Kenelm stood in the middle of the bright green grass at Gayhurst, directing five farmhands who were carrying a vast column, obelisk-shaped, and bound in old tarpaulin and ropes. "Avast! Heave-ho, ho, ho!" cried Kenelm, who kept forgetting he was no longer captain of two ships. Pope Sixtus V had once held a competition for the best device to winch obelisks into the streets of Rome; now Gayhurst would have its monument also. As the men heaved, the shrouded obelisk rose slowly, tilting like a giant peg.

Kenelm stepped into the house, where his brother was in the main hall, beside a stone sarcophagus, a primitive wooden faun, a crouching woman sculpted out of white marble with one buttock missing, a thick roll of tapestries, an immense shield furred with rust, a bundle of new French cutlasses, sticky-black in parts, seven superhuman-sized caryatids and a gleaming cardinal's sedan.

"Is this all?" said John, looking about him.

"Well," said Kenelm, trying not to rise to his brother, "there is also the matter of fifteen thousand pieces of silver, which I share with the Crown. And a little painted French harpsichord that I have already sent to the Queen."

"I like this one," said John, inspecting the crouching Venus.

"Oh, but you should have seen what we had to leave behind. The isles of the Cyclades are so full of statuary, John, it is as if a busy London street had been put under an enchantment, and everybody turned to stone."

But John was more interested in the French cutlasses, striking fencing poses with them, just to feel their weight.

"I also collected books, when I found them. There are some choice volumes in my study."

"Ah yes. Books. Most pirates go looking for books," said John.

Kenelm suggested that since it was fine, they should set out for their special place, the Old Dam bank, site of their fraternal games, where they used to build forts, and play swing-bobbin, and, later, where they went to loiter and smoke. On their way across the garden they saw the obelisk, now in an upright position, unwinding from its tarpaulin. A metalwork construction, pyramid-shaped, it bristled with small trapezoidal spurs, sticking out at angles. It was a beautifully constructed radio mast.

"I picked that up from a French fleet," said Kenelm. "They removed it from one of the isles."

"Which one?"

"I would have asked them, but I was busy avoiding being killed by their cannon. I believe it may have come from the sacred island of Delos, where no one is ever buried or born. I fancy it is some oracular rod, some instrument of divination."

Its metal filaments hummed with a breath of Buckinghamshire air.

"Did any take you for a pirate?"

"Plenty, until our letter of marque was in tatters through showing."

"Who fights better, the Frenchman or the Spaniard?"

"There's two reasons why the French are ill-served by their system of command. First, there are too many serving midships . . ."

They continued to talk in this fashion, as brothers do, while they walked through the orchard, which was glowing green and leaf-lit. Both bent under the boughs, being tall and well-made, and John broader than Kenelm, although he was younger. Fruit was already putting forth quicker than it could be collected, and apples and pears lay spoiling. In ten years' time, Gayhurst would be shut up because of the Civil War, and the orchard would again be full of rotting fruit, until locals loosed their pigs there, but this was the long peaceful summer of 1632, and the ripeness and bounty of fruit everywhere had led to indolence and decay. A high whiff of cider hung in the air. Sir Kenelm saw a perfect, smooth russet apple resting on the grass and bent to pick it up. A wasp flew out from its mushy underside.

"My wife is growing jealous of her face," said Kenelm. "She guards herself from view. She preserves the use of her face for great occasions only, and keeps it out of vulgar sight, by means of games light and dark and candlelight and veils and whatnot. She keeps her curtains fast in daylight. She flinches from my sight."

"It pains you."

"Yes, John, I think it does," said Kenelm, relieved to be speaking about this difficult subject. "I had intended to remove us all to London after two or three days, so I could take advantage of men's interest in my exploits, but she has it in her head that we must stay here yet another week. I begin to think she dreads going to town, John—being seen in company. It is the work of this new Italian mirror that she uses. It is backed with mercury, you know. Her crystal glass did no harm at all. Now she goes out hooded on the most innocuous errands. When she took the boys to see the shearing at Stoke Goldington, when she tended her little garden yesterday. Why? Perhaps she thought the ploughman would drop his bridle, or Joe the farmhand gape in wonder at her ruined cheek? I do not mean to be unkind, John, but I do not like this Sphinxy business of concealment. I love to look upon her, and I think that she should love to be looked upon by me."

"She is how old?"

"Five years senior to me. That age when a woman is neither young nor old: thirty-three. Forget I told you that—her age. She always has me say she was born in 1600, so she passes for thirty-one."

"But she's thirty-three. That's some way from the grave."

"Painting with lead does much injury. I think she fears her next climacteric."

"Her what?"

"That age which is by seven divisible, John. You know how it goes. Every seven years we are made again. A woman at her mid-climacteric is at a turning point. Remember Queen Elizabeth's Grand Climacteric at sixty-three? Our mother spoke of it. Such a dangerous age, it was thought to be, that there were celebrations when the Queen lived."

"Our mother had a new dress . . ."

"Aye, which she never wore again."

John split a cobnut between his teeth. Their mother wore no more gay dresses after their father was Undone. Kenelm remembered seeing all the servants leaving in a procession down the drive at Gayhurst, their belongings strung over their shoulders, and he thought at least Bessy or Nurse Nell might turn and wave to him or to the house, just to bid farewell, but none did.

Gayhurst House

After their father was executed their mother wore her stiff ruff and the same mourning clothes till the black washed out of the linen, and they lived quietly at Gayhurst behind thick fortified walls and scanty windows, scraping porridge from their old rough bowls, keeping the same Tudor household habits, labouring under their Catholic shame, and the new iniquity that attached to their name.

At Kenelm's majority everything changed. He came back from his travels and showed them how to become Stuarts, with fashionably floppy clothes and continental *politesse*, and he used all his money on getting his knighthood, and knocked dozens of windows into the house, making it his own. And he chose a wife whom everyone counselled against. John wondered if he would have had the courage to do any of that, but decided he would not have wanted to.

"So," said Kenelm, "Venetia fears to reach her mid-climacteric. Of course her mother, dying early, never reached that age."

"She never knew her mother . . ."

"No, and therefore she has no example of how to do it. How to age. It is proving a trouble to her, I fear, John."

"Venetia is still beautiful."

"Those very words do pain her. When I tell them to her, she turns and shrinks away. It is the 'still' she cannot stand."

"She is so vain?"

"She is a woman. No, come, it is the way the world has made her, John. She was 'a beauty,' it was her very essence and her designation."

"Now she is 'a mother.'"

"Aye, and a good one, but many women are mothers and only a few are beauties. It is a strange and cruel punishment, John, to be stripped of a title for no reason other than the movement of time. Imagine if you declined from 'poet' to 'former poet' within a few brief years. Or if you were 'scholar' then 'still very scholarly' then 'once a scholar.'"

"Scholar, poet, these are titles earned, not born . . ."

But Kenelm was in his stride. "Consider how her mother died when she was a few months old, and how she never found another mother but was passed around like a poppet, and stroked, and made much of, especially by great men. That she never turned into a lisping, painted chit is only because she has a character of great depth; indeed, her immortal soul is as profound as a man's, I do believe."

"Why then will she not make peace with this? With her decaying beauty? She is a part of nature as much as you or I or this tree. She cannot step aside from time and nature. Nor more than you can, Ken."

Sir Kenelm sighed. "That argument if rehearsed enough would have kept us from inventing paper, and wheels, and cannon, and wearing clothes . . . You would say to the man Leonardo, on the brink of creating a practicable flying machine: 'Oh stop, sir, you cannot step aside from nature.' We meddle with nature all the time, John, in the breeding of hounds, in the cultivation of potatoes in our English soil. In the creation of this orchard, even. As I am a production of the Almighty Architect, then is not everything I do with a pure heart also a production of His?"

Sir Kenelm liked saying this. It excused his presumptions: his alchemy, his experiments in natural magick, his manipulation of the rays of the sun and moon. He believed himself to be within the Catholic definition of Natural Law in so much as he worked, always, to advance the greater good. If he could find the Philosopher's Stone, he would share it, spread its wonders wide and bring about a Universal Cure. He searched his heart regularly, held it up to the light, and tried his conscience—but still he felt the sting of vulgar eyes. He knew that he and his wife were seen as brash, a dubious spectacle. But he did not wish to stand in line with other men just for the sake of it. If he could raise the white sulphur into exaltation, he would do it; if he could hasten the Age of Gold, he would.

"My wife and I," said Kenelm slowly, pausing before they strolled through the orchard, towards the house, "are both spoiled goods. We are bright, fine-worked pots, but crack'd inside and fixed with clay."

Venetia stayed late abed that morning.

This was uncharacteristic, but she found she could not rise.

Perhaps she was still angry about the spoiling of the apples. Mistress Elizabeth had not directed the farmhands to it and three barrels at least had been left to mulch. She shouted at her, and then she went to her room and cried. For what? For mouldered apples?

Yesterday she was in her knot garden at the front of the house, clipping the box-hedges using her dainty silver shears—play-gardening, as Kenelm called it—when a youth in the livery of the Earl of Dorset arrived. She put down her basket and smiled her famous smile at the livery boy, the smile Ben Jonson had written a sonnet about, and Peter Oliver painted; the smile that was so much in demand that a royal writ was put out to send any unlicensed copyist to prison, and still copies came. She stood there, her hip askew, so confident, the breeze in her flowing hair, her loose country dress full and soft. "Madam," said the boy, bowing like a silly sapling, then looking her full in the face. "Could you tell me where to find her most gracious beauty Venetia, Lady Digby?"

He was holding a tall fair lily—a gallant reference, she supposed, to the single fleur-de-lis on Kenelm's coat of arms—and aflame with nerves and excitement, he glanced back and forth at the house, as if he thought the great dame herself might at any moment appear in a cloud of golden light.

Venetia laughed it off and said, "Why, that lady is before you." And as the youth looked at her with disbelief, and as his face turned from disappointment to, yes, repulsion, she remembered, as she had to keep remembering, that she was no longer herself. Her teeth were going, though they were always so good, and she had not yet learned to smile without showing them. She saw, in the mirror of his face, as the young boy's pupils shrank, how much she had changed. And still he did not present her with the lily. Did he think she was a presuming and ironical chambermaid, testing him?

Edward Sackville must have talked up her beauty to his livery boy. It was his way. Since he became an earl his talk carried more weight. The boy had been expecting a treat: to see the woman with the smallest waist in London. Once that had been almost true. Now . . . "Have you no mouth to keep your tongue in, or do you stand there like a dimmock?" she snapped. As she heard herself speak, she felt ashamed. This is what it is, she realised, to become bitter, to spit out rude gall because your bones are turned to brittleness. She turned and took off her embroidered gardening gloves, while her rage subdued, and then she reached out and took the boy's hand, as if it belonged to her.

"Forgive me," she said, leading him inside the house to her drawing room, intending, by allowing him into her feminine bower, and by spending a short time asking him questions about his life and opinions, to make him adore her for ever. But after their spiced cup arrived, and she had poured it, she went upstairs to fetch her fan, and while she was looking for the fan, she found an old keepsake from Sir Kenelm, and soon she became unaccountably sleepy. It was already dark when she awoke, remembering the boy downstairs, who had vanished, leaving that long, drooping lily beside her cold cup of spiced wine.

Venetia was surprised at herself. She knew she was voluble and impatient, and many men found her too bold—except Sir Kenelm, who loved her strength—but she was not usually careless enough to abandon a young boy so thoughtlessly. But sometimes carelessness is a way of getting out of what we cannot do. She had always thrived on company. Now she was beginning to conceive a dread of daylight.

No wonder she went out veiled these days. It was a necessary precaution. She wiggled her toes in the cambric bed-sheet, to check she was still alive. "The rising sun / Which once I saw / Is now high in the heaven." She often made up madrigals about nothing at all, just to make her thoughts musical. She really ought to rise. Chater must have led matins without her. She would tell him she had been at private prayer.

What was it Dr. Donne preached, which had so affected her? They went to so many funerals she could not remember whose it was where Donne had looked so thin and shrunken standing in the pulpit, his voice so slow that as he began a new sentence, one feared he might not live to finish it. And yet the light and dark began to mingle in his speaking, and promise answered question, so that questions died away, and on the flow of his speech he carried them, speaking so kindly, so privately to the very heart of each of them, until all were moved to glad wet tears, and the inverse of the doctor's face, black-skulled, with bone-white burning holes for eyes, remained imprinted on her mind's eye even now.

Her pillow book was buried in the covers beside her, and she turned to the page where she had copied down that delicious passage: "That which we call life is but Hebdomada Mortium, a week of death, seven days, seven periods of our life spent in dying, dying seven times over. Our birth dies in infancy, and our infancy dies in youth, and so forth, until age dies and determines all."

Ripeness, she thought, is but the first sign of rot; there is no rest to be had anywhere on this planet. Since it turns, and turns, how can we ever be still? Sir Kenelm had the blame for that. He was the first to tell her that the earth was a hazelnut tossed in the air.

She could feel a new coarsening in her hair, which Kenelm had always stroked and made her laugh by telling her that the Greeks said a soft-haired creature was a soft-hearted one. Throwing back her blankets, like pulling off a plaister, Venetia considered her famous feet, once described by one of James I's Scots poets as "wingèd dreams, each toe a wish," splayed out fat and graceless on the counterpane. In private she sometimes made horrid faces in the glass, and wobbled her puckered thighs, deliberately tormenting herself. This morning she could not be bothered even to do that.

Ageing is imperceptible. It happens as gradually as a stone staircase wears, or a fan kept in sunlight fades. But to Venetia it had happened slowly and then suddenly, like a huge stock of water drains for a long time, hardly depleted, till the last swills vanish quickly.

I can bear it, she thought, because my husband bears it. He sees beyond the skin. He has deeper vision than most men. Why else would he love me, spoiled as I am? Each day we remain here together, before we go to town, we become more like a family, and he and I grow close again. We kiss each other every night; we wake together every morning. To my love, my husband, I am like a tree he sits beneath; he does not perceive my leaves a-turning.

Every day, the lowing cows in the valley told her it was almost noon, and every day their lowing seemed to come round faster. She rang for Mistress Elizabeth, and set about the business of dressing, unfastening and fastening, and refreshing her curls, thinking of her boys and her husband and preparing her face for the day's duties of smiling, as Elizabeth tied her stays and fixed her overskirts, and once apparelled in all the fine and starchy fabrics of her station, Venetia felt more like herself. But as the cows bellowed across the far fields, she caught a view of herself in the glass, and screamed a silent scream.

> "That incomparable Sir Kenelm Digbie's name does sufficiently Auspicate the work. There needs no Rhetoricating Floscules to set it off."
>
> George Hartman's Preface to *The Closet of Sir Kenelm Digby Open'd*, 1669

Pop! went a woodlouse on the fire.

Scrunch, escrunch, replied Sir Kenelm's comfortable nib. He was writing up his private notes from the last meeting of his clandestine university, the Invisible College.

Ten Solutions for the Condition of Man, he wrote, *as identified, proposed and debated by select fellowes of the Invisible College at their meeting last in ____shire.*

1. *The Transmutation of Base Metals into Gold.*

To this entry he added underneath, with a loose calligraphic flourish:

—*Already almost perfectly achieved.*

A log on the fire collapsed with a sigh.

2. *Perpetuall Fire.*

Kenelm checked his notes, crossed out "*Fire*" and wrote "*Light.*"

A wasp on the window sill rubbed its forefeet together with an infinitely small squelching noise.

3. *The Emulation of Fish—the art of continuing long underwater and exercising functions freely thereof, without Engines, by Custome and Education only.*

4. *Flight—the Emulation of Birds. Note that King Bladud, magus, flew unaided at Bath. His skill—quaere.*

He could half-hear snatches of Mistress Elizabeth and Alice outside, chattering ". . . lost her bloom." "What bloom?" "Blooming long ago." He rose and pulled the bottle-glass casement shut.

5. *The Cure of Wounds at a Distance—by means of the Powder of Sympathy viz. Kenelme Digby's private receipt.*

The laden bough of a pear tree sagged a fraction lower in the orchard. Sir Kenelm's sleeve brushed rhythmically across the paper; he drew the title with a dragging curlicue. This was his special topic: his legacy. He believed he had the means to cure wounds from a distance, without even meeting the patient. His method was to treat the weapon, not the wound. A bullet, knife, musket, or any vicious instrument could be conveyed to him, and he would treat it with his most precious Powder of Sympathy. The patient writhed and the wound burned as the Powder was rubbed across the blade or bandage; then, if the wound was left open, cleaned but unbandaged, it received the healing Atomes through the air.

"Pray do not think me peradventure Ineffectual or Superstitious . . ."

Digby always introduced his Powder carefully, because so many men suspected him of sorcery. It was a powerful cure, and Digby felt the burden of being its first practitioner in England. To pass his knowledge on, he entrusted the Invisible College with (almost) all his arcane and valuable material pertaining to the cure, which he delivered as a lecture concisely in two hours, before the Botanists completely stole the show with their diagrammatic explications and so forth. His signet ring clinked against the inkwell as he made notes of the Botanists' suggestions:

6. *The Acceleration of production of Vegetables from Seed.*

7. *Attaining of Gigantick Dimensions in persons, animals, vegetables.*

8. *Great strength and agility of body exemplify'd by that of Frantick, Epileptick and Hystericall persons.*

The lid on a pot in the kitchen rattled.

Sir Kenelm shuffled the scrap-paper notes he made at the meeting; his head produced as if of its own accord a low humming noise of concentration. His armillary sphere, sitting on the corner of his desk, seemed to respond, and as one of its brass zodiacal hoops shifted of its own accord, the earth's attitude moved by half a degree.

9. *The making of Armour light and extremely hard.*

10. *Varnishes perfumable by rubbing.*

Number 10 was another of his own contributions, based upon the Duke of Tuscany's writings. Perhaps varnishes could make base, dirty places fresh, or conjure the smell of a distant loved one—he had taken with him to sea Venetia's kerchief, but its incense-scent was soon gone. It worried him, and he feared she had expired, and taken the scent with her to heaven. Only her letter brought him relief.

His nib protested with a squeak as he wrote:

11. *The Making of Parabolicall and Hyperbolicall Glasses. Already practised though without the requisite exactitude.*

Some Glasses could be used to perform natural magick, such as the Burning-Glasses of Archimedes, which whipped the sun's cavalry into lined formation and so set fire to enemy ships three miles away.

12. *The Making of Glass Malleable.*

This, in his private estimation, would never happen.

In the scullery, a maid rent one of his old shirts loudly in two.

13. *Potent drugs to alter or exalt Imagination, Waking, Memory and other functions, appease pain, procure innocent sleep, harmless dreams, etc.*

14. *Pleasing dreams exemplify'd by the Egyptian electuary.*

The Egyptian alchemist Zosimus had a herbal formula for pleasant dreams which some of the Invisibles were working to re-create. Kenelm believed that men's minds were enlarged by dreaming, because then they breathed the spirit of gracefulness, or pneuma.

In the kitchen a pan of water came to the brink of boiling.

15. Freedom from necessity of much sleeping.

Geese panicked; wood smoke laughed out of the tall chimneys at Gayhurst; wind played notes across the neck of an old bottle. He was now writing fast, from Imagination.

16. The recovery of youth, or at least some of the marks of it, as new Teeth, Hair coloured as in youth.

A cockerchaff spun on its back, whirring like a clock. One of the piles of books in his study crashed to the ground. He thought he heard Venetia scream. He reached out to touch the armillary sphere on the corner of his desk and sent the earth's girdle spinning.

17. The prolongation of life itself.

Sir Kenelm felt a shadow fall, and he knew Mercurius had left the room. He put down his nib and closed his eyes.

Fame

"Venetia Stanley was a most beautifull and desirable creature . . . She was so commonly courted that it was written over her lodging one night in *literis uncialibus* [in capital letters]: 'PRAY COME NOT NEER, FOR DAME VENETIA STANLEY LODGETH HERE.' . . . She had a most lovely and sweet turn'd face, delicate darke-browne haire. She had a perfectly healthy constitution much enclining to a *bona roba* (near altogether). Her face, a short oval; dark-browne eie-browes about which much sweetness, as also in the opening of her eie-lids."

John Aubrey's *Brief Lives*, 1669–96

"When she raises her eyelids, it's like she's taking off all her clothes."

Colette, *Claudine and Annie*, 1903

TEN YEARS AGO, when the sun revolved around the earth and James I was King, crowds used to scream when they saw Venetia's carriage approaching. Girls and beardless boys would wait hours for the chance to see her pass. In those days her face was always at the window of her carriage; she would even cross back and forth between both windows, to give all-comers a chance to see her. She was more spoken of than seen, like a great sight of nature, a cave or a crystal, Wookey Hole or the Badbury Rings. Except unlike those monuments she would never stay still, and her life was a constant kicking up of dust, for she was very often undertaking journeys, to preserve herself from rakes and bloods and panting nobles, so she said.

Sometimes horseguards had to clear the street to let her pass. Serving-women dropped their dishes and crossed themselves when they saw her; men who met her either became so bold and eloquent they would not stop talking, or lost their train of thought and coloured. She had a face luscious enough to make her most banal remark seem profound, and she had grace and pride besides, a self-sameness, which was hers and only hers: a *haecceitas* in Latin—a "thisness." Venetia Anastasia was noble born, of course, and yet she would not walk stiffly, like so many ladies, but loose and smooth, and all her hair and flesh was hers, not stuck with patches or white-faced with fard or sewn with horsehair. She was warm and live, and there was carnality in the slowness of her blink.

Venetia by Peter Oliver, circa 1619

No wonder women would not let her near their husbands. When the nobles referred to her between themselves, they whistled and drew curves in the air with their fingers. They called her "*bona roba*," which sounded like a compliment, but implied she was light. Her name was often abbreviated familiarly to "Venice"—especially by knaves seeking to play up a small acquaintance. Kenelm's mother would rather send her son to Madrid than suffer him to marry her—and it became fashionable to remark, saucily, that though Mary Digby sought to send her son to Spain, he had as lief stay at home in Venice.

The bloods of the English court were then in Madrid kicking their heels pretending to hasten "The Match" between Charles of England and the King of Spain's daughter. Elaborate Habsburg protocol had clouded the matter, but the English were beginning to recognise that the Infanta was not to be wooed. They never saw the Infanta, except behind a screen. Charles wanted an opportunity to appeal to her, face-to-face, and he discovered that every morning she walked with her ladies barefoot through the dew of her private garden.

Kenelm was the boy in the tree who gave the signal to John Suckling that the Infanta was come out walking; Suckling leaped over the wall, and broke Charles's fall after him. And so England's heir jumped, rolled through the rose bushes, and accosted the Infanta he would make his bride, who ran away screaming.

While Kenelm was in Madrid, Venetia became celebrated at court. Both Sackville brothers pursued her, and songs were made up about her, and women copied her hair, and her clothes. She always favoured intense blues, and as she grew more scandalous, receiving Richard Sackville's kisses, and his younger brother's favours, the shades of blue she wore grew stronger. She was seen in a shocking new draper's hue that flashed like a kingfisher's wing, a very Papistical blue, unreliable, continental, the *ne plus ultra* of blues. It was made from a pigment of lapis lazuli—it would have been cheaper to buy a dress of beaten gold—and when she wore it in the sun she seethed like one of Kenelm's alchemical mithridates. The new blue was called "Ultramarine," a word that rolled about country folks' mouths too much, so they called it "Venetia's Blue" instead.

In Wiltshire once she stayed upstairs above an inn, as John Aubrey recorded, with high-born gents attending—Sackville, and some of his roaring rakells—with only her cousin George Stanley as keeper of her modesty. The landlord was delighted and put a sign outside the tavern (in capital letters), which pretended to warn people off, but only served to advertise her presence. Crowds assembled. It was on the feast of St. Philip, close after St. George's day, and there was mischief abroad and summer dust in the air. St. Philip's day used to be the old feast of Floralia, and women were decked in flowers, coronets of daisies and scabious and viper's bugloss, and they gathered outside the tavern, for women were always as wont to see Venetia as the men. Before nightfall the innkeeper was drunk dry. Men from villages as far as seven miles away—strangers, never seen before—were drumming on the empty kegs.

Venetia peeped out of the upstairs window wearing a borrowed servant's cap and shaking out a dishclout, so those below, certain it was not she, shouted up clamouring for news of Lady Venetia and she, quite sullen, shouted back, "There's no such fine lady here, only wenches and strumplings tonight!," then disappeared inside and slammed the window.

Eventually the magistrate's men came and dispersed the crowd for public affray. Her roaring friends adored it, but the innkeeper wanted compensation.

Her beauty made her almost wild. And her wildness made her beautiful. She could do as she pleased. Sometimes she wore her hair loose and half-tangled, sometimes she slouched and sucked her cheeks. Sometimes she danced when there was no music. She was never sluttish, and to kiss someone she did not love was an abhorrence to her, except when she felt like it.

Men had a passion then for the paintings of Titian, which they would keep hidden in their closets, showing them to one another as favours, by candlelight—and there was a something of the Titian about Venetia, whose pomegranate smile's red and whiteness was a splitting fruit. Her black fur cape was always about to slip to show her shoulders, like the girlie in the painting Stradling brought back from Madrid and carried always with him in his travelling trunk. Other times she was all froth and fancy, Fragonard's slipper already flying off its swing, a hundred years too soon.

She was no great reader or writer, but that can make a person's foxy instincts sharper. She could feel when she was being looked at, even in the dark, and she had a sense for secrets. She was impatient, and restless, and most men found nothing wifely in her. Neither Sackville brother wanted her for marriage, though once she let the elder walk with her alone in public, which gave the gossips much to munch on.

Higher delights and sweeter fancies she always sought, till, surfeiting of joy, she held an Evening of Melancholy, to which all the guests wore black. From the astrologer-physician Richard Napier she bought candles that were mixed with puck's fog, so they flamed with silver light, and she set smoked mirrors round her black-draped room, and in the brittle black-and-white light, she glowed like a siren of the silver screen, whose every film is lost.

She was named for the opulent, liquid State whence dark impassioned canvases came. Once in a court masque of the Great Rivers called Tethys Festival, she played Venice. Her Grace Lady Elizabeth Stuart was the nymph of the Thames, and the Countess of Essex the nymph of the Lee, and the Viscountess Haddington the nymph of the Rother, and Venetia, just fourteen, was the nymph of the Grand Canal. She was meant to be part of the set dressing, playing a cloud, but James's Queen, Anna of Denmark, picked her out and promoted her so that she might walk solo across the stage wearing a Doge's cap, very still and solemn, pulling a long, heavy green train behind her. Before she left the stage, she cast one deeply knowing smile back at the audience.

"F'neesha! F'neesha!" the women waiting to see her chanted as they waited to kiss her hand. She was excessively, undeservedly venerated, which is a form of oppression.

She would not have understood why it should be considered that. She loved attention, sought it out. Great ladies, stars and princesses often believe that public adoration confers on them an influence or power, which it is their destiny to put to use. But Venetia did not have this do-gooding impulse. She went through the motions of charity only. She had the heart of a pagan pleasure-goddess, and her instincts told her to look after her own, and to hell with the rest. The adulation made her run faster and stronger, gathering power as she lost control.

But within Venetia ran a crack, which fame had covered, and now her fame was gone the crack showed again, deeper and wider. The attention she received curdled to scrutiny, the envious admiration to calumny, or pity. And that was only the beginning, only the first turning of the tide that would roll against her, now her name was two broken promises. In the year of her birth, only maggot-brained philosophers would repeat the heresy that the earth moved round the sun. But the printing presses shifted heaven and earth, so that our sublunary pit was re-imagined as a magnetic ball or "terrella," which rotated around the sky, and by the time she was thirty this was the new orthodoxy, and there was a new king.

No wonder she wore a mask and veil these days, now she had tired eyes, and even the new king was no longer new, and the earth moved round the sun.

> Dapper: I long to see her Grace.
> Subtle: You must be bath'd and fumigated first:
> Besides, the Queen of Fairy does not rise
> Till it be noon.
>
> Ben Jonson, *The Alchemist,* 1610

Bidding her coachman wait behind a brake of trees, Venetia climbed out at a spot near the Dingles, the bank of cottages beyond the loam pits at the far side of the village of Clophill, six miles from Gayhurst. Hooded, and wearing her tall wooden chopine platforms, she picked her way around a chicken-foot lying on the verge at the crossroads. She was undertaking to visit one Begg Gurley. Most tradespeople—hatters, seamstresses, apothecaries—visited Lady Digby at home, but Begg Gurley was not exactly a tradesperson. She did not pay calls, as she might be apprehended in the street for soliciting her devious trade; she left no footsteps for fear they would be filled with wax by her enemies and thus her feet turned lame. If Venetia was discovered at her cottage, at least it would be clear she had come of her own accord. Blind Begg Gurley was a wise-woman, and some called her Dame Kind, or Mother Nature, while others called her Witch.

As she approached the cottages, with their flags of chimney smoke flying, a mongrel licking its flank eyed her from one doorstep, and a dirty child ran away shrieking. She had been here once before, seeking advice on how to make friends with Kenelm's mother Mary Mulsho, and together they had wrapped Mary Mulsho's dirty kerchief up in string and buried it in the garden, and although Venetia had found the whole process a little embarrassing, still, who was to prove it had not worked?

"Is that my friend Lady Diggy?" she heard a voice call within. "Will she not pull back the curtain?"

Venetia did so, and as her eyes grew accustomed to the smoky room, she recognised the huge motherly figure of Begg Gurley sitting in her wicker chair, her head back, her eyes closed, her hands poised apart on her knees. As she felt Venetia's shadow her eyes flipped open.

"Oh my lady," she said quietly, looking straight through Venetia with cloudy white eyes. "You poor lady."

She stretched open her arms wide and Venetia fell to be hugged to her bosom. "There, there." Burying her face in the rough flannel of her frontage, Venetia cried a brief burst of tears that came from nowhere like rain in April. "There, there," said Mother Nature, patting her back. "Begg will make all better. Is it my Lord Sir Kenelm?"

"Yes, I fear his lack of love," said Venetia, sniffing.

"Is it my Lord's absence?"

"No. He is so good to me and I only hope he means it."

Venetia felt understanding radiating from Begg. She was even comforted by her purblindness because it meant she could not turn an assessing eye upon her face.

Afterwards, Venetia could not recall how Begg had seemed to know everything without being told. In fact, Venetia had spoken a great deal, and talked of many private matters, while Begg said again and again the word "yes" in little audible gasps, seeming to inhale Venetia's anxiety, her big body absorbing it like a bullfrog.

Sir Kenelm had done Venetia an injury she had been nursing like an ulcer. Now she could claim sympathy for it. He had brought her, as a present from the Continent, a pair of revolting snails, whorly and horned. "He said their slime might be taken as a cure for my complexion, 'to hasten its recovery from childbirth'—those were his self-same words." As Venetia started to cry, very sorry for herself, her perfect nose growing quite pink,

Begg's eyes focused on a spot above her head, so intently they almost crossed.

"And his books! He is a man possessed. If he can come by any book, in any language, he must buy it, though there is no shelf left at home, and he can never read them all. And yet he piles them about the house, and touches them fore and aft with his loving hands . . . Sometimes I wish I were a book, that he might make such love to me!"

Begg shook her head gravely, tutting, though Venetia was laughing and crying simultaneously. Thus unburdened, sniffing with satisfaction and dabbing her face, she followed Begg's eyes up and flinched as, right above her head, she saw a tiny spider descending from the rafters.

"Don't mind him, my lady, that's just my old spinner called Joe," said Begg. "Him'll stop his weaving once we have an idea of how to help my Lady Diggy." As Begg spoke, her empty fingers twiddled forwards. "I think you would do well to receive help, my lady, and it doesn't seem like many are there that can or will help you, except perhaps some little friends of mine." Begg reversed the direction of her twiddling fingers.

"As it happens, a great dame called Lady Lily Trickle is staying with me today. Perhaps you knows her, as fine ladies do tends to knows one another."

"No," said Venetia.

"Lady Lily Trickle," called Begg, ringing a bell, "wills you join us?"

There was a muffled noise of alarm behind the curtain to the adjoining room, as if Lady Trickle had forgotten to prepare herself in time.

Begg Gurley dropped her voice discreetly low, and said to Venetia: "My Lady Trickle is approaching eighty year old, but as you will see I have helped her stay a very dainty lady. She has been courted by a great prince in the past and she is very friendly with fairies."

Her ladyship struggled out from behind the curtain. She was between three and four foot tall, and her head was covered in a downy blonde hair, rather scant, and her face was round and waxy, like a mooncalf. She was wearing a damask kirtle and mochado waistcoat, and Venetia wondered how she dared. The local sumptuary laws meant that only an alderman or sheriff's wife could wear mochado. Still, she was the size of a child, and perhaps the rules were excepted for fairies' friends. Her eyelids were heavy, which gave her a look of insolent pride. She did not speak.

"Good afternoon, my lady," said Begg. "Pray, nod once to indicate you are a living person and not an happarition of conjurement!"

She nodded.

"Pray nod to indicate the truth, and stamp to shew a lie. Do you have help maintaining your beauty, my Lady Trickle?"

She both stamped and nodded, being confused.

"We shall try again, dear. Do you have help maintaining your beauty?"

She nodded.

"First, for the protection of our souls, are you in league with the Luciferian?"

She stamped.

"Good. Are you assisted in the care of your skin by right and proper tidy little people?"

She nodded.

"How do you pay them—with silver?"

She stamped her foot.

"With gold?"

She nodded.

"Thank you, my Lady Trickle, I expect if we are so lucky we will summon some of the tidy folk now to see if they can help our friend Lady Diggy in her trouble."

Lady Trickle stamped anxiously, twice.

"What is it pray? Oh, yes. You are concerned that the tidy folk will not come if Lady Diggy can see them. If you will, my lady?"

Venetia had neither given consent nor protested before Begg Gurley and Lady Lily Trickle tied a piece of cloth around her eyes, and she was put to lie back in the wicker chair.

"One to summon the lords!" Begg said, and a tiny tinkle-bell rang.

"Two to call the ladies!

"Three to bid them dance!"

Venetia felt feathery tickle-steps dancing across her cheeks, and the asthmatic wheeze of Begg Gurley, whose breath smelled of hazelnuts.

Venetia felt a laugh rising in her chest, like a fart that will out, and she had to try hard not to explode with laughter. She thought of crows and cold water.

"My Lady Diggy smiles to feel the little lords and ladies gavotte upon her cheek," said Begg.

"Aaaaye," squeaked Lady Trickle. There was the small sound of skin on skin, and Venetia intuited that Lady Trickle had been reprimanded with a slap for interrupting.

"Now they lay their habilements upon your forehead, their gowns and ruffs," said Begg in a syrupy-sweet voice, as if Venetia was a child at bedtime. She felt a light pitter-pat upon her face, as if fresh rose petals with a hint of mildew to them were being dropped upon her forehead from above. "La, la, la," sighed Begg, as the petals dropped.

"And now the little folks' chariots made of vegetables await."

Venetia could not resist. "Are they drawn by mice?"

"Oh no," said Begg indulgently. "My dizzy lady! You don't know much about the fairy ways. 'Tis a fine conker coach set with turnip wheels. Mr. Harry Long Legs draws this carriage, and he is bound with a bridle one hair thick. Now the fairies bow and leave you for the other world. They go to drink from a dew drop, one between eight of them. And so, farewell, addy-oo!" The tiny bell chimed again. "Addy-oo."

Blinking, breathing in the fresh air, Venetia returned to her waiting carriage. She had an armful of Begg's mulberry leaves, gathered as a decoy for her journey. She did not begrudge the ladies the piece of gold for their show, as long as it bought their silence too. She did not feel compelled to visit Begg Gurley again. Her invention was too crude, too much of countryside. She could not believe in it.

Venetia had sceptical Percy blood in her. Her grandfather was Henry Percy, Earl of Northumberland, whom they called the Wizard Earl because his doors were open to mathematicians and astronomers, and in his castle study he had drawn a new empyrean with compasses and formulae and reams of parchment. She remembered sitting on his lap as he told her a trinity is three, and a quaternity is four, and so forth. She was told never to say silly things or speak of fairies to him, for he would be angered by such talk. But her intuition told her that she could never make him angry, for they were good friends, and she would sit on his shoulder combing his hair, while he read aloud to her. He had a soft tongue, cut when he was a boy, which could not pronounce all the words correctly, but it made her love to listen to his voice the more.

She felt ashamed to have visited Begg Gurley. Venetia was not one of those refined London ladies who found the old village ways enchanting, a "natural" alternative to pills and modern Physick. And she was certainly not a villager who took it on trust. She did not desire to feel better—she desired to look better. She needed Physick. This visit had helped her decide that, at least. As she left the Dingles, Begg tied around her wrist a bracelet of valerian, a green root silvered with tiny hairs, which was to remind her, when it fell off her wrist by rotting, that it was time to visit Begg Gurley again.

Venetia cut it off directly using her sewing scissors. But she also checked in her looking glass, against her graver judgement, to see if her skin was any better.

Sir Kenelm Holds a Press Conference

"Sir Kenelm Digby was such a goodly handsome person, gigantique and great voic'd, and he had so gracefull elocution, and noble addresse, that had he been dropped out of the Clowdes in any part of the World, he would have made himself respected. But the Jesuites spake spitefully, and said 'twas true, but then he must not stay there above six weekes."

John Aubrey's *Brief Lives*, 1669–96

WORD WAS SPREADING of his voyage, and Kenelm received letters from men requesting to visit him, some wishing to see his treasures, others to discourse with him about his exploits, so that news of his discoveries might be spread abroad. Well, thought Kenelm, since Venetia keeps me at Gayhurst still, so let the world come to me.

And here they were, men with a strange thirsty curiosity that tipped so quickly between sycophancy and impertinence. Young scholars, who wrote everything he said down in tiny handwriting; older men, whose fighting days were over and made a living from telling tales as gleemen or pamphleteers. Some were genuinely interested in Kenelm's voyage, others merely keen to win his favour, or take from him something that they could use, for their weekly corantoes, digests, news packets, or their own prestige. They crowded round him, asking him to pose and to show off his treasures, and he happily acceded to their requests, for he never needed much encouragement, and soon he was standing upon the table in the great hall, demonstrating how he defeated the French and Venetians with thrusts and parries.

Yet he felt his visitors did not look upon him as a man like themselves, but saw him as if through an eyepiece or a view-finder: their interest fell upon him like white light, lightning fast and interrogative. And so, entranced and blinded by the imaginary flashbulbs and the glaring light of attention, Sir Kenelm gave his first press conference.

"Is it true you seized more than a year's revenues in your escapade?"

"How many French cutlasses brought you hither?"

"On what day fell this sea-battle at Scanderoon?"

"But how many French men died?"

"So, gentlemen," said Sir Kenelm, answering the question he liked best, "the great battle fell upon my birthday, the eleventh of June. I dare say some errant wit and companion of Ben Jonson—one of the Tribe of Ben—will make a pretty verse of that. Luckily 'June' goes well with 'Scanderoon,' as you see."

Digby did not mention that he had commanded his ships to sail around the Gulf of Iskenderun for two days, treading water and polishing their muskets, in order that they might attack on the auspicious day of his birth.

"Your crew were set about by pestilence?" asked one man, a Polack with a long nose called Samuel Hartlib.

"Yes, a swinish fever brought aboard from Spanish ships. We had not reached Gibraltar but three score of my men were already dead . . ."

This had them all scribbling in their wastebooks. Samuel Hartlib, who was compiling a grand Encyclopaedia, wanted to know about quarantine and the prevention of infection, and so forth, but most of the other visitors had no interest in long and complicated truth. They wanted him to say something quick and epigrammatic, preferably exciting or bloody or moralising—any of these would do.

"You're not the kind of man who turns back, though, are you?" said Michael Parkinson, ingratiatingly.

"Are you an authoritarian below decks? Do you swing the cat-o'-nine-tails?" said Jonathan Ross, a fool with weak "Rs."

"Ask my crew," said Kenelm.

"We did," said Ross. "Some of them liked it a lot."

Ignoring the hubbub, Kenelm told them how he picked up hands at Tangiers, poor Scots and English sailors whose liberty he bought at some expense. "I will be repaid by the Crown very shortly," he told the assembly.

There was a small communal sigh, as if the company did not believe the Crown honoured its dues, but none knew the worst of it, which was that the debt would remain unpaid until the reign of Charles II, thirty years later.

"And did you divide your profits amongst your crew?" asked Paxman, wincing with his own pertinence.

"Yes," said Kenelm. "On modest terms, their liberty being their main reward."

A soft Irish man called Wogan said: "I'd be frightened beyond my wits if this happened to me, but tell us, is it true your crew fell to mutiny?"

"Mutiny is over-putting it. It was a small act of lower-deck rebellion amongst my new crew, bold fellows, worn down by their privations. A skipper hurled his trencher at the galley cook because he would give him no more biscuit. Some other men rose and started shouting also. I resolved this by means of diplomacy and pickled beef. First I put this malcontent in irons, but then since I could not send him home, the English packet being days away, I resolved to break his will, so I had him ducked and towed behind the ship, after which he confessed to his secret guilt of having previously raided the purser's store, which was a great mercy since it made him only a thief, not a hero. To the honest men, I made a speech, praising them, letting them know they would all be fairly dealt with, and that our mission would bring us gold, and more than that, gold with the King's blessing, and all the men cheered, and I rolled out the kegs of salt beef I had been saving for just such an occasion."

"How came you then to land?" asked Dimbleby, trying to hurry him.

"By signals between ships, and by secret confabulation with my navigator Sir Edward Stradling, and Captain Woodcock, who commanded our third ship, the *Janus*, I resolved to change our convoy's course so that we might stop within seven days to buy provisions at Zante."

Never, never had he felt such relief as when they dropped anchor in the bay at Zante and he knew that full-scale mutiny had been avoided. When the old women came down to the harbour hawking their foodstuffs, and the men waded ashore eagerly, he could have kissed the deck for gratitude. He saw a turtle waving to him from the shallows, and he dived into the lapis-blue waters to take him for a trophy. Hermes had made a lyre out of a tortoise shell as a gift for his brother Apollo. What was it that Apollo had gifted him in return? Some choice planet. But then as he swam closer he saw the turtle appeared to be at prayer, with his flippers together, and his wrinkled eyes shut fast, and Kenelm knew he must spare the turtle.

"And how came you to do battle with the Venetian galleasses?" asked Anthony à Wood, scribe and antiquarian, who had lately incorporated the distinguished "à" between his born names.

"Well, sir, like a swan with young they hissed at us. They wished to protect their convoy of French ships, and I wished them to know that the French were our enemies, and our enemies' friends are our enemies. We drew back, gathered up our strength, and came down on them like Englishmen. The battle we fought was close to, or something like, three hours in length, and each fought well and bravely. Load, aim, fire! Load, aim, fire! We were working under Phoebus's glare, to which our Celtic skins were not well-disposed, but the tiger was up in our blood, and so we loaded, so we aimed, and so we fired—until very timidly, like a ladies' petticoat, the little white Venetian handkerchief rose . . ."

Sir Kenelm did not mention how furious the English vice-consul in Iskenderun had been. The first he knew of Kenelm's attack was the noise of his cannonade resounding across the bay. He called the angriest alarum possible. Kenelm's actions jeopardised years of his diplomacy, he said. "Your privateering, sir," he roared, "will cost the honest English merchants of Aleppo in fines, in lost trade, and in goodwill. They may never recover this route."

"I heard the vice-consul was full of condemnation," said John Aubrey, with relish.

"He was apoplectic, wasn't he?" said Paxman.

"Well, he lamented exceedingly the loss of his toy pigeons' eggs," said Kenelm, speaking slowly, with a subtle purpose. "A few of which were cracked by the resounding noise of my English cannonade, which made the hens and chicks afrit. We were in the midst of battle, but his chief concern was all for his pet eggs," Sir Kenelm said with a note of regret in his voice that the vice-counsel should be so odd a fellow. The company laughed knowingly; canned laughter rang through the hall at Gayhurst.

"So we routed Venice. None of my crew were lost, but one of the Venetians' number died, I heard. I was graceful in conquest and I did not burn or scuttle the galleasses, though I could have. But I was mindful of the harm this would do our British traders. So I left with honour only."

The assembled company raised a cheer and poop-pooped as if it were the Last Night of the Proms; Digby did not think it necessary to tell them about the reaction of the Venetian ambassador in London, or the royal summons he received shortly afterwards:

> "Sir Digby is to leave those seas and come home so that further opportunity for offence may be removed."
>
> Edict from Charles I, 1629

Instead, he demonstrated many wonders to the gentlemen of the press, such as the size and motion of a dolphin—which he re-enacted with his arms stretched wide—and, to keep them entertained, his oldest trick: picking up a chair with one hand by its leg, until he became red in the face and the veins on his neck stood out. He offered the chair to the nearest visitor, the Pole and polymath Samuel Hartlib—"Your turn."

By the expression on his face, Kenelm feared Hartlib had a physical deformity that he kept well hidden. But then Hartlib smiled, and said he must be heading towards Banbury before the light was lost. Kenelm felt sad and foolish that he had played the martial, warlike side of himself today, when he should have spoken like a scholar.

"Will you go hither again?" called out one of the crowd, holding out a black baton at him as if it were a poignard, aimed at his mouth.

"What present did you bring to your wife?" called another, not looking at him directly, but through the mask of an artificial eye.

"Snails!" cried Sir Kenelm. "For the restoration of . . . any lady's complexion, they are mightily good." He felt he had said a wrong thing, and resolved to comment no more.

"Do you still love your wife?" asked a woman with a notebook marked "Viper Wine," who had somehow infiltrated the throng.

"More than ever," said Sir Kenelm. "And who are you, miss?"

"I am the author," she said.

Exasperated with all of them, and wanting finally to communicate something that was close to his heart, his higher self, Kenelm told them about the archaic sculpture of Apollo he found on the isle of Milos. "I tried to bring it home with me, but a hundred sailors could not move it. These sailors must be kept busy, you know, or they will fall to other fancies . . ."

It was such a figure, this Apollo. So full of prophecy. His blank eyes stared and his hair was wild, flaring. As Sir Kenelm looked at his full lips, heavy with breath, he thought he saw Apollo speak.

"All men should seize control of their lives," said Kenelm, determined to finish on a rousing note. "Look, we change, or else we must be overtaken by change. It is my motto, you know—not my family motto, which is 'None but one'—but one far more meaningful to me, my own adopted aphorism, taken from Seneca—'*Vindica te tibi*'—'Vindicate yourself for yourself!' Or, indeed, 'To thine own self be true.' Or, my favourite rendering . . ."

Sir Kenelm, standing upon the table, staring, wild-eyed in imitation of Apollo cried: "You must change your life!"

"*Vindica te tibi.*"

Motto stamped on the books in Sir Kenelm Digby's library,
now held by the Bodleian Library, Oxford

"*Du mußt dein Leben ändern*"—"You must change your life."

Rainer Maria Rilke's "Archaic Torso of Apollo," 1908

"When I went on my voyage to sea, shee [Venetia] so wholly retired and secluded herself from the world till my return . . . All the while she kept only with her ghostly Father."

Letter from Sir Kenelm Digby to his sons, 1633

When he was first away, gliding towards Scanderoon, he was in love with the sea, with the changefulness and power of it. The *Eagle* leaped and dived, and he laughed as it threw him forward mid-step and jogged his hand as he drank. The sea teased him, and caught him out; at night, it rolled him over and about, until he retched and longed for land and puked into his hat.

At home, on the solid grass of Gayhurst, young Kenelm ran round and round, roaring, trying to become dizzy. Venetia stood on the steps as if she were watching him, but actually staring into the green-shaded distance, baby John over her shoulder.

Just off the coast at Deal, the spyglass told them that an enemy ship was rising on the horizon—their first prize. With greatest haste, the *Eagle*'s quadrant and maps were hidden, the men mustered, games of dice put away, salt pork stowed, muskets powdered, cannon loaded with ordnance, private prayers whispered, and everything made ready for attack. The ship was now so close it was possible to discern, with the naked eye, that it was a Dutch vessel, and therefore unassailable, neutral. Glumly the crew watched it sailing past.

When Kenelm had been gone a month, and no more letters came from him, Venetia deemed it time to give young Kenelm his present. It was a model ship, a galleass daintily made of wood and cork, with parchment sails and miniature oars and coloured paper bunting. On its deck was a built-in dish, designed to carry salt at a banqueting table. All its cannon were fixed apart from one which could be taken out and filled, if money allowed, with pepper. Young Kenelm took it as his solemn duty to look after this ship, which although it was as big as he could hold, he bore to his room at night and carried down with him each morning.

In harbour at Lisbon, Kenelm was woken urgently and struggled on deck to see one of his ships, the *Samuel*, glowing upon fiery water. One of its tall masts was listing like a falling tree, endangering the deck of the *Eagle*, and there was much shouting to lookey-loo as it creaked, and the wind threw smuts at them and blew the flames brighter. Thus the second ship in Kenelm's convoy was burned down to the waterline and scuttled and her thirty crew sent to try their luck in Lisbon or where they would. "The horizon is vast enough for each of us," he said, flinging a purse of coins to the sailors across the foreign sky.

Venetia's eyes began to get accustomed to the smallness of a new silk stitch. Her needlework, a bed-jacket decorated with leaves and strawberries, was designed in such detail that the berries were gilt with tiny pips, and Venetia had to unpick her too-crude work again, until her stitches were as small as pinpricks. Looking up from her lap to talk to her priest Chater, she caught baby John as he uncomprehendingly snatched at the toy ship, snapping away a splint off the mast.

The *Eagle* suffered. It came on quickly one night, during supper. The first mate sat with his elbows on the table and his head in his hands. Kenelm thought he was affecting Melancholy, or had lost his manners, until he saw several of the crew slumped in slothful postures, heads lolling, or laid out on the benches. A petty officer serving soup put down his ladle and grasped his belly, sinking to his knees as bloody bile issued from his mouth.

That same day at Gayhurst the sky split open with rain that played like a band of drummers upon the roof and puddled underneath an open casement in the Hall. Young Kenelm sat up from his afternoon sleep with a cry and ran out of the nursery and downstairs, as fast as his legs could go. As Venetia saw him she remembered, too—and clasping John to her breast as he gurgled she ran through the rainstorm to the middle of the lawn where they had left their rugs and cups and the model ship. Rain had pooled in its salt-cellar, and the paper sails were dark and waterlogged.

Before they reached Gibraltar, half his men were dead. The ship's surgeon sewed the corpses into their hammocks as shrouds, and always drew his final thread through the dead man's nose; a sea custom, a last chance. Every time Kenelm saw the surgeon sewing, and he knew the needle was nearing its final jab, he expected the body to sit upright and scream. But there was no such resurrection.

Venetia had Mistress Elizabeth make new sails for the toy ship, out of underskirts. They sailed her upon an old horse trough clouded with green weed. Venetia stared into its murkiness, and saw only her own reflection and a bottomless kingdom of water-fleas.

Passing the Barbary Coast, he entered for the first time the Sea of the Middle Earth, or Medi-Terreanea. Kenelm hunched overboard looking for monsters in the sunny waters. He saw a long pulsing sea-beast with a head like ribbons that he thought must be a squid, and a bristling silver ball of fishes followed by a train of seagulls. Kenelm watched out to see if the horizon inclined, now he sailed closer to the round belly of the world.

After stitching for so long, Venetia began to believe that the strawberry she sewed was the world, and each stitch a mile, and each seed a league, and the plumpness of the berry was the Equator, and its hasp the Polar Land of Ice, and the blood-drops accidentally shed by her needle were little planets, dribbled across the canvas.

Had the largeness of Kenelm's life diminished hers, somehow?

Although they are not subject to our sense
A world may be no bigger than two pence . . .
For millions of these atoms may be in
The head of one small, single, little pin
And thus small, then ladies may well wear
A world of worlds, as pendants in each ear.

Margaret Cavendish, "Of Many
Worlds in this World," 1650

Kenelm paced back and forth his creaking cabin, preparing a speech the night before sailing into battle.

Venetia paced up and down the upstairs corridor with baby John at her shoulder, rubbing his back.

Kenelm heaved-ho, squinting in the glare.

Venetia cried out in frustration and threw down her needlework.

Kenelm felt his sword run through an enemy body, like a knife into a peach. It was his birthday, 11 June.

Venetia swore to eat no more suckets and do no more sewing.

Before the letters could reach them telling of his victory at Scanderoon, the family observed mass in the chapel at Gayhurst, and prayed for Kenelm's birthday to St. Barnabas, and to St. Christopher and St. Lucy for sailors in peril. Young Kenelm solemnly brought his model ship to the altar, tattered like any treasured toy, and the family's confessor, Chater, held it up to the altar, so it dominated the chapel. Even though it was now a good deal easier for young Kenelm to carry, the ship seemed to have grown immense with significance. As the bell tolled his absence from Gayhurst, the model ship filled the chapel. And all the while Sir Kenelm lay sunbathing on the deck of his little barque on the silver-silk ocean, as gentle winds carried him through Cyclades.

"Now towards her latter time she [Venetia] grew fatt, yet so that it disgraced nothing of her shape."

Letter from Sir Kenelm Digby to his sons, 1633

THE DIGBYS WERE at supper.

"How are your studies, love?"

He nodded and munched. He was almost certain their dining room was smaller than before he went away to sea. Perhaps his senses had grown through exercise of Imagination. Venetia's habit now was to sit across the table from him, in the half-light. In their courtship they had sat so close they might keep hold of each other constantly; her stockinged foot in his hand, her finger dancing upon his gartered knee.

"What are you eating, dearheart?" she said, peering over. "Ship's biscuit again?"

She was so interested in his diet, wanting so much to please him and make him strong. Women had too much love in their bodies, he mused. They could not contain it, it made them solicitous and overweening in matters beyond them. You could see it shining in their faces sometimes. Women needed to disburden themselves of love, and they would smother any small person or furry beast with it, even a shrub, a plant! It was too much, and Kenelm wondered if they could be leeched of their love, as of blood. One of the reasons Venetia had so much power over him, at first, was because she seemed like a man, never fussing, never over-flowing in her affections, but cool and sanguine. She was—or at least, she had been—the very opposite of his mother.

Kenelm was eating bacon and eggs, with a Wagon Wheel on the side. He had developed a liking for these foodstuffs, which he had brought back with him from the Med, where he had obtained them through trade with merchants who were carried on strange tides and backward-blowing winds. They called these bright edibles "Returned Goods," but whence they had been returned—the New World? Venetia viewed with displeasure another foodstuff he had brought home: a suspect pink and tasteless meat called Spam. Odd roots and infusions were often arriving from abroad, and they either became indispensable, like potatoes and tea, or were never seen again.

Sir Kenelm kept recipes and instructed the kitchen. He pursued pleasure craftily, like a good master of husbandry. He paid lavishly for saffron and pepper; mace and nutmeg. Venetia bargained over every penny, for the satisfaction it brought her, but Kenelm believed that the best things were, invariably, the most expensive. He sniffed the good from the best; he checked the eyes of trout for clarity, and sent for virgin Hampshire honey, and green rosemary, agrimony and thyme. He tasted every dish before seasoning it, chewing thoughtfully; he craved umami, the fifth taste.

Eggs quicken—by contraries—the salt taste of bacon, he wrote, to himself, scrawling a brief note that brought the English fry-up into existence: *Two poched eggs, with a few fine dry-fryed collops of bacon are not bad for breakfast.* His arteries squelched appreciatively.

He never thought to publish his recipes: that would be done after his death in 1669 by an opportunist scribbler who played up Kenelm's connections. The book's contents page was a feast of namedropping. "My Lord Lumley's Pease Pottage'; "Hydromel as I made it weak for the Queen Mother." It was a rum sort of immortality.

> "Sir Kenelm Digby is remembered chiefly for his cookbook . . . it was the first to recommend bacon and eggs for breakfast."
>
> *The Encyclopaedia of English Renaissance Literature,* Volume I, 2012

The cook came to Venetia close to tears, asking if Sir Kenelm could be kept out of the kitchen, as he was always using up the best honey for his fermented drinks, or throwing away perfectly good potage, or telling the kitchen mort that she should use none but the best herbs, even for scullery work. He created a great amount of mess when he made his meath drinks, and this delayed the serving of supper till the boys were listless with hunger. But Venetia, who took no interest in the kitchen, would not say a word against Kenelm's cooking.

"How is your transubstantum, darling?"

"Not today. Today I have written up a list of desiderata."

"A long list?" asked Venetia, who often had to coax him into talking about his Great Work.

"Indeed."

"For your Invisible confrères?"

"Exactly."

"I wish you would tell me what you mean by desider . . ."

"Desiderata. My darling," he said. "I only mean a list of what we most desire. That is to say, the most pressing needs of man. Contraptions to help us remain underwater, powerful electuaries, and so forth. For unless we dream, how can we do? So we begin by dreaming."

She smiled. "I dreamed last night that we had a daughter. I had forgot that until now."

He wiped his mouth with his napkin, and beamed lovingly at her, and took a big bite of Wagon Wheel. He had bartered the biscuits for nutmeg in the Bosphorus, bushel for bushel.

"Our daughter was very like me," said Venetia. "Is that the sort of dream you mean?"

"Yes, but on a universal scale. The needs and wants of all."

"So I might dream that all women could have daughters if they were of a mind to, or sons if they had none, and we might put it on your list, and by being noted down it should by your efforts and degrees of Physick become true."

Kenelm nodded as he speared a slab of Spam with his fork—they were fancy eaters now, using continental eating irons, though they had grown up using knives and fingers.

"But I expect that is already on your list, of course. I must think more deeply . . ."

"The list was compiled by scholars and philosophers and I have added to it also," said Kenelm airily.

Venetia was quiet.

"A serum to rub on cats' noses, that would help us understand them speak?" she said, trying to make him laugh. "Or perhaps a fish that flipped out of its element every time your distant loved ones had you in their thoughts? So you knew that they were safe. A drink to make you full even when you are hungry? Now that would help with fasting."

Kenelm laughed at her, and shook his head.

"Teeth that do not rot?" she asked, thinking of her mouth. "Flowers that never die?"

"I know where those are plucked," said Kenelm, putting his arms around her and reaching to caress her in a manner that was firstly affectionate, and secondly indicated he wished her to stop talking.

"Cloths that clean themselves? Maids that sweep tirelessly and never eavesdrop?"

"Aye, those are golems."

"Artificial music, after Francis Bacon—music that no orchestra plays, but echoes for days, years. Ah, here's the best. Childbirth without pain?"

"But now we come close to heresy," sighed Kenelm, kissing her on the forehead. "It is the curse of Eve, and we cannot end suffering, they say, else we would not be human. Though I agree, my darling, if Bathsheba could speak she would have a tale to tell when she came back from mousing."

Venetia closed her eyes. "Enduring beauty?"

"My darling, you are the most beautiful of all the women in the world."

Venetia turned from him, nauseous because the compliment was overblown and false. But she could see by his eyes that he meant it kindly, and she forgave him. She knew he was treading carefully to avoid that phrase she hated—"still beautiful."

"Immortality," he said. "There's the rub. We are immortal souls in heaven, and on the earth we are immortal threefold-wise. In writing, which is our voice. In portraiture, which is our likeness. In children, who are the heirs to our bodies as well as our estates . . ."

"Threefold, yet you forget the fourth," said Venetia. "In memories. In the minds of the living, though we are dead, we walk and talk."

"Aye, and so we are never dead till all who knew us die. There's something in that, Venice. It may be that one day we will bring that memorie, that imprint on the mind, to material presence. To see the past or future in a scrying glass is already done. To take the imprint of the voices of angels on waxy tablets is already done. Why not the inner eye's projection also? If you can dream it, you can do it. There's something in that, aye."

Turning over these profound speculations in his mind, he wandered back to his study, and as soon as he went through the door everything his wife had said vanished from his mind, and so did her very existence, as he picked up his comfortable nib again and fell to writing: rewriting his list of desiderata, entirely the same, but a clean copy, ready to send to his confrères.

Venetia in her silver slippers stepped carefully up the darkened stairs to their children, thinking of the rank desires she knew but could not name to her husband. To fuck without issue, or fear of French pox; to remake one's body; to become another person; to live for ever; to turn base lead into gold for profit and never tell how it was done . . . She felt ashamed to think of them, as if He might be able to see her thoughts. Even thinking them might sully her complexion. These were the shadow-wishes that could never be told.

Kenelm's candle glowed on his quill and paper, and beyond them on the panelled wall their shadows fell very huge, his fingers like a malformed giant's, his pen a rod, his parchment a valley, and while his list of his predictions was precisely lit by candle, behind them lay a vast dark trench.

Late that night, when he came quietly into her bedroom, she was awake. He could hear her breath, shallow and agitated.

"Some women . . ." she whispered into the dark. "Some women . . ."

"Yes?" He was listening. The smell of manly warmth and ale-breath told her his face was close. As his eyes grew accustomed to the dark he was able to hear her better.

"Some women drink potions, do they not? For their complexion."

The darkness inhaled. "I brought you snails," he said.

"I want no snails," she exclaimed, into the blackness of their curtained bed. "I need Physick. I need a tonic, like the women drink at court."

She put her cold hands around his neck.

"Will you make me one?"

He sighed.

"Will you?"

Clouds passed over the moon. A bat flickered over their bed.

She asked again, her voice strangled with urgency. "Will you?"

"No, because you have no need of any potions, my darling Venice. I like you just as you are." And he took her in his arms, feeling strong and manly, and stroked her hair, and whispered goodnight.

They lay awake, their bodies crackling with frustration. She had suffered a double indignity, admitting her vanity, her weakness, and all for nothing. He had refused her. She did not understand it. Usually he refused her nothing. Kenelm, on his side of the bed, was fighting to stop himself feeling cross with her. He had come home in triumph; it was the very least she could do to stay beautiful for him. She was only five years older than him—many wives were older than their husbands. And if she could not keep her beauty, she should at least maintain her faith in her beauty, since that was the chiefest thing, was it not? After a certain age, did beauty not become an act of will, or character?

He did not want her to discover the cures that other women drank. He had seen the effects of Belladonna and the cure of Antimony. He had seen skin scorched by Ceruse—the vinegar in it as bad as the lead, no doubt—and cheeks raw with Fucus, which could be almost any chymicall matter stoppered in a gallypot, and what the courtesans called Pinchers, tiny pegs concealed under the wig which drew the slack skin off the jaw.

He knew the initial glow was followed by slow disfigurement, as the new smoothness turned to crusted immobility, or, in the case of Pinchers, he had heard that the skin slackened so at night, with the pin removed, the skin fell down upon the shoulder and breast. And he knew a corruption of spirit seemed to follow. These women were always forced by their pride to lie and say they pinched not, they painted not, and they were touched by Nature's hand alone. And everyone pretended to believe them, and showed them such hypocrisy, curtseying to their new face, but laughing as soon as they turned their back.

Gayhurst was silent as a stone, the woods were dark and still. Kenelm turned over onto his side, and sleep lapped gently over him, submerging his mind.

No, he did not want her drinking potions. They could be dangerous, corrosive. He thought of the woman in *The Duchess of Malfi* who flayed her face off to remove smallpox scars. Why had his uncle taken him to see *The Duchess of Malfi* when he was only twelve? He had nightmares for weeks.

Beauty treatments could lead to slipping in the wit-house, pitting in the droolers.

The radio signal has been lost.

"Desquamation of the epidermis, cornified desquamation, crythema (redness) . . . All these are possible skin conditions resulting from radiotherapy . . ."

Bleep! Re-tuning in progress . . .

He twitched and fell, reaching out to catch her. He thought he saw her face distended, a Picasso portrait. Word-torrents poured through his sleep, lists from past and future medical dictionaries.

> "For hardness in women's breasts, take a purge of jallop, or turneps boyled, and put linen with loose flocks of flax, so 'tis thick and warm, and make a cataplasm using an old mellow pippin. Administer three days after the full of the moon. With this a Lady of Great Quality cured herself."

> *"There was a lady in France that, having had the smallpox,*
> *Flayed off the skin to make it more level.*
> *And whereas before she looked like a nutmeg grater,*
> *After she resembled an abortive hedgehog!"*

As the actor from *The Duchess of Malfi* delivered those lines, the audience groaned in unison like a wave crashing, and groundlings round him crossed themselves. The girl in the blue dress had disappeared.

Here was someone else. Cleopatra. A Nubian Queen, tall as an Amazon. She had heavy, contemptuous eyelids and she smiled at Kenelm with heavenly symmetry. She came close to his ear, to talk to him in a whisper, and she put her arm around him, her hand on his back.

> *". . . I went for a face-glow two years ago. The doctor burned me. Have you any idea what it's like to have your face burned if you are a model? I had second-degree burns to my face. I didn't work for three months."*
>
> Naomi Campbell, supermodel, 2009

"*THREE MONTHS!*" the Amazon shouted.

Re-tuning now complete.

He woke because Venetia was stroking the smoothness of his lower back. He lay still and thankful for her caresses.

Her hand was looking for the dimples that she loved so well, on either side of his spine, above his bottom.

But she felt something unaccustomed, a patch of roughness. At the base of his spine, the skin was raised. Her fingers traced back and forth, trying to read it. What was it? It could be, yes it could be a disease he had picked up on his travels—a flower of the French pox.

Kenelm, awakened, sat up.

"My pouncing! I had forgot. My pouncing, see? In the south, the sailors have a custom remaining from the Greeks. 'Tis a noble tradition, which—"

"Enough! Just tell me what it is," said Venetia, hiding her face in their pillow, wretched with fear.

Kenelm struck a flint, which made the room instantly darker, turning out the moon. "Look," he said, handing Venetia the candle and turning over, wrenching up his nightshirt. Venetia pulled back the coverlets.

Just above Kenelm's bottom was a blue-black design, a dirty squiggle in a shape like a little horned man.

"Mother of God, what is it?" she said, trying to rub it away.

"I am pounced, my darling. Pounced and pricked with ink like a savage," he said, straining to look back at her across his broad golden-tanned shoulders, which were peeling slightly. "It will never come off. It is a custom of the Greeks and the Kings of Guinea, they told me. I had it done with musket lead by my captain, when we were recovering from our battle. We all had one."

"Did it hurt?"

"A captain feels no pain."

"Mercy, but you might have told me sooner," said Venetia, kissing it, but also cross that her husband's body should have changed for ever without her knowing, and jealous, somehow, of all those men away at sea together. He sat up and pulled off his nightshirt, though the room was cold, and he started undoing the small pearl buttons on the front of her nightgown.

She was quietly thankful that she had not affixed the vinegar poultice to her forehead, which she usually wore to sleep, as a method against wrinkles. She had worn it every night in his absence. He buried his scratch-bearded face in her breasts. They smelled of almond oil, which she rubbed into them every day, to try to make amends for what time and children had done. She feebly tried to delay him from pulling off her whole nightgown.

"Darling, will you make a beauty tonic?" she asked, as he reached for her thighs. "A youth-cure for me to drink?"

Kenelm considered it unsporting and feminine of her to ask him at this moment, and so he ignored her and continued with his endeavour.

When they were both naked, she felt like Eve in the mural of the chapel at Gayhurst, round and pink and poorly painted. Her feet were cold and when she wrapped them round his warm back he cried out, laughing. He did not allow himself to notice how tense she was, as it would put him off his stride, and he closed his eyes, and he was home, and she was his one true love, and all he ever wanted, and just as she was beginning to forget herself, it was over. They had coupled only twice in three weeks since he returned. His long absence had reduced his need of her. As she lay beside him, the black squiggle was still on her mind.

"What does your pouncing say?"

"It is like an amulet or sigil, darling, to draw heavenly influences to my backbone, and assist me in my Work."

"But who is the little man?"

"That is the alchemical sign of Mercury," he said slowly, on the brink of sleep. "Not very expertly done."

"Of course."

"Not your name, my darling. That is on my heart."

"Oh, very prettily said," she scoffed, and in a few moments they were both soundly asleep.

Moonbeams Are Cold and Moist

"One would think it were a folly that one could offer to wash his hands in a well-polished silver basin, wherein there is not a drop of water, yet this may be done by the reflexion of the Moon beames only. Hands, even after they are wiped, are much moister than usually."

"A Late Discourse by Sir Kenelm Digby in a Solemn Assembly of Nobles and Learned Men at Montpelier, Touching on the Cure of Wounds by the Powder of Sympathie," 1664

ALL WEEK, HE studied long and late in his laboratory. One night, when his candle guttered out after many hours, he was left in a bluish darkness to which his eyes quickly grew accustomed, and he saw it was a night as bright as day outside, and the gardens of Gayhurst were drenched in moonbeams. He stood at the open window of his laboratory, catching them in a glass bubble. He turned it wonderingly in his hand, sending two dashes of moon-juice chasing across the orb. *Moonbeams are cold and moist*, he noted in his ledger. *They leave an acquatic and viscous glutenising sweat upon the glass.*

He tipped the moonbeams onto the back of his hand, where he saw them dissipate into a silver sheen on his skin, waxy like the belly of a snake. Could lunar rays assist in safely beautifying a complexion? He made a private note in Latin.

The next night was cloudy.

The night that followed, he and his wife stood out in their garden under the huge moon, two owls in flapping nightgowns. Sir Kenelm held a silver basin up to catch the moon-dew, and Venetia dipped her face into the splashing shimmers. The pores across her nose and cheeks were picked out by the light, and he angled the basin, so the light caught the places under her eyes where the skin was very thin, the veins standing out like the underside of an ivy leaf. The softness twisted across her face, like an inverse sunbeam. If men tanned by daylight, wherefore could they not be healed by night light? As above, so below. "It is a potent moisture," breathed Sir Kenelm. "I can see the refulgent beams at work." Venetia shut her eyes and inclined her face deeper inside the basin, until a cloud on the silver formed in the shape of her sigh.

She looked up at him. The elms waved violently behind her. She was radiantly beautiful again. The cure had worked already. She was her Platonic self, ageless, transcendent. Or was she only softened by the moonlight? He reached out to put his arms about her, to claim and hold this sepia-tinted, black-and-silver Venus, but she was already gone, hastening back across the lawn to bed, her nightgown wind-swollen, her hair flying.

After a week of nightly moonbaths, she could discern no improvement in her complexion, although her husband maintained there was a new, subtle, luminosity. His well-meaning comments, his encouraging tone, hurt her more than anything. She found herself commenting on his alchemical work in a sarcastic, disbelieving tone, as if her pride were a debit and credit sheet. Come, she told herself, be bigger than that, but it was not easy.

On the Sunday morning, Kenelm lay half asleep in her bed, while she sat in front of her glass at her toilette, making ready for their private mass held by Chater in their chapel, with a few other recusants from the other side of the shire also in attendance. He asked her if she could see the good effect on her complexion. She did not answer. He suggested that he could see the blue vein on her forehead better than before, as this usually pleased her. It was one of her marks of beauty. He asked if she wanted to try the lunar cure again tonight. Silence. He looked at the stiff outline of her shoulders as she sat at her dressing table, and inferred there was trouble coming. Her voice was strange and cold: "I cannot go with you to court."

"Venetia, come—"

"I cannot bear it. I do not know why you persist in this nonsense of moonlight—this, ha, lunacy—when there are other, better cures available, which you well know."

"Other cures? What do you mean? Have I not provided you with every safe cure I know of? Have I not imported snails into our grounds from distant climes, at some cost? And yet you will not have them for healing purposes, neither taking their slime to drink nor submitting to have them crawl upon your face."

She turned to look at him, and her skin was blotchy with tears.

"I will not speak of those snails! I would have thought that you, a man of Physick, schooled in chemistry, would know better than to chase after village remedies."

Sir Kenelm leaned forward, very serious. "It is because I know the power of Physick that I caution you against it."

"Other ladies drink preparations."

"You have no need of other ladies' cures. You barely have any need of a cure at all."

"You do not understand."

"I do, my love."

"And yet you do not, my darling."

That evening, though the moon was a bright crescent, they lay abed all night.

Of Fountains and the Creatures in Them

"At Sir Anthony Cope's a house of Diversion is built on a small island in one of his fish ponds, where a ball is tosst by a column of water and artificial showers descend at pleasure. But the Waterworks that surpass all others of the country, are those of Enston, at the rock first discovered by Thomas Bushell Esquire."

Dr. Robert Plot, *Natural History of Oxfordshire*, 1677

"*Quaesisti nugas, nugis gaudeto repertis*"—"You were looking for trivial amusements—here they are, enjoy them."

Inscription on people-squirting fountain at Augsberg, recorded by Michel de Montaigne, 1570

WHEN KENELM WAS fifteen, and under the tuition of Bishop Laud, he was given leave to go home for the feast of Trinity, and spent a day riding slowly east across the sun-parched countryside. As he rode he felt freed, gradually, of all the stiff, correct conduct Laud enforced, and their continual, courteous conflict on matters of religion. Kenelm had smuggled a copy of *The Odyssey* out of Laud's library and plodding along, sometimes half-sleeping in the saddle, his mind drifted to monsters, whirlpools and mermaids' tails. But whence did they propagate, if they had no legs?

In Oxfordshire, on the homeward stretch, he rode up through Pudlicote towards the River Glyme and spied a fine church tower and brook. This would do as a place to water Peggy, his pony, whose real name was Pegasus, but who was definitely a Peggy. As he approached, the bells began to ring out.

"What church is this?" he asked a woman passing by.

"St. Kenelm's," she said, and left him standing all ablaze, as Peggy cropped the grass.

Such a feeling of special providence is always pleasant, but for a fifteen-year-old boy it was intoxicating. He had heard of the church, but had never seen it before. Well pleased with the form and shape of his church and particularly its solid tower, he surveyed it twice on foot in a circle, and lit a candle at the shrine of his namesake Saxon child-saint, before journeying further into the gold-green countryside.

He paused to cross himself in front of the lichen-mottled megalith at the crossroads, some giant's old plaything with flowers tucked into its pock marks, and a bowl of milk left at its foot for Robin Goodfellow. A long stately drive, unmarked, attracted his attention and he wondered if it was Neat-Enstone, famous for its pleasure park and water-grottoes, built by Thomas Bushell, seal-bearer to Sir Francis Bacon. Kenelm had heard about its marvellous fountains. He turned his pony into the drive, though he had no invitation, and with the impunity of youth, headed straight ahead at a casual rising trot.

The trees along the drive were alternately tall then squat, so they resembled, to Kenelm's eye, an Irish stitch. The trees barred the sun rhythmically so as he moved forwards he was dazzled by stripes of brightness, then shadow, brightness, shadow. The drive was quiet but he could hear in the distance, so he thought, a roar of water.

He tethered Peggy and proceeded down a curved, deserted forest path. Sensing he was being watched, and feeling, as teenagers do, that this moment might be of great import for the rest of his life, he removed his hat and ran his hand through his sweat-darkened hair. When he turned the corner he saw an open garden lawn before him, fringed with trees like a stage's curtains, and hung with a very fine mist, resting on the air. A perfect rainbow arched across it.

Kenelm's eyes welled at this sign of peace and forgiveness. Soon the rainbow would be dissected by Descartes, and anatomised by Newton, but from where Kenelm stood it was a symbol, mystical, allegorical. He knew, of course, that it was made of rain and sunlight and eyesight, and he knew that what he saw was an artifice, conjured out of carefully created spume. Because he had a mind that liked to understand what moved him—the type of mind that would, by degrees, create the modern age—he decided the water must have been forced through a very narrow fissure to create such a delicate spray, and he wondered how such pressure had been attained.

He thought he heard a laugh, or the rush of water, and turned around to follow the path till he could see, some way off, an ornate dwelling, perched at an improbable angle on the hillside, with rocks below it forming a cataract and tumbling cascade.

He followed the path onwards as it took him back into the hill, towards a fantastical grotto set into the cliff. It had been bricked all about, like a saint's cave built into a cathedral, but it was still clear that it was nature's work; no craftsman could obtain these molten patterns in the stone, curves and drips as from a frequently lit tallow candle. Inside the grotto it was cool and peaceful. He sang a few notes, just to hear the echo. Some of the rock-drips were protuberant, like long noses, polished by the action of water on them over hundreds of years. No doubt since the Flood. The villagers probably said a dragon had died here and these stones were formed by its blood trickling through the rock. In some ways it was a more compelling solution than "the sustained action of water on a particular rock."

Crossing a bridge he glimpsed, through the leaves of a tree, girls splashing in a pond—sunlit, laughing, dancing whirlygirls. Three of them were playing catch, the water dragging their dresses as they leaped about. They were of different ages—sisters, maybe. Two more girls were lying talking together on a rock shaped like a lily-pad. He did not like this attitude of being a peeping Tom, so he walked boldly towards the nymphs.

> "One cannot imagine Kenelm Digby being, at any age, not a man of the world."
>
> E. W. Bligh, *Sir Kenelm Digby and his Venetia*, 1932

Kenelm aged sixteen

They did not stop to notice him, and he saw that in the middle of the pool, there was an island, and on the island, inside an oversized, open oyster shell, lay a girl.

She was on her back looking bored, with her heels kicking at the shell's point, and her arms stretched slothfully behind her head. She wore a nymph's silk gathered dress, which was—Kenelm swallowed—wet through. She did not appear to have noticed Kenelm; in fact, her eyes were closed, but he felt sure she knew he was there. She was the apotheosis of this pleasure ground, the spirit of the place. She was part of the display, exuding sensual luxury and extravagance from all her parts, in her dark tumbling hair, in her amused smiling mouth, in her curved cheek, in her breasts, rising and falling as she breathed. Lucky air, to penetrate her body. He could bear it no longer. Approach her, his instinct told him, accost her! He reached out to do what only a boy would do when confronted with this apogee of beauty—to splash her with pondwater.

But before he could do it, a shaft of water bounced onto the path in front of him, as if aimed by a cannon. And the next second, cold and unexplained, another shaft hit him in the face, slapping him back. The indignity of it! The water techniques that delighted him had now been used against him for a sportive soaking. This was a very trivial garden indeed.

From the house there came a catcall of triumph and a smattering of applause. Kenelm had no sooner regained his composure than another squirt got him in the chest. He fell backwards on his bottom like a toddler, and heard the girl in the shell laughing at him. Her laugh sounded like sunlight on the sea. Would he have a chance to tell her this? They looked at each other in the eye for the first time, and he felt her look echoing into his past and future, through all the caverns of his soul.

For her part, she saw in that one glance that change was possible. Her life need not be spent idly lying in a shell, a job that any plasterwork nymph could do. She became instantly conscious of the dubious nature of her current situation, and decided she must do something about it.

In other words, they noticed one another.

But the people in the house were laughing, and Kenelm saw he was now part of the entertainment, punished as any trespasser would be for enjoying the private pleasure gardens, like a churl in a morality tale who reaches for another man's wife and finds her shrivel to a hag in his arms. Kenelm would fight the operator of this pleasureground, Sir Thomas Bushell, for this nymph's honour, any day, with any weapon.

Smiling so as not to betray his feelings, he raised his hat and bowed, offering a graceful surrender and apology. They could see by his bearing and his dress that he was no lout or roaring boy. Soon the host, Bushell, came down to speak to him. After establishing his family and his nobility, which interested Bushell but little, Kenelm asked him many intelligent questions about the manipulation of the water, the contents of a rainbow, and so forth, and Bushell was only too happy to describe the hydraulics, showing him the various water cocks that were turned behind the scenes, and the tricks that could be thrown up by fountains, and the highest they could shoot, and soon the pair were conversing very like equals.

All the while Kenelm was thinking of the nymphs, and wondering if they were kept by Bushell as his secret harem or if they were Ladies disporting themselves in the fountains because it was a hot day. It was hard to say which was more likely. Kenelm fancied there was an air of luxury, a whiff of licence about the place. He asked, as casually as possible, who the dark maid was. "Venetia Stanley," said Bushell brusquely. "My ward."

Later that day he finished his journey and was home again, sunburned and thirsty. He stabled Peggy, kissed his mother, and played catapult and Jack-a-rabbit with his younger brother, running together into the dead rooms of the house that had been shut up since his father's execution. He puzzled constantly on the name of Stanley, turning it over in his mind, until, at dinner that evening, he asked his mother if she knew it. Mary Mulsho, the widow Digby, stopped with her soup spoon half-way to her face. "Why, Venetia? She was your playmate, your little friend. When her family were staying at the Abbey, your nurses put you together so you would sit there gabbling at one another, all nonsense, of course, and she being older than you would crawl away, but you could only lie there gurgling . . ."

Kenelm went bright red, and told his mother please to stop, but he also felt a deep sense of calm, as if his planets had simply turned in harmonious alignment. "She is fallen into a rare dishonour," said Mary Mulsho excitedly, forgetting, for a moment, her own despised state as the widow of a Gunpowder plotter.

"Venetia's father having lost his faculties, Thomas Bushell has bought her wardship, and keeps her as one of his marvels at Enstone House, like a fountain or a fancy rock. And they say," she added with heavy significance, "that Thomas Bushell's friend Edmund Wyld has her portrait." She shook her head censoriously, and if that dear brother of Kenelm's, John Digby, had not at that moment held up triumphantly one of his milk teeth, which had just fallen out, and wanted praising as he beamed gappily at them, then Mary Mulsho would have remembered to forbid Kenelm from associating with his former playmate.

Instead, Kenelm rose expressionless, and went calmly upstairs, until reaching his bedchamber he threw himself down on the floorboards and started performing exercises, fencing thrusts and lunges, lifting himself up by his forearms to the roof-beam, again and again. He used as weights the precious stack of books in his bedroom, the heavy volume of Ephemerides and the Hebrew Bible. He needed to build up his strength before he saw Venetia again. He worked on his learning, too, to make himself worthier of her love, and was very often lifting one book at the same time as reading another. It felt the right thing to do as he passed the unbearable time while waiting to see her. And so it was that Mary Mulsho spent the summer believing her son was riding out every day to make an antiquary's record of the standing-stones and monuments in the district, as indeed he was. Apart from every hot day, when he went directly to Enstone House, to talk mechanics and hydraulics with Sir Thomas Bushell, and gaze discreetly, across the ponds, towards Venus in her shell.

> "It is believed Sir Kenelm brought edible snails from the South of France for Venetia, as these were thought to have curative properties . . . It is true that this species of snail is still occasionally found in the district."
>
> Stoke Goldington history society, 2013

THE HOUSEHOLD WAS in chaos, packing for London. Upstairs, Venetia was standing at her closet.

"Red shoes, red waistcoat, Bible, sal aromatica . . ." she said, passing the items to Chater, who stood behind her in black priestly vestments, his big sad eyes bulging, the better to look over her shoulder into her closet. He loved seeing all her apparatus of womanhood, the pads which shaped, the strings which bound. It was marvellous to think how this stuff came together to create a lady.

"Rosary, sweet bags, pearls to be restrung. Will you have command of bringing with us my writing things, Chater?"

Chater was relieved; as their private chaplain, he had been hopeful but not certain he was going with the Digbys to London. He had feared being put in charge of the spiritual care of the children and servants here at Gayhurst.

He and Venetia had been each other's boon companions when Kenelm was away, spending days together making designs for Venetia's hats, debating questions of philosophy, or gossip, telling each other poems and songs. Chater had good taste, and he was cultivated—he had even been to Rome. It was said he might make a cardinal one day. He was one of the few Catholic priests in England legitimised by a grace note of pardon from the Crown, and he considered the Digbys were as fortunate to have him in their service as he was to serve. At Gayhurst he was the perfect companion for Venetia's closet, full of advice on colours, styles and fabrics. She had her lady's maid—but for urbane conversation, and modish judgements, Chater was invaluable. And while Venetia enjoyed receiving his advice, to contradict it gave her even greater pleasure.

His main calling was to save their souls at prayers, but he also made her laugh. He called Buckinghamshire The Void, and all those friends who would not come and visit he called Avoiders. She wondered if his sharp tongue turned against her in her absence.

"We must finish the new Devotional Tract very soon," she said, reprovingly.

We? thought Chater. Pah. She means me. I write all her Devotions, every word, and then when they are circulated under her name, she forgets I had anything to do with them and believes the lie of her own authorship. My lady can persuade herself of anything. She is quite, quite magnificent.

Venetia continued listing her choices. "So, the sea-green, the farthingale in case the Queen still favours them, the fur hood . . ."

"This blue silk would do you very well," said Chater, picking out one of her dresses and holding it up to his body.

"The taffeta, the curling tongs . . ."

"But this is the blue silk that corresponds with my lord's blue silk."

"Yes, Chater, but I do not like it any more."

"It suits you so well," he said, putting his hand on his hip and stroking the full skirt.

"I do not like to wear it any more."

"It was commended mightily at court when you first announced your marriage."

"It pleases me no longer."

"Soft, my lord's horse comes, blue caparisoned, his trumpeter's cordalls also, and his girdle, bridles and banners—then my lady following on wearing this correspondent colour—"

"Stop ye," she said in a voice full of passion. "It does not fit me, Chater."

He looked at his shoes.

"It shows too much of me here, and here. It is immodest. There used to be less of my person, and now I can only wear it on its loosest girth and so the dress has none of its shape and purpose. I feel foolish in it. I am grown more like a woman, Chater. I like my new person. In some ways I believe, after all these years of compliments, I am only finally, now, become a beauty."

Chater made a small intake of breath. Oh, he adored her. Such lies she told, with such conviction.

"I used to look at myself in my glass, every hour—more. But I am grown in understanding of Venetia, and, yes, I say—I like her."

His jaw twitched as if he suffered from keeping quiet.

"I feel I walk solidly upon the ground now . . ."

She is right in that respect, at least, thought Chater, who could not suppress a smirk.

"Perhaps because of the love of my boys and my husband. But to wit: stockings, one pair of white, one scarlet . . ."

Chater decided this was his opportunity. He had been waiting for it for some time. He took a deep breath, made his voice low and matter-of-fact: "My lady has not been keeping Fridays for fish."

"No, she has not."

"She has not fasted neither."

"I have been with child."

"John is almost suckled, my lady. The wet-nurse has been here a year. We are all corpulent beings in the eyes of God, and the purification of the flesh by fasting would be remarkably beneficial to my lady's . . . spiritual progress."

Venetia threw a fiery glance at him. Traitor. Kneeling, picking up her old slippers in her closet, she fancied they were a tiny person's shoes that would never fit her again, and she felt a new thickness to her hands and wrists, and thought how typical, how characteristic it was of Chater to tell her the disquieting truth. He was very like a salamander who would tell no lies, even if he burned. He was a good friend, but oh, he had teeth for biting. She managed to speak quite naturally.

"Black jet bead cross, a present from my lord. I think I will leave that here. My Dutch fan, yes; my old kirtle, no. Chater, please take the things down to Mistress Elizabeth. Tomorrow you must advise me on the fasting that my spirit so requires."

"I will look at the liturgical calendar. There are a few important saints' days next month."

"I think a full day's fasting sooner rather than later, no?"

"I am, as ever, impressed by my lady's commitment to her faith." Chater bowed.

"Go on, sir, go on with you."

With a little snort, Venetia pinned back her hair cruelly and screwed open the jar on her dressing table containing her summer night-time face cream, a bright turquoise preparation made of verdigris, boiled calf's foot, myrrh, camphor, borax and finely ground seacockleshells, which she rubbed violently over her face.

Poor Chater. She supposed it was not very fulfilling for him, living here in The Void, so far from his Popish friends and brothers. Letters from Chater's mentor Father Dell'Mascere had arrived so frequently at first, each one putting him into a radiant good temper, but then the Father's letters came more scantly, and now not at all; Chater was losing his friends and taking the pain of it out on her.

It was darkening, and she had the sense of losing another day. Down on the east lawn she could hear Kenelm huff-puffing as he ran about the garden, skidding and back-tracking on himself, chasing the over-sized snails that raced away, leaving silver skids. Time was slippery for Sir Kenelm, who surfed its eddies and slip-tides. His snails moved super-fast.

Wheeling and diving after them, he called out to young Kenelm, who although he was only six years old, understood that his father was highly unusual. And yet he panted back and forth obediently in the half-light. "They are fast as Mercury tonight!" Kenelm shouted, as a great whorled murex disappeared out of his grasp across the lawn, skidding towards the dark undergrowth.

"Let us creep up on them!" Kenelm whispered to his son, who joined him, tiptoeing, in silent ambush of the bolting snails.

Venetia, sitting on her bed, re-re-read (for the third time) her latest letters, which served for company. One from Penelope was full of detail about her dogs, so boring it became quite amusing. There were two pages of an effusive letter in a smooth French script from Henrietta-Maria's lady-in-waiting Angelique, saying goodbye as she had been sent away from court. There had been a rout of the Queen's Oratorian priests and Catholic retinue, who were summarily exiled from the English court when a letter intercepted showed plans for a Counter-Reformation in England. Buckingham himself sent them home. Venetia burned the third page of that letter, where Angelique had written, with dangerous complicity, "you and I know this country is not kind to us." There was no need for that to linger in her closet. There was also a letter in the intense, effortful hand of Lettice Stanley, her little cousin. Had she replied? She could not recall.

She met Lettice at Tonge castle, ten years ago, when Lettice was a young girl who was in love with her, following her everywhere like a spaniel, gazing at her, sending billets-doux and leaving presents of rosebuds and sweetmeats under her pillow. Lettice must be twenty-two now, and she had not married, and yet she had not taken orders either. Lettice was ambitious and full of life, and stayed most of the time in Shropshire with her mother, who was frail, and when she came to court with her father, she would not stop talking, telling hugely long stories about people no one knew, and holding forth on her opinions on the estate of matrimony, of the conditions of the poor, and habits and customs practised in France, all topics about which she knew very little, and soon everyone at court was most fatigued by her. Thomas Killigrew nicknamed her "Mistress Furtherto-Moreover," which was picked up in many quarters, so she was also sometimes "Mistress However-Because" or just plain "little Nonsuch-Nevertheless."

But to Venetia she was still devoted, and what could Venetia do but accept her devotion? Besides, Venetia believed that beneath her anxious, unformed exterior, she was a dear person with a pure and thoughtful heart, and Venetia felt sorry when people avoided her at court, and she encouraged her fashionable friends to think better of Lettice; Venetia cherished Lettice, particularly because no one else did. She was her little Shropshire pony. Venetia had effected various introductions for her, well aware they would come to nothing, but trying, nonetheless; organising for Emilia Lanier to teach Lettice music, so that she might make friends with some of the Queen's ladies. And because Venetia hoped she might speak less if she knew how to sing.

The fourth letter in Venetia's closet was a legal missive—the last Will and Testament of Kenelm's mother. Venetia had it drawn up by their lawyers in London as a precaution against the future. Although Gayhurst and most of the family money had passed to Kenelm at his majority, Mary Mulsho, to call her by her maiden name, still owned land in Ireland, as well as the dower house. Venetia had a secret presentiment that her husband might convert to the Protestant faith, since Catholicism was now his only obstacle to high office. But if he did convert, Mary Mulsho might seek to disinherit him again, as she had tried to once before, when they were first married. So her Will was a sensitive matter that ought to be resolved. Venetia would arrange for Kenelm to visit the dower house, taking with him some other letters, and the Will to be signed, and some tasty present, a game pie or pudding, and Mary would be so pleased to see her son, her golden boy, that she would, most likely, sign.

Venetia was quietly mindful of these matters; she practised daily vital diplomacies which her husband never noticed, writing letters of thanks and love, remembering saints' days and confinements, negotiating tenancies on the estate, creating friendships and alliances. She hated mundane tasks, which she was expected to perform in order to leave Kenelm free to dream, and she did them impatiently, dropping them at any moment to follow her diversions. She was more likely to drape the room in yellow taffeta than she was to make sure it was swept and ordered. The household was comfortable because she had good servants who loved her. People were what she lived for, company, wit and friendship, whether it be playing with her baby John, or seeking out Chater to show him a new tiffany sleeve or dispute with him about a biblical commentary.

Venetia was wise as Solomon, except when she was foolish. In company she was often silly, laughing as if her head were full of nothing more than pretty bubbles, and she was beloved for it. But the better you knew her, the more you saw her methods, which were often deep.

She heaved herself out of bed, and took her letter box down to join the rest of her luggage, so it would not be forgotten in the rush tomorrow. By the main door she noticed a huge and ominous collection of books, at least fifteen or twenty large bundles tied together with string. For a second she could not understand what they were doing there, and then she was shocked when she realised that Kenelm wanted to take them—

all of them—to London, though Kenelm's bibliomania should not have surprised her any more. She knew what he would say.

"My darling, if I am without my private library I am less of a man. It is the apparatus that keeps my mind revolving, like the planets that girdle Saturn. I must take all these, as I cannot tell which books I may need next for my Great Work, for my poetry, my travels, my experiments in Hydrogogie, the study of water-works . . ."

La, la, la, thought Venetia, as she climbed the stairs back to bed. Well, this makes my great trunk of beauty seem a little less. I should have packed my second-best cape and some kirtles had I known the coach would need an extra pair.

Although her task of packing for court was done, she felt less prepared than ever, less able to face those inquisitive eyes and assessing tongues. Chater had made her feel no better this evening. She wanted some new project to consume her, as her love for Kenelm and then her babies had consumed her. Perhaps she should become devout—a hairshirter with a scourge always in her hand. She could minister to the poor, and catch the plague for her pains. Or perhaps she should turn bibulous, a mead-swiller or ale-sot. It would blunt her boredom, and lift her thoughts, but she had not the taste for it.

As the sky condensed to indigo, and Kenelm skidded after his giant snails in the last of the light, Venetia remembered there was a plate of stale quince comfits in her bedside cabinet, and with bored, then relishing bites, she munched them one by one till they were gone.

> "Imagination is more important than knowledge. For knowledge is limited, whereas imagination encircles the world."
>
> Albert Einstein, 1931

Kenelm lay sweating, victorious from his snail-chase. His snails were in their snail-urn, a huge pot he kept for their containment, until he cooked them up with rosewater as a stew. A nice hot bowl would be a cheering surprise for Venetia. Young Kenelm had been rewarded for his endeavours by being invited into his father's study, and father and son were lying in the hammock that hung from its rafters. Sir Kenelm, during his time at sea, had come to prefer a hammock to a bed.

He had decided to attempt to lay a foundation of alchemy in the boy's mind. It was early to start, but . . . "All imaginations are mirrors. Yours, mine, Chater's. But the alchemist's imagination is more like a mirror than anyone's. We see how every thing has its opposite twin, to which it is attracted and repulsed. 'As above, so below' is one of our rules. D'you see?"

Inconveniently, a young maid came in to lay the fire for them, and he had to wait until she had gone before continuing with his dangerously simple exposition, which any maid might overhear. "Vulgar secrets to vulgar friends, but higher secrets to higher and secret friends only."

"What does 'as above, so below' mean?" said young Kenelm.

"Perhaps it means that we are a looking-glass version of the heavens. Perhaps it means that everything operates according to opposites. But there's beauty of it. It can mean so many things according to your imagination. It is a precept which you have in mind to guide you as you do your alchemy. Do you be paying attention?"

"Yus."

"We believe in the *anima mundi*. Everything is ensouled—whether it is the wind or the trees, which are obviously soulful, or something like a jewel or a clock, which ticks or sparkles, and is guided by its own stars."

Standing by the armillary sphere, which was at his eyes' height, young Kenelm was gravely tapping it with his finger so the world turned, and turned, and turned. He had an impatient facility for the mechanism that impressed and disquieted his father.

Sir Kenelm got up, standing in front of his limbecks and retorts. "Here," he announced, "are the rudiments of the process by which, eventually, base metals may be turned to gold. First . . .

"Calcination." He rapped the furnace.

"Solution." Ping! He flicked the glass.

“Separation.” Shh. He slid a finger down the conical flask.
“Conjunction.” He bent on one knee as if to pray.
“Mortification.” He pointed sternly to the fire-pan.
“Putrefaction.” Rattle! He shook the slop bucket.
“Sublimation.” He waved the fingers on one hand.
“Libation.” He blew bubbles from his wet lips.
“Exaltation.” He held a bowl up ceremoniously.

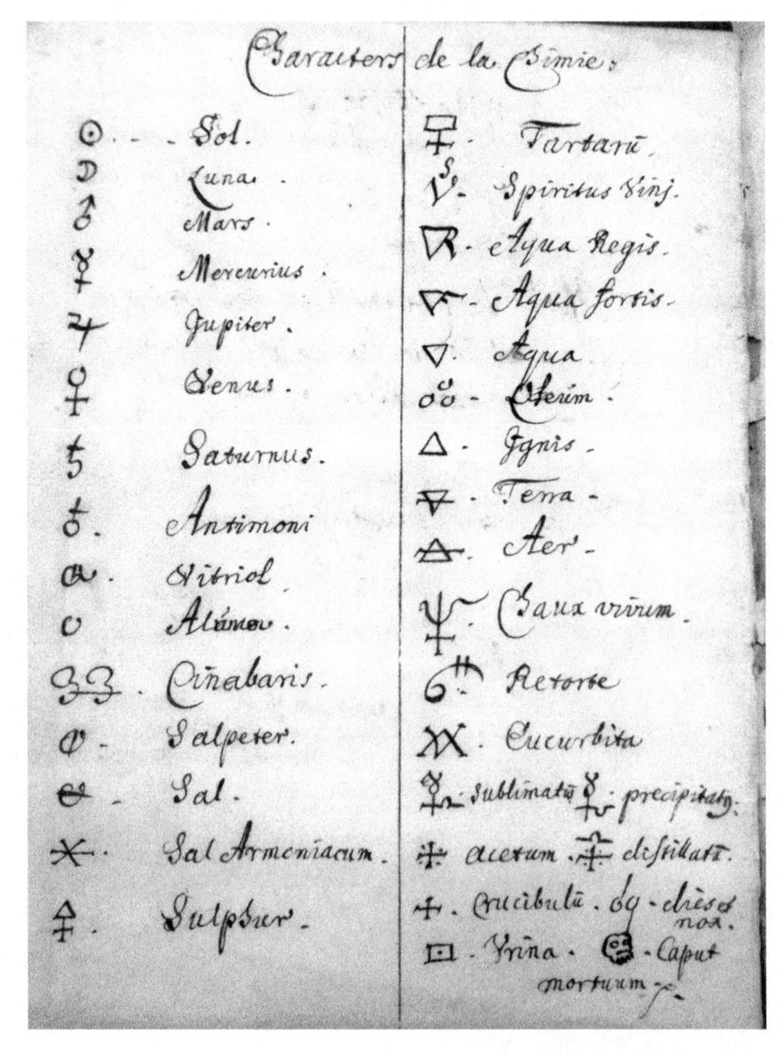

From the alchemical notebook of Sir Kenelm Digby

"Some stages take a long time: others are swift. We practise them like games of the mind. Each has a hundred different possible outcomes, depending on the conditions, lunar and sublunar."

Kenelm looked at Kenelm. He hoped he had not gone too far for one so young. The boy's mouth was moving; he wanted to speak.

"It reminds me very much of the brewing of ale that Mistress Elizabeth does down in the barn."

Kenelm's tufty yellow eyebrows rose very far up, as far as young Kenelm had ever seen them rise. He started putting away his apparatus quietly, humming to himself. "Well, sir, indeed. What did I say to you? As below, so above."

I Saw Eternity the Other Night

LATE AT NIGHT, while the household slept, Sir Kenelm was in his study, performing stealthy lucubrations. He was agitating quicksilver in a cork-sealed bolts-head, squinting as he followed the half-scrawled recipe, a loose page from his grimoire, a book in many languages, codes, formulae and Hebraic scripts, written in various hands, inks and fonts. The medicine he was preparing was a matter of urgency, since they must depart the next morning, but young Kenelm needed to be treated first, for it had been discovered that he had a slight but bothersome indisposition. In a word, worms.

Venetia recalled that a medal of St. Anne should be hung around the boy's neck, although she could not find one and used St. Christopher instead. Kenelm thought it was worth also following his private recipe. The village remedy of rosemary water he did not deem effective. He found this far superior recipe in his book:

> "For worms in children, take 1½ dram of the best running Mercury, put it into a bolts-head, spit fasting spittle upon it (from a wholesome mouth) and shake well. Then pour off the Spittle from it, and wash the Mercury clean with hot milk several times. Then allow the child this Mercury in a spoon with little warm milk upon it. Do this twice or thrice, intermitting two or three days between every dose."
>
> Kenelm Digby, *Chemical Secrets and Experiments,* 1668

Kenelm spat into the quicksilver, fancying he tasted its vapour, which was tart like blood. As he sat waiting for the milk to warm in the pan, he gazed into the shew-stone of the quicksilver and saw the distorted visage of his old tutor, Thomas Allen. He was wearing his gown and cap, and struggling to carry a great pile of papers, books and the wax discs that recorded his talks with angels, as well as a big heavy contraption with buttons marked with every letter in the alphabet, and slim mirrors, round in shape, marked Digital Versatile Disc. There was too much for Allen to carry and the pile was tumbling from his hands. Kenelm blinked and realised that he was only dozing and had been wakened by his own recipe slipping to the floor. He must go and see the old man in Oxford, before it was too late. Thomas Allen was eighty-nine.

Kenelm washed, and washed again the skittish silver liquid, then let it plop into a hornspoon. He could still see the face of Allen in the mercury, grimacing and distorting as the mercury spooled downwards and splashed into distinct globules, so there was a tiny Thomas Allen visible in each blob, and all of them were pulling different expressions.

Kenelm had proposed Allen as a member of the Invisible College, but the younger members rejected him because they feared the slur of sorcery. "We want no magi, no conjurations here," said young Pritchett. "He has the finest collection of mathematical books I have ever seen," said Sir Kenelm. "Do you believe the tittle-tattle that spirits thronged behind him on the college stairs like bees? Would you be like the maids of Sir John Scudamore's household, afrit of a ticking box?"

Thomas Allen was a guest of Scudamore when the maids there threw away his watch, which they judged a mechanical familiar. As they were cleaning his room they heard a ticking, emanating from a little black box that must be the devil, and so, without touching it with their hands but using their pinnies or dishclouts, they threw it out of the window to drown the devil in the moat below. Luckily it caught by its string upon an elder bush and so Thomas Allen's watch was rescued.

Sir Kenelm feared that the quick young Invisibles, with their hydraulics and botanical studies, were not schooled in Hermetic wisdom, so he filled in the basics airily for them: "Everything which is made is numbered in the mind of God. If the numbers that describe a toad were to be forgotten and fall from the mind of God then no toads should exist. Thomas Allen knows this mystical dimension of numbers, their mathesis . . ."

Kenelm said this speech, or something like it, to the company. But they stuck firm and would not have Thomas Allen, "nor the ghost of John Dee neither," said Sir Cheney Culpeper, and the Invisibles tapped their quills on the table in agreement.

"It is not that we believe Master Allen to be a conjuror," said another of the beardless wonders to him privately afterwards. "We do not. But the public tongue says he is, and therefore we put ourselves at risk if we take him into our ranks. We could be persecuted by the mob and our laboratories destroyed, as Dr. Dee's were at Mortlake. Or our patrons could withdraw their monies, or our designs lose their warrants. It is because we are Prudent that we do not welcome him, not because we are Superstitious."

Against everything, Digby took some pertinent volumes the Invisibles had in circulation, and sent them to Allen at Oxford. They returned two months later, pages somewhat dirtied and stuck together with soup, spindly incy-wee writing covering the margins. The old man's scrawl seemed to wheeze, rising and falling, illegible even to Digby's eye, once so familiar with his hand. The words he could read were indifferent to the purpose.

He was seized with an urge to go to Oxford almost at once to visit Allen, but he also knew that now was his time to be in London, his brief chance to shine while his naval exploits were news. He knew, from astrology, rhetoric and every noble discipline, that nothing could be achieved except if its timing were propitious. The stars must be in alignment before any new undertaking.

For example, the space-probes *Voyager 1* and *2* could not depart before the planets were in perfect order. Once every 175 years they fell into such orbits that their gravitational pull eased the flight of those great data-gathering insects so they glided effortlessly through the heliosphere. The *Voyagers* could have been launched in 1627, but no, Sir Kenelm was dozy; he was unprepared. In 1977 when the alignment came again, the *Voyagers* would surf the sky-tide.

An oak clawed at the laboratory window, and Kenelm rose and looked out over the blue expanse of grass, down to his obelisk, which was emitting a flashing halo of pale light. Circular rays were given off by every object, as the Alchemists knew. Time itself was circular, which was why Sir Kenelm was gifted with so many strange understandings.

"I saw Eternity the other night," he muttered to himself.
"Like a great Ring of pure and endless light . . ."

The radio mast bleeped intermittently, alerting Kenelm to Immortality, Eternal Youth and Perfect Health—all within his scope, if he would only turn his mind to his loved ones' advantage. He must think of his wife, but first, holding a candle and feeling happily paternal, Kenelm crept up the stairs with the hornspoon of night-bright silver medicine for his boy.

"Animula vagula blandula/ Hospes comeseque corporis."

The Emperor Hadrian's purported deathbed address to his departing spirit—
"My little wandering sportful soul/ Guest and companion of my body."

"Poor intricated soul! Riddling, perplexed, labyrinthical soul!"

John Donne's sermon on the day of St. Paul's Conversion, 1629

IT WAS TWILIGHT, and stray dogs and chained mastiffs were barking to one another across Whitehall; at Somerset House, cherubs with grotesque red cheeks were striking a French mechanical clock, calling Queen Henrietta-Maria's friends and household to a Catholic evensong. The laying of the foundation stone of the Queen's new chapel was to be celebrated, and it was the Digbys' first public engagement since they arrived in town. It was a difficult invitation, dangerous to accept, foolish to decline.

Kenelm paced the rose garden of their manor at Charterhouse, wondering whether they should go. Young Kenelm was cured of his indisposition, and the surly blots on his cheeks should not hold them back from attending. If they went, they would find further favour with their Catholic Queen and her Catholic friends; they would know everyone there, and it would be a good beginning for Venetia's return to public life. And yet Kenelm wanted to be more than the Queen's cavaliero. He wanted to make comptroller of the King's navy, but this would never come to pass while he played his Old Faith in public.

He and Venetia were usually discreet in their Catholicism; Chater ministered the mass to them in the chapel at Gayhurst in private, and they paid the fine for recusancy. That was that. To their neighbours they were "Catholics, yes, but not bad people." Kenelm was careful to be an irreproachable landlord because every slip he made, every stag disputed or grain sack overpriced, was considered a Catholic vice; the local people always looked at him sideways, and every long word he used in conversation was taken as a foreign secret or a spell.

Protestantism had his respect, and Catholicism his heart, but Hermetical philosophy, the Great Work, engaged his Imaginative soul, his deepest self. To be Catholic, to be Protestant—both seemed so limited when there was a Third Way. The real devotions he practised were in his laboratory, in the sublimations and transubstantiations, when the red sulphur died and the white peacock rose.

The Queen had been generous to them, though sometimes Kenelm wished she would be less so. Her talk of undertaking a barefoot pilgrimage in honour of Kenelm's "martyred" father grieved and embarrassed Kenelm. It could only open old wounds. He found himself snapping at her, Let it lie, madame—*laisse tomber, madame, je vous en prie.* After this outburst, he expected to fall out of favour with her, but he found she was fonder, warmer with him, and she began to call him her Chevalier d'Igby.

The fact that it was not a mass, only vespers, held outdoors, convinced Kenelm finally that they ought to attend, and Venetia threw herself into preparation, but their ambivalence showed itself in multiple mis-starts and delays to their journey—a lost pair of shoes, a carriage boy unbidden. The house was still in chaos with only half their things unpacked, but the business of the move seemed to have taken Venetia out of herself. She had found new strength, albeit superficial, glib and smiling, and in the coach she was full of chat and speculation about how changed their friends would be.

Young drabs and dolls and tuppenny-boys were gathered on the Strand watching the traffic of carriages arriving at Somerset House, and as the Digbys' escutcheoned coach turned the corner, many surged forward in unison to greet their goddess. Venetia, recognizing this crowd-frenzy that always attended her, clutched Kenelm's hand, saying "No, no!" excitedly, and shielding her face. But the crowd's movement had been motivated only by the opening of a beer-hatch on the lower Drury Tavern, and as they ran and queued it was clear they had no interest in the Digbys' coach at all. Kenelm, preoccupied by the royal halberdiers, barely noticed Venetia's mistake; Chater, whom they had invited to ride with them, bit his lip and looked out of the window.

Carriages rammed the street, and pikemen were checking every guest. The church chimes had already stopped when the Digbys finally entered the courtyard. The evening sky was like a stage-cloth, marbled pink and blue, and the air was Popish with incense, sweet clouds that hastened night and judgement on them all, as swallows turned tricks in the air, fast and faster till they became bats. Outdoors pews were packed with the congregation, whom Venetia ate up with her eyes, at least a hundred friends, or something like friends—so many massed and half-forgotten faces that Venetia had not seen for several years' exile at Gayhurst during her childbearing and Kenelm's absence. As they processed up the aisle of courtyard flagstones, Chater trotting in behind them, Venetia's eyes roved over everyone:

Master Stump's brow has become heavy since he lost his property. My Lady Cecil's face still has a lovely trusting turn, white as a legume, which never felt a moment's sin or pleasure. Dame Peterkin's jaw will not be trifled with. If those dark curls piled on top of her head are her own, then dogs can sing syllogisms. They're wired horse hair, I warrant. That fine lady, whoever she is, has an ale-sot's puffed and broken veins; this man eats too much meat and his eyes bulge. God forgive us all, for our souls are written in our faces.

There is my coz Lettice—red is not a becoming colour to her—let me reach to hold her hand briefly. Bless her, for she cannot have found any friends yet—there she is sitting next to two old matrons twice her age. Lady Vavasour has drunk the silver tincture cure for the French pox, and her skin has turned grey-blue.

Old Dame Overall has plaisters under her wig that draw the sagging skin tighter off her face. Dame Overall's friend, her sister perhaps, has not used any plaisters and looks softer, looser, older. Hard to judge who looks worse between them. One has fought, the other submitted. Both are tragic.

Venetia nodded respectfully at Aletheia Howard, the Countess of Arundel, thinking: She has filled her paps out with paper and her eyebrows are made from mink-hair and egg white, but she looks good on't.

Is that Olivia Porter? I do believe it is. Greetings, my dear. No sign of Endymion—he is more careful than to show himself here but he sends his wife alone. Olive looks unnaturally radiant. Like a fifteen-year-old girl who knows too much of life. And yet she is a mother of four living and more dead. I swear nature alone never made her cheek so flushed and peachy. I shall know more of this.

"Praise the Father, Son and Holy Ghost," said Venetia, bobbing to the altarpiece set up where the new chapel would rise. Yes, she believed in the reading of faces, which was why she was wearing a veil to church: I would rather they thought me modest than knew me blown.

In front of the altar stone, beside the candles, glowed bowls of new roses, fresh red. A blown rose had more grace and pathos than a crisp new rose, but no one wanted a blown rose. You wouldn't give so much as a penny for their soft, wide-open faces, and their petals, which dropped at the lightest finger-touch; their pale evening scent carried further than new roses, but was touched with tiredness and putrefaction. The saying jingled in her head like coin—*Against the blown rose they will stop their nose, that kneeled unto the buds.*

Venetia preceded Kenelm into their reserved pew. Oh Lord, thank you for giving us a good pew, near the front. Here we are again, foremost at the Queen's court. It is the very smartest place to be this evening, like a little piece of France. Forbidden Vespers practised *en plein air*, the very nerve. Oh Lord, forgive me for taking mass only at home, in private. Oh Lord, keep Kenelm safe and let him not fall out of standing in the eyes of men. Oh Lord, let him be made a lord. We can see almost everyone here from this pew. Oh Lord, who suffered for our sins, thank you. Oh Lord, let them not think my beauty gone. Oh Lord, protect my children. Oh Lord, forgive me always.

Their thoughts high and low interwove until the congregation's mind seemed to condense and take shape into clouds of incense hanging above them.

First came the Dismal Dozen, the Capuchin friars sent over by Cardinal Richelieu, hooded, and flat-footed, their censers swinging, ropes of tiny skulls knotted at their waists. Next, the Queen, looking as excited as a girl on her saint's day, accompanied by her favourite, the Scots Franciscan,

Father Conn. Venetia stood facing the altarpiece solemnly, refusing to look gawpishly at the congregation. She felt their eyes, hot with scrutiny: has Venetia had the pox? Is she with child again, or is she merely fat? Well, she supposed, some heads here must be at prayer.

As Father Conn prayed for the purification of the soul of the new chapel's architect, Master Inigo Jones, she heard a deep voice call "Amen" too loudly. It was Ben Jonson. Jonson and Jones were still at odds, then. The one could not make a masque without the other, for every setting needs a theme, and yet they loved to quarrel. She could see Jonson's great bulk in a pew also near the front. How that man swells! He must be close to 20 stones. Venetia could not resist leaning forward, to catch another look at his eyes, one of which seemed to have grown larger and lower than the other, perhaps because of a palsy. He winked at her—or was it a twitch? He was gross, distended, and yet the odour of the person he used to be clung to him.

They loved each other well, when they were both beginners, she a beauty and he a Coming Man of Letters, poor and hasty and a little self-glorious, but the quickest wit she ever knew. He could mimic a voice, or pick up a person's mode of speaking, as quick as walk in mud. They used to talk in their own language together, laughing in corners. Now, though they were both changed, her heart rose to meet him as ever before, and she knew that human love was stronger than decay. The platitude was true: love endured. Love overcame. Not in an empty, courtly, sonneteering way, but manifestly. She knew this—and yet she could not forgive herself for growing older.

While her lips said the catechism, Venetia thought of Olive, and her bright, peeled complexion, and yearned to know what change had overtaken Olive. Was she in love? Was she ill? There was something feverish in her eye, which showed unusually dark. She thought of asking Kenelm if he noticed anything different about Olive, but she knew the answer would be no. Seeing her standing glowing and pert at the corner of her pew, he might have remembered how much he liked her, or been struck how pretty she was. But he would never have questioned why, or how—or even observed his own observation. Half of us, she thought, are surface creatures; half of us have deeper understanding.

Veiled, Venetia was a riveting spectacle to the congregation. It was as if an arrow were pointing to and obscuring her face. People longed to see what had become of her. Those who could not help themselves craned their necks as she went past, longing to see her ravaged, no matter that they prayed for her beauty's preservation. There was even something compelling about the veil itself, the sheerest pale grey Cyprus that seemed to breathe with her. The veil was the perfect costume—demure, disguised. Reformed, perhaps. She knew she ought to pay lip-service to the idea that she was reformed now she was married and no longer infamous, and so forth, but she had always been impervious to the idea that she was scandalous in the first place. She had never been kept, never a courtesan. Her private wealth had given her outrageous freedom, that was all. There was nothing in her that knew how to apologise. She was so sure, so completely certain, as she entered any room, of her power, of her contribution to the sum of beauty in the world. And yet she had always been vulnerable too, wounded by the smallest slight, and turned into a pathetic self-doubting creature by such a nothing as a kind word left unsaid, or a sum she could not add.

Her unpredictability was like a drug to Kenelm. He was elated by her approval and fearful of her sadness. To hide these passions of his, he had developed a steady, watchful exterior which did not betray how much he regarded her opinion in everything, how very much he wanted her to have her own way. For her to be denied was agony to him. He believed she was always right, even when she was unreasonable. She was deft and sure in all her instincts when he was blundering and over-educated and obscure. Because she was excessive, he had always to play at being reasonable; because she was volatile, he needed to pretend to be steadfast. Thus he was become a man. He reached for her hand after the paternoster.

Kenelm's mind moved on to his Hermetic studies, as he looked at the bright green stones mounted on the High Cross ahead of them and thought of the mounted, valiant troops of winged horsemen, invisible to the eye, which stream forth in purposive armies out of precious stones, in order to heal, improve and refine—unseen and unseeing, and yet the air is full of them, as thick as motes of dust in sunshine. This put him in mind of the missing emerald tablet of Hermes Trismegistus, which had so much goodness emanating from it, and he considered—with the small inhalation that attends a new thought—if it might be discovered buried at the spot on earth where food is most plentiful, health most abundant and people live as long as Enoch who had 350 years . . .

Kenelm wondered where the King was. He had heard he might be here, in disguise. Charles and Queen Henrietta-Maria were good friends now, after their bad beginning. She had been stiff with jealousy of the Duke of Buckingham. Kenelm had seen it himself, when Buckingham was showing off to the King, doing some intolerable little dance for him, the Queen had walked out—furious, not looking back, taking with her a troop of ladies-in-waiting who followed one by one. But Buckingham was dead, stabbed by the ten-penny cutler's knife of a half-mad soldier, and in his grief the King had found the Queen, and he called her "Mary" and they represented themselves as Hermetic twins, as one person on all matters, except religion. The joke was even whispered at court, after it was censored from the script of Davenant's winter masque:

"The King is in love."

"With whom?"

"With the Queen."

"In love with his own Wife! That's held incest in Court."

Kenelm breathed deeply, as if trying to smell the royal presence. He scanned the congregation for a hooded person, a god disguised. Yes, there were a few cloaked nobles standing suspiciously together, high-ruffed and wearing hats, their heads down. Amid them, short, bow-legged, was that the King? The *Fidei Defensor*? Thus concealed, he could please his wife and yet not displease his people. Ha! We live, thought Kenelm, in playful times. Be mutable, be flexible, Ken. He wondered if the nearness of the King's body could be felt emanating through the congregation, despite his disguise. Perhaps his royal body also put forth streams of invisible noble cavalry, like a sort of human jewel.

Deposuit potentes . . . Exaltavit humiles . . . The congregation rose as the censer swung. Chater had slipped into a back pew along with a tutor he knew, and a moody Spanish ambassador. Chater scanned the congregation for people of note and fashionable hats. He noted that Master Wurbeck's hose were definitely too tight. The boys' singing rose pure and clear and the storm lanterns were lit down the aisle as the sky turned indigo. Chater noticed that Lady Margaret seemed to be with child again. Chater *loved* church.

He could spy Sir Kenelm if he leaned forwards. Sir Kenelm's tawny-golden hair was now growing wonderfully long, and curled so naturally. As the congregation knelt Chater caught a flash of Kenelm's strong stockinged calf. It was as if its veins were throbbing in time with Chater's heart. Chater shut his eyes. "God help me to love Sir Kenelm as my master," he prayed, "and to assist Lady Venetia in her spiritual progress and never think ill of her."

Holy water was scattered over the ground and Father Conn raised his voice loud to warn off the scourging angel of plague. And lastly, when night had absolutely fallen, there was a solemn prayer that all those present might be spared by the Lord to live to worship in the new chapel when it had risen from that spot, and in agreement, the congregation with one voice and one heart for the first time in the whole evensong, joined to say a true Amen.

"Venetia gave large sums to the poor, earning the money through gambling, in which pursuit she was both lucky and skillful."

The Oxford Dictionary of National Biography, 2012

"CLUBS," CALLED VENETIA.

"Oh, contagion," muttered Penelope.

"La, la, la," said Olive, thinking.

The three ladies had been playing Glecko all afternoon, first for almonds, and then for shillings and gossip; renewing, by this vicious game, their love and trust of one other. Venetia was their Queen. Penelope was blunt, decisive, plain. Olive was a graceful tree that bent any way in a wind.

"Did you ever see three knaves?" said Penelope, throwing them down.

"No indeed," said Venetia. "Now tell me their names."

"Ha," said Penelope. "They are Basket, Grey and Pippin."

"Those are dogs," said Venetia, "not knaves. But knavish dogs, I grant. Show us your gleeks and mournivals, Olive."

Olive, her strange new face glowing, surprised them by splaying a flush of four low hearts.

"What a fox she is," said Venetia.

Penelope swallowed her sweet sack quickly, so she might interject: "No, on my troth, I heard it said that Lady Anne Clifford is the fox, because as the proverb goes, the hedgehog knows many things, but the fox knows only one thing, and that is that she must have her estates.

"Her husband says to her, 'I love you and hold you sober in all things, except your land, which transports you beyond yourself and makes you devoid of all reason.'"

Lady Anne Clifford was known to be obsessed by her right to sue for to her father's lands, of which she was sole heir. She petitioned endlessly to the king, and had fallen out with her family and her husband over it. She had married the elder Sackville brother, who once courted Venetia, and since his death she had remarried and carried on her legal quarrel.

"Well," said Venetia, laying down another card, "I hear that it is better to be a prickler than a prancer."

Olive thought: They have the proverb the wrong way about. The hedgehog knows one thing deeply and the fox knows many things in passing. But Olive would rather be pleasant than clever, and did not speak this.

The cards spread flat, and mingled; they rose up into a church tower and were tapped down into a box.

"You are eldest," said Venetia to Olive, motioning that she should begin.

"I am not!" It was a little joke they liked to rehearse. The player on the left of the dealer was correctly termed "eldest."

"So tell me," said Venetia, "how is my poor Shropshire coz, young Lettice?"

"Little Miss Furtherto-Moreover? The great philosopher!" said Olive, pulling a face.

"Lettice and I are driving to Blackfriars to see the sheep shorn tomorrow," said Penelope coolly.

Thank goodness—she has made at least one new friend, thought Venetia, tapping her cards to change the subject.

"And what do we think of Lucy Bright, that is going to be Lucy Lennox?"

"Delightful," said Olive.

"So talented in so many ways," said Penelope.

"So many talents," sighed Olive, "you cannot count them."

"So fine it hurts my eyes to look at her," said Penelope.

"She sounds unbearable," said Venetia.

Venetia's shillings had run out, so she produced an Angel from her purse, at which the ladies made clicking, whirring noises with their tongues, which was a cock-fighting noise. None of them, being ladies, had ever been to a cock-fight, yet they knew the King was mad for them. Olive told her to put the coin away, but then took it out of her hand, to examine the archangel Michael and his dragon. Olive was a godly woman and she kissed the Angel quickly before placing him in the middle of the table.

Venetia took out her spectacle-glass, ostensibly to look at the Angel too, but mainly because she wanted to inspect Olive's face more closely. She saw with a quick glance that her skin was smooth, over-painted with egg-white and pearl dust no doubt, but wonderfully smooth. The problem was the pink, crusted rupture under her eyes where the treatment had stopped. "The Angel is at stake," said Venetia, and rolled the dice.

Spades, sweet Malaga sack; more hearts and more mournivals. The cards were flipped and spread into endless variations, like stars being shaken out.

"You ladies at court look so divine these days," said Venetia. "I feel very much a country mouse."

There was a little pause.

"Harbottle Grimston's wife has a special tooth resin come from France. I will give you some," said Olive, colouring slightly.

"Yes, I have some of that," said Penelope. "The gum of Tragamantha? It stings like Christ."

"Penelope, kiss the Angel," reproved Olive.

Penelope did so, and as she leaned forward they saw the hair below her cap was turned quite grey. She did not care about such things, being a practical and unaffected type of person, almost mannish.

The ladies nibbled almonds and studied their cards.

"What is the sweet thing all the ladies at court are taking," asked Venetia, her head on an angle, "to cure this new and mortal tiredness? To smooth the frown that lingers for no reason but habit. To make themselves visible again to men."

"Darling, you are almost as beautiful now as you ever were," said Penelope.

"There is nothing that can really be done," said Olive obscurely, tapping her cards. "Nothing, tra la."

"Which wise-woman ministers you your nothing? Which quack gives you nothing to put on your face at night? Not that I want your nothing, for I do not, I want none of it," said Venetia. "I feel I am only just now become a beauty, because of the love of my sons and my husband."

Silence.

Penelope chewed a candied fruit, slowly.

"I hear Lady Grimston drinks Viper Wine for her face," said Penelope, dropping a high card.

"I hear many birds sing in the trees," said Olive, discarding low.

"I hear the naming of secrets, and I raise you a Queen," said Venetia.

"There is to be a nautical display tomorrow," said Olive, folding.

"The Viper Wine is prepared by a city apothecary," said Penelope, playing two tens. "To an old receipt. I do not know which, mind. I think there is too much to lose to play at that quack's game."

"There is much to win also," said Venetia.

"Winning does not come into it, dearheart. It is merely a brief and dangerous postponement, that puts off losing for a little while."

"For the display on the Thames tomorrow, Endymion has got himself a new cape cut. In horrid yellow," said Olive.

Penelope, as she eyed the cards she had been dealt, had more to say: "If you have an ague or a dropsy or a gripper-the-chest, then get you to a doctor. As you have none, thank the Lord for your luck and Amen. That is what I say." And she folded.

"Thank you, dear ladies," said Venetia, collecting. "Thank you." She dropped the Angel back into her purse, and in the half-dark of that silken privacy St. Michael remained, forever on the point of spearing the dragon beneath him, which writhed in perpetuity.

When Penelope had gone, Olive and Venetia sat down together in front of the fire, and Olive with her raw, smooth face looked guiltily at Venetia with huge impulsive eyes. "I never told you lies! I hate to do it, Venice. But I do not wish Penelope should know the business of my face. I mean, my dealings with the apothecary. It would travel round the court faster than Orion and set all the teeth clacking so my Endymion will come to hear of it."

"You keep it a secret from him?" said Venetia, thinking: *He has not noticed?*

"Of course I do! I have to pay for it from the housekeeping money. He thinks I am visiting orphans in the stews of Greyfriars." She winked, and the tight skin around her eye rippled unnaturally. "Endymion has rejoiced in my good humour lately and"—her voice became softer, more confidential—"we have been better friends than ever." Venetia tried to put from her mind the image of jowly Endymion in amorous mood. Olive had once confided that he hurt her whenever he came to her bedroom.

"He is kinder to you now? Or does he still practice the unpleasantness upon you?"

Olive looked darkly at Venetia. "He cannot find release without it. It is something he learned from a courtesan, when he was a boy, I think. But the treatments of my face make me so much more willing. I feel myself more as he would wish me. It is a marriage cure, darling. But it is very sad—my apothecary has died." She giggled nervously. "By his own hand—I mean, by his own medicaments. So I would lief come with you to find another."

They embraced, and drank more sack, and Olive held up her glass and said, "To us!" and Venetia could not bring herself to drink before she asked, "But dear, what treatments have you been practising?"

"I have been peeled weekly with sulphur mithridate, and then every night I apply butter of antimony. It is said to counteract all the lead that has embedded in my cheeks from too much painting, which is the reason for my runckles . . ."

She started to cry a little, at the unfairness of it. No one warned her that painting with lead would be so injurious—it was what every beauty used. "The mithridate burns, to be sure, and sometimes welts a little, but I have grown to love its whip upon my cheek. I miss it dreadfully now I have run out. But my poor apothecary tried to cure his hot gout with drinking lily-water, and it did not work, and now his shop is shut up and he is quite dead." She giggled again, while wiping a tear.

"Who shall we go to, then?" said Venetia, ignoring her waterworks. "Who is the Queen's apothecary?"

"Theodore de Mayerne is a fart-britches. We will not go to him. He would put a cockerel on your feet and sing hallelujah. And for Sir William Paddy, we cannot trust him, as he will tell the Queen and she will tell Father Conn and he will tell Endymion. Besides, they are old men who follow Galen to the letter. They would bleed you for black bile or choler and send you home. No, no. We shall go to one of the new Physicians on Fenchurch Street who makes Viper Wine. I have been trying to find an excuse to leave my babes and visit him these past two weeks."

"Does Lady Grimston go to him?"

"I think so. And Lady Grimston has had the run of the Medici doctors. She knows all the cures. Her sister was first to recommend me frog's jelly for burning cheeks, and I have used it ever since."

"Shall we go, then? To the Fenchurch Street physician?"

"Yes, without delay."

"Oh, thank God. I am to be healed." Venetia crossed herself with relief. She would pay for this with the Angel in her purse; her pot of profit would thus be put to good purpose. The apothecary sounded expensive, and she would not wish him any other way.

The two of them embraced again, and close to her ear, Olive whispered "Secret!" and gripped Venetia's arm so loving-tight that her nails dug little half-moons in her flesh, the ghosts of which were still there half an hour later when Venetia went to bed.

Night covered the sleeping faces of London, blackened with pox, flowered with scurvy, or twitching as their muscles relaxed. Some mouths were sawdust-rough with scabs, some heaving with slack snores, others pinched like carp-fish in tight oblivion. Venetia slept sitting up against her pillows, with one eye half open. Olive's face, larded in lavender-scented butter, had disobeyed her will again and crumpled itself into the pillow, although each night she tried to sleep on her back, which was held to be better for the complexion.

Under darkness, the faithful turned, sighed, snuffled, sagged, creased, smiled—without gaslight or sodium streetlights or camera surveillance, without digital winking comforters or tiny breathing phones glowing next to them all night like mechanical familiars. Instead they were kept safe by their consciences, which censored and guided their dreams, and put them to sleep with a routine prayer, and sleeping they drew, suckling, on communal reserves of power and goodness, which would in time be replaced with literal circuits of cable, recharging their mechanical familiars. But even without navigation maps, they were not lost because they felt that God, looking down, knew where each of them slept, and saw their hearts pulsing evenly, radiating their presence on the map of His kingdom.

Yellow Submarine

MARS WAS IN its long winter, halfway through its year of ninety-two weeks. In the calendar of Buddhists it was 2176, to the Coptics it was 1348, and to the Japanese Kan'ei 9, but by common consent in London it was 13 October 1632. But whether it was the sixth year of the reign of Charles I or the seventh, no one could agree, because some adhered to the Old Calendar, and hated the continental fiction of the New Calendar, while others thought the Old Calendar outmoded, and many changed their minds between the two. Clocks kept different time across the country, suffering drifts of fifteen minutes either side of the hour, if they struck at all.

Time was personal, and so was the rule of Charles I who for two years now had not summoned parliament, and the taverns were full of gentlemen saying it would not do. But it did do, and that morning the sun still rose, and played upon the Thames, which was then at mid-flow, and the dandelions by the docks at Chelsea were downy globes, and the shadow on the dial in the courtyard at York House was short and sharp-edged, and upon the water-clock in the King's own garden, the decorative plaster spaniels had only just begun to chase the mallard. In other words, it was bright and early.

Beached upon the foreshore of the Thames was a strange and terrible creature, very like a whale, but made of stitched-together leather stretched over curved ribs of wood. There were six oars like fins protruding from both of its sides, and from a jaunty turret fluttered a white ensign. Rumour said it was going to sail like a fish, under the water rather than upon it. It had appeared overnight, manifesting itself upon the bank of the Thames. Cornelis Drebbel was the inventor of this strange ark, this bathysphere, this submarine. Drebbel was an old man, preoccupied with the details of his dreams, but his son-in-law, Abe Kuffler, with an instinct for showmanship, made sure all the pulleys and equipment used to transport it to the shore had been removed before daybreak, leaving it lying there alone, humming where it sat, a fat leather apparition from the future.

Drebbel the Dutchman had turned up a decade ago at the court of James with many Ingeniose devices, perpetual clocks, magic lanterns, and a camera obscura, and so on, which had much pleased little Prince Henry, then ten years old and already playing Maecenas, so that he took Drebbel into his employ at Eltham Palace, where he created artifices for plays and masques. But his imagination had a practical turn, and he invented temperature regulators for the ovens in the palace kitchens, and a "hatcher" for bringing forth chicks out of eggs, as well as his famous double-lensed artificial eye, which let you see very small things as if they were very big. And everyone called them different names, as "occhileto" (little eye), "engyscope," "brood oven," and "heat clock"—although Sir Kenelm pronounced them microscope, incubator, thermostat.

Crowds had gathered on both sides of the Thames, townsmen holding their children up to get a view, and gentlefolk yawning to be up so early, and groups of young men jostling each other to see better and get closer, experiencing something like lust for this fabulous machine. A solo drummer beat an unrelenting rhythm that kept the crowd's expectation ticking over. Up and down the strand, a Peter Pie-man hawked pasties made in the shape of the boat, shouting, "Sub, sub, submarine pies, fresh 'n' hot 'n' tasty."

There was a frisson amongst the crowd, as at a happy execution. When a pig's bladder burst, two women screamed. Was this vessel really going to submerge and sail beneath the waves? All the way to Greenwich and back? How would it pass the river's suck at London Bridge?

"It will never do it."

"They will all be drown."

"They done it last night in a rehearsal and the King himself done ride in it, too."

Rumours kept people occupied while they waited for something to happen. Some said it was the skeleton of a whale, preserved with glue, while others claimed it was a Papist spying ship that had been apprehended at Dover. A lord temporal watching from a balcony at Whitehall told his manservant the machine had "infernal eyes."

Meanwhile, a professional crier wearing leather livery that matched the boat was pacing up and down beside it, shouting points of information at the crowd. "Self-sealing gaskets of leather cover heach and hevery hoar," he cried, pointing to the paddles. "Her skin is held in place by clinkers, a kind donation from the Wherry Forge at Richmond, my lords and ladies, a kind donation . . . The craft is made to sink by pumping pigs bladders full'o water, and it is made to rise by God's will and the pumping of the said bladders empty-oh."

"How's they breathe then?" called a voice from the crowd.

"In the old model, each oarsmen be breathing through a tube bobbin' upon the surface of the water by means of cork, but this time, for the first time, ladies and gentlemen, for the very first time, air within the craft will be replenished by a burning hwick of nitreous, or salt-nitre. That's right, a burning hwick, a double-you, aye, see, kay." He seemed about to spell out "nitreous" but then decided against it.

The voyage had been carefully timed so that the strong neap tide would draw the vessel swiftly to Greenwich. "She shall slip around the eel-ships in a trice," he said. "There'll be no grounding of this craft in the mud this time neither, no sticking here, sirs, oh no, sirs—the craft has been made to be nimble and sleek like the dolphin, ladies and gents, like the dolphin . . ."

A curved, close-fitting door in the side of the machine popped open, and the crowd gave a smattering of applause. Drebbel, drawn and preoccupied, was checking it was seaworthy one last time. Then the pikemen beat a tattoo to announce the approach, down Whitehall, of the Seven Proud Walkers: the noblemen who would sail beneath the sea. These very Jonahs, set to travel in the belly of this whale. Devil-daring, machine-crazed, superheroes! Modern-day Athenians, about to ascend to the new Pantheon of mechanicians! Here they came, swaggering along the strand, preceded by sheriffs and pikemen in formation, their pikes and spurs clanking with the deep bass beat: Daah. Da-da. Daah. Da-da. Daah. Da-da.

All the nobles were masked and wearing matching doublets and yellow capes, each with a personal power symbol on their chest, a lightning flash or lion couchant, taken from their coats of arms. Kenelm had his fleur-de-lis. They assembled on the strand and then ran down together to the foreshore in formation, moody, powerful, oblivious to the crowd. They lined up on the strand in front of the vessel, and started performing squat thrusts and striking fencing poses. They were like dancing illustrations against the morning-lit sand. The crowd cheered and applauded, some for the spectacle's sake, others with feeling, as the troop bent their knees and stretched their hamstrings. Endymion Porter—his shape gave him away, for he was biggest—performed his stretches with stiff seriousness. Another of the masked nobles came forward alone and pranced about, displaying his muscles.

"Is that one Devereux?" the women asked. "Is the other Carew?" The younger ladies grew flushed and excited. The beat of the drum, and the swagger of the display, and the imminence of real danger combined to make one girl faint.

Ben Jonson paced up and down the sand, reading aloud a paean in praise of the men about to set sail, and the craft itself, which he referred to as *The Magus*. He spoke importantly, and the verse fell off with the heavy jingle of coins, not the living poetry of his plays. But he was clapped and cheered, as the greatness of his name resonated still.

On the terrace just down from the palace, the submariners' wives and betrotheds stood together, watching and laughing and waving. They were a gay party, some decked out in yellow and orange silks correspondent with their husbands'; Olive was wearing a jaunty hat that was meant to be the shape of a submarine, but which had clearly been sewn by a milliner with no conception of what one looked like, so she kept having to explain ("The vessel, d'ye see?").

Venetia cut a strange figure, since she had two dark green glass plates in front of her eyes, held onto her face by a metal and leather contraption, ostensibly to rest her eyes from the glare. It was clearly a nod to the theme of the day's festivities—designs and mad mechanicals—but it gave her a look of a blind, nocturnal creature, as if a parasite had attached itself to her pale, half-hidden face, and was feeding on her spirit. *I would rather they thought me odd than blown*, she thought. The younger ladies, lately come to court, who knew her by reputation only, did not mingle round her, but kept in their own girlish clusters, as if her predicament might be catching.

Maids distributed fresh nosegays, although after half an hour by the Thames they were already inured to its fester. No one knew where Penelope Knollys was, and they joked that she had masked herself and joined the submariners, "making an unlucky seventh aboard their boat."

Someone suggested that Master Hudson, the Queen's dwarf, should have a miniature submarine built for him to follow behind the large one down the Thames. "That would be a very good use of the Forced Loan," replied Lucy Bright tartly, and everyone laughed, but the laughter subsided into an unhappy sigh as the party considered the finances of the Crown.

Venetia asked the Earl of Hitchin three times if he knew what o'clock the submarine was due to land at Greenwich, but although he went through the motions of politeness, he did not listen to her question, and thus he never told her the answer, being more busy making sure that Lucy Bright had somewhere to sit, even though she was not yet married.

There was some raillery about the dwarf Jeffrey Hudson, whom they called Lord Minimus, hunting for a wife. Venetia remarked that there were too many Ladies Maximus, and some of the girls laughed. Next when they were talking about Ben Jonson she said knowingly, "He is a bricklayer's son, which means his hands are great," and the girls laughed again, as if they were beginning to understand her, but the Earl of Hitchin looked past her with an expression of distaste, as if bawdy did not suit her so well now.

The nobles in their yellow capes and masks lined up, ready to board the vessel, and as they did they sang a strange marching song about their submarine sailing under the sky of green, and sea of blue. A horn pooped as they clambered through the portal. A cymbal crashed, and with their friends all aboard, yes, every one of them, the little door in the side was jammed shut. Muffled singing and laughter inside the craft could be heard, as Drebbel's sons-in-law ran out, sealing the door with red wax. After an unbearable delay of about three minutes the men pushed the contraption down across the sandbank to the tide, which caught faster than anyone expected, and dragged it backwards into the river, while the crowd gasped. It bobbed on the surface, then quickly, gracefully, the submarine began to descend.

Going.

It was a thrilling and somehow peaceful sight.

Going.

The crowd let out a long cry of wonder.

Going.

Was this a mutual hallucination?

Gone.

Only the ensign remained above the flood, attached to the vessel by a long string and wooden float, bobbing swiftly down the Thames. And the race was on. A Royal Navy observation boat and rescue skiff cast off and skulled after the ensign, whistles blowing to keep their rowing in time. All the busy traffic of the river raced to the wharves to get out of the way of the magnificent machine. The crowd pursued the underwater ark along the riverbank, pointing and racing, boys streaking ahead, ponies and carriages clattering along, children tottering to keep up, and everyone pushing each other, for they all were at least two ale-cups down already, and mothers following, gathering up blankets and baskets, and old men finally hobbling after, all trundling down the main roads together and darting down the narrow alleys that gave onto the Thames, or running down the wharves to the water's edge, where they hung over the river squinting for a sight of the brave white ensign.

On the terrace at Westminster, some of the ladies were crying and Lucy Bright was encouraging them that all would be well. "Though what authority she has I do not know," exclaimed Olive, becoming fractious in her anxiety. As for Venetia, she had torn off her sunglasses and was already racing through the corridors of the palace to find her groom, so she could give chase to the boat by carriage.

> "About 1620, Drebbel constructed an oar-driven submarine . . . In this boat Drebbel travelled down the Thames from Westminster to Greenwich under the surface of the water . . . He refreshed the air

in the boat by heating saltpetre in a retort, which—as was known—gave an 'air' which one could breathe."

The Oxford Dictionary of National Biography, 2012

Stepping like ghosts out of their bathysphere, but leaving real footprints in the sand, the submariners disembarked at Greenwich, cheered by a raggle-tag band of onlookers, congratulated by a delegation of His Majesty's naval commanders, and observed by an artist making sketches of the whole event (later lost in the Fire of London). The nobles were bandy-legged, dizzy and laughing from the nitreous gas, and they staggered, listing and clasping each other, into a tent of green cloth of gold. Ned Denny was ghost-pale, having fainted during the voyage in the "stinking slave-bows," as he described them. They lay on cushions and drank white bastard, while meat carbonadoes were prepared on coals. Fatigue, relief, kinship and alcohol made them merry, and their talk turned to vaunting anecdotes.

They toasted Cornelis Drebbel who got up anxiously, struggling with his thick black smock, and told them all was not well—my Lord Denny must not undertake the return trip, and there were too many aboard besides. One other patron must forgo his place and return by horse or foot.

"Nay, this stands not!" and "Shame ye" cried the nobles. They each wanted to disembark *The Magus* at Westminster, with the show and splendour that was their due. All of London would be waiting for them. James Lennox got up to speak, calling Drebbel "old man" and laying a discernibly false show of deference over his attitude of wanting what he had paid for—all who sailed in *The Magus* had contributed handsomely towards the project.

"Sirs," said Drebbel, "your rowing is at fault, not my mathematics." Jeering ensued. The argument was abated by one of the sons-in-law who said, without conviction, that they would all sail, but not till a few hours hence, when the river-tide had turned.

Endymion Porter and Edward Carew went off to climb the ferny Greenwich wilderness up the hill about the tower, or glimpse the ruins of the old Plesaunce palace, while others lay about under the awning, chatting, but in an off mood, disputatious, doubtful. Kenelm wandered for a slash behind a tree.

Legs unsteady, his head aching from the submarine, he laced himself up and headed back, slowly, pausing to inspect the shoresmen's horses, careless talk from the awning was carried on the breeze towards him. Their voices were guilty with gossip.

"Aye, his father. Pale, he looked, and his eyes very puffy, but he made a goodly show of it."

"At Powles, was this?"

"Aye, he was dragged through the street behind a horse's tail. The other plotters were jackanapes. They were ill-made men. Not him. He looked more like a thing of heaven than of the other place. The crowd was oh, deathly quiet as he bade farewell to each of his former friends by name: 'My Lord Darnley, long have I loved thee'; 'Dear Lady Segismund, goodbye,' and so forth, just as easily as he was wont to do when he went from court or out of the city, to his own house in the country."

"He was as fair and fine a man as I have ever seen."

"As fair and foul. He tried to kill our fathers, mine certainly, and yours, and yours."

"When he was convicted he cried out to the jury, 'Do you forgive me?' And to a man, they answered, 'Aye.'"

"He was awake to till the very last?"

"Yes, hung by the neck only a little, so he saw his bowels turned out in front of him, and then the hangman went to work on his vitals, and leaned on his knife to get purchase on his heart, and held up before the crowd, so!"

Kenelm heard his friends make low tutting noises. He shut his eyes before the sun and saw shapes pulsing red and melting white. It was a tale he knew well; it was his father's execution.

"Then the hangman gave his cry, 'Behold the heart of a traitor!' To which the man himself replied: 'Thou liest!'"

The company made groaning noises; someone thumped upon the table. "Nay, nay," said one voice, "I do not believe it." Another voice: "Francis Bacon saw it."

Sir Kenelm could take no more and strode into the tent. "Gentlemen," he said, and only a stiffness in his neck showed he was not himself. For a second the three men seemed to think they had got away with it.

Ned said, "Ken, we thought you were up the hill."

"Aye," Kenelm said tightly.

"We meant no insult by our talk, I would have you know that, Ken, I would," said Ned, rising.

"Aye, you would," said Ken in a playful, frightful voice. Then he put on his hat, backwards, and picked up a half-eaten lobster from the table and made it dance like a puppet, waving its claws, and saying in a high pip-squeak voice: "Oh, Lord Darnley, oh, Lady Segismund, farewell, it seems I am a traitor. I never meant to harm ye . . ." Ken put the lobster's face right up against Ned's. "I would have warned you if I could, before we made our little firework display . . ." The three men laughed, loudly and uncomfortably. The lobster's two black eyes shook on their stalks and his empty carcass danced, as it looked around at them all, full of wonder and pathetic malice, and Kenelm had him sing "Eeee" in a creaky voice, like the puppet Mr. Punch, while the lobster, consumed by anger, started bashing its head against the table, sending shell-shards flying.

"Eee, I would have you know I was played like a puppet by the plotters," said Kenelm in his lobster falsetto. "My wife?" The lobster looked urgently in the face of Sir James, then up and down his body assessingly, and the uncomfortable laughter grew. "No, you are not my wife." It turned to Ned Denny, and looked him inquisitively up and down as well. "No," he said sadly. "You are not my wife either." The lobster shook its head. "My son?" it said, looking around again, then seeming to have seen its own puppeteer, threw itself on Kenelm's own neck. The others jumped back, laughing, embarrassed. Then the lobster looked again sad and alone, squeaking: "But now, aye me, I am undone, I am for the pot."

And Kenelm threw the lobster on the bright red cooking coals and then tipped a cup of bastard over him so the whole mess sizzle-screamed and smoked. The men cheered and tapped their signet rings against their tin cups, so they ding-ding-dinged. But they were mighty confused and their blood was up, in case at any moment Kenelm turned upon them with a poignard.

"I meant no dishonour by it, Ken."

"The dishonour is all my father's, sir," said Ken, smiling, not looking at him. He bowed graciously, which was harder still for Ned to bear.

Ken insisted on renouncing his seat on the submarine, and did not stay to watch it sail. Instead, he climbed the hill at Greenwich, to stand on the line marked by standing stones and menhirs where the time was once told by the sun. He marched up the steep knoll easily, breathing deeply, rabbits' scut-tails bobbing ahead of him under the racing sky. It did him good to see the runic stones, to run his finger over their long-carved patterns. He felt as if his time was set to a new o'clock. All things pass.

He wandered next through a sweet sunlit dell where through the bright-lit green he heard a bird cry: Milk, milk, milk today?

He paused. It was the London milk-sellers' street cry, sung by a bird. It came again, swooping and familiar: Milk, milk, milk today?

Another bird replied: Cherries! Cherries!

What was this? Street cries, from tiny feathered throats. The words were indistinct, of course, but the tune was the same as in the market. Had a family of crooked streetsellers been bewitched and sent to live in a nest? Or were these traitors turned skylarks, men's lying tongues poured into quick little dust-bathing bodies?

Meelk, meelk, meelk?

Che-rries! Che-rries!

The bower was green and silent and Kenelm turned around, looking for the birds, feeling he was being tested like a knight in a fable, who must resist enchantment.

Pipit, pipit, cherries!

Another bird joined in, like a wherryman: Sideside, ho; sideside, ho.

Milk, milk, milk. Freeeeeesh.

Sidey-sidey bankside, ho, pipit.

Perhaps they were rare sentient canaries, escaped from the old Plesaunce palace below. Then how would they know the street cries? More likely—yes, this must be it—they were birds once caged for sale on Cheapside or Seething Lane, who had heard street cries all their lives, and were now either released or escaped, and come to hide out in the trees together and rehearse their cries in strophe and antistrophe. Perhaps that was why they were so tame, singing close to him and yet never letting themselves be seen for fear of capture. Kenelm made a mental note to record this. He recalled something similar in Montaigne.

And there was another strange bird call, Brrring! Brrring! Bright and tight as a bell. Brrring! Brrring!

Speaking? said Kenelm. Hello?

He knew that birds often imitated bells and whistles, calls and ringtones.

Beep, beep.

Ping!

With his arms raised to heaven he span around the glade in a circle while the birds quizzled and cheeped and sang to him in tongues, and his spirit resounded with joy because he was a knight who lived by reason and logic, and knew these birds were not mechanical trifles from a sorcerer's foundry, or enchanted prisoners of Circe, but only poor little living creatures, escaped. He felt as if he had cut himself free from cobwebs of illusion, and he was resolved to live without them, in the open air of rationality. Experiment, observation, inductive reasoning—these were his methods. Metamorphosis was Ovid's way, a classical delusion. The ancients' age of prophecy was over. No longer would men live by myths and children's stories.

When Kenelm descended from the hill, healed as ever by the efflorescence of new ideas in his fertile mind, he saw that the green silk pavilion had gone, and there was no sign of it except for a stain on the grass, some charred debris and a few loiterers. Chater was waiting with the horses, and Venetia too, her head poking out of the window of her carriage alertly, like a lapdog; confident and hopeful that she was about to see him arrive safely, yet physically unable to relax until it happened.

As she waited, watching the trees blowing, she sang to herself at first, and then, growing bored, and fearful, she thought of all the things she would like to say to Kenelm: first, there are too many books in the house, there is not room to shelve them all, and yet you insatiably buy more, at what cost? All the penniless antiquarians know you for your tender heart and come to our door hawking books in Aramaic script and suchlike fustian babble. And this business of the bathysphere. What fantastick invention will you ride next upon the waves? A harnessed dolphin, or torpedo . . . ?

Staring at the Greenwich grass, she was so expectant, consumed, for once, with looking rather than being seen, that she had forgotten that her face was bare and unadorned, with the morning's paint worn off—until the moment when Kenelm appeared, when the strain seemed to widen the crack in her nature, and she remembered to half-cover her face and look coquettishly at him. They held each other tightly, and pressed their cheeks together. In her happiness she forgot every complaint she had against him. When he held her close, his smell touched her like a drug. He breathed her sweet pomander, and closing his eyes he saw

OR7D4

in his mind's eye, and he knew it to be the codename given to the isolated genetic olfactory receptor in Venetia's blood which made her swoon for his tired body's smell, because they were mathematically matched as lovers must be, their sequences interlocking, their separate selves fractions and the sum of their parts a whole number, prime, indivisible.

Chater looked on with long face and bulging sad eyes as they embraced. Venetia went on ahead in her carriage, trundling lightly over the grassy tracks, while Kenelm mounted the horse brought for him by Chater.

Kenelm felt wrung dry. Today he had breathed underwater and drunk sunlight, he had been cheered as a hero, taken part in an enterprise worthy of a new Atlantis—and yet at the last his old dishonour had come up, bringing out the bitterness in his blood. Chater intuited something was amiss by Kenelm's stiff bearing, his troubled eyes. They talked as their horses ambled home, and gradually Kenelm spilled his heart to his family chaplain, as if in an open-air confession.

"Of course, I have heard people speak about my father's crime all my life, talking, supposing, casting slurs or looking at me with a curious eye . . ."

"Were you there that day?" asked Chater. A good priest knew one essential question would open up a story, like a key.

"At my father's ending?" said Kenelm blankly. "I was." He kept a heavy silence, but Chater could feel there was more to come.

"I saw him tied to the wicker hurdle, face-down that his breath might not pollute the common air, as the sergeant put it. My mother drew my face into her skirts, but I peeped a look anyway. I was not yet three. He was hanging by his heels, his face twisting, very red. I think I thought it was some horrid game. There was a great noise of halberdiers' drums. I remember nothing else. Later, my mother told me she held me up to see him for the last time. We were not allowed to touch him, only stand in the crowd and shout. There was another plotter—Bates—whose wife forced herself through the guards, and flung her arms around her husband, who whispered where his gold was hid. We were not so canny. I'm told my father smiled at me and that he told me to look after my mother. Though I have never done so. I am a bad son to her."

"Come, sir, that is not true," said Chater, hoping Kenelm would go back to the more interesting matter of the execution, which he did.

"We did not see his ending. My mother and I were led out of the crowd quickly, so we might be spared the next sight. The crowd they say was very silent. That was a great comfort to my mother: a silent crowd."

"You are very brave."

"I am not brave, nor was my father brave, nor my mother unfortunate. All these words are forbidden if your trouble has been brought upon yourself by plotting and powder. You bear it, no more, no less."

Their horses snorted to one another, sharing irritation at the early-evening flies.

"They say my father's heart was plucked before his eyes. The man who looks at his own heart and speaks is a candidate for Catholic sainthood. There are other examples recorded. But as Laud would often tell me, my father was a good man misguided. He did not wish to kill the King and Parliament, only to frighten James. It was the others who were treacherous. I like to think it might be true. Laud said my father was the kind of man who believed that every beggar deserved payment; he was too tenderhearted. Once when he was young he came home shoeless, because a poor boy had asked for his shoes. Two hundred years ago they might have canonised my father. Instead, he is a two-penny pamphlet, a shudder, an effigy for the bonfire, a tale to tell while feasting, no more."

Chater did not like to see Sir Kenelm so disconsolate, and wanted to say something cheerful. "Still you were exceeding fortunate."

"Of course. To keep his lands and property was more than we had right to hope for—to be his son and yet be knighted, that was a true kindness. He liked to make a show of forgiveness. *Beati pacifici* was James's motto . . ."

"Blessed are the . . ."

"Cheesemakers," said Kenelm.

"Peacemakers, surely . . ." said Chater hastily.

"I only meant to have my sport with you, Chater," said Kenelm. "Perhaps the old Scot bore my father love. He'd an eye for a lovely lad. You know those men who dote on men."

"Aye," said Chater, looking down at his bridle.

"They have in the composition of their bodies too much blood, it is said. In Siena the Duke of Tuscany's old apothecary assured me that leeches judiciously applied—you need not ask to which part of the body, sir—took away those desires that they wish to be rid of, by destroying the excess of manliness and laying siege to those particular atoms charging about their blood—and so restoring them to their wives. But occasioned by the use of male leeches only, I am told."

Chater looked uneasy and made an equivocal expression of interest, and in his momentary distraction he let his horse pause to crop the green grass, and fell behind Kenelm. In silence they trundled back to east London across the Isle of Dogs, where the King's kennels yelped as the knight and chaplain passed by, silhouetted against a peachy early-evening sky.

Side-Effects May Include

"I wax now somewhat ancient . . . one and thirty years is a great deal of sand in the hour-glass."

Sir Francis Bacon, 1593

TWO LADIES WEARING fashionable vizard-masks were walking along Cheapside, in fast and purposive unison, towards the physicians' quarter on Fenchurch Street. They passed three children fighting for a farthing in a puddle, who stared up at them as if the ladies were creatures of a different species. A manservant stepped aside to allow them passage, deferentially looking away. A woman collapsed in a doorway watched them, her eyeballs liverish yellow.

"No one has seen us," whispered Venetia, clasping Olive's arm. Venetia had taken the precaution of wearing mourning clothes, so as to be more anonymous. Her dramatic soul enjoyed this and she declared that she was dressed "for the funeral of her own honesty." This was the first time that she had deceived her Kenelm. Well, the first time she had deceived him explicitly. The first time she had deceived him explicitly in a long time. Quite a long time. There were always matters untold between a man and a woman, of money, and trifling secrets of past affections, were there not? And all those abstruse points which one already understood, and facts one already knew, but allowed him to explain high-handedly, because it pleased him to do so. But this was disobedience. She trod a little faster.

The artist William Peake, son of the court painter, had lately come to take their double portrait. Venetia felt kindly towards him ever since, ten years ago, he made a divine little painting of her in masquing costume at the request of the Earl of Dorset. This time, she began the sitting in good faith, putting her confidence in him as he turned over his sand-timer to measure out his fee at four-pence the hour. She felt they presented a goodly show to the world, a handsome couple, on the cusp of new things. They sat for him in brightest daylight by the window of their great hall, which warmed Venetia, and helped to calm her.

> "How are the cheekbones? Do they need shadow underneath? Is the make-up excessive? In colour shots, this is disaster. If the jawline is dubious, try to avoid being shot from below. If you cannot relax, for heaven's sake, take a tranquilliser before shooting starts."
>
> Princess Luciana Pignatelli,
> *The Beautiful People's Beauty Book,* 1971

Peake sketched while looking at them with an unkind intensity, as if he saw them as planes and surfaces and colour-contrasts, rather than as people. It made Venetia feel, she whispered to Kenelm, as if she were "a cut of veal-calf."

Kenelm's moustaches twitched but he suppressed a laugh. They both sat very still, listening to Spenser, which Chater read aloud, while Master Peake's light-maker held up a frame of white cloth, to reflect the best of the winter sun upon them, and Mistress Elizabeth hovered, as instructed, with a box of pearl-powder and a mortar of egg-white, ready to tend to Venetia's face if she asked for it, as he sketched them, first with chalk on blue paper, while an assistant mixed his paints. Halfway through, Master Peake asked her to *relaxez-vous, madame.*

"I feel perfectly relaxed," said Venetia, "so what can you mean?"

He asked Venetia if she would mind showing a serene countenance.

"I am filled with serenity, sir, it flows quite through me!" said Venetia.

"No, no, madam, just . . ." He gestured with two fingers to his forehead, as if wiping away a frown. Venetia did not reply. She did not think she had been frowning at all, sitting here with Kenelm, holding the attention of this roomful of people, *The Faery Queene* echoing in her head. With a muscular effort she widened her eyebrows, to remove this alleged frown. After a minute or two, however, with her mind on the Queene's noble knight Artegal, her face must have fallen into repose, because Peake made again his encouraging hand-gesture to her forehead.

"Sir, do you not need those two fingers for your painting?" she said, through her teeth.

There was only the noise of his brush on canvas.

"You might do better to change your painting rather than my countenance," she said. This artist had made an ominous beginning.

Perhaps her hands were ill-positioned, but it was too late to move them, and soon she lost the feeling in her left little finger, and then her whole arm. Her head swam with Spenserian dreams. Kenelm nudged her twice, because he thought she was sleeping.

It was not until the end of the day that they saw Peake's double portrait.

His sense of perspective was very poor, so that while Kenelm looked fit and lean, she had been rendered plump and dwarfish, with chins that redoubled and a non-existent neck. Her eyes were flat and gazing, like a dead hare in a Dutch still life, and the expression in them was nervous and doubting, while her lips smirked and her cheek was sallow. Poor artist! He could not manage to bring off a face at all any more. He had, admittedly, done her hair well.

"Master Peake, we have wasted your time," she said.

Kenelm started to say something, until she gave him a look.

"I think you are more suited to painting cheeses and pieces of fruit, no? At least they have no friends and relatives to say whether it is a good likeness or no. No; dear sir, you would make a lovely painter of inanimates. But for women you have no longer the knack. We are so sorry that you shall not have this commission from us, for you are a good man and you used to be a good painter, I remember. You will have your money for today's labour. But your skill today, sir, why is it so much less than when you made my portrait last time?"

Peake was already packing away his brushes brusquely, and he stopped to look Venetia significantly in the eye.

"Madam, it must be because I am ten years older."

Peake's words echoed loudly in the panelled chamber, so resonantly that everyone must have heard him, through the household and beyond, and in the garden the leaves on the trees trembled, and the dandelions shook, and the clodded earth rumbled, and even further away, in a Hollywood screening room, Marlene Dietrich froze with fury as she turned to listen to her cameraman deliver the same wasp-sting words. Sir Kenelm ducked out of the room, pretending he had not heard, leaving Venetia in charge, as usual.

She took pleasure in dismissing Peake. He was lucky to be paid at all, frankly.

Venetia thought of the old pagan goddesses with their smashed noses and their broken arms. The acolytes turn against their queen, she thought, once her powers start to wane. The old statues have to be desecrated, reviled, to make way for the new.

So here she was, marching through Eastcheap in search of medicine that would improve bad painters, and cause rude old courtiers to remember their manners, and turn her inside out, so the serenity she felt was visible again. They came onto Fenchurch Street, where the physicians' premises were close beside each other, signed by the mortar and pestle. Some had reassuringly expensive facades, painted with College crests and appended with prestigious names: here was a foreign physician; there was Robert Fludd, under a Barber Surgeon's sign. The clients going about the street—a gent with a bandaged jaw: and a man and woman holding each other closely, with shy hope on their faces, as if they had come for a cure for childlessness—seemed to be persons of quality. There were no beggars with wailing brats or old women selling heather, as there usually were hanging about outside an apothecary's. They entered a door under the sign of a star, painted with the gold letters LANCELOT CHOICE.

Inside the air was close, spicy, and tickle-your-nose. In spite of the dark atmosphere, the ladies did not remove their veils. They stood silently in front of the grey-haired woman who climbed down off a ladder to serve them. Venetia and Olive both drew breath, but neither spoke. It was unexpectedly difficult to say for which preparation they had come.

The old woman introduced herself as Mistress Choice, and said softly, "Is it a private audience you are desiring?" They nodded. In a sweet bedside voice she said, "Then I will procure the master for you." She stepped back from the counter, and hollered down the stairs on solid lungs: "Here's CUSTOM!"

In the privacy of the doctor's consulting room, the ladies unveiled. It was tidy, stacked with tiny drawers and ceramic pots, and hung with fashionable embroidered fabric. There were none of the old apothecary's trophies, no stuffed monstrous fishes or clouds of desiccated herbs, not even any pulled teeth or false limbs or old plaisters lying about. A window let in the cool light of day, and the room smelled faintly of soap.

"Well, ladies," said Mistress Choice, putting her hands on her hips. "Is it the usual?"

Olivia and Venetia looked at each other, unsure what to answer.

"Your courses are late and you're wanting a help-me-along?"

"Oh, no," said Olivia, colouring. "No, no. We want your Viper Wine." Mrs. Choice looked surprised and gratified, and made a little nonjudgemental curtsey. "Pleased to be of service, ladies. I'll just fetch the Physician." Mrs. Choice went away quickly, being certain not to look too closely at them, since she knew ladies who came for these treatments were often sensitive.

Mr. Choice entered. He was tall, and handsome, and he knew it. "Thank you," he said, dismissing Mistress Choice. Was she his wife or his mother? Venetia guessed wife. He had the air of one who liked to be the more beautiful one in a relationship. His face was remarkably well made up and smooth for a man. His hair was long like Kenelm's except he wore, as a modish affectation, one lovelock behind his left ear, loosely plaited into a little tail. He was not wax pale, like some, but his paint matched his skin colour. His blush was subtle and his eye twinkling. Venetia felt the inadequacy of her own paint, hastily applied that morning. Perhaps Lancelot Choice drank his decoctions himself. He, and not his wife-mother, was the bait for business, the model of what could be achieved. He greeted them warmly with a deep bow in front of each of them, then relaxed into his chair, which like a throne commanded the room.

"I hear you are Viperish," he said.

They laughed nervously.

"We live in a wondrous age, my ladies, a golden time in which it is no longer necessary to present the marks of ageing and decrepitude. We improve our treatments all the time. You will find no puppy's piss here—that charm is by the by. We have only the most infallibly efficacious cordials, wines, salves, unguents, ointments and still other guaranteed means of enhancing your beauty, and with ladies such as yourselves it would be a deep privilege to be of service. I will make a quick investigation first. If you would . . ."

He beckoned Venetia to the window. He gently held her chin in his soft hand, breathing sweetly on her face. She saw up close his perfect skin, and felt a stab of, what, jealousy? He angled her cheek to the light and stroked it professionally. He asked her to smile, and she obliged. "So polished, perfect, round and even / As it slyd moulded off from Heaven . . ." These words Ben Jonson had written about her face. He had compared her smile to the rising sun. She felt it shine a little weaker every day. "I'll give you something for the teeth later," said Choice. He recognised her, of course, but did not show it. He placed his finger between her brows, and asked her to frown. He made a light-hearted hum.

The same procedure he repeated for Olivia, who laughed flirtatiously at the coldness of his fingers. He took this in silence.

"First I must warn ye, and I shall warn ye as follows. The Cure you ladies so desire, which we know to be Viper's Wine, but I shall hereto term only as 'The Cure'—The Cure may act upon ye as it has acted a thousand times before, which is as you ladies desire, but it may also act otherways, namely in the occasioning of fits, ague, local dropsy, grand dropsy, or a great increase in . . ." Choice said the word with disapproving relish, "Conker-pezzans."

Olivia turned to Venetia, who murmured, "Concupiscence." Olivia looked down into her lap, smiling.

"Ladies, I must continue to warn ye, and I shall warn ye as follows." Choice spoke as if thoroughly bored. "The Cure, if wrongly administered, at the improper time of the moon or in poor faith, bad temper or impious attitude, or if administered in conjunction with other cures that have come not from Lancelot Choice, nor are not known to Lancelot Choice, may result in twitches, conniptions, mild scratching of the body and face, or delirium tremens. It may result in tempora-ra-rare-y frantick distraction, delightful dreams, an *aurora mirabilis* that emits a gentle rose-coloured light around your person or in your water—"

"Rose-coloured piss-pots?" exploded Olivia.

"Shh," said Venetia.

"—or excessive use and consumption of The Cure may result in the unwonted acquisition of a Life Immortal, by which I mean a failure to decay or die, and now, ladies, if I can ask you to submit to some formalities, please. For the arrangement of credit, I require the head of your household's name, his escutcheon, tokens armigerous, and so forth. But for prompt payments I require no more than your coin and your smile."

Venetia tried not to wince at his patter and said tartly, "We will pay you today."

He nodded. "For your teeth and gums I can also offer an excellent preparation made of salt of pearls, salt of coral, musk, civet, cloves, Malaga sack and Canary Wine."

"Sir, we are not here for dentifrice," said Venetia.

"Indeed. Then for my dedicated services, weekly proffered, without exception, and for weekly supplies of my potent drink distilled here in these my well-appointed premises, and for the delivery of said supply, by discreet and speedy messenger, to my ladies' own dwellings . . ."

"Come to it, sir," said Venetia.

". . . I shall put a price on what is priceless then: fifteen crowns a week."

The ladies blanched inwardly, but nothing could stop them now, and they nodded.

"I will have my wife prepare the vipers for the stills tonight."

The ladies shuddered pleasurably.

"Did we meet your wife . . . ?" asked Olivia. "Downstairs?" And in that last innocuous word she somehow conveyed a world of judgement upon that lady's appearance.

"Aye, that is my Margaret," said Master Choice without expression in his voice. "You will have your potion, ladies; it will be ready to be fetched tomorrow."

Venetia thought "fetched tomorrow" was a lovely phrase. It promised so much. And yet she had still not decided if she trusted this apothecary.

"Sir, of what is this Viper Wine composed?"

"It is composed, my lady, of skill and faith. No, look you: it is a crafty extract. You know how a viper sheds its skin, I think? You have seen the adder's lacy stocking, a delicate membrane wriggled loose, and lying discarded upon spiky grass? Aye."

"Aye," said Venetia.

"So will we shed our skin alike, leaving it behind us perhaps on Cheapside pavement?" giggled Olivia.

"No, my lady," sideways-smiled the apothecary, "but the same rich liverishness which restores the viper's skin will act upon your own complexions."

If it worked, it was surely to be paid for again hereafter. Venetia was well acquainted with the tale of Faust. These things do not come for free. And yet. She had taken mandragora in childbirth, had she not? And it had eased her pain and done no harm. And for fevers she had been helped by many remedies. She did not like this man, but she would take his Physick.

"Ladies, I must have from you a nickname for my book, to guard your privacy."

"Call me Proserpina," said Olive.

"And me . . . Anastasia," said Venetia, thinking her middle name suitably exotick for this purpose.

"Ladies, your cure will be delivered to you discreetly in a crate that might as well hold strawberries as a miraculous potable venom known as the Venice Treacle, the Teriaca or sometimes, to initiates, as *Benzoardicum Thericale*."

He continued at a normal pitch: "You may do as you think, but it would be most beneficial to take this drink with the right hand on the left side of the mouth, thus, and to begin the treatment at the waxing of the lunar cycle, thus"—he pointed a long stick at the blackboard beside him, where was etched in chalk a diagram of the phases of the moon—"in other words, AS SOON AS POSSIBLE—and ladies, I will lastly advise you to put your good faith and deserving trust in me, for no Physick works without the will. So tell me how you like your drinks next time, sweet ladies, adieu."

He gave a very deep bow with his hands set together, like a priest. Soon they were vizarded and dashing home through the rainy streets.

"I am so glad we went."

"So glad," said Venetia.

"So very glad. He is such a handsome man," exclaimed Olive, as if she could not keep it to herself any more. "I really am a little in love with him!"

Venetia looked at her friend sharply. "But Endymion . . ."

Olive said that Endymion was never at home, being so often on the King's business, that she saw him not once a moon.

"He is busy with great affairs, I suppose."

"He is busy fetching the King's fancies from Spain, paintings and rugs and whatnot. I see no harm with visiting a beauteous, courteous, humane apothecary . . ."

"Secret," Venetia warned, gripping Olivia's hand, eyes flashing under her vizard.

"Ouch!" said Olivia.

When Venetia came home, there was no one about. Living in London was suiting Chater very well. He was spending much of his time at Westminster, arriving home in high spirits. His friend Father Dell'Mascere was giving him instruction again, and he had befriended the Queen's Dismal Dozen, picking up some of their Capuchin intensity. Well-cut cassocks, good art, fine wine, gossip from Rome—it was all exactly what Chater needed. He had developed a new dramatic style, quoting Revelations and the eschatological parts of John. His homilies on Sundays had become quite riveting.

She took the spare key from the parlour box, and let herself into her husband's study. The door would not open fully—stacks of books prevented it. She was shocked to see how the books had multiplied. His bibliomania was almost an illness. He seemed to feel responsible for all the orphan books sequestered by the monasteries after the break with Rome. To be sure, illiterates made use of the old manuscripts for wrapping crab apples and lining shoes and cleaning muskets, and she could see why Kenelm wished to save some—but this was insanity. One could barely walk across the room.

On the long table by the window were arranged limbecks and curved retorts, full of coloured waters, but they looked dusty, and she wondered how much Kenelm used them. Upon his desk, where his ledger was open, she saw his wastebooks, letters and scrawled memoranda. She could not help seeing a bill—forty groats for his leather shoes! But beyond that she looked no further. She was no Percy Pry-snout.

She only wanted to take a particular precaution. At his shelves, she found the works on herbs and Physick—the English Leechbook, *The Secrets of Master Alexis the Piedmontese*, *The Breviary of Healthe*, *Galen's Art of Physick*, *The Greek Herbal of Dioscorides*, John Gerard's *History of Plants*, a new copy of John Parkinson's *Garden of Pleasant Flowers*, with the pages barely cut. And there it was. The book that drew her hand was the nameless grimoire, bulging and tattered—her husband's own scrapbook of remedies, copied one by one over two decades or more. Her heart pricked with tenderness to behold the care young Kenelm had taken with his handwriting. Although his writing was smaller in his youth it already had the rhythm and confidence of his spoken voice, putting forth occasional vain flourishes. Some receipts were blotted and stained with chemicals. The pages were many, and she let herself pass an idle moment on the advice to procure conception—purslain, nettle, candied nutmeg, powdered root of English snakeweed, and so forth, thrice daily—but it did not indicate how to beget a daughter. She turned on till she found a page marked "Viper Wine—*Benzoardicum Thericale*."

> Take a viper, hold her fast by the neck so she cannot stir or wag at all, and with a pen-knife cut her throat open, so you may be able to tear out her tongue and innards. Prepare a great many vipers after this fashion. Separate their tongues, hearts and livers. Bake gently overnight in a furnace. Add opobalsamum, or Peruvian Balsam, little by little. Take some good opium, well chosen, dry it very gently till it be friable, and crumble. Sift through a hairen cloth, with a good spirit of wine tartarised, and the stale of a brood mare in foal. This quintessence is of extraordinary good virtue for the purifying of the blood, flesh and skin. Preserves from grey hairs, renews youth, etc.

So Lancelot Choice was, at least, no quack. She had seen enough. If Kenelm would not sanction this, why was its recipe in his collection? Some elements of it worried her, though. The stale of a brood mare in foal—was she to drink a horse's gilded piddle? The dogs barked, but it was Chater's voice that she could hear nervously chiding them. Kenelm was not come home yet. With fast and urgent fingers, she turned the book around to read the scrawled marginalia:

> "Conjugated equine oestrogens have been used for several decades for post-menopausal hormone replacement. The preparation is in the form of an extract from the urine of pregnant mares . . ."
>
> *British Journal of Clinical Pharmacology,* 2000

She had seen enough. She closed Kenelm's book, kissed it, put it back on the shelf. Making ready to leave his study, she heard a small rattle behind her, and noticed it came from the lid of a pot that had been left in the fire—probably some opiate or rare balsam he was baking dry—and she made a mental note to tell him not to leave his bonoficium unattended, until she remembered that this would betray her trespassing, and so, like a guilty thing, she slipped away, and the rustle of her silk dress, she fancied, sounded like a hiss.

Of Sunflowers and Sealing Wax

THE LAWN AT Charterhouse was scattered with daisies, and Sir Kenelm Digby and Antoon Van Dyck were treading delicately, careful not to crush a single flower. The grass had put them forth overnight, as if to welcome Van Dyck back to England: star-spangles thrown across the green.

"Our chain has been broken too long," said Van Dyck, stretching out his hand to Kenelm. In the strong morning sunlight his fingertips glowed with illuminated blood.

"Only a few years," said Sir Kenelm, reaching towards him. "'Tis as nothing, if you consider that the golden chain of knowledge that joins us both also travels backwards from Zosimus and, through us, oh infinitely forwards."

The men continued across the grass together, holding hands. Their friendship was Masonic, sealed by the chanting of an Orphic order behind a curtain in Tuscany ten years ago—and whenever they saw one another they spoke freely of the ensouled world, becoming at times perilously high-minded, with the unselfconscious pleasure of men who hold each other in mutual regard. They did not talk of family life or love, or even why Van Dyck had come to London. They talked of the new telescopes that revealed daily new Magneticall sun-spots and shadow-valleys of the moon.

Upstairs in her closet, Venetia peered at the sun-spots and craters on the dead planets of her cheeks, vastly magnified by the instrument of horror that was Kenelm's magnifying glass. She had never met Van Dyck and she was preparing for his scrutiny, leaning over her mirror with the magnifying glass. Every day, a new way to mortify herself.

Downstairs, on the lawn, Kenelm fell on one knee and put his eye to a daisy, which was open and gazing at the sun, beaming back the great orb's power from its tiny yellow copycat planet. The black aperture of Kenelm's eye—his pupil—shrank to behold the daisy's brightness. Hermes Trismegistus said that the sun was a god made visible. Kenelm could almost see the powerful magnetic rays communicating between this plant and the sun: therefore he did not trample on these tiny fringed observant *day's eyes*, which opened and closed with the light.

Van Goose! A sudden remembrance of Ben Jonson's nickname for Van Dyck came to Venetia. It was a masque-night foolery, to turn a Dyck or Duck into Goose. Perhaps she had met the artist before. She could not remember. But if she had met him, or if he had seen her acting, which was more likely, it would have been more than twelve years ago. She pulled an evil face at herself in her mirror.

Kenelm looked around him, to check they were definitely alone, and that Chater was not listening. "So you believe," said Kenelm, "that there is something reasonable in this heretical claim that earth goes around the sun?" With a curious swivelling motion, all the daisies on the lawn turned their faces towards their conversation.

"Indeed I do," said Van Dyck. His Dutch voice always struck Sir Kenelm as so musical. The gold ring on Van Dyck's finger, passed down to him by generations of faithful Catholics, flashed alarum as he ran his hand through his hair. "It is a pity His Holiness will not accept it."

"I cannot accept it," said Sir Kenelm, shaking his head. "It goes against everything. I respect the theorists but not the theorem. Besides," he said, "I am attached to my armillary sphere, my world of brass. I do not wish to buy another one just yet. A universe is costly, you know. And my planets are in harmonious alignment just as they are."

Van Dyck never quarrelled. He shrugged. "I have a friend arriving here later today who perhaps can tell us more about this. My guest is coming by sedan chair, and he is almost seven feet tall, and he knows more of the sun than you or me." A smile played around Van Dyck's lean chops, but Kenelm was annoyed that he would not have Van Dyck to himself all day. Antoon was a hither-thither kind of fellow, really—he had not been a good correspondent while he was away. But that was artists for you.

"The *Sidereus Nuncius* is to be tried for promoting his heliocentric heresy," said Sir Kenelm. They always called Galileo *Sidereus Nuncius*, the Starry Messenger.

"So he says it is a mathematical fiction," said Van Dyck, "and continues to refer to it as frequently as he likes."

"Ha! Very good," said Sir Kenelm. "But for how long?"

They sat outside talking thus for some three hours, surrounded by eavesdropping English daisies, sitting first in tree-shadow, then half-sunlight, then full glorious sun—until the dogs and calls from within alerted them that Master Van Dyck's guest had arrived.

He was travelling by sedan chair, but he was so tall that the top of the chair had been extended, and the seat removed. Had the gout led him to ride standing? He was haughty, or afraid of the unwholesome London air, perhaps, because he hung a cope of red velvet over the front of his carriage, so as to travel unseen. His two chairmen were also liveried in red. So who is this fellow, wondered Kenelm, who knows so much of the sun?

"He has come from the New World," said Van Dyck. "I hope he has not been too much fatigued by his journey."

Venetia and her boys ran downstairs to watch as the mysterious visitor was helped out of his chair with great care. Finally his footman drew aside his covering. He stood inside a wide terracotta pot, and his body was long and furred with pale sticklehairs, and his face was wide and staring, framed with over-wrought green tendrils and shouty yellow petals.

"Madam, I present," said Van Dyck to Venetia, "the Peruvian Chrysanthemum." The family clapped and cooed, and Mistress Elizabeth ran to fetch water. "Also known as an Indian Marigold or *tourne-soleil*. It is also called, but rarely, heliotrope or sun's flower."

It was clear by the way that Van Dyck looked tenderly at the whiskered sunflower that he adored it, although to Venetia its blank face, broad as a bedpan, looked brash and vainglorious. Its size was gigantique, almost frightening. She thought it did not appear to be a very intelligent flower. There was plenty of vegetable in its countenance, she thought, although it had novelty on its side.

"Heliotrope," she said. "Might do well as a name for a daughter, if she were plain."

"Now, sir, well, sir, what of that?" marvelled Kenelm. He had never seen a sunflower before, except in sketches.

"It is a gift for you, madam, in honour of your husband—a plant which, like him, turns to the sun to receive Enlightenment, being mightily Sympatheticall in its nature."

Kenelm was deeply moved by this presentation. Being the keeper of the Powder of Sympathy in England was a thankless task, and there was too much naysaying and calumny around. Van Dyck was good at presents. He used them as substitutes for his presence, for he never stayed long in one place or country. "I hope it will flourish in your garden of daisies, madam," said Van Dyck, bowing.

Analogies chimed like angelic bells in Sir Kenelm's mind. "Nature is so infinitely rhyming," he muttered. "It is as if one link in the chain carries within it a suggestion of the next, as one rhyme leads the way to what the next must be." The sunlight seemed to stream down on Kenelm like a golden chain, which twisted before his eyes into a double-helix. He saw the chain of Hermetic knowledge extending backwards to Zosimus, and forward, oh, to Crick and Watson, and onwards to men who made homes out of sunlight, harnessing its power to their purpose. Beside him the sunflower swivelled its alien head to receive the signal of the sun.

"Shall we sit, my love?" Venetia was holding Kenelm by the hand, leading him down the corridor to the dining room, where the table was set with game and soppits. "He is overcome by your most kind present," she said over her shoulder to Van Dyck, in a smile-warmed voice.

"He was nicknamed '*il fiorito*' in Siena," Van Dyck said to Venetia.

"Because of the fleur-de-lis on our coat of arms?"

"And because he wilted in the sun, or turned a rosy pink."

"And furthermore because I was tall, and said to be the flower of English manhood," retorted Kenelm.

"Who called you that?"

"Marie de' Medici!" And the men laughed and while Venetia was out of the room seeing to some complaint of the boys', they repeated the old story of how the Dowager Empress had fallen in love with Sir Kenelm, even though he was twenty-six years her junior.

"She wanted me for her pet, and made much of me, and had me sit with her in her private garden, and bade me sing to her, and then when she heard me singing, bade me recite verse instead."

Van Dyck put down his mug in expectation of laughter.

"The ageing coquette! She was very taken with you."

"There was no taking of me, I can assure you."

"She had that slavering expression whenever she saw you."

"And her chins wobbled with desire."

"And her eyes crossed through passion. And she applied more and more paint to her face the deeper in love with you she fell."

"And her voice was very shrill when she called to me, '*mon petit gentilhomme anglais!*' "

"*Mon concombre!*"

"*Mon petit pain!*"

"She sent me a map purporting to lead me to a great library," said Kenelm, "wherein she said I might read the book of all creation. I followed and it led me only to her silken bedchamber, where she patted the pillow next to her, as if to say, Come!"

Venetia returned to the dining room, and the gentlemen changed the tenor of their conversation.

"Now she is mother-in-law to your King," observed Van Dyck.

"But ah, I am glad I did not have to paint her likeness twenty-one times for the Louvre."

"Marie de' Medici, twenty-one times! That would have been a terrible misfortune!"

"Truly, terrible."

"Worse than anything."

They all knew that the commission, which had gone to Rubens, would have been the making of Van Dyck, and that he would have done it gladly.

Van Dyck, meanwhile, was looking at Venetia, anatomising her face. Venetia stared back at him, although her tender self shrivelled within her. She hoped his painter's eye was kinder at least than William Peake's, that poor artist whom she had so abruptly sent away. She wondered if he could tell that she was three years older than Kenelm, or if he already knew that. She wondered if his heart sank as he thought: Here is another former beauty I must flatter.

In fact, he was thinking: Umber, mink and charcoal for the hair; orpiment, very watery; bismuth white, perhaps, and lead for reflexion, leadvole for the eyebrows, chalk-lead and ground seed pearl for the skin . . . He could not stop himself. It was how his mind worked when he saw a noblewoman's face. He liked the plumpness to her chin, her indolent, almost sickly pallor. The hint of tiredness in her eyes was wonderfully worldly.

"I would so much rather paint your likeness than any Medicis," he said. "I hope I will have the pleasure."

Indeed he would. Sir Kenelm cared not for money, and in consequence he had already disbursed two fortunes. Now as a token of gratitude for his privateering, the King had granted him a third: a monopoly on sealing wax in Wales and the Welsh borders. Anyone wishing to write a personal letter, or sign a document, or seal a contract, needed a melting pool of wax to put their seal upon, and for every stick of sealing wax sold, Sir Kenelm collected a penny piece.

Van Dyck was not convinced this was worthy of Sir Kenelm.

"Can many read in Wales—or write?" he asked. Van Dyck had not ventured further than London.

"Ha!" laughed Venetia.

"Indeed some can, and more are learning all the time. You remind me of the Earl of Strafford."

"Ah, yes . . ."

"Who on being given the monopoly on soap by the King, said he feared the kingdom is not given so much to cleanliness as to raise this to a high consideration. No, come: this is why my monopoly is so fortunate. It is a trade that can only increase. The demand for sealing wax has doubled in a generation. I durst say in three, four hundred years, sealing wax will be carried by every man in the land."

Digby was invariably wrong about business matters. He was unusual because many of his judgements were mistaken, yet many others were right, so his insight and blindness flourished side-by-side, and were even part of the same plant, like a flower putting forth a dark and a white bloom on the same stem. Most people develop a habit of being right or wrong, and stick to it, but Digby's character was to be everything, at once.

"So we will indeed sit for you, Antoon."

"Anthony. I shall be English in England, I hope."

There were a handful of skilled Dutch painters already in London, and Van Dyck did not wish to become another of them, an exile. He wanted to be at home amongst the English cavaliers, to become the King's own painter-in-ordinary. He did not know he would become ill in England, spleen-aching at Blackfriars, his golden chain broken for the King's war chest, his funeral rites read the same day as his baby daughter's baptism.

"Once you are finished with the King's portrait, we shall be next to call on you at your studio. Blackfriars, by the river, no? I have in mind the idea that we should sit for you in a family grouping very like the King's," said Kenelm. "True likenesses, very *au courant*, but composed just so, in harmonious alignment, with my zodiacal armillary sphere sitting beside us, to indicate the assent of the heavens. We shall form a tableau of living beings. As if you might see, if you but peeped a little closer, the blue blood under our skin, the pulse of it at our temples, the rise and fall of our chests. To be painted by my friend with my love and our sons, during England's not unhappy years of peace. I think that will be the very pinnacle of my life!"

Venetia laughed at Kenelm, and kissed his hand, and Van Dyck felt their happiness enclose him also, so they made a sufficient little trio. He was glad to be in London, out of the long war that raged through Hungary, Saxony, Bohemia, Prussia, the Palatinate . . . It was hard for him to know which court to attend next.

"The Thirty Years War," Kenelm called it, which made them all look at him askance.

"If you say it will last so long . . ." said Van Dyck, shrugging.

The three of them made a merry dinner, although the elegant tiredness never left Venetia's eyes, as Van Dyck noticed. She was remote, preoccupied.

Once she had been a pert young miniature, painted by Peter Oliver on the back of a playing card. Van Dyck saw Digby's copy years ago, in Italy. There was no modesty in her gaze. Shamelessly she challenged you to breathe upon her, take her in your hand and lift her close to your face. He disparaged the copyist's technique—it was apparent here, and here, that the painter had dragged the stoat's tooth through the paint to make her hair—but there were magnets in her eyes. No wonder the Lords had all sought to pop her in their pocket.

Now, she would make a full-grown, stately portrait, large as life-size—and never looking at the painter, or the reader of the painting, but always obliquely past, beyond, her mind on higher matters.

Venetia knew she came across as grand, but in truth she avoided Van Dyck's eye because to look at him was to be seen by him, and she was too tired for that.

That evening, Kenelm felt his cheek aflame and realised he had caught the sun during their three hours' conference outside. It was never any nobleman's habit to wear his cheeks ruddied, and yet he felt this was a good omen: the sun-planet was fitting him for worldly power and advancement. Pray Lord its rays might advance his suit for naval comptroller, and bless his conception of their family portrait. It was, indeed, a Sun-day, and he had been wearing yellow, and his golden signet ring: these were all conditions favourable to the sun, and in return the sun had coloured and blessed him, and left its ambitious heat tingling within him. Nothing could begin without the sun's ignition—not a fire, not a burning glass, not a man's career. Just as an ear of corn was ripened by the sun, so man was brought to full advancement by sun-bathing, till he shone with burnished glamour. In time, everyone would know this.

The Queen's private chambers were all a-brabbling confusion of floating featherdown, clouds of new white wool and bits of paper scrunched and cherry-blossoms made of silk. White streamers hung from the rafters, and the floor was covered with white cloth, pale straw, clary flowers and young maidens, tumbling about. That morning, the room had been dressed to resemble a sweet white fairy bower. A tray of milk cakes had been knocked over and a few squashed. One or two girls were singing, out-of-tune, and thumping a stringed pandora, while another poured a fat white rabbit into her friend's lap.

Outside in the corridor, Venetia could hear laughter and noise. Why was she so often in corridors now, looking in? She used to be always in the midst of things. Today at the Queen's morning prayers, she had mentioned to Olive that she would come and find her before she left the palace of Westminster, but it now seemed evident Olive was busy playing with the younger ladies at court. Henrietta-Maria was at the Star Chamber with the King, but here her ladies were disporting themselves. Venetia considered going home and leaving the new clique to their play, since they seemed so happy without her, but a deep, social homing instinct pressed her on.

A maid carrying a tray of white sack went into the room, and Venetia caught a glimpse of Olive, being fed a sweetmeat by a girl she did not recognise. Venetia threw open the door and sailed inside.

"Ladies, I come from the Queen," she said, off the top of her head. "She has news for you."

Lucy Bright sat up. "What?"

"She says to tell you that you are her angels of Platonic love," said Venetia.

Lucy lay down again and carried on singing.

"Philomel with melody / Sing in our sweet lullabye . . ." With these words the ladies on the floor rolled over, singing, "Lulla, lulla, lullabye, Lulla lulla lullabye . . . So, goodnight, so goodnight with lullabye."

"What sport, girls, is this?"

But no one answered her, in the giggling and commotion.

"Oh no, my fairy wings are crushed."

"Sweet pea, you are sitting on my foot."

She noticed that young Lettice was there, in the middle of them, still wearing that unbecoming red dress but quite happy tickling Lady Mary Somerset's face with a sprig of blossom. How pleased she ought to feel to see Lettice so at home.

"Venetia, we are to be fairies at the Queen's new masque," said Lucy Bright, while the other fairies continued tumbling in soft heaps. They were meant to be rehearsing for the masque by arranging themselves into the initials HM, for Henrietta-Maria, but they were too giddy for that.

"We would very much like you to help us," said Lucy. "You are such a brilliant actress. We know you can do it." She said the shocking word "actress" casually, because the game was always to refer to the court masques as if they were the theatre. "Will you, will you help us?"

Pleased—and yet a little doubtful—Venetia sat on the floor, beside her, and said she would.

"Oh wonder. Here's the thing, darling. We are to represent a chorus of fairies, but we need someone to take on a bigger role. Someone with Experience. You see, it is really quite a demanding part. We need someone to play the Spider Ariadne."

Lily, Lady Hutchinson, snort-sniggered at these words, but in a bid to pretend she was laughing at something else, rolled over onto little Marion Cavendish, tickling her fiercely. Their combined years did not make Venetia's.

The high tide, the rushing ebb, and then the low, low sand. Later, Venetia could not remember how she managed to hold herself together. When she was a child she had always made people laugh, playing the pretty noodle. When she was beautiful she was famous for her irony. It was the grain of salt that made her beauty taste. She was still ironical, but people seemed not to notice; no one listened hard enough. And so the time for clowning was come again. It was no longer the time to be Helen of Troy. Now she was Thersites. She must play with these girls as she played with her sons, making them laugh by snapping her teeth and blowing out her cheeks. It was time to make her body serve a new purpose. She looked Lucy deep in the eyes, as if to say, I will not forget this—and then she laughed, shrill, gurgling, chesty, hoo hoo hews, haa haa haas, and she made a show of trying to stop herself laughing, and then finally she collected herself. "But who will play my flies?" And she opened and closed her lips in smacking parps of pantomime menace. Lucy loved her from then on.

"Nothing could give me greater pleasure than to spin a little web for you," said Venetia, though what she was really thinking was, I must drink that Viper Wine, as soon as I can, so help me God. But she continued: "Am I to play in the masque or anti-masque?" Meaning: Am I alive or dead to society? The anti-masque was disgraceful. Lords and ladies appeared in the masque; only hired actors, mummers and professional grotesques performed in the anti-masque, playing parts like "a runaway chicken drumstick." For Venetia to be in the anti-masque was impossible, and they both knew it. An idea struck Venetia before Lucy had time to reply. "Perhaps I should play the harp? A very spider-like instrument, I have always thought."

As she heard more of the plans for the masque—Ben Jonson was to write the speeches, and an actor from the Globe would come and help some of the women to speak them aloud—it became clear to Venetia that even if she had to play a scuttling, spinning arachnid, she would at least be at the very centre of things. And everything was reversed in a good masque. Ladies played boys; kings played gardeners; pale dames blacked their faces, and Moors lost their colour; the moon danced and flowers sang. It could have been worse. She could have been asked to play Medusa, with a nest of real snakes in her hair. That was the headpiece that Queen Anne had insisted the least beautiful of her ladies-in-waiting wore when Venetia played the Grand Canal at Tethys Festival, the Masque of Rivers, twenty years ago.

That afternoon they sang roundels, and Venetia sat by Olive, the new, smooth-faced, baby-ish Olive—and Lettice sat loyally at Venetia's feet, because Venetia would not move over so she could sit beside her on the bench, and as the singing master drew them into time together, Venetia's voice secretly choked at the sound of the young unmarried ones' high pure notes.

As they were singing, two persons slipped into the room: a little hooded couple holding hands, their faces obscured. Next came a scratching at the door, and a pair of spaniels bounded in, anxious to be with their master and mistress. Then Lord Arundel came discreetly into the room, and the game was up. The little couple pulled off their hoods revealing the smiling faces of their Majesties, and the ladies managed to carry on singing, although some faltered and laughed excitedly, as if they were children performing at a concert recognising their parents in the audience. After a minute or so a clanking sound echoed in the corridor, and the King's guard of a dozen pikemen came into the room, trying to move quietly, although they were much encumbered by weaponry. "Oh," said the King, dejectedly. "They have all discovered us, Mary," he said to the Queen, pulling a faux-sad face.

After the madrigals were finished, the girls went up to their Majesties in little groups, curtseying. Venetia and Lucy Bright were both determined not to let one another take precedence in this, and Lucy actually linked arms with Venetia, so as to hold her back from reaching the King and Queen first. And so it happened that Lettice, Venetia and Lucy Bright all came before the King and Queen together.

"Are you the mother of these two, then?" the King gamely asked Venetia.

The Queen nudged him with her fan. She was no great speaker of English, but she had a ready understanding.

Venetia decided, with an effort of will, to take no offence. The King was famously tactless, and a king's kick hurts less than a beggar's. She could grieve for his comment later, when she was alone.

"I am a riddle, if you will, sir—I am the state vanquished by mine own husband," said Venetia, because she knew the King loved a puzzle, especially one he could solve. Charles liked to be the clever one: his elder brother Prince Henry, who should have been king but died at eighteen, was bold and easy in himself and good at jousting, but little Charles was known as the scholar. Besides, she meant to remind him of Kenelm's victory.

"Every woman is vanquished by her own husband," he said, stroking his chin, enjoying the game. Lucy Bright was unable to summon any of her quick speeches, and she could barely take her eyes off Venetia.

"My husband defeated me at Scanderoon," said Venetia.

"Oh, ho ho," said the King. Now he knew who she was. She used to be the sweet bird Venetia Stanley. He recollected his elder brother, Prince Henry, talking about how he she made his mouth to melt, and how he had a will to stir her pudding, and various other drolleries, sincerely meant. Things had changed since then, to be sure, but she was still a sniff of heaven. The King was about to make a clever saw about the passing of time being cruel to us all, but his wife, sensing this, interrupted.

"Venetia, whose husband has defeated the Venetians!" cried Henrietta-Maria, and the King looked genuinely cross she had got there first.

"We hold you and your husband in our heart," he said to her, stressing the "h" in husband as if to remedy his wife's French accent, and laying his hand briefly upon her head, to let her know her audience was over.

Leaving the palace, Venetia went straight home to Charterhouse, where she crawled into bed, although it was afternoon, and pulled its curtains close as a burrow.

> "If the ceiling was falling down in your living room, would you not go and have it repaired?"
>
> Eighty-one-year-old model Carmen Dell'Orefice, 2012

It was like a love-ache, an unbearable absence. Venetia lay in her curtained bed all the afternoon. Sleep was impossible and so was waking: she felt heart-sick, as if for the loss of someone dear to her. But who?

This new character she had was unacceptable. This plainness. It was not suitable to her. She was not like other women. She was famous for what was called her "fatal beauty." Edward Sackville had lost a finger for her in a duel. He bought a spit of land for the purpose in the Low Countries, and the land was still known by the name of the man killed there—Lord Bruce. She had barely even spoken to Lord Bruce. The business was more between the men than anything to do with her, she knew now, and yet when she was sixteen, she took it very much to heart, sickened and enthralled by the news. A dead man, a severed finger and a ruptured lung—these were her tributes, laid across her dressing table with her favours and garlands.

She moaned into her pillow, missing her youth drink, though she had not yet drunk a drop of it. She hoped that when Kenelm came home he could not see the spider-ish look about her. She had to pretend to him she was still Helen, else how could he be Paris? How could she be anything less without disappointing him and the boys? She did not want to be a hag-mother, web-wound and scuttling. She felt the bitterness of it thinning her bones.

She managed to rise and repair some of the sadness that besmirched her face, and to leaden a little, and to paint a rosy lip, so that by the time

Kenelm returned, she was ready to smile at him like he was the new sun rising. He went down on one knee before her, and buried his lion head in her lap and she suffered herself to put her arms around him like the unicorn of old, and she hugged him tightly against the spinning of the world.

He said he was likely to make naval comptroller to the King, as his exploits at Scanderoon were finally come to the King's notice, and the King was interested in using *The Magus* as a possible model for a navy that ruled beneath the waves as well as above. "Ah, my nonesuch," she said, stroking his mane. "My none but one love."

There was one obstacle.

"My darling . . ." said Kenelm, and she knew it was important, by the way he was holding her hands, as if testing their weight. "Please you take this in a good and loving spirit and be not afrit?" She nodded; she knew this tone of voice. Although he seemed to be telling her something, he was asking, looking for approval.

"I am of the wrong faith. I will be received into the Protestant communion on the feast of All Souls at Westminster."

> "Moved by ambition, [Sir Kenelm Digby] has recently abandoned his Catholic faith and become Protestant."
>
> The Venetian Ambassador to London,
> *Calendar of State Papers* (Venice) 1629–32

Of course, Venetia had perceived two years previously that this might happen, and she had already managed Mary Mulsho's will so that it would be harder for her to disinherit Kenelm. She had played a close hand with her Queen and the court ladies-in-waiting, never wholly renouncing or embracing either faith but keeping a subtle counsel with both, just as she collected hearts as well as spades when she played at Glecko. But then a presentiment like a chill settled upon her, a feeling of a long, cold separation from her Kenelm, who, as a Protestant, could not be buried beside her.

"*We* are of the wrong faith," she contradicted him.

"No, my love, you will keep the Old Faith and the Queen's good counsel. I will take the new faith, and so support the King, and obtain promotion. I have to do it, Venice."

He was thinking of the worldly benefits. "This will settle the question that hangs over me and my loyalty, once and for all. My father's crime would be finally forgot . . ." Venetia thought this unlikely, but said nothing. "And can you imagine, my darling, what we could also do if we were preferred at court? We could put up a new wing in this house, my Experiments would be preferred . . . It is," he kissed her hand, to comfort himself, "all to the best, I do believe. I nearly converted when I was in Laud's care, but he said I should wait till my majority."

Venetia wanted to ask Kenelm what the Synod ruled for couples who died in different faiths: would they be reunited hereafter?

But then the dogs barked, and a bell at the back gate jangled.

"A late hour for deliveries," said Kenelm.

"No, no," replied Venetia, leaping up. "Just a parcel from my Lettice, I think. Who will receive you into the new faith? Will it be Laud?"

"He has been waiting these twenty years for the occasion," smiled Kenelm. "I must write to him now."

Sip sip, she thought, sip sip, as she rustled upstairs carrying her delivery, a small crate marked STRAWBERRIES and sealed with the fat worm-like viper seal of Lancelot Choice. The crate was neither light nor heavy, but just so. Sip sip. We raise the transforming wine-cup to our lip. She locked her closet door and used her paperknife to split the seal. Inside, under straw, seethed seven vials of purplish red liquor that had separated into bands, vermillion at the top, clotted black below. So every day would be a serpent's Sunday: seven days' supply of pagan sacrament. Should she drink it?

It was easier for Doktor Faustus, she thought, because he knew the price of his pleasure. No woman would complain about a bargain she had struck herself, with her eyes open, but Faustus had raved regretfully about it for three hours. If we, like Faustus, knew the price of our desire, life would be easy. Desire is dangerous because one never knows its price, nor its cost. Thus Chater preaches against desire.

She stowed the crate in her closet, and closed the door. She caught sight of herself in her spotted glass. She smiled. It was like watching a piece of parchment folded, creasing. She smiled again. The crease was deeper. Each time it took a little more, like a wave claiming a cliff—such a harmless action, repeated to death.

Downstairs, her husband traced again the astrological chart of their nativities using an Aztec divining scalpel, which bent and danced from point-to-point.

She had smiled so many times. Smiles at nursemaids, smiles at wet-nurses, smiles to be fed and smiles to be wiped, smiles to make them pick you up and smiles to make them put you down.

He traced the house of Scorpio under Mars; the Ram in Venus rising on the day of his birth when she was already three years old.

Smiles to be noticed, and not to be sent away, and to be not such a bad little poppet to have around, and to be a good grateful girl, and smiles to show she would not bite. Smiles to say, I am yours.

The broken tower and the seventh moon; her strength was for a long time unchannelled even as her star rose.

Smiling was like paying again and again from a purse that seemed endlessly full. And only now she realised she had squandered. It was the insincerity that cost so much. The real smiles, the ones she could not help, they came for free and took no toll. They were traceless, silent. The other smiles, the fake ones, sounded like a peach being ripped open. They cost. They were female currency.

The celestial prophesy, made under a martial sign. They were both fighters.

And her smiles at court, liberally distributed like alms, smiles that said, notice me, beware, come hither, go away; smiles that flashed with power, that took and gave at the same time, that disarmed and bristled like a set of knives. Smiles even when her eyes were hidden by a mask—smiles that could have come from anyone, smiles that no one needed; wasted, extravagant smiles, like wine thrown onto grass. Why do it? It was what she did now.

She was finally come to join him in Gemini, bless her. But she would not stay there long, being destined for the eclipse of Cancer.

In the great hall at St. John's she caught sight of a woman reflected in the casement and wondered who the old dame was.

The full moon in Venetia Anastasia's ascending house landed on Jupiter. Kenelm's compass traced it again to check. Yes, Jove, signifying strength of spirit, determination, desire beyond reason.

She realised the old dame was her, of course. Soon she would spy a hag.

Kenelm's compass told him he would receive a blow, a bereavement perhaps. He thought of Thomas Allen, and crossed himself.

Venetia twisted a curl around her finger and pulled on it too hard. When she was low, all she had was self-hatred, and she could charm no one, do nothing, be nowhere. She heard the music slowing, and only an act of will could speed it up again.

To stay ourselves, we need to change.

Face-down, she buried her head in the silken pillow, faintly mildewed from being shut up so long while Kenelm was away. She pledged this to herself: she was resolved.

In the forest at Gayhurst, an owl hooted. Out in the middle of the wine-dark ocean, the tide turned.

She sat up, and she went to her closet, and she took out the cork-stoppered bottle filled with wet rubies, black-red coagulate that glowed as she held it up to the candle. Her throat pulsed as she shut her eyes and drank.

"For thine is the kingdom," said Kenelm, practising the unaccustomed Protestant version of the prayer for the first time. "For thine is the kingdom, the power and the glory. For ever, and ever . . ."

"Amen," gasped Venetia, putting down the empty vial.

From that instant, time galloped on apace.

"Everything flows, and nothing stands still."

Heraclitus, 535BC–475BC

They began, as we all do, as tiny seedlings. Naught but little weedy shrubs. When the Digbys took up residence in Charterhouse Precinct that summer, Kenelm drew up a new design for a parterre in the garden, pegged out with string and planted with sixty tender seedlings.

Kenelm obtained letters recommending himself and sent them to the new lord high admiral, the rear admiral, the captain of the fleet, the naval high commissioner and the chief petty officer. He petitioned the lord high admiral in person at Westminster. He wore out three nibs with letters of enquiry.

The seedlings were soon a foot tall, green and shrub-like, apart from two of them, which had been dug up by dogs.

At Rotherhithe the embroiderers' needles flew, stitching flowers and insects into a counterpane for Venetia's bed.

Father Dell'Mascere and Chater enjoyed many conversations on the subject of Purgatory. A bridlepath from Charterhouse Precinct led to St. Giles Cripplegate, green grass all the way, and Chater and his friend idled there often. They walked close, and each time their shoulders brushed, Chater burned with happiness.

The seedlings thickened and their trunks grew silvery.

One week Lancelot Choice sent a small case to the house marked MULBERRIES, the next ABRICOTS. Their hidden fruit: seven glowing vials.

Baby John tottered about the garden, reaching up to tug the leaves off the shrubs, and trying to eat them.

Venetia published a pamphlet edition of her Thoughts and Notions (composed by Chater). While staying away from religion by necessity, it offered pious advice on fasting, household management and marital love. She distributed copies amongst her friends, at their church, and at Powles churchyard, where they were sold for a penny each, as alms for the sick of the Capuchin monastery at St. Malo. The title was *A Mirrour for a Modest Wife*.

Kenelm still heard nothing from the admiralty.

Half the shrubs began to be tinged with autumn colours.

A scrawled letter arrived for Venetia, calling her a Catholic whore who spake the Bible with an unclean tongue. Kenelm took it from her trembling hand, and threw it on the fire.

A black sheep was shorn, out of season, giving its dark thread to finish Venetia's bed hangings, and butchered the next day.

Kenelm noticed Venetia's teeth were staining red. She said something about beet-root. Young Kenelm was wrapped up and taken out to ride his own pony for the first time. Street-boys hawked hods of stenchful manure, which the gardener bought to thickly fertilise the shrubs.

Kenelm took his first Protestant communion at Whitehall, while Chater and Venetia observed mass at home. They spent a quiet day together play-gardening, re-potting the mulberry bushes before the frosts came.

Outside, the shrubs were well-established, knee-high and healthy.

That night, when their bedcurtains were drawn, Venetia's lips were cold when they touched Kenelm's ear, his new Protestant ear, and his cheek. "What if . . . ?" she said. "What if one of us should sterve?"

She used the old word, out of superstition.

"Would we be separated?"

"Never," whispered Kenelm. "We both have our health, pray God, and this is a peaceful country. We shall be reconciled in our faiths one way or the other soon enough. Either you will join me, or I you. It is"—he shut his eyes—"all to the best, I do believe."

She wanted to know which was the True Faith, and which Expedient, but he would only repeat that Mercury had their souls in his keeping.

In the morning, standing at their window overlooking the flowerbeds, you could finally see the purpose of Digby's design. The shrubs had grown and been trimmed enough so that from above, they looked like a fleet of ships. Tawny copper beech leaves were the ships' boughs, and dark winter grass their sails, and they sailed upon a sea of hyssop. There were three of them, in reference to the fleet Kenelm had guided home, and they were flanked by an Arch of Destiny, fashioned from quickset bound in willow, from whence the garden path led either to the compost heap or to the Terrace of Honour.

Venetia entertained three wives of Naval commanders, who came to sit with her and eat an Autumn salat. The garden was festival-bright, the leaves scalded yellow and pink. Venetia wished that women's hair could turn scarlet and orange with the seasons instead of fading into discolour.

Kenelm took his oath of allegiance at Trinity House, and received a royal warrant commanding him to become a Commissioner of the Navy, and he started going to Greenwich every day.

PEAPODS and SWEET PIPPINS and NUTMEG—every week Lancelot Choice sent the vials under a new name, and they were taken up to Venetia's room by habit.

Ben Jonson's latest poems were circulating the court, and Venetia was lent a copy by Penelope, who liked it no more than a shrug. Venetia took it upstairs and read it with growing dismay. It was a paean of praise to the Countess of Bedford, which was not in itself a crime, except that it was so badly written.

"My Muse bad Bedford write, and that was She!"

Venetia read and reread, trying to find a subtle game or satire. Nothing. His style was cloying and glib. It was flattery, shameless and venal. He was writing for money—even the rhymes were terrible. It was as if he wanted people to know he was not trying. There was a word for this—yes, doggerel. Here was Poet turned Poetaster.

"The Humble Petition of Poore Ben, To Th' Best of Monarchs"—she was not even going to read that one. She wanted to slap him into sense, and she raised her arm to hurl the book across the room, but did not throw it. The book did not belong to her. She growled with fury instead. This deathless poet, this immortal bard. He should drink a potion for the rejuvenation of his wits.

The meadow and bridleway between Charterhouse and Cripplegate was now full of half-built houses, donkeys and shouting builders, and Father Dell'Mascere and Chater could linger there no more.

At night, Chater slapped himself in the face until he bled, scratched by his finger ring. He had been advised in his youth that this was the best way to subdue the devil in his thoughts. He dared to hope that Father Dell'Mascere was hurting himself in the same fashion, while thinking of Chater.

Venetia slept soundly under the deep white snowdrift of her new winter coverlet, sewn in black embroidery with flies, and bees, and flowers. She slept a great deal, and dreamed that she was sleeping.

After drinking her Viper Wine one evening, she forgot to put away the empty vial, but Kenelm did not notice it.

One morning she awoke feeling as bright and quick as when she was a girl. She touched her skin and found it plump. She looked down at her hands, and saw the liver spots had blanched away. The veins were flat and smooth, the fingertips plump again. She hurried like a child to the window in her nightshirt, and looking down upon her winter garden, she saw that the flotilla of shrubs, and the Arches of Destiny and Honour, had become nothing but bare blackened sticks.

My Name Is Mary Tree

My name is Mary Tree, and I am on my way to the biggest city I can think of, which is Totnes. I have been walking these two days and I have not yet eaten my cheese, though I have oft been tempted. It is beautiful marching weather and I have seen a great flock of starlings moving like a blanket being shook. I have also seen a dead crow, but I will tell you no more of that. Starting with "Green Grow the Rushes, O!" I have been singing all the songs I know by heart, except in the early evening when mites of the air fly in my mouth, so I keep it closed. Sometimes I skip contrariwards, so I can see the sun as it sets at my back. I have seen no goblins.

And then I remember my strange and mortal purpose and the thing I am carrying, strung from my shoulder in its purse. It is the dagger-shaped shard of glass that cut Master Richard, bound in the bloodied linen of his garter. And when I think of poor Master Richard, and how his lips turned quite white, I tread faster, my skirts draggled dark with grass-juice, and the shard bounces off my shoulder, like someone chiding me to be quick.

My mother being called to Heaven when I was eight years old, I was sent to live with her kinswoman by marriage, my late uncle's wife, Lady Pickett, at her family's estate named Endcote Early. There I learned all manner of useful habits, how to darn and pluck and bake and carry and how to not be seen while doing any of these things, since the seeing of me put My Lady on her nerves. At first she would hold her fan before her eyes rather than look at me, possibly on account of my Mark.

Many things put My Lady on her nerves. The use of a spoon on an earthenware dish, raised servants' voices, the barking of dogs, Papists, and saying "thee" and "thou," which is uncouth. I tried to guess what would please and what displease her, until I came to see that displeasure was her natural condition, and that to sigh and cavil gave her greatest satisfaction. And so as soon as I knew I could do no right, we began to be friends, and she would have me plait her hair and talked to me of how she was once to be married to a man who was lost in the Armada, and she would make noises as if she was crying, though I could see she was not. Mrs. Able the cook told me later that he was not lost, only lost to My Lady.

My nickname in the house was "Only By Marriage," since My Lady used the words so often to describe me. When she had company, she would say it hushly after my name, and sometimes also when there was no company, so I would know my place. So "Only By Marriage" or sometimes simply "Only By" was my name, and I would laugh about this with the other Marys, two servant maids also in the house. Other times I thought that "Only By Marriage" was her way of explaining that she had no consangernooty with the Strawberry Mark that sits across my cheek. I have not looked often at myself in a glass, but I have always known my Mark is there. First because my mother used to kiss it and tell me it was a special prettyness and that a fairy had touched me there to protect me always. Later, because I was so often looked at askance, and held at a distance.

A surfeit of pilchards eaten on a Sunday brought My Lady very low, and she was sick for weeks, her mind tending in a curious direction, namely against those who would help her. Sometimes she would abuse us, and once, in her lady's maid's face she tipped hot caudle. Another maid she—no, I should not tell such tales. But one by one, her servants quit her, knowing that in her Will and Testament there would be nothing left for them, due to the entailing of the property, so the servants took with them divers plate, trinkets, bellows, and so forth, till it was only me and My Lady Pickett living together in that once-great house with no cushions upon the chairs or pots upon the fire and even some tiles pulled up off the floor, to cover unpaid wages, so they said.

I tried to keep her comfortable, and from the village John Tupper brought us fish from the stock pond and helped chop firewood too, for he was a kind fellow, and he was unafraid to look me in the face moreover.

I found some companionship in books, as I have ever been a great lover of books, and when My Lady was ill, I would sit with a book beside the fire some nights, or to seek out new favourites from about the house where they were half-hid, as silver might be. Books are like a special kind of silver, the shine of which only some can perceive. In all, I had three books, one prayers, I think, one of flowers and one in tight little script which smelled like tree-bark. My mother was also fond of books and like her I love to hold them and regard their pages, although I cannot read.

Our vicar, Dr. Jonas, came to sit awhile with My Lady (she was meek with him, mercifully) and afterwards he took a cup of plain posset with me and told me he had been thinking that I would take passage. Take passage? Said I, though I knew his meaning, which was to send me to the New World. I quickly said I could not leave My Lady, and as he went on talking, saying (as I recall) "well, well, we shall see" and "there are many better girls than you sailed already" and "you would do well to be useful, a girl like you," and all the while my head was filling unexpectedly with all the things I did not want to leave behind, as the firm English soil, and a good pot of gravy, and even John Tupper's freckled face, as I confess ye now.

Some days before My Lady died, the sun was bright, a dazzle-day for February, so I cast ope My Lady's curtains, though she always pleaded for the dark. The light in her sick room was like the sudden violence of angels, and My Lady covered her eyes with her skeleton hand, aghast.

"Damn thee," she mews and I do not reply, for she is not well, mind nor body.

Some portion of the curtain, rich red oneside and sun-stained pink the other, has come away in my hand, and I look down to see the fabric turned to mealy matter, all string with tiny eggs a-laid in. A Mothy creature has made of it their home, and quite all of it had, so I saw, tiny worms struggling through the tatters, squirming against the daylight. As I gathered them up for burning in the grate, I considered how they came to be growing there, these white little live things, and I felt sorry for them as they popped and browned.

My Lady starts conversing with herself, or with an absent other, a phantasm from her youth, perhaps. She smiles flirtishly, and talks of spring and laughs and then her mood changes and she looks serious and names me "Mary, my husband's sister's child—by marriage only." I had thought that

I had served her so long I had become something more like kin to her, but "only by marriage" was I ever. I cannot help but smile. "What a little vole of virtue," she says and sighs and seems to look right past me.

"Poor lass," she says. "There's none will take her. We thought the towns-man John Tupper might, but he's appalled of her, they say." She sucks at where her teeth once were. "No man will take a girl as plain as her."

I don't suppose she meant to be unkind. The strawberry mark on my cheek burns as I brush away the tear which has fallen out of my left eye, and quickly my mind fills with thoughts of the curtain. My next duty should be to tear the curtain down and make of it a bonfire. But I look back at My Lady, who is sunk back into a snoring sleep, her mouth agape. I have already salved her gums that morn with aniseed. And I say aloud, "Mary, let these curtains rot."

I left them hanging. I cared for My Lady and fed her broth, and comforted her through her final days, though she never spoke again, and the departing of her soul was very slow, so for several days I was not sure of whether she was there or not, and I ope the window to let her soul out and when it went, pray God it was upwards.

They say the truth shall set ye free and with her harsh words My Lady loosed me like a hare from a trap. I no longer had so much doubt of myself, and I was content to please myself, since I would please no man; and I made a promise that since I would not be loved nor give love to any one, that I should endeavour to be good friends with every one and all the world.

I shall tell more next time, but now I must rest in this warm under-tree hollow, where the sheep have left white wool-trails on hawthorn hooks. I can journey on apace tomorrow. My dear kinsman, the closest I have to kin, lies sick of a wound at home, and his only hope rests in me. I seek the Keeper of the Powder of Sympathy, Sir Kenholme Diggy. I do not know where he resides, nor whether he will be able to cure my friend's mortal wound. All I really know is his name, and this, I trust, will be all I need.

"There are no ugly women, only lazy ones."

Helena Rubinstein, *My Life for Beauty*, 1966

AS WINTER DREW in, each day dawned colder, but Venetia awoke feeling stronger, and more hopeful. Venus was in her smile again. The highways frosted, and the geese's down thickened, and every day the garden died a little, while Venetia grew more pert. It was like an artificial spring. The mirrors that she had packed away, turned to the wall or stacked in the cellar began to reappear about the house.

Every day, she drank her Adder juice. It thickened her veins, and filled her up with all its magical properties—later understood as iron from the vipers' blood, ascorbic acid from the tartar, artificial hormones from the urine of pregnant mares, and hope, faith and comfort from the dribble of delicious opium.

Venetia even took a bath, her first since spring, turning the house into steaming, rose-scented commotion of slops on the stairs and the maids running up from the scullery to the dining room where the tub was set, the males of the retinue obliged to busy themselves away from the house, and all the housemaids waiting to use the hot water after her in order of rank, and preparing to be sewn into their winter clothes.

She was suspicious of baths—it was often said that the last thing Lady so-and-so ever did was take one; or that Master this-and-that was never the same after his bath in 1603. A bath taken for too long seeped in through the skin and damaged the organs; it was important not to wallow. On the appointed morning, she held young Kenelm especially tight and kissed sleeping John's feet, muttering a blessing of love over them.

But who could not enjoy being immersed? It was like a second baptism. She lay bobbing back in the tub looking at the withdrawing room—

fireplace, ceiling, tapestries—from this new angle of repose. As she rose steaming from the waters, which were grown cloudy and scummed with petals, she glimpsed herself naked in the mirror—pink flesh like hot roast gammon, curved and wobbly as Rubens' Susanna bathing. She grasped the sponge to cover herself, even though there was no one watching but her own reflection.

She saw that Venus had breathed upon her, reddening her cheek, plumping the flesh around her collarbone, and stroking her neck softer and smoother. Her whole form was wet and strong and smoking in the shaft of light penetrating the room above the curtains. She felt unexpectedly forgiving, as she looked at this person's pink, vulnerable body. She had a waist again, she noticed. There was certainly less of her than before. Her worst fear—an incipient dowager's hump—seemed to have been allayed by the rubbing and palpations she had lately required Chater to perform upon her shoulders. She stood a little straighter, then turned so she might look back at her bottom. It was a good enough bottom. She exhaled. It was not a reconciliation with herself, but it was a truce.

Two grooms were at that moment sitting outside in the mews, eating a pease pottage and talking about horses' flanks, then cows' arses, then women.

—I'd say she was like two fine shaddocks.
—Aye, like a great big pompkin.
—Cleft before and aft.
—And soft as you like.
—Heavy to lift and good to taste.
—Not the greenest.
—Nay but sweetest.

At the naval office in Greenwich, Kenelm put down his pen and daydreamed about his wife. He imagined her lace garter, and the soft bite it left on her thigh. He thought about her plumpness, and her seashell-smelling parts, and her grip and her buck, and then a maid came in with his ale, and broke his reverie.

When Venetia was upstairs recovering from her bath, Chater came to her door as directed with a pot of quicklime and arsenic mixed with water into a depilatory paste. Kenelm had these in his laboratory but Venetia was too proud to borrow them for her purpose and she sent Chater out to buy them from the apothecary. Chater stood at her bedroom door, with one hand across his heart, frozen with anticipation of being invited inside the sacred boudoir. His eyes were very large, trying to take in everything at once. Venetia shut the door casually in his face. She tested the quicklime with a feather, and while she was waiting for it to be ready, she rubbed rose wax on her heels and nipped her eyebrows, looking intently at the gluey white root-tip of each black hair. She wondered if all women's hairs had these, or if hers were especially disgusting. She checked the quicklime and saw that all the feather had dissolved, leaving a wand of cartilage, which meant the mixture was ready, and she spread the gas-smelling paste across her legs, knees to ankles, while it curdled and bubbled. The quicklime should be left on the skin for no longer than the time it took to say three Ave Marias, and Venetia whispered them as she lay there, rigid and sweating through the burning. She knew well this friendly agony. The more it hurt, the better it worked. She smelled the pleasing whiff of shrivelled, sizzling hair.

Holy Mary, mother of God, pray for us sinners now and in the hour of our death, Amen. Holy Mary . . .

Next she spread across her hairline a blue preparation of blackberry leaves, walnuts, gull turds and cypress nuts, to try to touch up the greys. It stung her scalp, and she tipped her head back so it might trickle further, like a path of delicious fire-water across her brain. Her scalp would scab and then she would idly pick it off, feeling the fascinating grit of it between her fingers. Oatmeal, bran and lily water were pasted across her face when she answered the door to Chater, who had come to take away the ill-smelling package of quicklime. She showed him her face, painted dead-white like a mummer's.

"Well, sir," she said, "does you like my new look?"

Poor Chater stammered tactfully, and his confusion was so entertaining to her that her face-mask cracked into a thousand tiny lines.

Finally she rang for Elizabeth to help her get dressed. Her costume must be put on each and every day. She sat at her dressing table, painting. *God hath given you one face and you make yourselves another*, she heard Hamlet's angry words in her head, and she thought what a tiresome person he was, licking the tip of her sable brush and dipping it in carmine. Poor Hamlet was ever a booby. The poison-pen letter she had received had gone into some detail about her painted lips, "her rubious o, her bright fornicator's mouth." She wondered if the writer of the letter had formerly been one of the boys who chased after her carriage shouting hallelujahs.

As she went about town that afternoon, helping Chater distribute her pamphlet of domestic wisdom, *A Mirrour for a Modest Wife*, she was both pleased and displeased by her unaccustomed cleanliness. It made her feel brand new but invisible, as if she had no shadow, no presence. The comforting musty aroma of self was gone. It would take weeks to recover it.

That evening, Kenelm called her his strange new wife, and kissed her curiously. Usually Mistress Elizabeth unlaced her but tonight he did it himself, pulling at every string and bow he could see, even the decorative ones, and doing it badly, like a boy, unlacing everything in the wrong order, and tearing a few stitches in his hurry to see how clean she was.

A few months ago, she would have doubted him, wondering why he was so excited, tormenting herself with suspicions and asking if his male psyche was pretending she was another woman, some cheap young doll or katy.

But now her power had returned, and none of these cruel thoughts bothered her. When she was naked, she slowed him down, staying his hand and keeping him back, until he was the kind and gentle lover that she had taught him to be in their early years together. And finally, well pleased with one another, they fell asleep under her new coverlet, with their legs entwined the whole night through, waking only sometimes to kiss one another, as they had done at the very beginning.

A cart had drawn up in Charterhouse Precinct, and men were fetching piles of books into the house. Sir Kenelm was amongst them, coming and going, his voice commanding where the next consignment should go, his arms filled with books, his face wet with tears that he did not seem to notice, as he continued to lift and stack the books into pillars, piles and tottering columns.

There were vast folded maps, as tall as young Kenelm; flapping incunabula and sheaves of illuminated manuscript, not bound but tied with string, like parcels; doll-sized prayer books and gospels; Indian mandalas and Islamic calligraphy and books of Aztec illustrations marked "Ægyptian." The sole extant copies of Anglo-Saxon poems were mixed in with tattered sheaves of church accounts and Medieval tithe books, alongside dozens of annotated books of geometry, bound in black with no markings, in order to disguise their dangerous content. It was the entire library of Thomas Allen, who had finally been released of this life in his rooms at Oxford, where he had been found dead in his chair, as if asleep. He had got up to put on his best clothes before he died—his Magus's cloak of blue and threaded with silver stars.

"It is as if," Kenelm said, pausing to wipe his face, "as if we carry his heart, his lungs, his spleen, and every part of his body into our house."

Venetia, who had come down from her bedroom to discover this excess of books, and her husband in tears, took in the situation immediately. "He speaks figuratively," she explained to the men. "He is only sad for the loss of his old tutor and friend. Whiles you are with us," she smiled airily, flashing her old power, "could you do us the great good action of moving this big old chest here, so, and heaving this cabinet here into the upstairs chamber . . ." And thus Venetia had the men running about rearranging the house as well as filling it with books.

> "Like a number of mathematicians, Thomas Allen was popularly supposed to be a necromancer . . . As early as 1563 he began acquiring manuscripts and gradually built up one of the largest private collections in Oxford . . . which he bequeathed to Sir Kenelm Digby in 1632."
>
> *The Oxford Dictionary of National Biography*, 2012

The books were in Digby's mercy now, bequeathed to him as a child to a godparent: a blessing but a burden of care. They had come to him because he loved books; so our passions gather their own speed. Over the next weeks, he would furiously reprimand the servants of his house for using the books to hold doors open. It was the way people treated manuscripts, since the monks were driven out. He found a beer pot placed upon an Illumination. "I will not have these papers abused," he insisted. "Who harms my books harms my very person."

The air that night was sulphurous and syncopated with burst-bladder pops and bangs. A loud one, catching everyone by surprise, made the carthorse stamp, and the windows rattle. It was the fifth of November, and the commemoration of the Gunpowder Plot was enforced by law, though the Digbys always spent the night holding vigil at home, even though one of them was now a Protestant. Kenelm was of the opinion that Venetia should retire and draw their bed-curtains against the noise, in case she was with child again, and the explosions marked their baby—he knew that by looking at an execution once, a mother had given birth to a headless child. He found he was crying again, for the woes of the world.

Digby paused beside a stack of books in Italian, noticing a little volume wedged underneath, as big as the palm of his hand, in stiff goatskin the colour of dried blood, tooled with naïve, off-centre round Celtic designs. He held it gently, became caught up in its first pages, and fell to reading.

The men moved back and forth past him, shifting and shouting, and one of the men put out his back through heavy lifting, and made a cry about it, and Venetia ran to get him a pretty medal of St. Christopher from her own closet, only a little mouldy, and his to keep, she insisted. It was not worth a penny, less than the worth of the work of furniture shifting they had done, and yet the man went away well pleased, and sweet on Venetia.

Outside the war-like sounds continued, and the smell of a hundred good Protestant bonfires drifted across the city, but Sir Kenelm was still absorbed in the tiny ox-blood volume. He held the book to his riddling, turnover heart. He had an inclination to believe it was the gospel of St. Cuthbert, buried nine centuries previously in the saint's coffin, in the salty earth of the holy island Lindisfarne, and used in many Catholic miracles since it was disinterred in the claw-like grasp of the saint's crystalline, salt-preserved body. With the smallest flick of his tongue Kenelm licked the top cover of the book. It was salty. He wondered if he might be struck dumb with tongue-rot, so he could say no more Protestant prayers.

He realised the men had gone and it was dark, and he looked up and saw he was in the dining room, trapped in the midst of his old tutor's precious library, and had to shift two stacks of books to get out. He kept the Gospel tightly in his palm. This little volume had not yet achieved all its miracles. In a few hundred years it would raise buildings and save souls.

> "The Society of Jesus has sold the St. Cuthbert Gospel to the British Library for £9 million . . . Proceeds of the sale will support Jesuit schools in London, Glasgow and Africa."
>
> *The Tablet* newspaper, 2012

Kenelm climbed to the highest window in the house, where ashes from the city's bonfires blew into his face like black snowflakes. Over the river a display of sparked-up military firepower spluttered, low, golden and bloody, like a demonstration of what the state could do to your guts, if it was so minded.

It was a potent celebration, this festival of fireworks—almost alchemical in its method. For it sought to convert a substance into its direct opposite. Powder had been a means to murder, now it was re-deployed as a means to delight. Screams of agony became screams of excitement. An act of terror became a celebration. A literal thinker would never have created this commemoration. Suitably for a Protestant occasion, everything hung on analogy.

As Kenelm's private thoughts flared and sizzled, the display on the river seemed to grow out of control, fizzing ever higher into the sky, and just as he began to be afraid for the city's safety, Kenelm thought he saw his father's golden hair shining across the heavens, fading out of sight like a bounding Leo, for his father was born on the cusp of August. The bright form of the leaping lion was still there when he closed his eyes.

"What is happening?"

It was young Kenelm in his nightclothes. "Well," said Kenelm, taking him onto his knee, "tonight is a festival in memory of your grandfather."

It was almost true. There were some things that would need to be better explained to the boy, certainly, but he could start with the grand concepts. The detail—his grandfather's treachery, trial, and so forth—could be filled in later.

The boy hid his face in Kenelm's clothes.

"The city is celebrating your grandfather with fireworks," he said. Less true, but never mind. "If you watch the sky you will see him glimmer and wave to us."

A spluttering fusillade meant neither could speak or hear, then golden limbs streaked across the night.

"He's a Starman, waiting in the sky," cooed Sir Kenelm, as little fireworks whizzed round the sky like fiery maggots.

Over the music of crashes and rocket whines, he spoke urgently to young Kenelm. "I have told you that we Philosophers of Alchemy say that we are all Starmen, you know, and our bones are made of stars, and after we die we return to the stars."

Young Kenelm nodded.

"La la la . . ." sang his father, plucking words out of the sky, "He would, in Kenelm's consideration, blow their minds."

Kenelm hummed the song to his son, a lullaby he must have heard in his own childhood, a Buckinghamshire air, perhaps. The boy's limbs became heavy, and the sleeping Kenelm was carried to bed, while outside, tortured rockets whined across the sky.

Mary Tree: 22 Miles Travelled

I TELL YOU, THE world is wider than you would ever think possible. The cruel shard I carry, which wounded Richard Pickett, is already tar-blackened, with no red on its bandage, and I have not even left the county of Devon. But I have learned so much. To begin with, I now know the proper name of the man I seek, the Keeper of the Powder of Sympathy: Sir Keyholme Digbin. A mighty pleasant name.

People in towns are very kind, I have discovered. I stayed in Totnes at an inn one night, where I paid the extra that was demanded so I might be in the warm company of many others, rather than in a drafty room of my own. I had expected the cost to be the other way about, but the inn's hostess explained me my error. She seemed barely repelled by my Mark at all, but talked to me as any other. It was she who corrected me so I had Sir Keyholme Digbin's name better. She said I should seek out one Sir Mungo Stump, who knows of all the great Men of the Age, and will blab about them moreover. And so I was sent onwards by cart to Dawlish, and as we ride I will tell something more of my strange business.

I saw to it that My Lady Pickett was funeralled and the bell tolled as she wished, even though Father Jonas was doubtful of such high ceremony. Being of a mind to pack me off to Virginia with the Puritans, he said he would come and see me that evening, and I said I feared I would be too busy and sorrowing, and he looked me deep in the eye and said it wasn't a long business that he needed to do with me.

I went home and started to pack to leave at once, so I might evade him, and perhaps go into service at some house in Cornwall. I was considering whether or no I should take my three books with me, and I left without them, as they were not properly mine, and then went back to fetch them, when I heard a commotion at the gate and peeping from the window I saw a cart outside, with two horses, and a boy running after, and in the midst, a man, holding his feathered hat to his breast and gazing up at the house.

Richard Pickett it was, My Lady's nephew, and a gentleman, come to claim her estate. He was bluff and pink-faced and with two thick grey whiskers, in the manner of a cavalier. His woolly dog, grey whiskered also, asked me with his eyes for a drink so I fetched him one. "What is his name?" I asked Richard Pickett, but he ignored me. He was dressed all in black, but when I told him he had missed My Lady's funeral he did not care and swaggered past me as if I had not spoke. I was afraid he was a strange man, possibly contemnable, to be so heard-hearted, until I discovered he was slightly deaf due to "service in the cannon's mouth," as he termed it, and he motioned to the right side of his head, by which do I mean the dexter? Yes, and on tiptoe, into this hair-sprouting ear, I shouted that My Lady was already buried, at which he looked most contrite and asked to visit her grave.

The loss of My Lady must have brought out a new boldness in me, for next I spoke quickly, into the same ear, that our vicar, one Dr. Jonas, wished to transport me hence to the New World this evening. "And do you want to go?" he asked, directly, which made me silent, unfamiliar as I was with questions concerning my wants. All I could do was shake my head. "Ye shall not go then, miss; ye shall not go," he said, and continued directing his boy with carrying in his books and properties.

And so I remained at Endcote Early, with Richard Pickett and Asparagus his dog, and though I was perplexed by them, and maddened too, they were the finest friends I ever had. As I journey now to Dawlish, the sword in the bag at my shoulder, I pray that Richard Pickett is in no pain. He is a man full of theorems and Ingeniose strategies, learning and deep thoughts. But aye me, he is a bodger. He could not milk a cow without receiving a kick, nor catch a fish without drowning himself. In London once at his friend's house called "Tradescant" they let him hold in his palm a Phoenix's egg, from Araby-land, and as he told me the story I was full-fearing he drop't it.

His gait is rolling, like one who has been too long i'the saddle, his hand is constantly cupped behind his ear to hear better. He is an antiquarian, and can see far into the past—he could converse with the Caesars, were they to visit Endcote Early—but he cannot see his own porridge without peering. He is followed everywhere by Asparagus, who pretends to be lame also out of sympathy with his master, but is able to run well enough on his own. Sir Richard is fanatical of naval history and soon after he arrived at Endcote Early he was out, striding about the lower paddock, prodding a stick in the turf and measuring distance with it as if he were prospecting for gold, or planning to sow the growing gold of wheat when, in fact, he was planning how he would dam the River Stickle and flood the lower paddock, the better to re-enact a naval engagement there. All it would take, he said, was six weeks of rain together, and I was thankful for the dry spell and his forgetting of the plan meanwhile.

Once an officer, always an officer, he says—and in the forecourt at Endcote Early he raised a standard. His greatest pleasure on a sunny day was to whistle through his teeth and mark upon his tabor a rhythm, while me and the little boy called William from the village would march up and down the garden with Sir Richard Pickett leading us and commanding—"Leftwards, HO!" and "Eyes RIGHT!" and sometimes, tapping me on the neck with his drumstick, shouting, "Shoulders back, sir! Should I take you for a scobberlotcher?," by which he meant a dreamy jakes.

Supper he cared for not so much as the tobacco afterwards—a pipe and conversation were his favourite dishes. In the evenings sometimes he would read aloud passages of sulphurick philosophy, which reminded me of Mrs. Able's receipts, but for a devil's larder, stocked with possets of mercury, pies of flux and fiery matter and cordials of moonbeams. I liked to listen, though I knew my questions were poor, and that Sir Richard wished for company.

Master Richard and me and Asparagus living in that former great house together must have made a strange picture to the village, but it suited us. After I stopped asking John Tupper to cut the elder-bush and the bindweed, a green-tangle grew up all around the house and the windows were hard to open. Tradesmen ceased to visit. Sir Richard noticed no difference, while I felt safe behind the overgrowth.

We marched to the tabor's beat on the parade ground, for so Sir R called the paddock, although the little boy William did not join us any more, perhaps forbidden. In the evenings Richard would read aloud, mostly tales about matters very big or very small. It is either the heavens this or a grain of sand that. Sir Keyholme says the air is full of flying prawns that fit one hundred to a needle's eye. He only told me of the flying prawns late at night when he was in his cups.

I asked him to tell me tales about the great personages of the day, the fine lords and ladies, and he would begin with the histories of their titles, lands, estates and tithes, slowly moving on to the detail of their heraldic arms, while I yawned greatly, but tried to make it look as if I only exercised my face. Once he told me of Sir Keyholme Digbin, the Keeper of the Powder of Sympathy, which could heal wounds at a distance, by means of acorns passing through the air. At least, I think he said "acorns."

I sat up when he told me of Sir Digbin's lovely wife, Lady Venetia, who he said was very fair, but more than that, all he could recall was that her grandfather was a so-called Wizard Earl, which sounded promising but soon moved back to Logick. Richard could remember nothing of Venetia's shoes, nor whether her hair was curled or no, nor even whether she was an orphan.

He would only shake his head, and say she was a Beauty. I have seen many sights of beauty in my life—a hazel with every leaf frosted, a bowl of gravy with steam rising off it, and a sticky chick newborn, but I have never seen a Beauty, except the old carved Virgin at Snittlefield, who looks very kind but—I know I shouldn't say so—she is squink-eyed with a long nose, God forgive me! I have seen how a loud and comely woman can work on a man—there is Moll from the village, chased by all the boys—and I saw a townswoman with a great forehead which they said she kept high by plucking, but I have never seen a Beauty, or a Fine Lady. And I wished then that I might behold such a lady, that she might walk close past me, if only once in my life.

Richard told me that Sir Keyholme's mother disapproved of Venetia as a "libertine," but when I asked Richard what it meant, he said we had talked the fire almost out and the man in the moon was wondering at us.

How could this dear man be done such harm? Some boys wanted to come to the house for naval training and drill, which pleased Sir Richard.

He loved nothing more than to call commands, which made his voice quavery with passionate remembrance. "Stiffen your sinews," he would growl at the boys in their smocks. "Summon up the blood . . . Are ye not Englishmen born?" They would try to stand taller than each other till they were fit to burst with holding breath. Sometimes their older brothers would come to visit also, and sit on our gatepost like jackanapes. I heard them calling Sir Richard "Ricketty Picketty" and "R-r-r-r-ick—A-Pick-A," and such like. None of them dared look me in the face, being afraid of my Mark, or so I guess.

But Richard wanted to school the bigger boys in musket practice, so that those who wished to might know a little of it, before the press master came to town. And so one afternoon we dried his powder carefully and the next day in the morning, some lads came by, three skinny pips and one big butcher's boy, all very meek and none of them daring to look us in the eye or say aught but "Yis" and "Nay."

When the musket fired first, all four boys went leaping in different directions, made witless by the noise, if they had any wits to start with. The big one sat down panting. But little by little as the sun grew powerful and Sir R told tales of his expeditions, their fear gave way to boredom and thus to high spirits, and they began to whisper and snuckle among themselves, which Richard busy with his musketry could not see, and certainly could not hear. Richard went indoors, I think to visit the heads as he calls the privy after the naval fashion. While he was gone the naughty boys made a war-horse out of the butcher's boy, who was romping on all fours with one of the skinny boys clung to his back. "Ride the elephans, ride, ride!" shouted the other boys, and the skinny boy scrambled and waved the musket.

So there was I, shouting, and Asparagus, barking for the first time in years, and then a great bang comes, and a shatter of glass as the musket ball hits the upstairs casement. And I heard a high whine of horror, and there was Sir Richard still upright and walking from the house into the green garden, except as in a dream, out of his side protrudes a great dagger of glass. And as the wound's blood spread, the colour drained from his face, till it was blanched and looking down I can see each pore on his white cheek as he lay in my arms. Two boys were running as fast as they could for the road while the other two were still climbing over the gate. At first I thought they were running for help but when no help came I realised they were only saving their skins.

"Gus?" said Sir Richard, calling his dog, who dragged him a marrow-bone. While Richard gazed at Asparagus, I tugged the glass out of his side, which left a wound very long but not so deep, though I saw some of his yellow guts revealed. I staunched the bleeding with the nearest cloth to hand—Sir Richard's garter. Then I wrapped Sir Richard like a dolly in a blanket and lit a fire for him, although it was a hot summer's day.

He bid me go to London, and make my way in life. I told him it was only the wound talking, and hushed him. But he insisted, more strongly as he grew weaklier, that I should go and find Sir Keyholme Digbin, and prevail upon him to save him, by exercising the Powder of Sympathy upon the glass shard that stabbed him. He said I should know Sir Keyholme when I saw him because he looked very like the Angel on the Rood screen at West Wycherley, except his feet were not on fire. He could give me no other directions for finding Sir Keyholme, and told me the world would help me there.

I could not leave without making arrangements to keep him safe, in case the Powder of Sympathy was not immediately effective. John Tupper's mother promised me she would take care of his victuals, and Midwife Barker I paid well to go and tend his wounds, so his healing might begin before I was home.

And so you understand a little more of my journey. Sometimes I fancy I can hear Asparagus keening at me to be quick, and yet I have many miles to go, and there could be no slower beast than this poor carthorse, bless its withers. My next task is to find the lodgings of Mungo Stump in Dawlish. I hope it will not prove too great and busy a town, and that he will receive me without displeasure. In Totnes I came close to seeing my reflection in a drinking-glass, but looked away at the last moment, having no need of that.

Sir Kenelm's Infinite Library

SIR KENELM HAD the builders in.

This meant a great deal of coming-and-going in boots, which offended the floors and therefore Mistress Elizabeth, and cold drafts, which offended the baby, and noise of hammering, which offended everyone. What was worse was when there was no coming-and-going, and only the ominous silence of unfinished work, and deserted workbenches and dust sheets in the hall.

Kenelm had commissioned the finest private library he could design, with thematic shelving, harmonious proportions and a black-and-white chequered floor. Here, Universall Knowledge might come at last within the Grasp of Man. "You have my word of honour, I'll not pay you another penny until you have completed the World, Americas and France," said Kenelm, when the builders' foreman finally appeared.

The foreman, Thomas Clack, considered pointing out that Sir Kenelm had not yet paid him any pence at all, since he was working on credit as usual. Sir Kenelm had provided his material, forty good oaks from Gayhurst. "My forest—a fine crowd of old trees—has been cut down for our purpose, and I must have my library, or where will my poor books winter, in stacks on the frosty floor?"

Together they toured what was already accomplished, going in through the new double doors to the long library, with new ceiling supports, of wood, painted as marbled columns in the Doric style. The room was cold, paint-smelling and echoey, but its new casements gave onto the garden, and there was also a little door, so that in summer Sir Kenelm might wander, book in hand, out of the library and through the scented Path of Contemplation, to join his wife where she sat eating cherries in the breezy Roman Pergola, their summer reading house (as yet unconstructed).

Across the walls of his library-in-progress were marks in red chalk betokening where his pantheon of Poets would sit—Horace, Seneca, Spenser and the rest. Their busts were in commission. The Emblematicall paintings of Actium and Tiphys, sea-battles to reference Kenelm's own at Scanderoon, were already sketched into their porticoes by the scenery-painter, and the master letter-writer had been tasked with rendering Epigrams in a clear hand across the upper parts of the walls, thus:

One Small Step for Ma

But he had been interrupted, so that the charcoal cartoon of the lettering only went so far, and the rest was whitewash.

"*Man*," said Sir Kenelm. "*For Man*. And where is the rest?"

Clack put his chalk in his mouth while he rubbed his hands, shrugging.

". . . *One Giant Leap for Mankind*," said Kenelm. It was depressing to see this noble phrase incomplete.

"Yep," said Thomas Clack. "He's only gone for his dinner."

"The calligrapher went for his dinner last week and has not come back."

"He's a good lad, he'll be with you later today or tomorrow, sir." Thomas Clack was not himself a craftsman, but he was an able general manager, and he knew how to pacify his clients.

"And your cloud-painter, is he come yet?" said Kenelm, pointing to the ceiling, where Zephyrs should be disporting through heavenly Afflatus.

"Now, Bill the Cloud is high up in the Worshipful Company, and he's much in demand. First there is Master Suckling's Love Temple, which needs many, many more clouds if the flying maidens are to have any modesty at all, and then he is painting Lord Arundel's heavens, which was meant to be a quick job but are now required to the degree of storminess that they will put forth lightning. Then he must finish the Passion for Mary Abchurch, or there will be no Christmas altarpiece, and the people must look at our Saviour suffering upon an empty sky of plain red clay—do you wish that to come to pass because you have such need of your own library?"

"No," said Kenelm wearily. "No, he will come when he is ready. I had not realised London was so much in want of clouds."

Kenelm had at first had the idea that the library ought to be constructed in the Vitruvian fashion, after Michelangelo's library in Florence, with all its proportions following the golden archetype of Man's Corporeal Body, with a cranium in the middle which was a cupola inset in the rafters, with the light of consciousness let in from the sky, but over time Kenelm contented himself with this more prosaic library, yet his cherished plan was that the shelves should cohere to the Continents of the World (as, Roman, New World, English, and the like) and just as there was *terra incognita*, so there would be dark, empty shelving held for works as yet unacquired and unwritten: biographies of men or even women unborn, Atlases of countries undiscovered. Only a complacent and heretical library could present a closed frontage. No library should ever be full.

Thomas Clack was waiting to speak. "Sir, your *other parts*," he said significantly, "are being worked upon."

Kenelm had asked Clack, who was often employed by Catholics, to build him a mirror-frontage concealing private shelving. Clack took the commission with high seriousness, presuming the secret books to be seditious tracts from Rome, manuals of equivocation and Counter-Reformation. In fact, the most precious books in Kenelm's collection were on the Pope's Index of Prohibited Books. Contradiction and countermand were intrinsic to his soul. Clack frequently reassured Kenelm, under his breath, that his designs had been noted, and were being put into practice. Clack even winked at him in reference to the pornography he presumed would also lodge there, but Kenelm missed this profanity, assuming he had dust in his eye.

As part of his duty of care for Thomas Allen's books, Digby was having them re-bound in leather and gilt. When he first became custodian of them, he thought he could never wish for any more books—until he went to visit the bookbinder at the Blue Bible, who showed him other rare volumes, which must have come from a great philosopher's library: *The Opus Majus of Roger Bacon*, Aristotle's *Secretum Secretorum*, a pharmacopœia, and Rolle's *Pricke of Conscience*, tooled in gold and red calf, as well as volumes in esoteric languages unknown to Kenelm, who looked them over with a grim kind of pleasure, since these must also be added to his library, even though some were duplicates of books he already owned, and yet he must have them.

The windows, being the eyes of the building, must not let too much brightness into this place of contemplation, nor must they keep it unduly dark. It was ideally to be somewhat like a gentle forest dell, wherein new thoughts might grow and weedy distractions wither . . . The windows were to be painted with scenes that appeared Emblematicall, though they were sweetly personal to him and Venetia, depicting moments from their courtship. Two fat cherubim, playing together; the lion with the thorn in its paw, in remembrance of how he once took a thistle out of the heel of Venetia's hand; the Laurel of constancy, the Mulberry of patience, the Cherry of Virtue, the Maple of her suitors' rotten hearts. In the final window, there appeared the Fig-Tree of deliciousness.

His library would be never-ending, thanks to *trompe-l'œil*: at the far end, he hung his Dutch perspective painting of the great library at Leiden, which played with the eye from a distance, and the great grey architraves of the library looked so permanent, and its books so material, that if he hung it half behind an Arras curtain, anyone might think that it was a portal to another library, and hence from Leiden, one might wander into another library, and beyond that ever forwards.

When he peered into the painting, Kenelm fancied he saw amongst the lean, dark-hatted scholars the figure of Thomas Browne, working for his doctor's gown in Leiden. They knew one another from Oxford days, when they were acquainted only by reputation. The queer thing was this: Browne moved. Sometimes when Kenelm looked at the painting, Browne was pacing about. The next time Kenelm looked, he was daydreaming in the scriptorium. Sometimes Kenelm peering very close into the painting fancied he stood at Browne's shoulder and he could see, as his nib moved across the page, that he was writing his Bibliotheca Abscondita: his list of books that either were lost or had never existed:

The song of the sirens
The paradoxes Berkeley invented about time but never published

The lost language of the Saharan Garamantes
The proof of Pierre Fermat's last theorem
The unwritten chapters of *Edwin Drood*
Aeschylus's *The Egyptians*
Homer's comedy *Margites*
The secret and true name of Rome
The Gnostic Gospel of Basilides
Works of David Foster Wallace's dotage
The perfect translation of *Eugene Onegin* into English

Over the page, his notes continued:

The book of Lilith
The ending of Mrs. Gaskell's *Wives and Daughters*
Queen Nefertiti's edicts
Jane Austen's *Sanditon*
Sylvia Plath's destroyed journals
The works of Ada Lovelace on the Analytical Engine
Letters of empresses, queens, noblewomen and ordinary women
Diaries of the same
Masterworks of the same
The letters and papers of Venetia Stanley

Leaving Browne at work, Kenelm began to explore the library at Leiden, pacing as in a dream through the cold, stony labyrinths, looking at all the unreachable volumes, until he came to the back wall, where there was a curtain, which Kenelm drew back, to find another large painting of a library, so well done it might have been a window, and by gazing, Kenelm moved into it, propelling his mind forward with the same effort one might use to lift a weight, or pull a rope.

This was a very magnificent library, in a new classical mode, on a circular model, so one might turn about, looking down the walls of books like spokes in a wheel. Rotating with some mental effort, as if he were trying to write with his left hand, Sir Kenelm began to feel giddy, and clung to a wall, where a sketch hung, an architect's plan for the best library in the New World.

Gazing into this design, he saw on the shelves some of his own books.

> "In 1655 Digby sent a gift of about forty books to Harvard University."
>
> *The Oxford Dictionary of National Biography,* 2012

From there he was drawn onwards, through another window, into a drab, clean library, in which there were no books at all, only a humming emptiness. The users of this library were not present, but Kenelm could hear them working, making thousands of tiny clicks.

"Every book ever written is inside me," he heard a slim shape on the table say, as its mouth lit up.

"You can take me anywhere and turn my pages with your eyes." The machine fluttered as if a dove were trapped inside it.

"Most people have access to all the books in the world. They carry their libraries about in their pockets."

Kenelm smiled with relief—Utopia was come to pass.

"No one *reads* them—are you crazy?"

Thomas Clack coughed, to bring this hare-brained one back to reality. Of all his dreamy clients, the Catholics were the worst.

Kenelm swallowed and ran his hand through his golden hair.

"And above the door, here, dominating the room, I plan to hang Master Van Dyck's portrait of our family grouping, which is soon to be completed," said Kenelm.

"It will be a fine enough place," said Thomas Clack, "in spite of all the books."

"Spare no cost, sir, and make it the finest," said Kenelm.

The Apollo Room at the Devil Tavern

"CUP US TILL the world go round, the world go round," sang Suckling and Davenant, arm in arm, doing a little dance down the steps of the Devil Tavern.

"Our careless heads with roses bound, roses bound . . ."

Gatherings of the Tribe of Ben usually ended in chorus numbers. They had been feasting in the Apollo Room upstairs all day, producing sonnets extempore in the first flight of wine at noon, exchanging couplets over beef, speechifying, toasting and boasting, and finally, succumbing to hiccoughs and singing.

Jonson left early, so they bowed to his bust, and set a napkin over its head when Carew's verse was bad. "I trod a tough hen on Monday last," sang Shackerley Marmion, "of thirty years of age . . ." And Kenelm silenced him with a raised hand. They were not coarse braggarts; they were gifted adepts of the Quell and Stile. Ahem. The Quill and Steel. They would defend their honour, leaping from balcony into walled garden, displaying terrifying swordsmanship, and write it up with embellishments before morning in Apollonian hexameters. Thus they were—Kenelm said the word with an Italian flourish—*Rhodomontades*. Young Thomas Killigrew was joining them for the first time, and the Apollo Room standards should be maintained. And William Davenant was there too. He was unexceptional in his versifying, but there was immortal blood in him. He was Shakespeare's bastard, after all.

"But the world has gone dark—has Phoebus fallen out the sky?" Young Killigrew ran out into the street, shouting and wheeling faster and faster, a loosed piglet, until he fell over into the mud, shouting: "And now the earth has tilted on his axis, and thrown me off!"

Kenelm saw he was, at least, more sober than Killigrew. He found the cold air of Fleet Street refreshing to his face. He was conversing with William Cavendish, and he knew their discourse was of mighty import, only his understanding of it would not keep still, but came and went like the sea's surf.

"Everything depends upon the circle and the straight line," said Cavendish. This was not an original thought, but one of the tenets of Dee's Monas Hieroglyphica.

"Everything," said Kenelm, suppressing a belch. "Observe the molecular structure of water."

Cavendish did not notice this anachronism. "Indeed," he said intently, playing for time while he swayed a little. "And now, if we were to hit upon the right symbol."

"The symbol of essential wholeness," said Kenelm.

"According to the Fourth Letter . . ." said Cavendish (this was their code for D—John Dee).

"The symbol would, if perfectly engraved, enable us to achieve just that," said Kenelm heavily.

"Achieve what?" said Cavendish.

"Gnosis," said Kenelm, swallowing the "g."

"Whazzat?" asked Cavendish.

"Divine Regeneration!" whispered Kenelm, suddenly thinking he might be sick.

Mary Tree: 41 Miles Travelled

I FEEL SURE I am closer on the trail of the Keeper of the Powder of Sympathy now, and all thanks to Mungo Stump who is the most free-hearted gentleman imaginable, though somewhat given to flummery. He is tall and flax-haired and wears a Saxony doublet and boots with lacy tops that match his collar's falling bands. He is a great patron of tailors and horse-dealers, and so forth, which is why he has so many tradesmen coming to call on him, sometimes in the middle of the night. The whole inn was woken up by their hammering last night, and he explained to me today that this is because of his famous knee-turning deportment, which makes tailors so keen to have his custom.

He bid me welcome to his table, where were already one or two other women, maids or married women I knew not, but their presence encouraged me to accept his invitation to sit down. He listened courteously to me as I told him everything. Worry not—I did not tell him of my mother, or my name "Only By Marriage," or John Tupper. I only told him of Richard Pickett's plight and my search for Sir Keyholme Digbin, which provoked in him first explosive laughter, which I did not understand, and then a thousand recollections.

Sir Keyholme, he said to the table, was a great personage at court. "Why, a nobler gent, with a finer leg, and a prettier wife, I have never seen!"

"Are they now married?" said one of his companions, Humphrey de Habington.

"With two brats, I hear," said Mungo Stump.

To me, he added, "Her name is Phonecia, and she dresses in heavenly blue."

Phonecia! So I had her name off wrongly. I kept this embarrassment to myself. Before I could ask any more about Sir Keyholme, Mungo Stump had started off on a story about how the Queen was surprised on her birthday with a great pie.

"The pastry of the pie was broken from within by a tiny halberd fighting its way out. And there he was, a little person," said Sir Mungo, "a dwarf-kin, a fraction of a man, positively jumping out from the pie!"

"Aye," muttered Humphrey de Habington, "I would not doubt it if the pie was hot."

"The manikin is now a great favourite at court and goes by the nickname 'Lord Minimus.' "

I tried to steer the conversation back to Sir Keyholme.

"He is a great unmasker of the recondite mysteries of nature," said Humphrey.

"He knows how to raise spirits," said Mungo, topping up my ale.

"But the Powder of Sympathy works?" I asked.

"Oh, undoubtedly," said Mungo. "Naturally and without Magick to ease a patient's wounds, though the patient were not present, and never seen by the physician."

A log collapsed on the fire, and I almost rose to stir it, before I realised I was not at home.

"This Powder saved the life of one Mr. James Howell."

"Never heard of him," said Humphrey de Habington.

"He was injured trying to separate two of his friends in a duel. Both were greatly upset when they saw his wound, put their weapons off and Sir Kenelm—I mean, Sir Keyholme—bound up his hand with one of his garters."

"Not a new garter, I do hope," said Humphrey, wit-like. "They might have used one of their own."

"The staunched wound turned to gangrene, and the garter was bathed in the basin wherein was dissolved the Powder of Sympathy, and Mr. Howell's wound felt refreshed; when he put the garter before a great fire, Mr. Howell felt burning. Within four or five days the wounds were cicatrised and entirely healed, and the choicest wits stood astonished."

"Indeed," said Humphrey, "it could give a gent some courage in duelling . . ."

"You know how when a wet-nurse's milk is thrown on the fire her dugs ache? Is it a cure after that fashion?" said one of the women at the table, whose rouge, now I saw her at closer hand, made me uneasy.

"The principle is the same . . ."

"Explain the workings of it," said Humphrey de Habington. "The wounded party stays at home, while the bloodied bandage goes forth?"

"Yes, because the cure is effected through the air. It is for this reason that Sir Keyholme says it must not be enacted in a cave, nor hiding hole. Nor priest hole, I expect he means, for he is one of *them*. He says the Aire is full of Atomes, fine and feathery motes that are not perceptible to our eyes, except in bright sunbeam of course, when we may see them charging about like cavaliers. These tiny messengers flow in formation through the air, carrying the healing particles with them. Thus the Cure is effected."

I had many questions, such as—why we do not breathe the wingèd cavaliers into our noses? But I found myself asking: What colour is Lady Phonecia's hair?

Mungo told me, "Somewhere between a chestnut just sprung open, or a mahogany bay mare in sunlight, and very fine, and curled just-so. Her born name was Phonecia Anastasia Stanley, but now she is Lady Digby. She is altogether"—he whistled silently and drew womanly curves in the air with his fingers—"*bona roba*."

I tried not to blush, especially when the other women at the table made whistling noises too.

And her face? "Oh, sweet as milk," said Mungo, and Humphrey de Habington said, "Aye, it is," gravely, not to humour me but as a word of truth.

"Phonecia Anastasia Stanley," I said to myself, like a charm.

Although I wanted to know a good deal more, I did not care to impose too much upon the conversation of the table, and I fell silent, resolving to ask more tomorrow, and the company's talk moved on to trade and treatise, and like Asparagus when he is lying by the fire I felt my eyelids growing heavy. The next I knew, I was stirring from sleep. Luckily one of the other women at the table had my purse in her hands when I woke up, or else, as she told me, I might have lost it as it fell out of my pack.

Mungo Stump offered to see me upstairs, which was kind of him, but I had my own candle's sufficiency. When I refused his help, he called after me that I had the Keeper's name wrong: Sir Kennel Dippy was the man I sought.

I was not so foolish as to believe that. Nor did I listen to him when he shouted up the stairs to tell me he was called Sir Kenelm Digby. Mungo Stump was in his cups, and I shall not be so easily put off my search for Sir Keyholme Digbin.

Sir Kenelm's bilious moment passed, and he and William Cavendish took a restorative pipe of tobacco under the stars.

"Have you heard of the cure-all 'Venice Treacle'?" asked Cavendish. "Our women drink it, you know."

Kenelm thought of the backstreets of Venice, where he had seen the apothecaries of the guild flip their wooden rattles and display cages of live snakes outside their shops, showing off their writhing ingredients, as a sign they would soon be producing, for sale, the one, the only, the authentic Theriaca: a thick tarry still with a purple sheen to it that looked and smelled to Kenelm as noisome a slobber as he had ever seen. The vulgar called it Venice Treacle.

"Theriaca, sir; it is called Theriaca by me. I stayed in Venice a short time in the brewing season. Theriaca is a long-known cure-all. I believe Trajan's doctor dreamed it up. It has treated poison bites since before the birth of Our Lord. Made of powdered vipers, rare balsams and other salves. Because, of course, the poisonous snake is not poisonous to itself, therefore it contains within its body the antidote to its own gall. And thus they claim it gives the life eternal."

"Have you any with you?"

"No, sir, I see no snakes in London."

"But death, sir."

"Oh, this is always and never with us."

"Oxford has a plague again, they say."

"God save it. I prefer my own methods—my metheglins and life liquors. My plague water. I can give you my receipts. I have a book of 'em. I don't take the Theriaca myself. I heard that a batch from the monastery San Giorgio Maggiore, adulterated with tar or wormwood, killed a fresh young girl who drank a pottle of it for her health."

"Bad," said Cavendish, striving for a profundity he did not achieve. "Bad and sad." He shook his head. "They drink it here, you know, our women. The Venice Tipple."

"I would not drink it without giving it first to a dog."

"I mark you, sir, I mark you." Cavendish was swaying again, looking at the middle distance, since upon the stars, his eyes would not focus. He nodded: "'Tis a dog's drink!"

"Though any dog who tastes it might outlive his master," said Kenelm.

"Then like the Ægyptian, mummify the dog and put him in a pyramis," said Cavendish, full of mirth.

"Cup us till the world go round, the world go round," interrupted Davenant, singing and twirling.

"A piss on your pyramis," said Suckling, lurching at Kenelm, who turned to him with his fists up.

It was lucky that neither of them were wearing swords, out of respect for the *Leges Conviviales*—the convivial rules of their club—which held there were to be no rough words, no breaking of windows.

"No swordplay between Brothers," said Cavendish. "No digladiation. But simple fisticuffs, now there's the spirit! Have at thee, sir!"

While Cavendish cheered them on, Davenant tried to pull them apart, crying, "*Eruditi, urbani, hilares, honesti!,*" as if these words from the *Leges Conviviales* would bring them to their senses.

Suckling swung his left arm at Kenelm, missing wildly and grabbing his hair instead. Kenelm's hat, unnoticed, fell into the gutter. Kenelm retained Suckling's arms behind his back in a wrestling lock, and roared. Thus the erudite, urbane, happy gallivants began their evening.

Venetia, dozing in bed with her book open, knew that Kenelm was come home because she heard him singing at the house gate, then a great jangle as he dropped his keys. She heard a hollow thud as he walked into the water butt, said "My pardon, madam," and finally unlocked the front door, muttering.

She came downstairs in her nightdress and nightcap, to check he was well, and to witness what a state he was in, so she could enjoy censuring him and maybe laugh at him. He had lost his hat and there was a little mud around his face. She saw by his dear eyes, which had a haunted look, that he was wild with sack.

"My love, how are you?"

"Darling, did I ever tell you about the Malaga wine I have hidden under the old boxes in the cellar? It's very important that it is not put out to the household. It's a fine, fine beast of a wine. Which is to ask why? First it roars, no, first it purrs, sweet as a cat . . ."

"Kenelm, what have you about your person, under your doublet?" Her face, shiny with borage-oil night-cream, loomed over him; Venetia could see that he was unshapely, his doublet distended by a sideways angularity that was nothing like her husband's body.

"Then the wine begins to growl, which is like the bigger animal. Then—"

"Kenelm, tell me what you have hidden in your midriffs."

Kenelm looked up to heaven, and said, "Nothing particular."

"Well then, my darling, the Malaga sack—should I pour it away tomorrow?"

"Ay, ay, ay—no, madam! Be not so hasty. It is the wrong time of day to pour away perfect cordialls."

He had seen off Suckling, neither of them sustaining much more injury than a sore lip (Suckling) and popped fastening (Digby). Suckling was reduced to trembling, roaring in pain when Kenelm pulled his hair. Both enjoyed the panting, coursing elation of the unexpected fight, although Suckling had to savour the bitter taste of his own bloody lip. They ended their brawl by embracing one another, pushing their heads hard together like bullocks, while Davenant and Cavendish reconciled themselves to an end of sport.

Then Suckling and Davenant retired together to a house of ill-repute, and Kenelm celebrated by going with Cavendish to the bookbinder at the Blue Bible, and hammering hard at his door, and calling out that, if you please, Digby was come for his books.

Kenelm stood up, put his hands round Venetia's waist and puckered his lips to kiss her. At that moment, a whoosh and a clatter surprised them both, and they looked down to see that his doublet had disgorged four volumes, which lay tumbled on the floor—Roger Bacon's *Opus Majus*, a pharmacopaeia, *Piers Plowman*—and another book, which fell open so as to reveal pages that were written in a script that, as they both looked down, neither of them could read. It was covered in stars, slashes and disjointed sentences of Java Source Code, ready to run on any standard-linked computer. Kenelm looked wonderingly at it, forgetting his surroundings as he hunched over the book on the floor:

```
response.setContentType("text/html');
  final PrintWriter pw = response.getWriter();
  try {
     pw.println("Hello, world!");
     } finally {
        pw.close();
        }
  }
}
```

The letters seemed to him like a spell or symbolism more than a story: hieroglyphs, in a word. There was a bare beauty in them. Perhaps these were corrupted, or an ill-copy. They might be inscriptions from an obelisk, too faithfully translated. If he followed each of these directions, Great Work might be done. Perhaps it was a Mayan calendar. It was hard to keep up with all these discoveries of the New World—no wonder his library overflowed.

"Dearheart." She pronounced the word with a crisp, married tone. "We have spoke of this! I have nowhere to put my second nursemaid, she must needs sleep with the cook, we are so full of books. We have a whole houseful of books arrived the other week, and yet you come home with more? It is beyond all reason, Kenelm. I love your learning but this is madness, darling." Again, the endearment: tartly said. "I am going to bed, and doing so I walk past stacks of books along the way. I am surprised I must not yet sleep with my bed full of books, my pillow stuffed with them . . ."

Thus lamenting, Venetia made her way upstairs, stopping resentfully to blow a kiss back at him, at which Kenelm ran to her, knelt, or rather subsided before her, and clasped her hand to his cheek. And they tarried a while together, embracing, until she said, fondly, that he was ripe as a brewhouse and she was going to bed.

In the hall, he picked up his volumes unsteadily, and went to his study, where after many attempts, he lit a candle, found his quill, and settled down to drawn the symbol, the image of life eternal: Divine Gnosis.

His quill was remarkably poor, much worse than it had been that morning, but he took care to cover one sheet with insignias of the circle and the straight line, along with divers occult marginalia.

The dots, in the shape of the quincunx—the sign of five. An ancient signification; a pattern used for the planting of fruit trees in the garden of Cyrus.

As he drew, the dots seemed to disappear in front of his eyes.

When he could inscribe no more he staggered to his hammock and dived headlong across it into heavy slumber.

In the dry-parched morning, before he took his cup of ale, he looked for the sheet he had drawn on for so long, and found it blank.

When he looked in the mirror, would that be blank also? Had all his solid parts been blasted, as his penmanship, to vanishment? This seemed as Magick, and yet it must have an explanation in Natural Philosophy. He seized the sheet again.

When he held it up to the light there were craven scratchings and marks: signs of a quill at work without any ink.

"One spoonful of this beauty elixir every day has much greater bio-availability than a capsule so it's readily absorbed into the body and can help eliminate wrinkles from within . . ."

Fountain: The Beauty Molecule—a drink containing Reservatrol, extracted from Japanese knotweed, launched on the UK market in 2013

Venetia continued to be nurtured by her secret advantage, holding it close like a trump. Three mornings a week, the ladies came to Venetia's salon: tapping cards, clinking coins, exchanging sharp talk. They liked to see one another, and to drink posset, but more than anything else, they liked to win at cards. The sweetness of winning, the desire to taste it in their mouths, brought them back to the table again and again. Penelope and Venetia felt a longing for it in their throats every morning. Only Olive amongst them had some deficiency of will or surplus of self-restraint, and played for fun, not for love of winning—but the other two needed her to make up the table, so she become a gambler too, out of friendship.

With Venetia's returning confidence came her old habits of sociability, and she had a whim to see young Lettice at her card table. Besides, it was her duty to include the poor child. Lettice arrived unconscionably early—from her bedroom window, Venetia saw her standing on the doorstep in a new bonnet, what, an hour ahead of time? Venetia felt oppressed, sometimes, by Lettice's adoration.

It soon became clear that Little Miss Furtherto-Moreover had picked up fashionable ways. She clasped Venetia close in a loving embrace, then without looking at her, flung herself down on the daybed in an affectation of exhaustion. She had, she said, been dancing her very slippers out, though when Venetia pressed her, it seemed the revels had taken place more than a week ago, so Lettice's exhaustion could not have been a direct consequence. Certainly, she found enough energy to regale Venetia with many opinions as they took their spiced cups of caudle.

"Penelope, I adore that woman, she really is my dearest creature, and to me her plain, blunt manner is simply who she is. I insist you cannot take her any other way, because she is born to be like that. We were out in Hyde Park last week with our new mufflers and she looked at my muffler and said, 'Yours is an ominous colour, because it is yellow, because Mrs. Anne Turner wore it when she was hanged.' She said so, just so! Anyone who did not know her as well as I do would think it was an insult, but she and I have a most special understanding, so it made me love her all the more . . ."

Venetia was an indulgent patron to Lettice, and she was used to her importunities, and glad she had forged new friendships. It was sweet of the girl, really, to talk as if she were unaware that Penelope and Venetia had been close friends for a decade. Venetia hoped Lettice's nerves would soon abate. But a tray of sweetmeats gave her second wind.

"There is something particular about my feeling for French music," said Lettice. "I do not say that I have any talent, it is simply that I have a feeling for it deep in my heart. When I stop singing, people ask me why I have stopped, that is all. I do not know what they mean by it. Master Warwick asked me how long I had been singing, and I said since my birth, practically . . ."

Venetia found herself reaching, surreptitiously, to pour her Viper Wine into her cup, so that its rich, liverish taste might comfort and distract her.

It had revolted her at first; now it was half-disgusting, half-delicious, and she was drawn to taste it again and again, as if every next sip might bring her to decide if she liked it or no. She supped from her caudle-cup slowly, with an opaque look, nodding as Lettice spoke.

A jangling at the gate announced Olive and Penelope had arrived, at last, and they came into the salon exclaiming about a dozen things at once while Mistress Elizabeth helped them out of their furs and tippets. Penelope was in her usual grey twill, but Olive was wearing something new, of yellow, with frills and rosebuds adorning it. She had stuck her "heartbreaker" ringlets down upon her forehead, as some of the younger ladies did at court. She looked very much the new penny, and she seemed to know it. She came close and as she embraced Venetia, she held her at arm's length, the better to view her, and making a loud noise of approval.

"My sweet," she said significantly, "you are the very picture of beauty today." Then, embracing her closely, Olive whispered in her ear, "Your teeth are red!"

She turned away to sit down with a meaningful swish of her skirts.

"She is always the picture of beauty," said Lettice loyally, without looking at Venetia.

"But today she has never looked more beautiful," said Olive, winking. "Has she, Pen?"

"Well," said Penelope, getting ready to equivocate. Then she looked up at Venetia and seemed struck by her appearance.

"You do look rather pert. Are you *enceinte*?"

"No," said Venetia, swallowing the hot caudle she hoped would shift the viper stain from her teeth. "More's the pity—I would love a little girl."

"She's newly plucked maybe," said Olive cheerfully. Discreetly, to Venetia: "Has Kenelm noticed?"

"He notices a change, but not the reason for it," replied Venetia.

The lovely cure was taking effect. Life could be resumed, and with it everything she had put off wanting for so long. New clothes, new portraits, the court masque—all these trivial activities, as well as the business of being alive, and being adored, for really they were one and the same, were they not? She could lift her veil and shine her light upon Edward Sackville.

There was the distant sound of horses stamping in the mews; winter sun glowed intensely on Venetia through the casement above their card-table, lifting her dark hair so it was momentarily bright copper.

Penelope was about to cut the cards when Chater hovered into view, his hands on his prayer book, clearly about to address them. He had been in the room long enough to sense that they had been talking about secret things. He looked at Venetia and Olive, at Olive and Venetia, and he saw that they shared a conspiracy, and that it was a personal matter that went to the core of their feminine selves. Chater had enough secrets himself to know one when he smelled one.

There were a few prie-dieu chairs in Venetia's drawing room, against the wall, but prayers were not required today—Pen and Olive were both Protestant—and so Chater simply read aloud some of Venetia's book, *A Mirrour for a Modest Wife*. Chater declaimed sonorously and with style.

As he spoke he looked often at Olive. Her pretty, too-tight face was frozen into a rictus of concentration. If she could have frowned she would have frowned, but instead her face had settled into an expression that looked somehow stunned. Chater could not help looking at her more than was seemly, examining her face with an unwilling, morbid fascination. While he was concentrating on speaking, he had less control over his eyes, which returned to Olive again and again, as a tongue returns to search a chipped tooth. He was drawn to shiny, broken people.

After he was finished, Penelope immediately started dealing the cards, while Olive laid her hand on Chater's. "Father, that was most beautifully said."

"My lady, if you ever feel you would benefit from a spiritual conference, or private prayers . . . Or even a walk and a long talk, I am more gentle than I look; indeed, I can even be quite a pleasant companion," he said, laughing at himself. "I can resist from delivering any thunderous sermons for, oh, at least half an hour." He could be so sweet; no wonder the ladies loved him.

Olive smiled at him sadly. "You have my sympathies but we are not of Rome."

"Venice, did you really write this book—all those purple passages?" asked Penelope.

"No, that which we just heard was taken from Chater's own little book, which is a work in progress, but what I hear I like," said Venetia, patting Chater encouragingly on the sleeve.

Chater coughed with disbelief. So Venetia had not read her own book before it was published. He had just declaimed some of its star passages. It was currently on sale in Powles Churchyard under her name—both her names, Venetia Stanley—writ large—and Lady Digby—a little smaller. She had remarked that she did not intend, so late in life, to lose names, only acquire them.

"Chater, my dove, I fear Kenelm needs you—he was asking for you earlier, as soon as we could spare you . . ." Venetia knew how to play Chater. He headed for the door without demur.

Chater had no sooner left the room but he heard them begin laughing and casting dice. Kenelm's hat was missing, which meant he was out. He had been duped, again. Oh, she was magnificent! He walked off, fuming, getting his revenge by thinking about Olive—yes, putting Venetia entirely from his mind for a moment or two. He wondered how he could obtain a personal appointment with Olive. She should not be wearing quite so many bows and rosebuds in such bright, divers shades. He loved her for her daring, but he could not let it continue. She should wear cream or goose-grey, with a plain stomacher. None of these virago sleeves, thank you. He would help her find a new safe apparel. She was a lost, brittle thing—perhaps he would be able to steer her to the safety of the Old Faith. Her conversion would be a great coup.

Olive's face had been meddled with by a physician, that was evident. She seemed proud of the fact; she presented herself like a gift to the world. She had the air of one who felt they had got away with it. He admired and envied her, and yet the righteous part of him wanted to smite her vanity. Yea, smite with a thunderclap and lay bare her real face, which, however raddled, would be more beautiful than the painted, fake version—more beautiful because it was, above all things, true. And then, when her finery was gone, she would need Chater. He imagined Olive weeping for him through the night. Then he would lead her, through suffering, to His redemption.

Chater whistled as he walked through the garden and about his business, knowing none of this would come to pass, but daydreaming about how he might attend church with his convert, the new humble, penitent Olive, who would be modestly dressed and leaning on his arm.

Inside, the ladies were absorbed in a new game. For a few weeks, it had been Glecko, then farthing-gleek and toe-gleek. Then they had moved on to beast, and angel-beast, which diverted them for a while. Now they were playing one-and-thirty, which called for more subtlety of method, and projects of collecting and discarding, which the ladies enjoyed. They removed the eights and nines from the pack and threw them on the floor; they sipped their Malaga sack and focused on their hands, except for Lettice, who was full of information.

She told them about the Queen's new pet, a Welsh giant called Evans. Lettice had seen him and been too afraid to approach. "I do not know what it is in me that holds back when everyone else is leaping forth, but I could not approach the giant, could not accost him. Could not!" She then told of the damage done by fire to Master Jonson's lodgings, reciting with great sadness an inventory of all the masterworks the great man had lost to the flames. When Venetia observed, showing the suggestion of a smile over her cards, that it was typical of dear Ben to make the most of any calamity, Lettice replied pertly that these were uncopied, unpublished works, and Ben had told her so himself. She sighed quietly, as if Venetia were sadly ignorant of Ben's talent, and said to herself, "A very great loss."

Venetia felt a small comforting throbbing at her temples, which reminded her that the Viper Wine was at work. When she was annoyed or discomforted, she often let herself listen to the Viper Wine's good music, beating in her veins, across her brow. As she assessed her hand, she tried to listen to Lettice, who was still talking.

"Ben Jonson has told me that he will write it whether or no the Earl commissions it, as he has the rhymes of it already in his head, and conceived to do it the first time he saw me . . ."

"To do what, Lettice?"

"Write a sonnet sequence in my honour. I am to be set within a talking garden, a pleasant place, where all the vegetables have voices, a bed full of herbs and sweet plants—for my name, of course. It is to be a celebration of all things new-grown."

Venetia put down her cards. She started to speak, and then could not. "My dear . . ." The truth was that Ben had always written for rich women, or women that he thought might have rich suitors or husbands, or when he spied an occasion for self-promotion. And he so seldom wrote from his heart, as he had done for her, Venetia, back when he was half in love with her, and they used to speak in their own language together. And at any rate, whatever he wrote these days would be empty, worth having only because it was by Ben Jonson, not because it was good. None of this, to be sure, could be expressed to the sweet little leaf sitting opposite her, so very pleased with itself.

"A garden that talks! Of course. What a lovely idea, and lovelier still if he were not to profit by it," she said crisply. She had gone too far: the child's smile chilled.

"Are you quite well, Venetia?" said Lettice. "It is just that, every now and again, your face twitches, and the pretty blue vein on your forehead throbs."

But Venetia was absorbed in the delightful patterns of her hand of cards, which she had carefully swapped and traded so it was a perfect flush, spread neatly across the baize. The sight of the cards themselves alone gave pleasure. They were so regular, so impervious.

"I think we are ready for some more hot caudle, ladies, are we not?" she announced, with satisfaction, as she stood up and scraped all the coins in her direction, and everyone gave in, and started fishing in their purses. They did not begrudge Venetia her winning. It was expected. How could she lose? She was herself again, and they felt more beautiful just by being near her.

A long and powerful rat-at-tat-at-tat at the door did not trouble the ladies, as they bet a higher stake on their next hands, which was in turn higher than they had bet yesterday. But when Mistress Elizabeth answered the door, she found no one there, only a huge nail, rammed into the wooden door, skewering pages of parchment that flapped alarmingly in the wind.

Kenelm found this letter on his desk when he came home. It was a censorious age, and they lived with a good deal of show, and Venetia attracted a number of correspondents with faltering itchy-scratchy nibs and raving minds. She had already been told by one that she was a celestial harpy, and that her "cunning device" of keeping her wings underneath her dress did not fool this correspondent, oh no. He culminated with the leering: "I seeth you as the lord seeth you." She had inflamed enough hearts in her time—and now their ashes were returned to her in twists of parchment. Only mad people wrote, because only mad people dared. Kenelm and Venetia could easily have the authors arraigned before the sheriffs, but instead they shrugged them off. They took the attitude that burning the letters destroyed their malice, so it became no more than smoke. In Kenelm's Sympatheticall universe, the authors felt their minds tingle as their letters were consumed by fire, and the hands that wrote them blistered.

This letter was headed "Hoplocrisma-Spongus, Or, a Sponge to Wipe away the Weapon-Salve." It ran to ten pages of tiny handwriting, all disparaging Kenelm's Sympatheticall Cure. He scanned the looping, regular script; the author, one Parson Foster, a Protestant divine no doubt. "A treatise wherein it is proved that the cure late-taken up amongst us, by applying the salve to the weapon, is magical and unlawful." So this was war.

"Blimey," said Kenelm, meaning to say "Blind me" but coining the modern version accidentally. He read the treatise against him in full, and stormed upstairs to find Venetia, and then he stopped outside her bedroom, hesitating to show her the letter with all its injurious claims. He told himself it was because he did not want to worry her. He also knew it was because he needed her admiration, and did not want it shaken. His world of happiness, his mighty encompassing O of safety, was all in her belief and trust in him. With the letter's angry words ringing in his ears, he walked out of his garden, and through the streets, at odds with the tide of people who were hurrying home against the gathering rain, and yet he pressed onwards to the Thames's bank, where he climbed out upon the jetty of Garlickhythe. The busy river seemed to pause, and the docks were unusually quiet. The wind inflated Digby's collar, lifted his hair.

He tried to make his thoughts methodical. The problem: many mistook his Cure of Sympathy for a Magicall Art. The reason: it appeared to work upon an object like the witch-cures often did—a shoe strung up to warn a spirit off, or a sleep-worn pillow chanted over, or a cup buried, to stop a man drinking too much, or a clock to be set at the time of a robbery to help return some stolen goods.

These were the Old ways, and yet there was truth in them. He believed they were possible, because the air was thick with purpose. The air was full of Atomes, tiny invisible particles, the smallest part of matter, also called Minims, that moved through the air, tumbling and whirling, moved by Heat or still'd by Cold, constantly turning, had we but vision to see them . . .

It was fanciful talk to most people. King James I had suspected him of witchery. Kings are often suspicious, and James had the habit of seeing black magic everywhere. He was on the very point of knighting Kenelm, with his royal sword ceremonially drawn, when he paused and asked him if he dealt with the devil, believing the nearness of the sharp steel would put Kenelm on his mettle. Kenelm answered frankly, looking him directly in the eye, and telling the King that his Sympatheticall Cure worked by means of Art and Nature, harnessing the cavalry of the air that charged about unseen. At which the King had looked askance, but knighted him, and all the court exhaled.

Plenty of men found him Overreaching, or Heretical, because he believed the air was full of thousands of tiny invisible particles, darting about in the void, giving life and breath, without divine direction. This was clearly heresy, and the Jesuits even made a prayer to deny it: "Nothing comes of Atomes . . ." Kenelm had doubted it himself, at first—who could easily believe that the air was not empty, but vastly manifest and substantial?

But then he read Lucretius' *De Rerum Natura*, lent to him by Sir John Scudamore one night with a wink and a candle as he went to bed. And Digby stayed up until dawn reading of Venus and the urge to reproduce that overtakes us all, and how the stars are made of the same matter as us, and we of them, all tumbling together in a universe in which the divine spirit was immanent, rather than directed. Kenelm drank it in one intoxicating draft, committing as much as possible to memory. He never saw the book again.

To possess *De Rerum Natura* was heresy in Tuscany, punished with a fine and a personal invitation to eternal damnation. In England, it was a secret that people passed around and kept to themselves, and used as they wished. After reading it, Digby became an Atomist. He did not let go of any of his other beliefs or callings. He was a Catholic by birth, a Protestant by education, a melancholic by affectation, an alchemist by vocation, a Rosicrucian in aspiration, and an Atomist by imagination.

> "Digby . . . joins the Medieval to the modern world."
>
> Introduction to *The Closet of Sir Kenelm Digby Open'd*, 1910

The wind tore over the sludgy Thames, and he was lit up by a flash of purple-neon lightning. He would, in time, become a so-called crypto-

Catholic; a "Renaissance man"; an emblem of mourning; a dilettante *avant la lettre* (and before "*avant la lettre*"); a touchstone for Nathaniel Hawthorne, named in *The Scarlet Letter*; a cameo in a novel by Umberto Eco; and, possibly, the hero of a subscription-channel costume drama.

Born in the 116th year of English peace, he was one of the rose-wreathed cavaliers, unwitting architects of the cataclysm of Civil War. His name would be used by Aldous Huxley to sum up the backwardness of the seventeenth century. It would be used to invoke the fertility of the Renaissance mind, and its happy union of disciplines artistic and scientific. He would be ridiculed as the last of the crackpot experimenters before the Scientific Revolution. He would be the subject of a reverential biography written in 1932 by an infatuated don, in prose that yearned for Sir Kenelm, but also for his successors, lost in the trenches of France and Flanders. He inspired myriad fantasies.

> "Sir Kenelm Digby . . . loved to talk in six languages. He was a bold, sexy pirate, a wide reader and an even wider knower."
>
> Diane Purkiss, *The English Civil War: A People's History*, 2006

Kenelm was haunted by the future, which announced itself in echoes and pratfalls, in twitches as his body fell asleep, or hypnagogic visions as he fasted or daydreamed, when ideas from the far future sounded to him as if they came from the near past.

His modesty did not prevent him from wondering if he was an angel. Angels were said to live in many times concurrently. While heads were bowed in pews, he scanned the fiery-footed angels who flared across rood screens and murals, looking for likenesses of himself.

To him, time was circular, and alchemical Wisdom was a golden chain, never-ending, eternally returning. The ourobouros eating its own tail was an alchemical cypher, later taken up by mathematicians. To Kenelm, the mathematical symbol used by Einstein to represent infinity was instantly legible:

$$\infty$$

Sometimes, in the right conditions, when he had an empty belly and a clear head, and he was moved by singing, poetry or the heart-suck of his wife's kiss, Sir Kenelm grasped the roundness of existence—its simultaneity—encircling him, and he knew that he lived concurrently with what had been and what was to come. Most of the time, though, he felt the blessed lack of hindsight each of us needs to be at peace.

Kenelm stood on Garlickhythe jetty, breathing the fish-ripe Thames, his hair rising in the wind like tentacles around his ears. He was convinced: if the air was full of invisible Atomes, then extraordinary things could be accomplished through the air. Messages and thoughts could be conveyed, signals given.

In times to come, everything would be done from a distance. Power would be maintained, peoples directed, healing performed. Signals would be sent and received, voices heard, hieroglyphs exchanged.

Sir Kenelm heard a metallic swishing of the wind, so bright it sounded almost musical, very like the noise of the wind playing his obelisk at home. He wondered if it was a sign or portent, come to him across the air, to tell him that his Cure was right, and Parson Foster wrong. He thought of his Pylon, his Mast of Divination standing in the garden at Gayhurst, the wind playing it like a lyre, and he felt certain he could hear it, jangling sweetly.

He had a vision of power cables and pylons bridging the countryside, singing in the wind, like vast Aeolian harps.

The wind hurled a drop of rainwater in his face, then another. He wished to know if he was practising quackery, or if his Cure was a just Cure, a true Cure. He screwed up his courage and asked the obelisk:

Do Atomes travel in the air?

The sky looked full of thunder, and Digby held his hands out in front of him, in the position of the alchemist at his labours, and at that moment the wind reached into Digby's purse—and while Digby did not cause this, neither he did not stop it—and the wind caught one of the sheets of Parson Foster's letter, raised it up and away, down the Thames, and then another sheet peeled off, and another, and another, until the Hoplocrisma-Spongus was scattered and floating down the rain-swelling river.

> "Honey bee venom is used cosmetically to fool skin into thinking it has been lightly stung with the toxin melittin . . . Experts collect bee venom by placing a pane of glass alongside a hive and running an electrical current through it which encourages the insects to sting the surface. Because the bee's lance remains in its body, it does not die. Tiny quantities of venom are so valuable that it costs up to £30,000 for one ounce . . . The Duchess of Cambridge and the Duchess of Cornwall are already fans."
>
> *Daily Mail* newspaper, February 2013

Venetia was lying on her daybed, exhausted after her game of cards, and Chater was sitting at the other end, rubbing her feet.

She was teasing Chater, because she had discovered that his Christian name was Posthumous.

"*Thomas* Posthumous, my lady."

"Why did a letter come for Posthumous Thomas Chater, then?"

"My mother is old, she becomes confused, she has them the wrong way about." His eyes bulged when he became agitated, so Venetia made an effort to hide her hilarity. She perceived his name had been a trouble to him in the school-room.

"I know the reason for your name is solemn, Chater."

"My mother would have done better not to compound for me the loss of my father with such a name."

Chater kneaded the sole of her foot.

"My lady seems so happy," he said reproachfully.

"My Chater seems happy too," she parried.

He made an equivocating wiggle with his head.

She had no idea; she did not know what it was to behold an angel of love, bearded and strong like a prophet, and to talk soft words with him, and burn with feeling for him, and yet not to be able to hold him, or touch him, though the will to do so was as strong as Holy Fire, which raged over him and yet would not consume him, so he stayed blazing all the livelong day, like the priest in the temple at Jerusalem, because Chater was righteous, and would not touch Father Dell'Mascere. But her—she was married to her love. What a waste. Sir Kenelm would have made an excellent priest.

"My lady is fortunate that she is not like the other ladies at court," he said.

"How so?" she asked.

"Some of them wear their improvements so openly, it is hard to see the woman behind the handiwork. They are like St. Paul's—an old cathedral with a new frontage."

Venetia laughed, but she knew he meant to disquiet her.

"Oh, how lovely that you compare them to that holy place. It is true that some of the women at court are as celebrated as St. Paul's, and they have many devoted pilgrims, too . . ." She laughed naughtily, thinking to make a bawdy joke about the ladies' suitors going always in and out, but then she looked at Chater and decided that was going too far. He was become more pious since they came to town.

He was now reacquainted with his bearded friend Dell'Mascere, and this had brought him to a higher pitch of feeling, so his joy was spiced with pain. She knew Chater was chaste: she could tell by his tension and the bile in his voice, and his fastidious nature. But she guessed it cost him. She detected a struggle constantly taking place within him. Mortification was part of his Order, and she knew he whipped himself under his soutane. She hoped he was not spoiling the second best bedroom's sheets.

Chater saw she was not going to give up without a fight, and rubbing her feet a little harder, he continued: "It is so sad, so very sad, to see a lady destroy her face by means of artifice. Have you noticed how those who do it are always those who were formerly the most beautiful?"

"Aye," said Venetia, enjoying Chater's ministrations to her feet. "But if they were already former beauties, then the artifice is simply a third thing, no worse than decay."

"No, my lady, I must disagree. It is a crime against your Maker to render your cheeks immovable with lead. Decay is holy, in its way."

"Oh come, Chater. It is not forbidden for a woman to improve her condition, is it? I remember no Commandment, thou shalt not paint."

"The Puritans will not have paint."

"The Puritans will not have anything."

"Paint is one thing. Irreversible embellishments are quite another matter. They are far worse. They might render a woman unrecognisable to God on Judgement Day. Think of that."

"Chater, have you been reading Savonarola again?"

He put his weight into twisting her foot, so she gasped. She would not show it was painful.

"Excellent footwork, Chater."

He looked serious. "There is something Florentine about the King's court here, yes. Now, take my Lady Porter, what has she attempted?"

"Many things in her life, I should say."

Exasperated, Chater cracked the joint of her big toe, and worked his way down to its fellows.

"Has she taken Dr. Scoderu's Virginal Milk perhaps, of sorrel and fucus? I have heard that is quite a puissant mixture. Except it would not make her face to blister . . ."

"I know it not," said Venetia, twisting as he pinched her little toe.

"Or perhaps that ghastly Alexis of Piedmont's recipe is still in vogue, the one that calls for a young raven from the nest, fed for forty days with hard eggs only, and then distilled with myrtle . . ."

"Are you interested, Chater? Do you wish for my recommendations? But your brow is still smooth. You have a few pretty greys, mingling with the dark . . ."

Chater involuntarily raised his hand to the back of his head, and stroked downwards with aghast tenderness, but in no other way did he give Venetia the benefit of a reaction. Seamlessly, he went back to massaging her feet.

"My lady, I am responsible for the conduct of your soul. I cannot let you abuse your beauty without speaking out."

"What do you mean, Chater?"

"My lady understands me well enough."

"You are full of insinuation, Chater," she said, stressing the "sin" with a sibilant "S."

He was afraid to call her on it. He needed her friendship so deeply, he did not dare to ask her outright if she was taking any medicine for her skin. And yet he had been bold enough to come this far. Poor Chater. She felt quite certain of it, now, looking at his face contorting as he manipulated her feet, that he knew she was beautiful again, and that she was restored to Sir Kenelm's love, and she was regaining her old place at court, and that he did not like these changes, because he did not understand them, and he felt redundant, and rejected, because he had no power over her now. Before she drank her potion, they were two broken, clever creatures together, both surplus to requirements, somehow, and complicit in their loneliness and their little games of Scripture. Now she was a juicy plum again, but he seemed sadder than ever.

"Sometimes I worry you mortify yourself too much, Chater. I went into the laundry once and I saw a bloodied undershirt they said was yours."

"It is the duty of true believers to mortify sin all their days," said Chater. "Mortify, make it your daily work; be always at it while you live; cease not a day from this work, be killing sin or it will be killing you."

"John?" said Venetia, weakly.

"Galileans. Should I need to remind you?" He exhaled, and gripped her ankle with his hand. His fingers could almost close around her ankle now; she was become so slender of late, the bitch. She used to be his plump darling but now she had no use for her Chater.

Venetia looked at his long face and realised that he was angry with her. She had expected him to love her more because she was beautiful again, and to follow her around adoringly, because everyone loves a beauty, do they not? Apart from those who prefer to keep you in your place, where you were less powerful, because they need you for themselves, and do not want to share you.

"I hope you have not been listening to idle chatter, Chater."

"I hope you have not been visiting any meddling herbalist no better than a quack."

"No, i'faith," said Venetia with honest indignation. "If I were to go to anyone, I would go to the best."

Chater realised: she was trying to tell him that Sir Kenelm gave her a potion. It was what he had long suspected.

In fact, she was on the cliff's edge of telling him about Lancelot Choice and his blood-red decoction. It would lighten her secret to share it, and renew her friendship with Chater besides. It would be entertaining to see his eyes pop when she told him. But Chater was embarrassed because he thought he was trampling upon Sir Kenelm's business, and he did not let her speak, interrupting her angrily: "My lady must resist the vain society here. It is not wise, nor fruitful to be afflicted by fashion."

"Is Chater now so wise he would have me in a nunnery?" She laughed, relieved to find that her urge to confide in him had gone as quickly as it had come.

"Chater! That hurts!"

He laid down her feet and rubbed them soothingly back and forth, with the flat of his hand.

Mary Tree: 170 Miles Travelled

When I arrived in London, I was lucky to meet Bess Bottomly almost at once. She hath but one hand, but she is so quick with it, you barely notice. She came up to me as I was praying beside the fine Cheapside Cross (three storeys tall with a great golden cross and a dove on top!), thanking the Lord for my delivery from the bone-shake of the coach, and praying for Richard Pickett. When Bess Bottomly saw I was at prayer she kept back until I had finished. Then she asked if I wanted to stay at her house until I found lodgings of my own. I knew she would want paying for this—I did not think her a saint—but I was grateful nevertheless. There were many other girls staying with her, and often they have visits from gentlemen who are their suitors for marriage, so Bess told me.

I was so pleased to be safe and warm and in the company of women, all of them merry enough, as far as I could tell. Bess's lieutenant, so-called, is one Anna Trapper, who sits and minds the door of Bess's lodging-house. Last night I sat with her, talking.

"An Abraham man came this way today," she said, "and then changed his mind and became a Ruffler."

This is a test, to see if I have conned her correctly.

"An Abraham man begs by feigning to have been mad," I said. "And a Ruffler pretends he has been in service in the wars."

"Also known as?"

"An Uprightman."

"Good. And what do those beggars who pretend they cannot speak be called?"

"Dummerers!" I crowed, for I like to get my answers right as much as the next good girl.

"More Rome-booze, my darling," she said, meaning "More wine," so I filled her up.

"Who demands for glimmer?"

"Those who pretend to have lost all their belongings in a fire."

"And what do I mean by a Counterfeit Crank?"

"One who dissembles falling sickness and so beg for alms."

"For alms? For alms? No, no, no, doll. No! No Abraham man, no Counterfeit Crank, no Ruffler, no Dummerer, no none of them wants alms. They wants money. Brass. Gilt. Dust. Counter. The old cross-n-pile. Right, let's see. A Prigger steals . . . ?"

"Prancers."

"Prancers being?"

"Horses."

"Foisters, Nippers, Lifters . . . ?"

"Are common pickpockets."

"And Churbers?"

"Are burglars who use long hooks to steal by."

I was doing well, and I was frequently told by Anna that I needed to learn all this, for my own safety. By the way she looked at me and my Mark—once she licked her thumb and drew it across my cheek, as if she were trying to remove it—I could see she knew I would never find the protection of any man. So I was grateful for the education she was giving me. And yet in my heart I knew I was becoming versed in the muck of the mire, and as much as I wanted to make my way in the city, for Richard's sake, I also wished to shut my ears and go home to Endcote Early.

Many gentlemen suitors came offering marriage that night—some of them half-drunk, I believe. One gent came in to Bess Bottomly's discreetly hooded but with long, yellow-gartered legs on show. *I know those knees*, I thought. His face confirmed what his legs suggested—this was none other than my friend Mungo Stump. He was not so pleased to see me as I expected. He looked aghast, in truth. By his face I began to see for certain I was not in a place of good repute. I told him I had not yet found

Sir Keyholme Digbin, although I went out marching the streets enquiring after him every day. He coloured bright red under his flaxen hair.

When Mungo Stump was upstairs imploring his lady love to marry him, Anna Trapper's conversation went beyond its usual bounds.

"What's a cony-catcher, then?"

I blushed and shook my head.

"What's a marigold-picker, eh?"

She poked me in the ribs.

"A young wench not yet broken by the Upright man is a dell. When they have been lain withal by the Upright man, they be doxies and no dells."

I did not like this talk, but I tried to be civil.

"Oh yes," I said, without interest.

"A kitchen-mort is a young girl, soon ripe, soon rotten . . ."

I can barely think how long this talk continued, while I endured it, sorrowing all the while for the girls—my new friends—whom I realised had already been broken by an Upright man. And I realised that I should also have been upstairs with a gentleman, had I not been Mark'd across my face, and not for the first time I was wholly thankful for my affliction.

But Mungo Stump came downstairs quickly, as if he had thought again on all his doings. He told me that my aunt Lucy wanted me to stay with her this very night. I am not so innocent as some, and I knew after only a moment or two that a lie was required here, and so crossing my fingers behind my back, I said, oh yes, I must go to my aunt.

My leave-taking began, and with some coin, and the laying on of more Rome-booze for Anna Trapper, it was accomplished quickly, as I knew it must be, before Bess Bottomly was back. In my haste, I was frantic to think I had lost the shard that wounded Richard Pickett, but then I found it under my pillow.

Mungo Stump took me to stay with his old housekeeper. He told me, somewhat shamefaced, that I had the name of the Keeper of the Powder of Sympathy wrong, and that I would have better luck in my endeavour after I enquired for Sir Kenelm Digby. I suppose he thought it was good sport to mislead me all those weeks ago at the tavern in Dawlish. But perhaps there is a special providence in his doing so, and thus feeling guilty enough to rescue me from Bess Bottomly's.

Sometimes I feel a cold hand at my shoulder that tells me I am running out of time. Richard Pickett's groans are often in my head, and yet I feel further than ever from Sir Kenelm and his lovely Lady. Her life must be full of such gaiety and ease. When I feel like giving up, I dream of becoming her lady's maid, and it keeps me walking. I went to the Great Cross on Cheapside again today, and tied a little piece of Richard Pickett's bandage around its railings, to see its whiteness flutter hopefully beside the Cross.

The Great Cross on Cheapside had been well-beloved some four hundred years, and it had grown tatty with love. Pilgrims had tied devotions and ribbons to it, and stuck holly berries in its niches and bread and wine at its foot, and in turn these attracted birds and rats, and the saints' niches had grown soiled, while the city's soot turned their emblems black. The Lord Mayor usually maintained the Cross, but he was Puritan in his sympathies this year, and he preferred not to polish the gay old shrine, but let it fester. Venetia had no ribbon but she tied some thoughts of hope around its railings, making a quick prayer, and picked her way onward through the puddles on Cheapside.

She passed a horse and a stunted child, working the barrels. She saw a prostitute with a false nose, and a gang of rakes from the Sponging-House on Wood Street, stamping in puddles at people for fun. She longed to watch it all, but for fear of being recognised, Venetia put her vizarded head down, making quickly towards Fenchurch Street.

She knew she must look like an adulteress—thankfully, she had more originality than that—but she felt monitored by the eyes of God and her husband. God and Kenelm were often conflated in her mind into a living He. He was her better part, her salvation and her eternal hope. Despite Chater's good work, she struggled with God—but her love for Kenelm came so easily to her, so naturally, that it helped her to understand all the other loves in the world, the divine love called Agape and Christian Caritas, and so forth. To love Him was obvious. It was there in every breath.

But to obey Him as well—now that was impossible. The reason being that He was so often wrong. At the moment, He imagined that He preferred her not to drink Viper Wine, but she would get round Him. He would soon see that she had been right all along.

Margaret Choice was not in evidence, and Venetia went straight up. Lancelot Choice rose to meet her when she came in.

"Did you receive my letter?"

"Madam, do come in."

She stood in the centre of the clean-smelling salon, which seemed to have been freshly painted, and lit with more candles than before, giving an impression of increasing prosperity, even luxury. Master Choice came to her. He lifted her vizard tenderly, first loosening the strings from around her ears. His finger touched her neck and she felt an involuntary shudder.

He guided her to the window, flinging back the drapes to provide better light. He searched her face with his eyes. "Superb," he breathed. "But I cannot comment until I have seen your water."

"I will send it hereafter," said Venetia, flinching as his thumb lifted her chin, and he inspected her cheek. Her pupils were large, which he was beginning to see was a consequence of the Wine. It gave the body all the outward signs of pleasure. It made the lips redder, the eyes engorged, the nipples pert. So some of his bolder ladies reported. He suspected it put something up their skirts, too. He also prepared it as a venerous drug, to sweeten the bed, but it was as a Rejuvenation Tonic that it was selling best. Desire, being plentiful, is cheap. But men and women will pay a higher price to quell their fears.

"Your eyes are very black. Have you been taking Belladonna?"

"No, a few years back I used the droppers, but not since then," she said.

"Good, because you are my patient," he said, holding her by the chin, "so you take only what I prescribe, of course. You must never taste Belladonna, by the way, because it is Deadly Nightshade."

"I am familiar with Belladonna."

"Very good. Now, my lady: what a change. Your skin is remarkably improved. Do you know that?"

Venetia nodded at the praise she was due, and smiled.

"Have you not been using the dentifrice?"

Venetia covered her mouth with her hand; she had been famous for showing her pretty teeth, and she found it hard to change that habit.

"Did you read my letter?" she asked.

He returned to his desk and looked through his papers, trying to find the sheaf that was hers.

She remembered: *He is my only, but I am one of his many.* This made her feel sad, for a moment, but it also reminded her that she was a paying customer, which held its own power. As he continued to search for her letter, she interrupted: "Your vipers—do they multiply?"

"They thrive. They would breed faster if they were mindful of my lady's beauty," he laughed.

"Would they breed faster if they were mindful of my lady's money?"

"You would like a higher dose. This is a step we cannot take without due analysis, and it calls for . . ."

Voices outside on Fenchurch Street broke the silence of the consulting room; an everyday, street-bustling sound, but it pricked Venetia's ear.

Venetia knew that voice better than she knew her own; its notes, its rhythm. It went to the heart of her and in a spasm she followed her strong, quick reflex to save herself, and she ducked out of the view of the window, hiding behind the curtains.

Oh hell, thought Lancelot, *another Bedlam-ite.*

But Venetia had reason. One of the voices floating up from the street was her husband's. She peeped around the curtain and through the light deformation of the glass she saw his golden hair, tawny by candlelight but blond by daylight, and his cornflower-blue corderalls, his well-made shape. He was standing talking loudly in the street, looking up towards the house. There was a note of choler in his voice.

Please to Jesus he had not followed her.

"My lady—" said Choice.

"Shh!" said Venetia urgently, but smiling, trying to make light of it. "Pray ssssh!"

She ducked down again and whispered savagely: "If he calls, tell him I am here for dentifrice. Dentifrice—yes, Choice?"

But Lancelot Choice could not keep up. "Tell who, my lady?"

Venetia fell upon her knees. "Oh Mary mother of God. He has discovered your trade and my deceit and we will both be undone."

She felt as if she had been caught selling the family silver. Her beauty was his as much as hers, was it not? And now here she was planning to melt it down, to trade it in for something new. *I was forced to come here,* she silently rehearsed—*you would not give me any remedy yourself. You made me do it. I did it for you.*

To Venetia's guilty eyes, Kenelm appeared to be looking straight up at the house of Lancelot Choice, but in fact he was calling up to the window of the physician Robert Fludd, whose rooms were next door.

In the open air, the wind catching his voice, Kenelm was saying loudly: "The very same came to me this morning." Or something like it, Venetia could not catch every word. "So let me come up," said Kenelm, his hand on his sword. "Are you not with any customer? Aye, so I shall."

And so Kenelm was gone from Venetia's sight, stepping into the house of Fludd.

Inside Fludd's hallway there was one of his famous automata: the dragon and St. George, its metalwork very fine if now a little dull with age. Kenelm wondered if it was still in working order. He looked about the hallway, but there was no one watching him, and he tipped with his finger very gently the lance of St. George, which made the snakeskin-bound dragon rear up and backwards—his articulated wings spreading with a smooth and subtle motion—and then after a click let the counterpoise within the dragon spring, its mouth shot forth a long red fabric tongue. Kenelm was disappointed; this creature did not appear to be ensouled, only clockwork. The best Thaumaturgic models surprised you, since you could not see their workings . . .

Then, poof!

A tiny flare of flaming gas issued from the creature's nose, burning up all the dust in the air with a bang, and startling Kenelm so he flinched. A thin thread of satisfied smoke issued from the dragon's warty nostrils.

"Ha!" said Fludd, who was watching from a mirror positioned at the top of the stair.

Fludd was a dragon-tamer, and a bull-keeper (he had also made a Minotaur that bellowed and ground its hoof) and he was master of a lyre that played itself. He was the esteemed author of the *Catholica Medicorum*, which ran to five volumes already and was not finished, and though he lacked the personable, solicitous nature that some require in a physician, he had built up a considerable practice.

No doubt that dragon trick is played several times each day, thought Kenelm. He suspected that during the evening hours Fludd was also a Philosopher, practising the Great Work, but by day he was a physician who cured by means of metallurgy, healing plants, natural amulets and, yes, weapon-salves. He was Kenelm's foremost fellow practitioner in this, though the two of them preferred to be unique than to be allied, and they maintained a watchful, distant cordiality, preserved by the fact that they did not often meet.

They sat in front of Fludd's fire upstairs, under a dozen bladders that were hanging up to dry, and Fludd fetched them a small tot of plague water—"Keepeth me, keepeth thee," he said, knocking it back.

"Is this the receipt of de la Porta?" asked Kenelm, after he had taken a sip.

"No," said Fludd. "It is my own, of rue, agrimony, wormwood, celandine and sage; of mugwort, dragon's-eye, pimpernel and marigold, clarified with featherfew, burnet, sorrel, scabius and wood-bellony. After it is steeped in avence, tormentil, cardus benedictus and rosemary, with angelica, burdock and green walnuts." Fludd had such punctiliousness in his personality, he was himself rather like an automaton.

"Delicious," said Kenelm. "Let me have the recipe? But to the matter of the moment. May I see your letter?"

Fludd, glowering, pulled the Hoplocrisma-Spongus out from under a cushion, and Kenelm saw as he scanned it that they had received documents that were very like.

"The Parson Foster, hungry for fame, it seems, has already published this at Powles."

Published the Hoplocrisma-Spongus? Kenelm smote with his fist the chimney breast that abutted the room in which Venetia sat. She did not hear it, though in Lancelot Choice's grate, an ember collapsed.

"I intend to respond with a pamphlet vindicating my method," said Fludd. "Or else my practice will fail by it. I must write a Spongus-Sacerdotus—a sponge to wipe away the parson."

"You must, Fludd. If I may, I will pay for the printing. We ought to stand together in this bad business. He says—look, here—that in the process of our weapon-salve, we anoint th'offensive weapon with moss grown on a human skull."

"Now did I tell you, he's a jake's-head."

"He also has it that we apply the flesh of a hanged man."

"He's an imbecilic syphilite."

"And he says that we require the sacrifice of a cockerel."

"Maggotty-brained abortionist."

"And he says that we use magical invocations rather than natural Physick."

"Injurious toad."

"He also says we recommend the wound be washed in the patient's urine."

"Ah, now there he is not without reason."

"Oh, suffer me," muttered Kenelm, who had long suspected he differed with Fludd on matters of the application of the salve. "You still practise that old habit? You will tell me next that you dress the wound with suet."

"A nice and proper setting of suet does help the wound to become incrust."

"And you bathe it with turpentine and camphor?"

"Indeed, it must be bathed thus every day."

"This is abhorrent to the rules of nature, Fludd."

"This is often the only hope for saving a desperate man."

And thus the two of them fell to disputation, calling one another very curtly by their surnames, until Digby told Fludd his malpractice had brought the parson down upon them, and Fludd told Digby that without camphor he would suffer a mouldy grave. Digby said he had seen men die of it in France; Fludd accused Digby of being a Catholic conspirator, and got up and showed Digby to the door, where Digby bowed angrily, although Fludd would not look at him, resembling, in his wobbling and ill-suppressed anger, an automaton with a valve or spring missing.

Venetia, still in Lancelot Choice's study, heard the door slam, and she started as if she were attached to it by a string.

"Is it him? Is he coming?"

"No, my lady," Lancelot Choice said, standing suavely by the window, watching her husband's form striding off down the street, his hat in hand. "And so he is gone, and we can continue." He smiled, showing teeth that came from the bottom of the ocean.

She did not feel relief exactly—the double-quantity of Viper Wine that Lancelot Choice had given her protected her from such vulgar emotion—but she felt a warmer glow than ever. Choice had spent this half-hour or so asking about her health, which interested him to the minutest detail: her new disposition to take only broth until dinner, and how much vigour she had now, compared to the old tiredness she used to feel when she was fasting, and so forth. It had been a pleasant enough way to pass the time, and she almost forgot he was doing it for reasons of professional flattery. It did not occur to her that he asked all these questions because he knew so little about the workings of the Wine.

To allay Venetia's fear of discovery, Choice had got Margaret to draw her a large cup of newly decocted Viper Wine from the stills, which scalded and burned her throat; she could feel it altering her as it went, flaying the back of her mouth into a new texture, and sitting on her heart like a lump of iron-ore. She made a burp that was richly purple, and tasted of thin metals. What moreish torture! It was what she needed. If she was not to be caught by her husband, she had better be punished by the Wine.

The bell of St. Michael Paternoster sounded, and she was glad to think it was pealing for her reprieve. She was passionately grateful she had escaped discovery. But then her mind swerved in a doom-laden direction, and she imagined the bell had a different purpose in its tolling, and in her self-involved way, she began to dramatise in her mind this day, this hour, this instant, as the turning point, the moment she could have been saved, but was lost.

Choice seemed to enjoy the drama, and put his feet upon his desk, showing off his ankles in their fine new thrummed satin stockings. He told her that he was in receipt of a stronger, more efficacious beauty treatment, by which she might easily profit.

"Your friend, with whom you first visited, whom we call discreetly Proserpina . . ." said Choice, although he now knew she was Olivia Porter. "I cannot say she has taken the benefits of the Drink so well as you have. You have not such a history of tending your beauty already as she has. You are a fresher canvas. And you have taken the Viper Wine up into your breast, your cheek, your brow. There is no stop to what we might achieve," he said, stroking his thumb thoughtfully across her forehead. "We have means of going deeper. The Viper Drink is only the beginning. But for the giddy instant, my lady must rejoice that so much of her beauty is restored."

As a lady she did not handle her own coin, except at cards, but her will to secrecy meant she had brought a full purse, to pay for this session, and for her next three months' drink in advance. The coins seemed to her so bright and slippery, and counting them out was harder than usual. "I am faster at the card table!" she laughed. Margaret Choice helped her into her over-clothes, which Venetia laced with trembling fingers, and leaving the house of Choice it struck her out of the fresh blue sky that there were so many places she wanted to visit, now she could put a face to the world again—so many friends and former suitors whom she longed to behold, to hold in her arms. She would go to the Tower later and pay a visit to her old step-granddam, whom she had not seen for years. She passed a market stall with little cloths hung up for sale, embroidered with mirrors, and although she had seen this sort of cloth many times before, she was drawn to these, marvelling at them, touching their rich fabric.

"Cry for a beautiful lady, cry for a beautiful face!"

An old beggar woman was shouting at her, thrusting something into her hand, a lavender bag.

"Cry for me, lady, for I'm almost dead and gone."

Venetia walked on, not looking at the woman. Passing a stall laid out with tubs of beans, she threw her hands into them, just to feel her fingers in amongst their round smoothness, until the stall-holder shooed her away.

She knew this for what it was—a heightening of mind caused by the Wine. The Wine had made her concupiscent, yes, but not for any man.

She was mad for the whole world, the great jarring sensuous wonder of it. She had never walked the streets like this before, as a man might, without direct purpose, simply free to wander. She was becoming brazen.

A tradesman sharpening a knife turned to stare at her, and she gifted him a smile. She had smiles enough now, smiles to spare. *I should be punished for this*, she thought, as she drifted down the street. So much pleasure cannot come for free. She saw a donkey's load about to slip off its back, and she ran across the richly muddy road and righted the pack with a huge heave of her arms, and when the carter thanked her, she lifted another heavy box over to him, just to feel her new strength and suppleness.

I will pay hereafter, she thought. My wits will wander; surely I will come to grief. And yet—she clutched her purse—I am safe, I have my senses. It is my sensibilities that overflow. Ahead of her, a bucket of filth splattered onto the road from on high with slow, luxurious inevitability. As her nose twitched it felt as good as scratching an itch. In a morality tale, I would lose my way, here in the streets, and be brought low, and punished—but this is not a morality tale. This is my brief and insignificant existence, God forgive me.

Venetia stopped at a fabric shop and asked if they sold Ultramarine, but the shop girls looked blankly at her.

"The colour made famous by Venetia Stanley," she explained.

"There's no call for that shade any more, madam," said the shopkeeper. Perhaps she meant, it is too expensive for our clients, Venetia thought, as she walked off, humming a favourite jig as she went. She wondered if they would play this jig at court, after the Candlemas Masque, during the dances. But then she realised it was an old song, which had been popular when she was first come to court twelve—no, fifteen—years ago, and she guessed that it would not be played any more. And she remembered that she could not follow her plan to visit her Percy granddam at the Tower, because she had died last spring, and Venetia felt suddenly old, older than she looked, and out of step with herself, as if she had a double rhythm to her dance.

Seeing Tuttle's Fields she knew she was nearly home. The chill air felt delicious on her hot lungs, and the early-evening darkness struck her poignantly, a deep, animal reminiscence of all the winters of her past.

She was preternaturally thirsty. The sky began to spit sleet that settled in cottony clumps upon her cloak, but as she looked on them they turned into the wettest black-wet water-drops.

When she came into the house, Kenelm looked at her intently. "Venetia?" he said.

So here we have it, she thought. Finally he notices the new enchantment about me. She walked daintily over to him, and took his hand. "Yes, my darling?" she said, with her eyes closed, waiting for his words of love.

"Have you not heard the news? There is word from Sir Francis Knollys about Penelope. She is sick with smallpox."

"Please God she will not be pitted," said Venetia.

"Please God she will not die," said Kenelm.

> "To prevent marks after smallpox: Take oyl of sweet almond newly drawn by expression without fire, and with a feather or other fit means anoint all over the face and that it runneth down backwards by both ears, as the party lyeth on their back. Cover carefully with gold leaf—wherever there is a defect of Gold there will be a scar. Leave 10–12 days until it has grown to a hard crust. Do not cover the eyes, but come as close as you can get to the hair."
>
> Sir Kenelm Digby's *Receipts in Physick*, 1668

Burning the cushions in her sitting room, and burning the cards they had played with, and smashing the cups that Penelope might have drunk from—all this was probably in vain, and yet Venetia did it anyway, with a fast and trembling hand.

She was furious with Penelope, and burned the things that Penelope had given her, the handkerchief she had stitched for her and a book of poems set to music. She sprinkled lavender water in the places Penelope had walked in the house, and she set fire to a fistful of rosemary and waved it around and about her doorstep in a circle. She drank a draft of Viper Wine, and then gulped down a foul pox-repelling tincture of rue, wood worm and antimony, which Kenelm prepared for her. She had never had smallpox, and to catch it now, at her age, would be less life-threatening but could lead to face-pitting, pock-marking, cheek-scabbing, a life of wearing patches and black spots, of people peering at her with curious pity. At her darker moments she felt the easeful shadow of death would be preferable to scarring. Venetia prayed for Penelope, to be sure, but she cried for herself. When Kenelm caught her crying, she hoped he would think she was moved with anxiety for her friend, but he knew her better than that.

"Venice," he said, holding her, "you must not be afeared. I have a recipe for the pox so it leaves no scars."

He imagined the patient, mummified with gold, like a Myrmidon. He would use the Highest substance to purify the skin. His fingers danced to get to work.

"I call it the cure of *aurum dixum*. 'Tis of mine own devising, based upon receipts from the Duke of Tuscany. I would take more care over your face, my darling, than Rubens does of his ceilings. I would make you a perfect mask of gold."

"Thank you," sniffed Venetia.

"And afterwards, I would have the gold melted into a tiny spoon, and keep it in a drawer at Gayhurst."

"Have you ever tried this cure before?" she asked.

"Not yet," said Sir Kenelm, trying to hide how keen he was to try his cure out upon Penelope. "Not yet . . ."

"I tell you this," said Venetia, her voice low and awful, so that even a dog would have understood she was angry. "You will not bring Penelope's pestilence into this house. If you tend to her bedside, you shall not come to mine."

Sir Kenelm found he was very busy with other matters.

Venetia had a new friend in Morpheus. Oh, how she slept. Sleep had never been so exquisite to her, and she could pass whole days in its arms, rolled in bright drifts of dreams. She was able to wake up, perform some little action, kiss her boys and say a prayer with them, perhaps, and then dive straight into the depths again, taking up her dreams where she had left off, chattering into her pillow and smiling as she slept, while her bones stretched, and the incipient dowager's hump she dreaded disappeared, her shoulders dropping, her spine straightening, her marrow regenerating. Sleep seemed to heal her from within. Her dreams were more vivid than daily life.

"How does she do it?" remarked Aletheia Howard to her dog Lemuel, as Venetia trounced her at Glecko. Now Penelope was sick, Venetia needed to look elsewhere for card-playing companions, and she had been picked up by Aletheia Howard, Countess of Arundel, Surrey and Norfolk, who loved to have a quick young woman playing at her table. Indeed, she seemed almost pleased to be beaten by her, more amused and admiring with each trump, calling "Good girl!," as if she were allowing her to win, except Venetia knew no gambler ever allowed another gambler to win. The sums Lady Howard played were more than Venetia was used to, and this quickened her enjoyment, sharpening her mind.

Aletheia was the granddaughter of Bess of Hardwick and she had inherited both her desire for independence and the fortune to achieve it. She lived most of the year alone in a mansion near the woods of St. James's called Tart Hall, where her husband the Earl was not allowed to visit. Tart Hall was like a nest, full of strange objects Aletheia liked to keep about her. A gondola was suspended over the doorway to the main hall, and one chamber was titled the Diana Room, for its friezes of the huntress showing muscular thighs in sportive poses. In the Peacock Room were set many-coloured tiles arranged into Moorish arches, and there were tall teapots and a Venetian mooring post of striped red and white, and feather fans and letters and miniatures and a weeping head of Christ set with rubies, and Aletheia sitting in the middle of all this on a low daybed, eyeing her cards shrewdly, pausing only to draw upon a Tobacco Pipe, and narrowing her eyes against its smoke.

She spoke relentlessly about any subject that took her fancy, and today it was Van Dyck.

"He was the fastest I have ever sat to. So fast, and so 'cute. Oh, he's the best of them all. He's a *diminuendo* of a man, not much to look on. You'll see. He'll adore you. He'll paint you uncommon well, Lady Digby."

For a fraction of a second, Aletheia looked sideways at Venetia's bosom, which was swelling so much lately, because of all the pregnant mare's urine she was drinking in her Wine. Venetia felt herself rising voluptuously against her gown every time she breathed. She was so much thinner now, she had her waist back, and yet her bosom had expanded pneumatically, so she was really something like an hourglass, a parody of womanhood, even without much lacing of her waist.

Venetia explained that Kenelm had already commissioned Van Dyck, and they had both sat to him together. Every week they expected delivery of their portrait, but because it was a double canvas, requiring many hours' work, it was delayed; and besides, the royal commissions took precedent.

"He's too much in demand. First it was Mantua, Venice, Antwerp. The Gonzagas shall have no more of him, at least. The Barberinis will probably get their hands in next. But when you do sit to him, Lady Digby, you shall mark my words: take the thing away with you, for little Jesus's sake. Oh, you must, you must."

"What thing?" asked Venetia.

"The *pittura*. The *canovaccio*, the canvas, Lady Digby. Unless you do you shall never see it again. There were four years before I had possession of my Venice portrait by Rubens, and we've not seen the Earl's Van Dyck since he sat to him. Never," she tapped her Tobacco Pipe out on the floor, "never let a portrait out of your sight. Take it with you. Even if the studio folk tell you, 'Oh, it is not dry yet, it is not ready.' " She was as vehement as if Venetia disagreed with her, although she had done nothing but nod and say, "Indeed, indeed!" Aletheia tutted and shook her head. "Take it with you," she insisted.

Venetia caught Aletheia's companion, Dorothy, also glancing at her bosom. Venetia sensed something hanging in the air, with the Tobacco smoke, and though she did not entirely understand it, she liked it, and she was perfectly happy here at Tart Hall where menfolk never visited. She felt she could spend all her life with women, and it would be so much the better. Women adored her as men did, except with more understanding.

Aletheia caught her eye. "You know I carry many titles, Venetia," she said, adding, *sotto voce*: "One of them is Baroness Strange."

Venetia hoped to become more like Aletheia as time went on, to cultivate her style and her queer brusqueness. What a wonderful thing it will be to be an old and magnificently rude woman, she thought. To be an old, rich, magnificently rude woman—now that would be even better. And in the conduct of her marriage, Aletheia had avoided the usual indignities, without any rancour between her and her husband, only distance.

Aletheia asked Venetia, out of nowhere, if Sir Kenelm went behind her back.

Venetia took this very calmly. "No i'faith, and it means he is always at my front," she said, as if she were weary with his desiring. But Aletheia's question opened a problem she had considered closed. Was it not obvious to all that, in her gorgeous condition, she had full control of Kenelm? And yet Venetia remembered, in that moment, that even the most beautiful, most seemly wives are sinned against. Perhaps a man does not want rich jewels and satin every day. Perhaps—but no, Aletheia did not know what she was talking about. Her marriage had been a set-up between noble twelve-year-olds, stiff with silver.

"Kenelm and I married for love, against our families' wills," she said.

"Mournivals and gleeks out, please," said Aletheia, by way of reply.

They showed their hands.

"Well, *you* can never come back," said Aletheia, snorting, as Venetia took up her winnings.

"How does she do it, Lemuel?" said Dorothy, asking the dog, who still could not answer.

Venetia reached for her pocket to stow away her winnings. The floor here was covered in rushes and Lemuel lifted his leg to squirt against the daybed. Venetia did not think animals belonged indoors. Neither of the ladies seemed to mind, their nest here at Tart Hall being more like a cosy den of the old days, stuffed with curiosities. And yet Aletheia could have had a splendid wing of Arundel House on the Strand to herself.

"Do you think it is a lovely helping of blancmange?" Aletheia asked Dorothy. "Or two jellies on a plate?"

"Aspic of pigs' chaps," replied Dorothy. "With two apricots on top."

Aletheia and Dorothy laughed between themselves.

"I fancy it is the Pope's own *panna cotta*," said Aletheia.

Venetia was not really listening, but she fancied she was being discussed, as usual.

"Or at the very least a cardinal's."

"Maybe it is a dish of pale broth," said Dorothy.

"With two piglets in it," said Aletheia.

After laughing they both sighed, as if their game was ending.

"Have you never been to Venice, Lady Digby?" said Aletheia, although she knew the answer. No women in London had been to Venice, apart from her and Dorothy and a few gypsies and ambassadors' wives.

"The Venetian trousers are the most famous export, and I have several pairs," said Dorothy.

"*Diminuendo,* please, Dorothy!" cried Aletheia. Venetia gathered it was Aletheia's favourite word. "Lady Digby does not wish to know of your trousers, Dot," she said. "She is every inch a wife, just look at her marvellous frontage. We are both quite entranced. Do you not lose things down there frequently, purses and whatnot?"

"Never," said Venetia. "Though others may lose themselves through looking."

"Oh bless her, for she colours! D'you see, Dorothy, she colours!"

Venetia was not aware of blushing; in fact, she was convinced she was not.

"No need to be bashful, Lady Digby. You have managed the Sackville brothers' advances, I am sure you are not bothered by little me. *Solo poco me!* And you and I have a better *affiatamento,* a better understanding than you might think. For I know your Method." Aletheia blew a chute of smoke away from the table. "Your Method of Beauty. Your *antidotum vitae.*"

Venetia searched her mind for slips or indiscretions she might have made. She looked up at Aletheia, feeling panicky and diminished, while Aletheia grinned at her like Goliath, her plucked forehead rising high up to her grizzled hairline.

"Come with me and you shall see my meaning," said Aletheia, leading her out of the Peacock Room by candlelight into an interconnecting room, draped with crimson, and down a brown-yellow corridor to the Dutch Pranketing Room, which housed a larder full of Delftware, and there, beside fly traps and cake dishes, stood an earthenware still. Aletheia removed its lid triumphantly, and peering inside, Venetia saw three large, whorled Continental snails.

"Your husband brought you the very same, no?" said Aletheia, looking at her intently, studying her reaction. "Their slimy serum costs as much as silver. You entice them to move across your brow, and cheek, and even further, hmm?"

Venetia laughed with relief so her white bosom heaved.

"Why, Lady Howard," she said, "you have unmasked me. Now we are sisters, and I can never beat you at Glecko again."

"You use the Murex, then?"

"I use all manner of matter for my face."

Aletheia looked at her with an offended expression, and put the lid back on the still. "Well, if you will not tell me, I will have it elsewhere," she said, off-hand.

"They tickle and kittle the temples terribly, do they not?" said Aletheia, trying again. "And it is such a long, slow march they make, even encouraged by *una mosca morta*—a defunct fly, placed upon the nose. Ha!"

Venetia, playing her hand carefully as ever, gave up her suit and told Aletheia that Kenelm had indeed brought her the snails, although she did not mention that she was too disgusted to use them. But she also hinted, as she took her leave of the countess at the side-gate of Tart Hall, that Kenelm now provided her with a much better remedy, which was to remain a secret of their marital union.

Aletheia declared her deep respect for the sanctity of marriage, all the while raising one eyebrow at Venetia. She did not subject Venetia to further questions, although inwardly she was already deciding how to find the secret out, as she let her go with a wink and a pat on her bum-padding.

The Opium Garden

ANOTHER LETTER CAME for Venetia from Penelope, delivered by a hooded plague doctor. Venetia's first impulse was to have it burned at once, but she had suffered a fit of penitence over her burning of Pen's last two letters, fearing that she had destroyed Penelope's final farewells to this world, or even admissions of florid secrets. This was unlikely, given Penelope's nature, but every imagination responds to an unopened letter. Venetia would not touch this new letter herself, but curiosity drove her to make Chater open it, in front of the fire, using tongs, while she watched from the semi darkness of the other side of the room, dramatically covering her nose and mouth with her veil, her hands clasped in prayer for Penelope. Straining by firelight to read the writing, Chater managed to make out a few phrases.

"Our Old Pippin . . . has had a ham bone. He had great pleasure of it, dragging it to his bed, even though his teeth are fewer than they were . . ."

Chater and Venetia's mood of spiritual earnestness cooled. The letter was full of platitudes about the weather, her dogs, and news of her embroidered bed-jacket.

"So we risk our lives for kennel talk," said Venetia. "She is on her deathbed, and yet I never read a more boring letter!"

But then Chater read aloud a few fond words of friendship, which touched her, as well as a passage in which she implored Venetia to come and nurse her, saying she would do well to catch the smallpox from her as it was a light visitation and not likely to cause much scarring.

Venetia thought Pen must be out of her mind with illness, but she decided to send her a comforting little present—some tansy from the botanical gardens at Holborn.

Venetia drank her draft of Venus Syrup—although she did it every day, it could never become so drab a thing as a habit—and an hour later, with the Wine stoking her blood, she rapped at the door of the Terrestrial Paradise, a small garden door in the long brick wall. It was known as Sir John Parkinson's Terrestrial Paradise because it was a place of rare beauty, arranged like another Eden with all the herbs in harmonious groupings. He made a play on his name and called it the *sole paradisus terrestris*, Park-in-Sun.

The bricks in the wall were deep red, and she was absorbed with looking at their marbled veins like lumps of beef, when a gardener appeared at the door, hooded, and carrying a broom.

The Terrestrial Paradise was largely dank earth, dotted with greenish shrubs, hawthorn spikes, reeds and mouldy, broken bulrushes. Some plants had petrified where they stood, crucified to wires, while others had liquefied to mush. A small pond was cracked like a mirror in the middle, and frosted solid around its edges. All was hung over with a pall of blue woodsmoke, issuing from behind the brickwork nurseries.

Venetia had forgotten, somehow, that the garden would be dead or resting, buried below the sod. In that darkness, as in the darkness of the womb, small seeds were swelling, kicking as they unfurled. Venetia tiptoed into the garden, careful not to wake the sleeping plants.

"Are you Demeter? It's winter now, until she come again, so tell me you are her, lady, and I shall give you a pomegarnet," said the Gardener.

As she smiled, she could taste the dry, metallic wine returning in her throat, making her giddy again, and she swallowed twice so as not to choke. They passed a snoring beehive, and a vicious black bramble, which had formed itself into an empty cage, and a pair of seedy yellow-brown pokers, formerly red hot, now weeping glue. The walked past a row of stumpy trees, pollarded like beggars, and then they passed under the ribs of a trellis arch, and a bush bristling with anaemic sprouts of Old Man's Beard.

"Those that decay I leave to rot," said the Gardener. "It's untidy, but Dame Kind likes it better that way. She's a mucky lady. She loves a bit o'mulch. It makes everything else come up fresher. The old shrivellers make the new ones come on faster. It's none that die but aren't useful to the rest."

They walked onwards to the covered nurseries where Venetia expected she would find Parkinson pickling peppers, perhaps, while he waited for spring. But when the gardener opened the nursery door and Venetia ducked under the doorframe, she smelled at once the foetid warmth of artificial summer.

There were sprays and blossoms here, green shoots and flung-open flowers. A bud-rose was splitting apart like a slashed doublet. Venetia could feel the pores of her skin opening in the wet warmth, her nerves relaxing. Titania wintered here, no doubt. Venetia wandered about the hot-house in a daze. There were miraculous little pansies, smiling, and tall papery blooms of Lady's Slipper. There were blowsy orange poppies that they call Welsh poppies, which Venetia pinched between thumb and finger to check they were real and not made of silk, so she tore half a petal, and left her thumbprint upon its delicate skin—but who would believe this winter flowering without testing it?

Spiky and shock-headed, comically proud to be alive, were a whole guard of daffodils, in December. And vegetables, too, peasquash, beans and marrows, putting forth bright yellow flags as if it were August. Parkinson's greatest patron was the Queen—it seemed he furnished her with fruit and flowers all year round.

"Are these goodly fruits and flowers," she asked the Gardener passionately, "fit to eat? Not hollow, or blighted, or corrupted by unseasonal flowering?"

The Gardener laughed and shook his head.

"They are real, in other words, and worthy of love," she murmured.

One plant was squat like a marrow but spined like a porcupine. It bit Venetia's finger when she touched it, and the buzzing of a blow-fly sounded very loud and large in her ear. As she walked unsteadily about, another bush reached out to pluck at her gown, and she turned about in time to see it recoil, its fronds whispering and shuddering.

"The best plant to eat in here," said the Gardener, "is the Vegetable Lamb of Tartary," pointing to a little plinth where sat a mass of wool and fern, somewhat like an old mop crossed with a dog.

"He is the reason we keep this nursery pen so warm, because he's a precious beast indeed. He's come from beyond the Alps, beyond the

Tartar Sea, from a place called the Ural, and he's thought to be about to issue forth live lambs, which will graze around him, joined to this plant by an umbilical stalk. We've feed for the lambs in case they come early," he said, kicking his foot towards a sack propped against the wall, "but there's been no bleating from this corner yet."

"Is he plant or animal, then?"

"A mickle of one and a muckle of the other, my lady," said the Gardener, inserting himself between Venetia and the Vegetable Lamb, so that she would not harm him through carelessness.

"Sometimes I make a melody, to bring him on a bit."

The Gardener turned and started sweeping, heaving his broom and singing:

"Only the dove and the lamb live here

Lions nor vultures nay breathe the air

Sweet music and nay narry distress

In the *sole paradisus terrestris*."

He carried on sweeping and singing, and he had such tenderness in his voice, she felt the Vegetable Lamb must surely grow with the nourishment of his tunefulness.

"Master Parkinson is fixed on bringing about the production of lambs from this plant," said the Gardener. "Namely, the production of meat from seed. He says none will go hungry if we can do it, and the taste of this lamb is said to be uncommonly good. Every time I sleep for more than a few hours, or our fire goes out, then he berates me, saying the Lamb is the Joy of Man's Vegetable Desiring, and I jump to my work again, because it seems likely that after the earth has discovered potatoes, meat should be picked from a tree."

Some visitors to the Park-in-Sun denied the Vegetable Lamb, and said it was no better than a bush wearing a wig, and called it a hoax and a nothing, and the Gardener heard them, and yet he kept his faith in the Vegetable Lamb.

As Venetia stood in front of it she was convinced she heard it gurgle. The Vegetable Lamb's tails hung from its stunted boughs, and as she looked at them, wondering what Kenelm would make of them, they began to shake and wriggle with the foolish happiness of cloned lambs, gambolling about transgenic laboratories where they were tended by a thousand white-coated shepherds. She blinked, looked again, and saw that the Vegetable Lamb's tails merely trembled where she breathed upon them, though Dolly the Sheep's great granddam (to the power of a thousand) already grazed on the Derbyshire vale. Moved by the strangeness of the Spirit, she performed a quick cross and genuflection, in front of the Lamb, and the Gardener followed suit.

"We always strive to build Utopia in our garden. For if we bring plants here from Every-where across the world, then here becomes No-where, a place that is only full of the best. And Utopia is a good place, and yet no-place, and so we have it here, where there are no seasons. My master always replies so: 'God would be much honoured if we could do it.' And so I say also, God would be much honoured if we could devise a true understanding of the parentage of grasses and reeds . . ."

Venetia wandered away, drawn to a peaky-looking lily that perched on the edge of a trestle of blooms. It was of an achingly sad, voluptuous disposition, its heavy head on an angle. She touched her cheek against its cantilevered petals. It smelled of summer, of Gayhurst, of Floralia, of her son's bare suntanned legs. The skin was fibrous with a waxy touch upon it. It had flourished by special pleading, and careful maintenance, and yet it was as beautiful as any woodland or hedgerow flower—more so, because in its plenitude and hot-house refinement, there was something overly sensual and rare. It had been kept constantly warm here, taken outside into sunlight and shielded from frost, cosseted and fed and watered, nurtured against nature into a constant bloom. It was a lily that had drunk of Viper Wine. She looked at its pert stamen, and wondered if it was barren.

The lily, looking back at her, creaked fibrously into bloom, exhaling a breath of musk and cream and incense, inviting Venetia closer until she could smell its glandular undertow. As she closed her eyes, its rusted stamen stained her neck with two brown imprints, fang marks that smudged into love-bites.

Tansy, or Mugwort, or Gold Buttons—by any name it was as helpful to a woman with the smallpox—was sprouting in the medicinal section of the nursery, and the Gardener cut her a good quantity. It cost, but of course it cost. They stoked the fires here constantly, and watered as frequently too: there was foetid greenness growing on the window casements, becoming thicker all the time, blotting out the light more now than when she had stepped inside, as if the pace of life in here were unstoppably quick, and oppressed by the close atmosphere, she darted outside into the wholesome cold.

The Gardener saw her scratching herself surreptitiously under her shawl, and he moved in front of her, blocking her path, looking intently into her eyes, scanning them with his own. Even in the garden light, her pupils were too wide.

"*Papaver somniferum,*" he said, more to himself than to her. "I wish you joy of your dreams, my lady." With a small bow, he pointed her towards the tiny door in the wall. "Take care to waken from them."

Penelope had her tansy by nightfall, but the lily pollen stains clung to Venetia's skin until evening when Kenelm, searching her body and breathing her incense-scent, found the yellow smudge of them on her neck, and removing them with his thumb and his hot tongue, covered that spot with loving kisses, which suck'd the vessels under her skin so gently she could barely feel them breaking, and pleasured in the feeling, until she realised what he was doing and told him to stop, in the name of her honour.

Now Venetia was herself again, Kenelm's life was full of luxury. He was like a greedy bumblebee rolling in pollen. At their table they took baked venison, from Gayhurst, cooked as Kenelm directed, so it could be eaten with a spoon. Gellied bones, and whipped-cream syllabub; veal with sweetbreads, champignons and truffles: what a banquet of the senses they enjoyed! He felt the fitness of his tongue through much licking.

He had the bare plaster wall in their chamber covered with leather, tooled into fleur-de-lis patterns, and its richness went in at the eye, yet pleased the fingers, without touching.

Godly men and women, Puritans so-called, preferred plain things, of lasting quality. But Kenelm was in love with decoration, opulent colourings and fretwork. To his mind there was nothing that could not be improved with a few swirls and spandrels.

He bought young Kenelm a pistol, inlaid with pearl and chased with silver. It had the enchantment of all miniature things, and its cartridges were pluggits of cork.

The sound of Venetia approaching made him weak: the sigh of her skirts, the lush heaviness of them. He pinched the lawns and tiffanies she wore between his fingers, feeling their fine grain, marvelling at the abilities of worms.

Whenas in silks my Julia goes
Then, then (methinks) how sweetly flows,
That liquefaction of her clothes . . .

Venetia's silks were a fetish for her admirers, who used to crouch at keyholes to watch the rhythm, the pattern of her walking, and the flare of her gown as she stooped or stepped. It gave young men a frisson to think that the silk moved because she had a pair of legs, independently articulated like a perfect doll, which (yes, no word of a lie) divided at the top . . . For Kenelm the doll was gone, replaced by the woman he loved, but an echo of the fetish remained, in the rustle of her silk, and the flow of her sateen, its indecent slipperiness.

Next, when I cast mine eyes and see
That brave vibration each way free;
O how that glittering taketh me!

Venetia's hair was curled with the expensive new pomander he bought her, which was spiced with bergamot and ambergris from the belly of the whale, a scent that came to define that time of their lives even as they were living it, so that whenever Kenelm caught it he sighed for last week, last month, last year.

He wondered: was his wife his greatest luxury of all? It was the other way round. There was no luxury without Venetia.

When Kenelm sat at his desk he closed his eyes and ran his fingertips over the tooled letters of his newly bound books, reading in the ridges and grooves the deep and light luxuries of his life, and imagining he was touching Venetia. He almost went to her, so they might roll all their sweetness up—but he stopped himself, and opened his book instead. They had time enough for that to come: tonight, after dinner; tomorrow; a lifetime, indeed. Was this not the blessing of marriage?

"It was [my] fortune to fall into the company of a Brachman [Brahmin] of India . . . which man was one of those that the Indians held in great veneration for their professed sanctity and deep knowledge of the most hidden mysteries of theology and nature. [The Brahmin enlightened Sir Kenelm so that] . . . after much patience, and by abstracting my thoughts from sensual objects, and raising my spirit up to that height that I could make right use of these powerful names which this art teacheth, I got a real and obedient apparition as I desired."

The Private Memoirs of Sir Kenelm Digby, 1631

"A button of gold could stretch, as thin as a hair, from Montpelier to Paris."

Sir Kenelm Digby, *On Bodies and the Immortality of Souls,* 1659

"OMMMMMMM."

Sir Kenelm was meditating. His pantalooned legs were crossed beneath him, his lacy cuffs rested upon his knees, his dark gold hair lay upon his collar, and his thumbs and first fingers pinched together into a point, like Bodhisattva's teardrop. His pale eyelashes were closed.

Thoughts of worldly advancement—Sir Francis Windebank said more monopolies were being offered by the Crown, for loans—entered his mind, and he cast them away. He breathed in light, and breathed out darkness.

Thoughts of the tightness of his garters entered his mind, and he cast them away. He breathed in darkness, and turned it into light—for was the meditating subject not using his body as a jordan? As a flask or alembic, for the transmutation of base matter into higher thoughts?

"Ommmmmmm . . ."

Sir Kenelm had come across his old chest of relics from his teenage travels, rare trinkets he had collected on his journey through Alexandria and Anatolia—tiny jangling bells from a temple; a representation of the evil eye; his Persian cloth, decorated with a design of palms that would in a few decades be called Paisley; some scented sticks that were even now giving off a thoughtful odour; and some rolls of parchment painted with Buddhist mandalas, which had greatly interested him, since they were so similar to English astrologer's wheels.

"Ommmmmmm . . ."

There was also a small holy statue which he had bought at great cost, having been assured it was an ancient relic, even though after purchasing it he discovered underneath it a small stamp saying "Made In China."

Sir Kenelm vibrated with the irenic sounds that the Brahmin had taught him would lead first to visions, then to Vedic flying and finally to divine Atman transcendence, as he fingered his Catholic rosary beads.

"Ommmmmmmm . . ."

Downstairs, in her bedroom, Venetia was standing, an empty vial in her hand, staring at a grey stitch. Innumerable grey threads, twisted together, created one grey stitch. Next to it was a yellow stitch, and next to that another grey stitch, then a green stitch, an umber stitch. Grey, green, umber.

There was no design or purpose to them. They were unreasoning, varicoloured stitches only. As she blinked, her eyelashes were like a heron's wings flapping.

Grey stitch, yellow stitch, green stitch, umber.

The colours were a jumble-pie.

She took a step back.

From here she could see that each stitch was packed together like sacks of wheat, making up the smoothish surface of a textile, bunched a little with the tension of warp over weft.

She blinked, and the glassy blackness of her iris tightened as she stepped back again, widening her field of vision.

From two steps away, she could see the dark stitches represented depths while the lighter ones were sun-glinting peaks. Each thread of colour served a larger purpose in the picture; her step backwards had created order out of chaos. Perception was everything. She reached for the word pixelated—but it was three hundred years away.

Three steps back, and she saw the stitches were part of the tapestry on her bedroom wall depicting the myth of Hero and Leander—Leander was peeping around a rich curtain, which was made out of yellow and grey stitches, its folds falling in dark green and umber stitches.

So one textile creates the illusion of another, thought Venetia. Each stitch both is a stitch and represents a stitch. And she went close to the tapestry again, and repeated the words, and together they made mad music:

"Each stitch is a stitch."

"Ommmmmmmm."

"Is a stitch is a stitch is a stitch . . ."

"Ommmmmmmm."

". . . is a stitch is a stitch."

As Sir Kenelm meditated, he flew about the world like one of Lucretius's Atomes, unfettered, unmotivated, drawn by forces of heat and light.

He felt tiny neutral particles, neutrinos, passing through his body, a million squared per second, perpendicular to the sun. The antineutrinos, shadow mirror images, passed behind them.

Venetia picked up one of her fallen hairs, long and gracefully curved, particoloured, silvery at the root and rich black thereafter, where she had coloured it.

A button of gold could stretch, as thin as a hair, from Montpelier to Paris, thought Sir Kenelm. He saw the string, reaching infinitely far like saliva, growing telescopically ever thinner. He plucked at it, and like a harp string, it played a note for a long time, vibrating back and forth across itself.

She took out of its velvet drawstring her black obsidian mirror, a scrying glass. A steel glass showed the truth unpartially, as Sir Walter Raleigh's poem told, but a scrying glass was much more sensitive. She breathed upon it, and when the white cloud cleared she looked into its deep lake, dark and still.

Kenelm thought about telescopic string, and how it stretched, and yet retained its usefulness, and how a tied piece of string was the strongest thing he knew, and he wondered if Atomes that sailed through the air were string-strung, flying Frisbees.

Venetia looked into the abyss, and saw you looking back at her.

The atom split. Kenelm's mind snapped back on itself like a rubber band and flew into the future, into particle physics, string theory, superstring theory, supersymmetry, Higgs boson theory, M-theory—all flashing fast and faster, turning like a zoetrope, changing and improving with every spin of the wheel.

Isaac Newton's mother, still only a child, danced around a maypole in the Lincolnshire countryside.

Venetia lying on her stomach, gazing into the dark lake, looked straight at you and asked: "Well, what did you expect? What could I do—except become Narcissus?"

Kenelm felt a tug on the golden string that ran through him, into the future, in the direction of a unifying theorem that reconciled general relativity with quantum mechanics, which they called A General Theory of Everything. Currents of exhilaration pulsed through his vibrating body. Ommmmmm. Alchemy's Great Work might yet be achieved, three hundred years hence.

Ping! Sir Kenelm lost his concentration momentarily, and celestial spam arrived in his brain: "14cm black Wiccan obsidian scrying mirror, highly polished both sides. Dispatched within 1 day, seller guaranteed . . ." He tried to clear his mind by breathing.

In her mirror, Venetia saw acres of Dark Matter, streaming like fast-forwarded clouds, vapid cosmic gas, the ego in sublimation. She saw herself in eleven different space–time dimensions. At eighteen, at twenty-one, at thirty-three. She saw herself as others saw her, not directly, but in the third person, as object not subject. The string between the first person and the third person broke, and she saw herself as a stranger would see her, with an objective eye. Venetia fished into the darkness and trawled up photographs.

Now she took Sir Kenelm's hand and made him look into the mirror also, so he could see them streaking across the skies.

Sir Kenelm soared amongst the Dark Matter of the heavens, the distant shores of the cosmos that had no name and no definition, and he was as happy there as he was exploring the *terra incognita* on his own maps, the Dark Lands beyond the known perimeters of the Indies and the Americas, beyond which a man might found a kingdom in his own image, or at the very least, in his own name.

She dived deep into her glass, falling into her scrying mirror plundered from an Aztec kingdom, made of obsidian glass polished by the excrement of bats—half-digested beetle wing-cases, baby bird bones and enzymes—which had scrubbed its surface into a mirage of almost-wet smoothness, potent as an LED screen.

The Dark Matter swelled and irradiated, bright as sky coral. Venetia and Kenelm fell out of the sky together and landed on their bed, holding each other fast, their ideas tumbling over one another like clattering shells. The signal was lost.

A mouse ran, a dog barked, a bell rang and the display screen flickered and cut out. The visitor from Porlock had arrived, and Mistress Elizabeth was knocking at Venetia's locked door, calling that Olivia Porter was here and was refusing to take off her outer-garments, saying she was ready to accompany her to the Strand.

Venetia Furiosa

In which our Heroine, together with her lieutenants-at-arms, makes an attack upon the British Bourse.

The scene: the New Exchange, or Britain's Bourse. A proud building on the Strand, housing a great covered market, designed by the same hand that built palaces and chapels-royal (Master Inigo Jones) and shamelessly modelled upon a Mohammedan market-place or Turk-like Bazaar. It is the Greatest Market ever to be filled up with such piles of specious rarities, toys and trifles. All the Exquisites and Epicures of London are gathered here, to see one another and to be seen; to see, to touch, to want, to wish, to buy and, on going home, to lose, break, spoil and forget.

For Venetia and her friends, it is a place of surpassing vulgarity, which they fondly scorn, even as they hurry to visit. Entering by carriage, they pass through jostling sedan chairs and hot dung piles, shouting traders calling them in, and Puritans calling them away.

Bourse Boy: What lack ye, ladies? Fair cut-work falling bands, vardingales, periwigs, polking sticks?

Praise-God Jones: Leave Him to furnish you with everything you need—

Bourse Boy (louder): China chains, china bracelets, china scarves, china fans, china girdles . . .

PRAISE-GOD JONES (YET LOUDER): Enter not this house of luxury, for all your food comes from Him—

BOURSE BOY (LOUDER STILL): Birds of paradise, muskcads, Indian mice, Indian rats, China dogs and china cats . . .

PRAISE-GOD JONES (SINGS VERY LOUDLY): For He hath regarded the lowliness of His handmaiden—

BOURSE BOY (SHOUTING): Umbrellas, sundials, billiard balls, purses, pipes, toothpicks, spectacles. See what you lack!

[Bourse Boy's words taken from Ben Jonson's *Entertainment on the Opening of the New Exchange*, 1609]

Shielding their faces and picking up their skirts, the ladies came through the din, Chater following behind. Once they were through the first portico they settled on the public seats, where one of the Bourse stewards gave them a cup of hot Bishop, while another kneeled and removed the pattens that the ladies wore to protect their shoes, and Chater went ahead to procure their small-change. Olive had clearly been waiting a while to speak privately to Venetia, and as soon as Chater was gone, she asked with big eyes: "Do you think 'He' will be here?"

When she realised that Olive was referring to Master Lancelot Choice, Venetia said firmly "No," and called her a ninny, and a nodgcombe, hoping her tartness would bring Olive to her senses.

Preparing herself for scrutiny, for eye-darts and gossip wounds, Venetia raised her veil, so it framed her face, and with a small deliberate exertion of her facial muscles, like an actress warming up, she raised her eyebrows, lifted her chin, and prepared a gentle, smiling countenance to show the world.

They had not come for anything particular, except for the easy fun of it, and she knew from experience that they discovered things they wanted to buy soon enough—that was the wretched cleverness of the place. But being efficient by nature, the ladies set out to cover the whole place in a clockwise motion, moving purposefully through the crowds and dawdlers. They only stopped to talk to friends, not every acquaintance, otherwise they would never leave. First, they toured haberdashery—fans, shoe-roses, a multitude of ribbons, collars and cuffs. They dallied, comparing prices and testing lace with their fingers. Chater followed, condemning every article as poor taste, sucking his teeth and shaking his head at the jewelled pill boxes and pink feather fans.

Venetia and Olive inspected a set of fine marquetry chests, pacing around them like two hunters around a dying stag. Chater found fault with their inlay. He was very taken, however, by some calfskin gloves, and the ladies left him deliberating between grey and orange. They joined a small crowd and saw a monkey with a little hat on dancing a jig, though not as nicely as the Queen's pet monkey Pug. The monkey somehow discerned that Venetia was his rival for the crowd's attention, and made a great play for her, prancing at her feet, bowing, and hiding itself in her skirts, to the crowd's delight.

Onwards the ladies walked to the sweetmeats, the suckets and sweet-salats and sugar-puffs and fresh fried pain-perdu, for which the hungry crowd was ten deep. Venetia made Chater go and wait to buy some, so they could pass on without him to the penny pamphlets, to browse the poems, songs, recipes and popular stories of murder and woe.

"Do you think he loves his Margaret?" asked Olive, out of nowhere, as if Venetia, too, were thinking constantly about Master Choice.

"Olive! I do not know," laughed Venetia. "They are a strange couple. One wonders if she had the money, or the apothecary's practice he wanted. I love those marriages of inequality. They fascinate me. And they are touching. If a handsome man loves a plain old woman, we should all rejoice."

"You are a very unfeeling friend sometimes, Venetia," pouted Olive.

"What, because I do not say only what you want to hear? I am beginning to feel our experiment in Cosmetics has furnished you with a soft cheek and an even softer head."

Olive shrugged. "Tender sentiments and a quick, trusting heart—these are what every woman wishes to regain. Youth is not a bow one can wear in one's cap. Youth is not a fard or fucus slathered on one's face. It is an attitude or *point de vue*." She picked up a decorative parrot and stroked its tummy. "It is seeing the best in everyone. It is being pure, and sportive, and kittenly. It is," she added with conviction, "the feeling that everything matters very deeply."

Venetia laughed. "But nothing much matters very deeply."

Olive made an appalled face at the poupette in her hand.

"Darling, say that is not so! Look at these dollies, so nicely made, it is as if they can hear us speaking."

Venetia was not impressed. "I don't know if I was ever young in the sense that you describe, even when I was a child. I always kept my own counsel. But I know this for certain: I do not wish to lose my wisdom, if I have any, only the outward marks of it. I want a milk-sweet forehead, not a milk-sop disposition."

Olive exhaled as if to say, I have too many thoughts on this matter to know where to begin. "But think of a man's view. He would rather you were sweet in your disposition. A man would prefer you to be the soft, impressionable creature you were when you were a girl. He would like you to think him the handsomest man in the world, and to believe him the best—the only—prospect for your future happiness. Instead, he has you full of wise disappointment, because you have found out the limits of his talents, and his capacities . . ."

"But I love Kenelm more and ever more, and his oddities, his failings, even, are the very things I love the best. It touches me near tears sometimes to think of him fussing in his study over his Secret Work, and sending for bat droppings or some other strange recipe, excited and full of high seriousness, and yet nothing seems to come of it, year in, year out."

Olive shook her head. She counted this little speech of Venetia's heresy against husbands. "Endymion is far wiser than I, and he knows more than I will ever know. This is how marriage is, Venetia, and how it should be."

Venetia was silent for a moment, and this pleased Olive, who was not to know that Venetia was thinking of Endymion's ruddy face and curt manner, and wondering if he had become a kinder lover, or if he still brought to their marriage bed the tricks of the stews, as Olive had confided. Venetia said in an inwards voice: "A husband's heart is a little glass bauble, coloured like the rainbow, and we must be careful to preserve it from our deep or wounding thoughts, and keep it from cracking with the heats of our disappointments, and guard it safely. This is an act of care, Olive, not of innocence."

Olive thought how Venetia always seemed wiser than her, even though she was a year or two younger.

"Does he still hurt you?" asked Venetia.

"Oh, always. Whenever we couple. I am learning to like it. He never gives me real pain. It is only close to pain—a game, really."

Venetia thought of the canvases Endymion bought, of Europa ravished and the Sabine women and the Innocents being massacred, and all those naked, flaunted, terrified women, and she wondered if art sometimes fed the appetite, rather than the soul.

They went on together towards the apothecaries' stalls, where Olive asked after Master Choice—Venetia could not prevent her—and when they were told he never came to the Exchange, they browsed the pots of paint and fucus, the horse hair-pieces and the patches for pock-marked women to wear upon their cheeks. There were black spots and stars and moons and musical notes and fleurs-de-lis and even, look, they pointed out to one another with appalled laughter, a tiny coach and horses! They asked one another a question with their eyes, and then burst into laughter again.

"Not for Penelope," said Olive.

"Oh dear, no, not the coach and horses."

"She will need a great many of the plainer sort though, like as not," snorted Olive, with ill-disguised excitement.

Venetia looked at her reprovingly. "Penelope recovers apace," she said, setting a more sober tone for the conversation. "Or so I gather."

Venetia did not think Olive needed to know about the letters she had burned.

Chater caught up with them carrying their *pain-perdu*, which they retired to eat in the counting house, where they sat and restored their senses so they were ready for the next round of commerce. Whenever Chater left them for a moment, Olive tried to talk to Venetia about Choice, or his Wine, such as: "Do you fancy it makes your water smell horse-ish? Like a breed mare?"

"No," said Venetia firmly, to quieten her, although the suggestion stayed with her, and she came to the discomfiting realisation that the strong, healthy smell she had noticed on her skin and in her breath did carry something of the stable.

The New Exchange being a better sort of place, its stewards tried to keep the criers and ranters out, and yet still they came, and people liked their spectacle, and it made the whole place agreeably like a theatre, so they were kept to the open-air courtyard in the middle, shouting themselves hoarse and distributing handbills. There was an apothecary called Dr. Dafft, offering small samples of brown liquor, which Kenelm had told her was no more than angel water with sugar in it: "Cure of life, ladies, precious tincture, drink ye down and rise again."

There was the tall, white-clad figure of Lady Eleanor Davies, the baronet's daughter who claimed to be the Meek Virgin of the Apocalypse. She pronounced to the Bourse that "Popish Priest" was an anagram of "Her Piss Pot." The pamphlets she printed illicitly in Amsterdam were arranged for sale in front of her on a little rack, although she was not here for commerce, but to answer her Calling. Since the execution of her brother Mervyn Lord Touchet for crimes too terrible to mention—even in anagram—her will to prophecy had redoubled, and she did it compulsively, in public, pronouncing to whomsoever would listen. "The letters cannot lie!" Randomly consulting her Bible, she spoke in short bursts: "The Beast's days not more numerous. The people, rapt. The saviour, come. Blood in the river!"

Venetia stood alone in front of her listening, absorbed. She was attracted to millenarian intensities, and this woman's abstracted words struck her with a kind of rough poetry. Venetia felt her face framed by her hood as she stood there dreaming and as a snow-crystal settled on her cheek, she became lightly conscious that she was making a lovely picture, and so she stayed there for a second or two more, holding the pose, thinking that a very good painting of herself in this attitude could be taken, and that its title might be *A Lady Considers the Fate of Nations.*

Repelled by the sight of a well-born woman speaking in public, most people passed by Lady Eleanor Davies quickly, but there was a crowd around an upmarket mouse-catcher and his prize cat. "Mices, rats, cockerchaffes—she wants 'em. She's the fastest cat in the country, ladies. She's caught three dozen rats in a minute, by the bell. Your bed shall be your own again, ladies."

The thickest gathering made its object hard to see, but Venetia, taller than most of the crowd, glimpsed a small baby-haired woman with a round head like a moon-calf, standing on a box and declaiming in a high-pitched voice that was hard to hear. Venetia was about to move on to another entertainment when a handbill was passed to her:

A MISTRESS OF NATURAL PHYSICK

IS ARRIVED in LONDON bringing her Country Cure and Kind Ways to restore the stale and tired women of the Town as she finds are very much in need of her consultations and advisings. Ably assisted by her clever little friends she can read water, remedy sores and dispense to ladies for heartache and distemper, with jallops and fever-few.

Shee is an auctoritee in the matter of BEAUTY Having lately cured a very Noble woman (whom out of sweet deference we shall term only Lady V.D. née. S.) of middling years of her Sadness, and Having restored her to Her Husband. Which was no small matter, Hee having been long away at sea fighting battles and Shee having gathered much dust during that time.

Yet after consultations the Noblewoman has Lately been seen in Publick with her Adoring Husband and Shee restored to all her former glory. What cure has this Lady taken? Natural Physick onely and dispensed by your own MOTHER NATURE, who shall be found at the sign of the Thistle, beside St. Mary Axe, and who goes by the name of Mistress BEGG GURLEY. She shall not stay long in London, so seek her out without delay.

Printed at Powles by the Saracen for Master Thomas Leake

As Venetia read the handbill, she realised the small woman talking to the crowd was "Lady" Lily Trickle, and she made ready to sweep her up with furious anger and carry her kicking by the braid on her little mochado jacket and bring the Lord Chancellor down upon her—except as she elbowed through the crowd she saw that Lily Trickle, her supporting gentleman with his handbills and, yea, even the box she stood upon had vanished, leaving her spectators dumbfounded.

"She's with Queen Mab," said one woman.

"She's scuddled," said another. "Creditors maybe."

"Poor little mite," said a third, looking at the handbill. "Do you warrant she restored the great Lady to her husband, or no?"

Olive appeared, slipping her arm around Venetia's waist, and Venetia quickly folded the atrocious handbill away, and put it in her pocket. There was no need to magnify this problem by sharing it.

Venetia said she was bored now, and Olive loyally agreed she too was bored.

The only sign that anything was amiss was a tiny muscular movement across Venetia's brow, which repeated of its own accord, like a tick or spasm. Venetia was angry, and yet the subtle potion she drank disallowed anger, repelling it from her face, blocking its pathways and its impulses, so that it took a deeper route, making a vein in her forehead stand out like a river on a map, and giving her eyes a frozen glitter.

Determined to leave this place, she fought against the crowd, Olive following behind her as she elbowed past all the happy, animated faces that looked blindly through her, thinking of this pretty China-bowl or that Pipe-stand which they must have, even as they stepped aside and bowed to her as a lady of quality whom they half-recognised. But a few ladies nudged one other, hiding their smiles behind handkerchiefs as Venetia came by. They had read the handbill of Begg Gurley, and looked at her sideways, with awed and credulous fascination. Venetia smiled haughtily and ignored them, furious with Begg Gurley for her cheek, and the indignity it brought upon her. Yet as the whispers spread, and more people glanced up at her, and as the crowd parted before her, deep in her heart, Venetia loved the bitter-sweet attention, and recognised the tinder spark of infamy from her past, when she was called courtesan one day and sweet virgin the next, and halberdiers used to hold back the crowds so she could pass.

She wanted to send Begg Gurley and Lily Trickle to the stocks, to the ducking stool, if they could find a chair big enough for Begg, and one small enough for Lily. She wanted to see mouldy veg pounding upon their faces and their heads covered in egg yolk, and leprechaun familiars laughing at them and pinching them. And yet she knew it would never do to prosecute Begg Gurley; that would only bring the whole debacle out into the open, so that Kenelm and all his friends knew of it. This was what Francis Bacon meant when he wrote of the Marprelate tracts—"He that replieth, multiplieth." Complaining would only ensure everyone heard Begg's slander, and found out about her other Viperish secrets besides. Instead, she would give Begg Gurley and Lily Trickle a scare; without a doubt, she would. Perhaps she would send one of Dr. Choice's worms to their lodgings at the sign of the Thistle. She would slip the live worm into a velvet purse, with a sickly sweet letter tagged to it, so they thought they had a rich jewel for a present, until they put their hand inside and touched a livid, hissing coil.

But for the moment, Venetia would live up to the attention, the gossip, the prurient looks, the half-sniggers. The handbill was out, escaped to the four corners of the Bourse, and she must assume that everyone would read it. Even Aletheia Howard, whom she noticed over in the eastern alcove, involved in tough negotiations over a set of Porcelain.

She looked across at Venetia and squinted at her, trying to work out what had changed about her. Aletheia had the eye; she could distinguish Titian's own work from that of his studio assistants. She could discern hair-cracks in walnut wood boxes, and she knew how Greek ikons were faked. Today, she thought Venetia was executed not by the Master's hand, but a close acolyte's. She was well done, indeed; but a little *too* well done.

Venetia consoled herself: this outrageous handbill had come about because she was herself again. Begg's chestnut-munching mouth must have hung wide open when she heard the talk of Venetia's restored beauty—and the old hag believed, no doubt, that she had managed to cure her with the power of pattering fairy feet and rose-petal rain. Ha!

Venetia threw back her head and walked about the market as if she were on the stage of a masque. Her face assumed that expression of utter thoughtlessness that had served her so well. She sucked her cheeks and tossed her head. She would show neither pleasure nor displeasure, so she would, in time, come to resemble a China-cup, or a Sandal-wood box, and she would be traded, her name called up and down the market, people clamouring for more of her, and handbills flying with her name on them, and yet she would keep consignments of herself just scarce enough, delaying them by means of continental blockades and wars, so when she came to market, she was much in demand. And she would walk back and forth, advertising herself, and there would be no end to her and no beginning, and she would be stacked as high as the hollow China Dogges on this very table in front of her.

"Madam, shall you buy this Dogge—on his neck a bell which rings?"

She was a very good China Dogge, because she was shiny, and she had glossy hair, and a sweet nose, and people wanted her, and because they wanted her she had a price. Otherwise she was useless. Was she not? But she could inspire people to part with their money, and therefore she was not useless. She shook her rattling head. Certainly she was not useless to Begg Gurley and Lily Trickle and—she checked the poxy handbill again—Thomas Leake, whomsoever he may be, the pouch-penny swine.

Venetia smiled at a pretty young woman, imagining that she knew her. She was her friend Anne Somerset from the court of James. But no, Anne was now mother of six boys, and living in the country. And then she spied a poor little gentlewoman with a rolling gait—Penelope. Was it? Yes. Venetia felt herself coming back to life, brimming with happiness to see her good old Pen, and she swept through the crowd towards her.

As she came close, she saw that Penelope was thinner, with a tougher expression in her eyes. She was wearing a mob cap as usual but it did not sit right, and Venetia suspected that her hair had suffered. She was pale but she was not pocked—it must have been a mild attack of the sickness. The King had also been spared, two years ago, when he sustained barely a mark. Sometimes the scourging angel's wings brushed gently. Standing with Penelope was Lettice, and when they saw Venetia coming, the pair of them stiffened in unison, and Venetia could see that they had become close.

"Pen, my dear," called Venetia, who reached out towards her delightedly, but stopped short of wanting to kiss her.

Penelope smiled weakly, and Lettice gathered her arm around her, like a swan protecting a cygnet.

"Thank God for your recovery," said Venetia, crossing herself.

"Oh, she shows an interest now," murmured Lettice, almost audibly.

A juggler tried to captivate them with his spectacle, but Lettice and Venetia shooed him away brusquely. Another man tried to give Lettice a handbill, and Venetia seized the handbill, tore it in half, threw it on the cobbles, and ground her heel upon it, just in case.

"I was laid low and plightful for two weeks," said Penelope. "And then it was over."

"She needed very careful nursing," said Lettice.

"'Tis mighty fine to be out again," said Penelope, smiling weakly.

"I sat with her night and day," said Lettice, shrugging. "I do not say that I have any feeling for nursing, I do not, it was simply a matter of my friend in need, so what could I do? Of course I helped her and I did it gladly—we had so many conversations, so many long discourses of debate—"

"The time passed very slowly," said Penelope.

"Did you get the tansy I sent? It was out of season," said Venetia.

"I had several cures sent me, dear," said the invalid, evasively.

"Penny was too sick to pay great attention to which token came from whom," said Lettice witheringly, gathering her pocket up on its drawstring, beginning to gently guide Penelope away.

Not in her whole life had Venetia ever heard anyone call Penelope "Penny." She was either Pen or Penelope. Venetia felt the blue vein begin to stand out in her forehead.

"Did I mention I sat with her night and day?" said Lettice. "But now she must rest, because this is too tiring for her, who is weak as a babe!" And with that Penelope and Lettice walked off, not, Venetia noticed, to the seats, but into the throng of the shopping, where they promenaded in front of the cats in cages, and the jailed canaries, communicating, by their posture and carriage, that they had been done a grievance, while Lettice pretended to enjoy the market entertainments, yet looked back over her shoulder every so often, to check if Venetia was watching.

The sadness, even distress, which she might ordinarily have felt after such a confrontation rose within her, and yet it did not blossom. It was blocked and disallowed by the new smoothness of her complexion, and having been denied expression, the sentiment withered and dwindled within her, so that standing there on the cobbles of the now-darkening New Exchange, Venetia experienced that phenomenon later observed by medical science, which tells us that those who cannot grimace feel less discomfort, and those who cannot frown, less vexation.

Tears were more slippery, since those who cried were usually eased and purged, and yet tears could redouble a feeling, too—in fact, the very passage of wetness down the cheeks could make one feel sad, as Venetia knew from experience, having noticed that the drops of sweet almond oyl she applied under her eyes at bedtime left a maudlin track. So soft and suggestible are we, she thought—men and women both—and there is so much about us still unknown, and yet people adventure into foreign lands. I would sooner go to the edge of a woman's tear duct, she thought, as to the great Cataracts of the Nile, to know the nerves behind a flayed man's face, before I knew Madagascar, or the moon.

Her serene expression allowing her thoughts to roam, Venetia smiled agreeably as Lady Aletheia Howard tapped her on the arm with her fan and bid her visit her at Tart Hall again, which pleased Venetia, and yet she still pondered this new, tight little alliance between Lettice and Pen, deciding it would probably last until Penelope recovered her strength. It was a passing inconvenience. Not a dram, not a scruple of guilt did Venetia feel for not tending to Penelope during her illness.

Venetia curtsied to the good folk who were still waiting to talk to her, and gathered her footsoldiers for their departure, interrupting Olive, who was on the point of buying a sprigged garter, and causing Chater to break off his animated conversation with Aletheia Howard's chaplain, and thus escorted, she sailed out of the arena, leaving the China Dogges with their eyes bulging and the caged canaries all agog. As candelabra in the likeness of a winged Athena were lit to keep trade turning into the night, Venetia quit the marketplace in triumph, all eyes upon her—and she had spent not one penny from her purse.

> "A clock face looks like magic—till I look on the other side and I see wheels, retorts, counterfoils . . . That every effect whatsoever must have of pure necessity some cause. We need not have recourse to a Daemon or Angel in such difficulties."
>
> A Late Discourse by Sir Kenelm Digby Made in a Solemn Assembly of Nobles and Learned Men at Montpelier, Touching the Cure of Wounds by the Powder of Sympathie, 1664

Kenelm was at his studies, drawing up a curriculum for his sons' education: a simple list of topoi taken from John Dee's Preface to Euclid. He did not want to be an overbearing father, like Montaigne's, who had made a project of his son by talking only Latin to him, till his teens, and teaching all their servants Latin also so they might not break the spell. An irony: while Montaigne's Latin was his first tongue, his writings in French are all one wants to read. To wit, a gentle course of study for his boys:

Zographie—painting, sculpture, architecture, &c. and their symbolical signification. The story of Zeuxis, and his murals of grapes, so well done the birds pecked at them.

The feather quill in Sir Kenelm's hand fluttered lightly, longing to fly again.

Trochilike—the properties of circular motion. Its use in wheels, mills and mining.
Helicosophie—concerning spirals, cylinders and cones.

Did all good fathers write a curriculum? Sir Kenelm had never had a father, so he could not judge.

Pneumatithmie—the study of pumps, air or water.
Hydragogie—or how to conduct water uphill.

To be sure, thought Sir Kenelm, his youngest son could not yet walk, quite, but he wished him to be native in these subjects—a child mechanician.

Menadrie—the science of moving weights by means of pulleys.
Hypogesiodie—underground measurements and surveys.

But then the son must be a scholar, too—so why not inculcate him in lightning-writing at a young age?

Brachigraphy—note-taking at speed, writing but one letter-sign for each word.
Horometrie—the art of measuring time by clocks and dials. As a boy learns to read a clock, so should he learn its workings at the same time. Therefore he has no Occluded beliefs, no Superstitions about Clocks, and knows that the soul of a clock, its animus, comes from the manipulation of weights.

Some had it that a child should not be loved, should not be celebrated nor encouraged, should be invested with no hopes, should be given no character, and no familial likenesses pointed out, no birthdays celebrated, no father–son matching outfits commissioned, and no astrological charts drawn up, because the risk was too great.

Navimaturgike—the art of navigation.

A child was not definitely of this earth before it was six. It could be recalled to heaven at any moment. But Kenelm did not believe in keeping his heart safely in a strong box . . .

Stratarithmetrie—the disposal of armies and soldiers in geometrical figures.

The boys would enjoy that study. It was important for them to be manly; scholarly, but not weak. Tomorrow young Kenelm was to be britched; he was six years old, full ready to cast off his baby's coats. The tailor had put together his first outfit, themed like a page, and to be delivered on the morrow. Young Kenelm would sleep no more in the nursery and be no more a mother's darling. He was now old enough to be out of danger.

A book tipped off the corner of Sir Kenelm's desk, and was drawn to its nearest soul-mate, which was the tiled floor, stand-in for the earth, to which the book, like all heavy things, longed to return. If it were a paper dart, and had more in common with the clouds, it might have gone upwards.

Statike—demonstration of the causes of the heaviness and lightness of all things.

The idea that there was an encircling and immanent power, a force called Gravity, by which God kept us bounded to this round and revolving world—now that, he knew, was fanciful talk.

He shifted his papers together and put them under the dead weight of a new-plucked dandelion.

Cosmographie—the whole and perfect description of the lunarie and sub-lunarie spheres.

A baby bumblebee bashed into his window, causing the glass to shatter.

Thaumaturgike—the art of marvels. The dove of wood, made to fly, peck and scratch. Vulcan's self-movers (with secret wheels). The iron fly of Nuremberg. Fludd's dragon.

He paused, and crossed out the entry *Thaumaturgike*. He did not want his sons to study this topic. Marvels had fascinated men of his father's generation, but their quality these days was so poor that they were now like trifling toys. Tools, plans, schemes—these were what his sons would take to Virginia and the other plantations.

Nanobiotechnology—

Sir Kenelm set down his pen, because he could hear a commotion in the hall. He went out of his study, and through the hall onto the stairs, where he found Venetia crying, because baby John had fallen on his head, and young Kenelm crying, and running around, angrily, protesting he had not caused the fall, and baby John howling his head off.

Seeing that no visible damage had been done, and that everything was in reasonable order, Kenelm shut his door against the noise and went back to resume and complete his syllabus for the boys. But when he came back he could not remember what was meant by *Nanobiotechnology*. It was—it was . . . He looked in his book again, but even John Dee seemed not to have it clearly in his Preface to Euclid.

Endymion confided once that he rarely went home, in order to avoid the constant havoc of family. Sir Kenelm felt that men should not be interrupted so much in times to come. Men would each have small marvels of perpetual motion in their pockets, like watches, which managed every interruption. These would replace the man in urgent communications, perhaps even impersonate him. Yes, in future times, men's thinking would be respected as much as their sleeping. In time to come, men would really be able to concentrate.

Mary Tree: 217 Miles Travelled

IF I HAD not come to Gayhurst, I would not have met Annie Braxton, and if I had not met Annie Braxton, I would never have stood in Lady Venetia's bedroom as I do now, looking at her glass gallypots and potions, her fine bed-drapes, her curling tongs. Annie goes in to dust and ope the windows once a week, and I have command of her dust-clouts today. The house is shut up, Sir Kenelm is abroad, the Lady Venetia is absent, all my long journey here was in vain, and Sir Richard is no more healed than before, and yet I feel strangely peaceful, as I wipe the motes off her bedposts, and shake out the sleepful hollows of her pillows. We can none of us do more than try in this world.

Annie calls from the closet that I should lie on the bed, to feel the feathers, but I cannot do that. Nor can I lean and look at myself in the mirror that sits in front of her dressing stool. Once you know what you are, you should live according to that knowledge, not against it. Father Jonas told us that some are saved and some are not, and there is little one can do about it. I am not sure—but Annie is calling again. She says that I should paint my face like a lady with fucus from the blue glass gallypot.

Annie Braxton, you are a minks indeed!

We both are laughing, and yet I think she has another purpose. I shake out the counterpane and watch the wingèd cavaliers of the air charging about. I think Annie wants me to cover my Mark, so I can see myself as I would be without it. Perhaps I should then learn to cover it with lead-white fucus every day, so it were only a slight raised welter on my cheek, not a liver-coloured botch where my Maker erred. But then I would still be botched, and only patched.

Annie comes through holding very carefully a feathered hat from Lady Venetia's wardrobe, that I might see the blue crewel work and the oily beauty of the dyed feather in the light, shining blue-purple. It must suit a lady such as her so well. And yet she has not taken it with her. Perhaps it is too good to take, I whisper, but Annie says it is more likely forgotten. When your life is full of splendour and love as hers must be, you take these things lightly, I suppose. I reach to stroke the feather but Annie pulls it away, for fear it spoils to my touch.

For all my imaginings of Venetia's life, I never expected she would have so many tools and instruments for her beauty—nippers, lotions, rose-and-sage-waters . . . Those globes that look like suet, Annie says, are Bologna balls, for the softening of her hands. I little thought her hands would be harsh! At the back of her bed where I am dusting I find a hidey-hole containing a little hidden looking glass—which I run the duster over carefully, holding its face down, so it does not bite me—and a thick-lidded pot, sticky with dribbles. I wipe it clean, then twist off the lid. Inside, the oil has pooled as from a marrow bone, but the pot is full of feathery-looking mineral twists, and the smell of vinegar and sulphur and metal—tin?—is harsh as a slap. My nose stings with the whiff of it.

"Plume-alum, it is," whispers Annie. "Takes the skin almost off the back of your hand and makes your eyes leak. She wipes it all about her face, though, fancy."

We are sitting on my lady's bed, and in the rich green and yellow light of the leaded casement, it is almost like being underwater, or in a shady dell. Annie looks at me, and for a second, I think that she is going to take a scoop on her finger and rub it into my cheek. Instead, I dash the lid on and screw it safely down. Better to keep the mischief in the pot than let it out to turn my head with hopefulness.

I get up directly and fetch the clout bag. There is so much else for Annie and me to do, for chambermaids must be washermaids and waiting maids when the house is shut up, and if they are to tolerate me here awhile as I wait for the London coach next week, I must be helpful to the household, as I well know.

NEWS FROM THE SERRAGLIO

A discourse on the Foul Foreign habit, now affecting our Fine Ladies

"Turn away mine eyes from beholding vanity, and quicken thou me in thy way."

Psalms 119:37

"They shall take up serpents; and if they drink any deadly thing, it shall not hurt them; they shall lay hands on the sick, and they shall recover."

Mark 16:18, *King James Bible*

Eve was the first to be tempted, and Shee was not the last. It is common for Womenkind ever to be practising Washings, Annointings, Fomentations, Tinctures and Frictions upon their faces. Even a Godly Woman washes her Person. But some Women be now Painting, Colouring, Nipping and Applying False staining of Spanish Paper, viz. Beetle Paint, to Mislead Menfolk and affect a Modest Blush. Save yr. Opprobrious Cries, for there is WORSE.

It is the Duty of this Author to report that many Ladies of a great age, often of almost thirty years, with Crump-shoulders, Crack'd Cheeks and Gobble-teeth, have lately appeared in a new form, as: Virtuous Young Maidens. Their Frontages unseemly Smooth, they Glide like Dancers from a Turk's Harem. The Cause of this Scandal is none other than a Libation or Tonic dispensed by a Physician in Fenchurch Street, where his premises beneath the sign of the Star are discernible by the sight of many Fine Ladies going in and out of his door leading many to wonder what is the cause of his Popularity. Alas, perversions as, the Iron Bodice, the Bumbost that gives Shape to Withered Haunches, the Spliced Cuttings of Other Women's Hair and all such False Representations—these dissatisfy our Finest Ladies who ought to be Serving their King and Husbands in Humble Duty, but are compell'd by Vanity to Please their Lords another Way and seek out a Drink which some say is made of the Entrails of Vipers, cook'd. Be warned, good people. So like the Creeping Adder the Ladies make themselves Unnaturally Anew. The Wine is feared to be a dangerous Intoxicant of the Male Spirit. Mark ye, all those who read, what is Here Expressed.

—The Author—

Lancelot Choice turned over the handbill, shaking lightly. He daubed his eyes, which had put forth a crocodile tear.

"My dear," he said to Margaret, "you are a mighty cunning woman, but this, this . . ."

He was beside himself, convulsed.

"How much did the writing and printing of this cost you?"

"Nowt," she said. "The cover charge for readers is one penny, so the cost is eaten up outright."

"Ach," he said. "Such craft she has!"

He put his hand over his belly, which ached from laughing. "We shall never want for custom now. 'The ladies make themselves unnaturally anew,' indeed. The prosperity of our endeavour is guaranteed."

Syringes and Lemons

When will you pay me?
Say the Bells of Old Bailey

AS FOUR O'CLOCK struck, Venetia was leaning gracefully over the prie-dieu, thinking of all the combinations that made twenty-two when the ruff was at stake: two tens plus ace plus one; a Tom and two Queens; a Tom, a Tib and a Queen . . . It made her mouth water, yes actually water, to think of holding the cards.

I do not know
Says the great bell of Bow

The bells made her conscious time was passing, and the day darkening, and yet Kenelm had not noticed how perfectly her pale bosom curved over the neckline of her dress, contrasting with the tightness of her waist. She sneaked a hopeful look at him, and even touched his foot with hers, but his eyes were so sweetly closed, and she knew this was his one moment of peace in a busy day, so she desisted, and said a little prayer for him, asking that he might be blessed with a better appreciation of her beauty, as Chater droned on, speaking so inwardly that she fancied the Holy Spirit lodged somewhere inside his nose.

"Yea, though I walk in the valley of the shadow of death, I will fear no evil . . ."

Chater watched Sir Kenelm's lips moving with the psalm. He was triumphant they still prayed together as a family, despite Kenelm's conversion. As he spoke, Chater imagined leading Sir Kenelm, by the hand, through the vaporous vale, and then showing him where they might lie safely together upon green rushes, in the care of the Lord.

Kettles and Pans
Say the Bells of St. Ann's

One by one, the churches of the city agreed the time, each saying their piece, like voices in a conversation. Only the Puritan bells sounded the hour plainly, without any pealing. Kenelm loved this multiplicity of bell-ringing in the city—the peaceful capital of the only peaceful country in the Old World. The bells spoke to him of religious toleration, not yet achieved, but not far off, he prayed. Let a thousand different birds sing God's name.

Brick-bats and Tiles
Say the Bells of St. Giles

The peals reached Fenchurch Street, scattering the birds of the air, and telling the vipers in their pits that their prey was soon to be delivered. As the bolt of the cellar rammed home, disturbing their warm solitude, they readied themselves silently, flicking their mouse-decoying tails by atavistic instinct, as if they were still in the fields, while Margaret Choice trod unsteadily down the cellar stairs, bearing her tray of chopped rat-meat.

Fillers and Needles
Say the Bells of St. Stephen's

Four o'clock arrived at Westminster, and anyone looking into the lamplit lower window of Tart Hall, as they were passing through St. James's, would have seen Aletheia Howard, sitting in her high-backed chair smoking her pipe with an inscrutable expression, and Olive next to her on the divan, rosy-cheeked and enraptured to the point of seeming idiocy, and both of them watching the figure of a gentleman, or at least a well-dressed man, who stood before them with his back to the window, gesticulating roundly, and holding up, for demonstration, first the delicate tubular slough of a snake's skin, and then a vial that looked like burnt rubies.

Olive was not given to betrayals, as such, but she was liable to forget old agreements that did not fit her new passions. Her intelligence, which was considerable, was firmly in the service of her feelings, which made her more dangerous than a less intelligent person. She was highly persuasive, utterly convinced by her version of events, and considered herself one of the most scrupulous people she knew.

She was unashamed, therefore, by her decision to introduce Lancelot Choice to Aletheia Howard. Yes, she had been encouraged to keep him secret, but she could not resist the double boon of pleasing Aletheia, while spending more time with Mr. Choice. He was so personable and his cure so efficacious—what harm could it do to extend their circle of confidence to include Aletheia? Besides, Aletheia had worn her down, prodding Olive for her beauty secrets with the force that her character and degree conferred, until Olive gave way. Aletheia had not yet thanked her as such, only given a long snort of satisfaction, and called her "good girl"; Lancelot Choice, moreover, merely treated this engagement as another job of work, rather than a special favour, but it was, she felt sure, a matter of time, before he saw her differently.

Syringes and Lemons
Say the Bells of St. Clement's

By the darkening river, at Blackfriars, in the studio of Van Dyck, a paid model wearing Venetia's clothes had been sitting with her left arm suspended in a graceful arc across her belly since noon. She gratefully heard St. Clement Danes strike a third hour, and hoped a fourth was coming. The Digby double portrait must be nearly done. Her arm's posture was intended to express marital fertility, but it was arse-work to maintain. She would be glad to get out of this horse-piss-stinking gown before dark. She was chosen for the elegance of her wrists, not her mind—that much was certain. Her long tapering fingers were seen on almost every Van Dyck beauty, and she slept in kid-leather gloves lined with suet.

The painter, who was not Van Dyck, but his hired fabric master, hummed as he worked; Van Dyck was next door with a new client, always too busy to paint anything but the preliminary under-sketches, the faces and the final flourishes. Margaret Lemon, Van Dyck's mistress, was pacing about the private side of the studio with her gown unlaced, chomping from a pot of pickled cherries. She ignored the paid model but stopped to watch the sleeves and kirtle of Venetia's dress fill out.

"Dainty work," she said, looking at Venetia's likeness closely, chewing, her head on one side. Feeling as if Venetia was watching her in return, Margaret Lemon ceased to chomp so noisily, and straightened her back, although she did not feel the need to fasten up her bodice, because in Venetia's example there was grace, but not correctness.

Absorbed in his work, the fabric master built upon Van Dyck's under-sketch with washes of azurite and smalt-blue, creating with utmost care the effect of casually falling fabric, glowing cloth which appeared to pour in random folds from Venetia's waist. It was the master fabric painter's job to ensure the viewer's eye was never drawn to the fabric, never questioned it, but only looked beyond it to the subject's face; he knew he was little better than a skilled scenery painter. And yet, breathing slowly, holding four paintbrushes in one fist, he was deep in the bliss of creation as he romped across soft peaks of sateen and wallowed in deep, blue-shaded valleys . . . Van Dyck would never know this suspended world, this peace, this playfulness, for he worked always on a knife's-edge.

Here comes the candle to light you to bed.

Dang!

The last bell in the city struck four.

Here comes the chopper to chop off your head.

At Tart Hall, Lancelot Choice prepared a soupçon of Viper Wine for Lady Howard.

Venetia crossed herself and prayed to win at cards that night.

The rat-meat fell into the adder pens, and the pouncing jaws began.

Lady Howard wiped the winedrops from her smiling, bloodied chin.

Van Dyck's studio boy lit a lamp, killing the daylight, and the fabric painter surrendered his brushes.

The palace of Whitehall, that august labyrinth of two thousand rooms, resembled a great hive or nest, built with blind diligence and no design. Each generation added their own improvements, so brick-built chambers extruded off the old stone halls like Gothic red growths, fashionable red telescopic chimneypots sprang out of old eaves, fingering the sky, and all was supported by half-timbered council chambers put up temporarily two hundred years ago.

The Queen's Garderobe was formerly a Council Chamber, where feudal lords once carved up the kingdom, and sleepy ministers scratched through endless dispatches, but its pews were now given over to the spectacle of the Queen's habiliments, where she was dressed in ceremonies of long and stifling intimacy.

It was important for every lady-in-waiting to attend, as no one wanted to give the impression they had been uninvited, and the Queen liked to have massed ranks of assumed friends around her. She spent a good deal of time changing in a withdrawing room, however, and there was no denying that the event would have been extremely boring for those ladies sitting in the upper tier of the chamber, had they not a million matters to talk of: friendship, and the hidden causes of things; the nature of their dreams, the habits of their servants, and the sayings of their children; of great occasions past and forthcoming, and, most of all, of who had said what, to whom, and what they really meant by it. The tone of their conversation was quick, informative and frank—at least, on most matters.

When the Queen emerged from her private room, many of the ladies held prospective glasses up to their straining eyes, the better to see her fashions, the pattern of florets and lozenges stamped in hot indentations across the cloth, or the pinking about the cuffs. But as the session wore on, her ladies turned these prospective glasses to other uses.

"I fancy Dame Digby has a brand-new face," said little Anne Ogilvy, slowly, glued to the sight of her.

"Cosmetic improvements are of no interest to me," said Belinda, Lady Finch, trying to take her glasses back from Anne.

"She does not exercise her face as much as she used to. It seems almost . . . immobile," said Anne, holding her ground, and focusing the glasses with her thumb.

"Smiling is plebeian," said Lady Finch, "and frouncing the brows together gives a woman a mannish look. I have long perfected the art of an immobile countenance. Give me back my glasses, dear."

"And yet there is something new-born about her, which I cannot place . . ." continued Anne.

Straining with barely contained impatience, Lady Finch's face was far from immobile.

At that moment, the Queen walked out in a stiff silk of butter-yellow, and the ladies clapped. The Queen appeared not to hear them, as she was caught up in an enquiry over the dress's hem length. Conversations around the chamber continued at a peaceable hush.

Venetia turned away from general view, inclining like a heavy-headed lily towards some confidence from her companion, Lucy Hay.

"And now she's occluded, and I shall see nothing of her," fumed Lady Finch. "It is all to the good, for I take no interest in the complexions of Catholics, be they never so fair."

She remembered that the Queen was Catholic, and said quickly, "I jest, of course. *Une blague*, ha ha."

"It is a shame and a pity when good women use medicines to make themselves new faces," said Mistress Daubigny, joining their conversation. This put Olive Porter in the middle of them, and without the least hesitation, she agreed with Mistress Daubigny.

"Oh, the abuse of cosmetics is a terrible shame."

All the ladies turned to look at Olive, and her tightly tweaked cheeks, and her dilated pupils, and her unnaturally smooth skin—and none of them said a word.

"I don't know anyone who does it," continued Olive, to fill the silence. "I would not myself, certainly."

They were kind ladies, and they all ignored her.

"It is indeed a great pity to meddle with one's face," said Lady Finch, squinting through her spyglass as hard as she could.

"It is terribly sad," said Mistress Daubigny, leaning dangerously far over the balcony, the better to see how sad it was.

"I think her neck is lovelier than ever," said Anne, unguardedly.

Indignantly, the ladies in possession of glasses scrutinised Venetia's neck. Intuitively aware of the attention, Venetia turned her face to the gallery, to indulge those who watched her, and display her most serene countenance. She fanned herself, looking upwards with a contemplative expression she copied from a carved Madonna.

"Oh," sighed Lady Finch.

"Ah," sighed Mistress Daubigny.

"Ha!" said Anne, with youthful excitement. "I told you!"

"I see what you mean," murmured Mistress Daubigny.

There was silence while all absorbed as much detail of Venetia's physiognomy as they could.

"There is not so much gold in the world that would persuade me to take whatever cure she has taken," said Lady Finch.

"There is no cure can do that. She is younger and more beautiful than I remembered, that is all," said Mistress Daubigny.

"Pah!" said Aletheia Howard, coming back from what she called "taking the air" outside (by which everyone knew she had been smoking her pipe). "Lady Digby has been at her husband's cabinet of medicine, I wouldn't doubt. She's married to an alchemist who supplies her with the *ultimo*, the finest treatment."

"What treatment would that be?"

"How so, what treatment?"

"Do tell."

"Indeed," said Aletheia, savouring this moment, "the one they say

'Ripens Wives.'" She smiled mischievously, and stroked the spot on her chin where the wine had dribbled.

"Ripens Wives?"

"Oh, there are plenty of them about. The ripening wives. They are everywhere!" She tried to catch Olive's eye, to wink at her, but Olive had busied herself with reading her prayerbook. Aletheia continued: "No, come, come—Ripens Wives is an anagram for Viper's Wine, which is her new beauty cure."

"It sounds like a most dangerous tonic, and I should have none of it," said Mistress Daubigny, her glasses still focused upon Venetia.

"Nor I, never, no, not a drop," said Lady Finch, also looking intently at Venetia, like a feline at prey.

Then one by one, they all said to Lady Howard, urgently, as if they were very keen to protect themselves from this dangerous cure, "Tell me again. What is it called?"

It was the last Levee before Christmas, and the Queen's costumes were grander than usual, and she now emerged wearing a dress of silver and gold, with a rebato collar, and yet the spy-glasses of all the ladies were focused not on the Queen's high collar, but in the wrong direction entirely.

"It must be a most choice decoction."

"It's the drink of choice, my dear."

"Indeed—Choice on Fenchurch Street."

"Choice would be a fine thing."

Choice, Choose, Chosen. A bird, a turtle dove loosed or lost from the royal cages, flapped around the hall, struggling to get out. Its beating wings against the high ceiling created such an atmosphere of distraction in the Chamber, that much delay and chatter followed, and the whispers of "Vein Wiper" and "View Repines" and "Ripen Wives" chased one another across the benches, as the letters were rearranged in the slipstream of its wings, and word continued to spread until the only male present in the room, the young Prince Royal, burst into loud tears, and the Queen's Levee was adjourned.

Inigo Jones's Motion Pictures

"These shows are nothing else but pictures with light and motion."

Inigo Jones on the court masques, 1632

CHRISTMAS WAS COMING apace, and Lucy Bright wrote to Venetia asking her to attend a rehearsal for the Queen's Twelfth Night Masque. Venetia went unmasked, wearing her silver slippers and her gladdest attitude. The court had removed to Somerset House for the holidays, and the north courtyard at Whitehall was like a builders' yard, all sawdust and commotion, with stage flats and props stacked against the fountains. Lucy Bright was in the courtyard, watching carters unloading a vast tree made of wire and silk. She came to greet Venetia as soon as she saw her carriage, and took her on a promenade of the set.

The palace, seat of power in England, was urgently busy: a joiner was making a chariot without any back, and two set-makers painting wooden trumpets. A queue of apprentice stagehands were watching a demonstration on the art of gently agitating false trees, so their silk leaves rustled as if in a breeze. From a wagon came bales of flocked azure sea.

Stepping inside the Banqueting Hall, the ladies found it semi-dark, the windows blacked out. A stage had been erected at one end, with rigging, ropes and a ladder 40 foot high. A huge consignment of boxes stood in the middle of the hall. "These are full of pink-coloured glass," said Lucy, opening one and holding up a rose-tinted glass candle-shield. "They will create the stage-effect of dawn. The effect will last perhaps three minutes, but the cost is almost a thousand pounds."

They exchanged looks. The cost sickened them both. It was wasteful, and wrong, and Venetia loved it.

"Worth every penny," she said.

Venetia opened a box containing mirrored candle-shields. "These are very like the ones we used for the Masque of Blackness," she said. "They caused a sudden *éclaircissement* when the deity appeared—Queen Anna was quite blinded by her own entrance."

"The mirror shields are another essential expense," sighed Lucy. "Though why they must buy new ones for each masque, I do not know. People hear the words 'for the Queen,' and pull a price out of the air."

"The Queen says the Medici have masques six times a year," said Venetia.

"And Valois, and Lorraine," said Lucy. The names were current and powerful, and simply saying them conferred sagacity.

"Ah yes, I have brought my gown," said Venetia, holding up a basket with a blaze of Ultramarine folded in it, her old treasure, her famous gown, now quite shabby, but highly coloured as a kingfisher. Lucy Bright had asked her to bring it for the Queen, who was considering a bright blue dress for the masque.

"Of course," said Lucy, taking the basket from her in a demonstration of her superior authority at court. Dressing the Queen's body was a matter of such reverential importance, governed by vast and elaborate protocol, that Lucy did not thank Venetia for bringing her dress, but Venetia thanked Lucy for allowing her to bring it.

Sweeping up the shallow stairs in their skirts, they climbed onto the stage. Even in the half-light, the Banqueting Hall was wonderful from this perspective, a model of Palladian style, representing a kingdom of order, proportion and symmetry, where everyone had their fixed place. To Venetia's eyes, its elegance connoted virtue. She felt safe and at home here; ready to shine.

"Master Jones, come down! I have Lady Digby," called Lucy.

Inigo Jones was atop the stage-ladder, hanging a smooth wood-slatted circular object from the gantry. He waved decorously. "Ladies, excuse me, I am raising a Harvest moon. If I desist now I will be eclipsed."

"You were eclipsed long ago," boomed Ben Jonson, lumbering out from behind a plaster urn, his big black smock pulled down over his tummy, his hands full of handwritten scribbled papers.

When he saw Venetia he began, as ever, to extemporise a new panegyric for her:

"Half the world in thy retinue would be too few

And leave the odd in war against the even

Competing to be the first to see thy face each morn . . ."

Venetia knew this one. He was re-using the same rhymes from long ago.

"As it slid gently off from heaven?"

"Yes, yes, that'll do," said Ben, closing his eyes for a time as if in pain or dull remembrance. "Now I must off and finish this play, Venetia," he said, shuffling towards the wings. "I've a play to put out, you know. Yes, me—" He broke off into one of his lyrics:

"Me, the tardie, cold

unprofitable chattel, fat and old

who hardly doth approach

but to break chairs or crack a coach . . ."

He spoke almost entirely in his own verses now. Since his recent palsy-the-wits, conversation had become impossible. He talked in old bricks, laid together end to end. His brain was become the maggoty, abbreviated book of his own quotations.

He kissed his hand to Venetia, a gesture he fancied was more winning than it was, and turned to the wings, keen to give the impression he was busy. Venetia followed after him, whispering urgently so that Lucy Bright might not hear her.

"Let me have a pretty part, dear Ben, and not be made to represent Night, or a hag, or a spider?" She cultivated, as ever, a charming tone of speech, but the smile in her voice was as unnatural as the painted wooden oranges on the scenery behind her.

"Night?" asked Ben, jowls swinging with confusion. With one eye bulging, he peered into the shadows of the wings, looking for his help. "Where's William?"

A young man was sitting on the prompt stool, and Venetia guessed this was William Davenant, who was assisting Ben with his writing these days.

He was wearing a collar in the style of his supposed illustrious father, and his hair parted in the middle, too, like the portrait in the First Folio, which struck Venetia as a pretty trick.

Instinctively positioning herself so that her hair caught the light that spilled from the stage, while her face was held in the soft shadows of the wings, she breathed deeply, and Davenant looked up at her. She let him have one of her most candid smiles.

"Is this him, at last? The young pretender. I have heard much talk of this Davenant who is to be crowned with a wreath of swan-feathers."

He was holding a quill pen, which she tapped with her finger. Davenant leaped up, guessing who she was.

"He has the inky mark upon him," she said, looking at his fingers' ends, which were bestained with black. "'Tis a pox can only be cured with candles and much parchment. I'll warrant he was born with an inkwell in place of a navel. If only we had use of this Davenant in days gone by, when we were playing festivals outdoors, all summer long, and especially when we made the Tethys Festival. It greatly wanted wit, Master Jonson being out of favour at the time—or was he in Scotland? No matter; they are the same. So the writing fell to Master Daniel, and he struggled and he strained and in the end we had few lines, but much music . . ."

She indulged Davenant with gossip about legendary masques and their writers, and he lapped it up, impressed by her experience, cajoled by her warmth and familiarity, and yet how grand she was, how grand! She made him feel he was nothing and something all at once.

When Lucy Bright called out for her, Venetia's work in the wings was already done.

"Write me some lovely lines, dearheart," she cried as she left the writers. Both thought she was talking to themselves alone.

"Dear hart of the forest . . ." Jonson began; Davenant gave her a comprehending look and a deep bow.

"Make them good lines, won't you?"

"Lines? Lines are of no account," interrupted a loud, disembodied voice that was Inigo Jones in the gantry, using a megaphone. "These shows are nothing else but pictures with light and motion."

He started the special effects with a signal. Hot white dots danced across the backdrop, then focused into concentric circles, as a mechanician in the pit played with candles and a mirror. "Spectacle and motion pictures—this is what they want," said Inigo, sitting in his director's chair.

Using a paper cut-out, the mechanician made Inigo's moon wax gradually into a round, bright Harvest moon.

"Light and motion," he said.

A diffuse glow spread across the stage, then turned pink.

"Motion and light," said Inigo. "And—action."

Outside, the sun had risen in the sky, and as the clouds shifted, an errant sunbeam thrust its way through the Banqueting Hall's black-out windows, piercingly bright. It cut through the hall's darkness to the stage, illuminating dust dancing in its beam, picking out Venetia's form and face in a spotlight.

"And there we have it," muttered Inigo, crossing himself. "All my invention is eclipsed by God."

"Women goe up and downe with white paintings laid one upon another soe thick that a man might easily cut off a curd of cheese-cake from either of their cheeks."

Thomas Tuke, *A Treatise Against Painting and Tincturing*, 1616

ON FRIDAY, NO delivery came from Dr. Choice.

Venetia shrugged it off, being busy with the household, but found herself out-of-sorts and listless. It was particularly hard to get through the afternoon, when she had a habit of sipping her Wine continuously, as if it were a posset cup. She reached for the vial three times, forgetting it was empty. The day seemed wasted, and she did not even feel like playing cards. By evening she was in her closet, licking the old vials for any remnants of liquor, swilling them out with angel water and gulping it down. She took herself off to bed early, and slept lightly, stirring at every sound in case it was her delivery.

She woke from angry opium dreams feeling full of self-reproach. She heard her boys calling for Mistress Elizabeth and chastised herself as a bad mother, and a tough old hen, not fit to tread the Queen's stage. How did she think she could compete? The more paint she applied, the more she would be a figure of fun, like the curd-cheek'd woman in the popular song.

Most people would tell you that vain women drank Viper Wine, and drinking made them vainer. But that only showed how little understanding most people had. The Wine had freed her from her riddling disquiet about her own appearance, so instead of squandering her time on looking in the bottomless glass, she could turn her powers outside herself, free to go into the world and do better deed, as far as she was able.

She reckoned that so much Wine was in her blood—that her veins were now made of Viper Wine—that she had the strength to be herself for the day, even without her dose.

She would put on her shield and vizor and go forward. It was vital to resemble oneself, even at home. From her private cabinet she took a pot of Spanish red, and a squirrel-hair brush, and drew herself a pair of rosebud lips.

Upstairs, Sir Kenelm was looking over his son's shoulder at his wastebook, and saw he had been copying the sign of Mercury, doodling, deforming the shape. "No," he chided. "Symbols have power."

She used a tiny trowel to mix up some ceruse, adding pearl dust and vinegar.

"Symbols work upon men's minds more directly than words," said Kenelm.

She used a sponge to pat white ceruse across her chest.

"Words equivocate, and words are used in sophistry, and words turn back and forth and obscure the truth . . ."

She worked the ceruse up into her neck and jaw, and patted it into her pores so she was as smooth as an ivory chess piece.

"But a symbol is worth a thousand words. Symbols, sigils, hieroglyphs—these are dangerous in and of themselves. They do not correspond to power. They are not analogous with power. They are not translations of power. They *are* power . . ." Sir Kenelm realised he was talking more to himself than to his son.

She clipped a pearl into her right earlobe, and tied black ribbon in her left. Thus she was adroit, *pas gauche.*

"If you write out a holy acrostic, it can protect you."

Now she spread a little blush into her cheek. She was coming into being.

"And if you write a low symbol, it can summon injurious notions, spirits and malevolent will."

Her finger slipped and she put a great dark shadow under her eye by mistake. She corrected this with honey water and a rag.

"If we could engrave the perfect symbol, the world would be made anew."

Young Kenelm sighed and scratched his leg.

"Cattle die, birds eat their young, it rains flies and the sun is covered over by the clouds for months when this sign is shown abroad," said Sir Kenelm, reaching to show young Kenelm what he had drawn.

Venetia's left eye was now blue shaded and beguiling.

Kenelm showed his son a swastika.

Venetia put down her brush and smiled at what she had created: the representation of a beautiful woman. Not quite herself, but certainly, a beautiful woman. For when we dress, we symbolise ourselves.

Kenelm ripped out the swastika and threw it into the fire. He then addressed himself to the page and drew it again, curving its spurs in a different direction.

"But this sign, its mirror opposite, means peace which surpasseth all understanding."

In the afternoon, Venetia played with baby John, who looked at Venetia's bright face wonderingly, and tried to pull off her nose. They babbled to one another, until he was taken away by his nurse. Venetia went to linger by the scullery door in the kitchen, watching the back path and listening out for a messenger's tread, hoping her delivery was about to arrive.

Mistress Elizabeth and the under-maid became very self-conscious, fearing she was checking up on them. Venetia started looking through the larder, out of boredom, and telling the servants it was organised all wrong, when a rap came at the scullery door, and Venetia looked up with a glad smile, and rose to answer the door herself. Mistress Elizabeth was brought to doubt her whole understanding of Venetia. Was she cuckolding Sir Kenelm?

Lancelot Choice was at the door, breathless and hatless, but with one hand on his hip, in affectation of a careless pose. He handed her a crate marked TURNEPS, which she took quickly out of his hand.

"At last," she said. "My turnips. I have been waiting for my turnips."

"I am sorry, my lady," panted the physician. "No staff, and Margaret indisposed, and—"

"It doesn't matter," said Venetia, ripping off the lid of the crate. Only her deeply engrained femininity prevented her from taking one and drinking it down in front of him. "They're here now."

"'Tis freshly culled, though not without risk. Our crop of living worms is not easily harvested. Margaret is bitten."

"Three vials only—you might have brought me a full complement."

"Indeed," he said stiffly. "And she shall surely recover." Venetia realised she had been talking without listening properly, or understanding his meaning, and she impulsively reached out and seized Master Choice's arm.

"Oh no," she said. The marriage between her handsome apothecary and his maternal, grey-haired wife intrigued and touched her. "Poor Margaret."

He nodded. "One escaped brute. Biding its time, brooding in the corner of the pits. Margaret, barefoot in her nightclothes, checking the furnace. In the dark she happened upon him, underfoot, but she swears the viper was laying in wait for her, and as he pounced, the other vipers in their pens were roused and joined in a chorus of hissing rebellion. I say she raves in her mind, but she swears it true. I made good work of him with a shovel, after he bit my Margaret."

"You lodge above the viper pits?" She had believed, for some reason, that the vipers lived in the countryside.

"Oh no, madam, they are farmed a good distance hence," he said, scratching the back of his neck. "We were with them not they with us. Forgive me, I am confusing you with my worry. I have dressed the wound with a good quantity of millipedes, washed in white wine and reduced to a powder. She will be perfectly cured withal. Her ankle is in a state of paralysis, though, my lady, so I must—"

He turned away, making for the road.

"Go quickly then, and . . ." She was going to say that she would ask Kenelm for his advice on snakebites and their antidotes, but she remembered she could not, for reasons of her own vain secrecy. "And thank you, sir."

She saw him walk off down the low brick path, by the South Ditch, which ran like an open sewer along the backs of the houses, a busy crossing for men and women who lived in the new tenements now built over the land between Smithfield and Etheldreda's at Ely Place, where Chater sometimes went to minister to the secret Catholic congregation.

She shut the door on him, and there, hidden in the dark privacy between the curtain and the scullery back door, Venetia, Lady Digby, scion of the Northumberland Percys, and the Shropshire Stanleys, Earls of Derby, set her lips around the cold neck of one of her draughts, her throat pulsating as she drank it down. Afterwards, she breathed a deep sweet breath, and her body felt at ease once more. As her strength returned, she ran to tell Master Choice that Sir William Paddy had once cured Prince Henry of a viper rash, her feet carrying her lightly across the road.

"Master Choice—"

Lancelot Choice had untied his horse, which was in a dancing mood. As he pulled its bridle towards Venetia, a sharp movement in the riverside bushes, a rat or a weasel, startled the horse so it bolted across the sewer-bridge. It was almost an open bridge, wide enough but built with scanty railings, and at that moment a young girl was crossing the bridge in the other direction. For fear of being trampled by the bolting horse, the girl, little more than a child, sprawled off the bridge and was sucked into the grey tide of the South Ditch.

Master Choice pursued his rearing horse. The girl was struggling in the water, almost submerged. Venetia looked around. This was the drainage for brewers and tanners, lime-burners and beet-boilers. It was scummed and murky. But there was no one else to do it. She did not stop to think of herself, or to face her Maker. The Wine had made her a virago. Doubtless the girl, a city child, had not learned to swim; Venetia had played a water nymph at Enstone House for a summer. She threw her fur off her shoulders and kicked off her slippers, and shut her eyes and leaped, and then she was cold, and wet, and she was grasping a handful of the girl's hair, and her coat, and they were kicking one another, strangers keeping one another half alive, as the river carried them along.

Venetia felt that she might not live to perform in the Queen's Twelfth Night Masque, and she imagined all the courtiers observing the briefest silence in her memory, before beginning their merry dance again.

As they seemed to be going under, Venetia felt the Wine kick in her gut, and give power to her shoulders. In childbirth or in feverish fits, she had clung to the thought of Kenelm, and how she could not leave him, and this had kept her alive. But now the Wine insulated her, so the violence of the water did not scare her. She could not die; the sweet Wine needed her. The South Ditch was deep and its currents were strong, and Venetia managed to cling onto a branch, but it was only floating, brought down by the autumn flood, and the current sped them onwards. The girl screamed. Venetia managed get hold of the bank just past the brambles, and to cling on, and so drag herself and the girl onto land.

They lay there, filthy and panting.

The girl spat brown water. Venetia had managed to keep her mouth closed.

"So there we are, lass," she said, rubbing the girl on the back.

"Ah-boo boo boo hoo," cried the girl, holding up her grimy skirt, and showing she had lost a boot. "Booo, boo, hoo." She cried like a bad impersonation of someone crying. The ill-tempered horse was now tied up safely, and Lancelot Choice approached them, holding out Venetia's slippers.

"You poor ladies," he said gallantly, as if they had both befallen a misfortune, but he had luckily come to the rescue. "Let me help you."

"Give me my slippers, sir," she snapped. "I shall carry them safely home. But I thank you for your kind consideration."

"My lady, be careful on the stony ground," said Choice, gesturing to the broken path that lay between her and her home.

"Thank you, but I think it can do me less harm than your horse can," said Venetia. "Besides, I want to get back to my box of turnips. And you to your Margaret, no doubt. My best to your poor Margaret."

Folk from the household were running out, calling alarum, and Venetia looked back at the sobbing girl, and considered taking her into her house and making her clean, so she would not be in trouble when she got home—but then she decided she could not be bothered with it, and sent the girl on her weeping way. The proximity of danger had focused her mind. Trivial things will take up your whole life if you let them, she thought. Let someone else see to it the child is washed. I have saved her life.

Mistress Elizabeth, out of breath and disturbed by all these odd occurrences, blurted out that to her mind, the girl was a baggage not worth saving.

Stinking and bedraggled, Venetia went into the scullery and, ignoring everyone, opened up her crate of seething red vials. She held one up and drank it down. She did not care who saw. Afterwards she wiped her mouth with the back of her hand, like a man.

Later, as Mistress Elizabeth helped her out of her dirty clothes, and wiped her body with a cloth—this leap into a running sewer did not seem occasion enough for a bath, which would be too dangerous to undertake so lightly—Venetia talked aloud.

"Women are precious vessels. We must comport ourselves carefully, and not spill or knock ourselves. With good cause. If any mishap befall, if you slip or sprain or twist, or get a fever, splodge or stain, then you are ruined. You are broken. It is not possible to mend any of us back again—no more men than women, but a broken man has given service, while a broken woman is a pity and a nuisance."

Mistress Elizabeth wrapped Venetia in a blanket, hoping to comfort her out of such speeches. Venetia tingled all over with strength, with pins and needles in her blood, and she wanted to run, or take another risk, or get out of breath, and she wondered what the drink had unleashed in her.

She did not tell anyone about this incident, not even Kenelm. She did not mean to hide it from him, but she did not see how to explain it. He would only worry. The servants never spoke of it again, above a whisper, and the household somehow ended up believing that an accident had befallen their mistress, but that a handsome delivery man had saved her from the Fleet.

In her head, the vipers were always moving, turning over one another, their hot smooth bodies restless and sleek. The three vials lasted her barely two days, and she went to fetch more from Choice's lodgings herself. It was her last chance before the rehearsals for the Queen's Masque, and she felt drawn there by the whispering silk-stiffness of her dress. She could have forced herself not to visit Choice, but it was so much easier to let herself go to him. As she walked, she could hear the vipers hissing in her skirts.

> "I go to Dr. Sebagh's and have the 'vampire facelift.' They take a phial of blood from your arm, separate the plasma, and inject it into your face. It helps the skin repair itself."
>
> Actress Anna Friel, 2012

At the entrance to Fenchurch Street she darted into a blind alley, because she saw Belinda, Lady Finch, coming in the opposite direction. She was accompanied by someone but Venetia could not see who it was; she heard a snatch of light voices as the ladies passed by. She wondered if another lady of the court was also hiding from Venetia, in a doorway, and another lady hiding from that lady.

Perhaps Choice was now beset by ladies demanding Wine. Could that be the reason he had not supplied her with a full consignment of vials?

Had she sunk so low in his esteem that the blood which was hers to drink went to other women first? Would the whole court now be growing dewy skinned, with deep black pupils? Indignantly she rapped at the door, which she noticed had been overpainted afresh, while above the door the sign of the star had been embossed in rich gilt.

There was no answer. Venetia bowed her head and slumped her shoulders, willing herself not to be noticed, nor to stand out. She tried to blow herself out like a light, so no one would see her. It did not suit her. She was meant to flame, not cower. At last, the door opened a crack and a young apprentice, a boy she had never seen before, peeped out.

"My lady, we can't be having you today—"

Venetia was not going to accept this. She laughed at the very idea that he would keep her on the doorstep.

"Move for me, or there will be all hell cut loose," she said in a very icy, smiling voice.

Stepping inside, she unveiled and, seeing a new smart leather book on the counter, which she judged was the book of appointments, she stood leafing through its pages avidly, while the apprentice shook his head and stammered. The clients were identified by initials and pseudonyms only, and she was idly puzzling over some of them when, screwing up his courage, the apprentice plucked the book out of her hands and hid it under the counter. To remove her from the main corridor, he showed her into the back room where there was a wooden chair. She sank into it gratefully. "Well, sweet boy, I must see your Master Choice. Where is he?"

The apprentice held his head in his hand. "I don't know. Upstairs. Oh, I wish you weren't here, madam."

"Are his other customers so much more important to him? Is he with a very great lady?"

In his anxiety the apprentice stretched his mouth very wide and started to devour his own knuckle.

"Is it the Queen? Why else would you be so indelicate with me? I was counted something in my day, you know . . ."

It occurred to her that Olive and Master Choice might be enjoined in adulterous bliss upstairs, while the apprentice guarded the door.

But then upstairs she heard deep voices that penetrated the floorboards like a rumble, and the sound of a chair scraping, and heavy treads on the stairs, and she realised she had misunderstood.

The apprentice stopped chewing his fingers' ends, and threw his hand at Venetia in despair.

"My lady, one of the Sheriffs of the City is upstairs interviewing Master Choice about his use of improper and Papistical cures!" he hissed.

She could hear them coming down the stairs with great clanking steps.

"Too many great ladies coming here, in and out, all day long. The Sheriff suspects a Popish plot. If, if, if he discovers you here, it will be so much the worse for us!" The apprentice was now dancing on the spot, performing a small jig of worry and fear.

Venetia looked around the room. She heard the Sheriff and his lieutenant in the hallway, and guessed they were about to come in. She ran across the room, unbolted a small door under the stairs that she took for a cupboard, and darted down a flight of steps. The door slammed shut behind her. A black stink brushed her face, and she guessed it was a curtain, which she grappled with, heaving it aside.

It was unexpectedly warm, for a cellar. It smelled of death and sadness, but then most cellars do. God help her, for she was having such a day. She could see nothing in the darkness, but she soon became aware of a presence in the cellar, betrayed by a small, soft sound, like skin passing across skin.

In darkness we are made, and to darkness we return.

The sound was constant but irregular, like the action of a thousand independent fingertips.

All flesh is grass, all grass is flesh.

The sound surrounded her, cosseting her senses, like the crested tempter at the ear of Eve. She had always known she would be drawn here eventually, into the darkness of the pit. She knew where she was, and what a multitude of scaly enamelled bodies she was amongst, but she could not see them, only sense them. As her eyes adjusted to the darkness, and she became aware of a soft glow from a furnace, she could discern an outline of tubs or pens, roughly knee-high, although she could not see anything inside the pens, but she could feel her heart beating all about her, as if she were split into so many long living coils, tumbling over one another.

She tried to imagine she was surrounded by old shovels, empty earthenware jugs and bottles of wine, as in any other cellar. But viperish thoughts crammed into her mind, and she feared for her little boys and prayed they never played upon rotten logs, nor squeezed inside the brackish caverns of decaying trees.

She wondered if the creatures recognised her as one of their own. Would they be attracted towards her in the dark, smelling the blood of their brothers in her veins? Would they hunt her like a rabbit or a mouse? She tried to make her breathing less fast and shallow. Snakes were creatures of the night. Could they see her in the dark, though she could not see them?

She stayed very still, breathing with forced gentleness. She fancied she heard a smooth unspooling, somewhere inside her chest, as if the enemy that had long kept itself coiled about her heart now wound into her throat. In front of her face in the darkness she felt she could discern the distant wet papping of a mouth opening and closing. She did not want to tread upon a soft lethal body, so she froze, resolved not to move until she saw where she stood. The cellar was pulsing, yet strangely calm, or at least she made up her mind to find it so. She told herself the poor creatures might be happy nestling together here, until their little time was up.

In the room upstairs, the Sheriff concluded his interview with Master Choice, that wondrous talker, and smooth-tongued gent, and the only sign he was unnerved was his crenelated necktie, too stiff upon his throat. The men shook his hand and wished him and his wife well. Margaret's wound was healing well enough that she hobbled to bid the Sheriffs adieu, her paralysed leg stiff like a strut beneath her. The blue had left her lips and the fever passed, but she swore she would never return to that place—the place where Venetia, at that moment, was crouching in the dark.

The commotion upstairs had roused the vipers, which she could hear rising up and hissing, expecting, perhaps, a fresh consignment of flesh, or baring their fangs in the latest battle of the long war that had dispatched so many of their gold-green brothers . . .

Take a viper by the neck, and hold her so she cannot wag or stir at all . . .

The door to the viper pit flew open and she saw daylight, and Master Choice, and his apprentice, and she raced up the stairs out of the cellar, without looking behind her. Lancelot Choice shut the cellar door fast and bolted it, so she might not see where she had been, and what amongst.

It was necessary for her not to look behind her, if she were to continue drinking her Wine.

Two Guessing Games

Prosopagnosia—commonly, face-blindness. A term first used in 1947 by Joachim Bodamer, a German neurologist, describing a young man who after sustaining a gun-shot wound to a particular region of the head, failed to recognise friends, family and even his own face.

IT WAS AN ignoble situation in which to find himself. But Kenelm could not recognise his wife. He thought he saw Venetia in a painting, or at the window of a sedan chair, or a balcony; as soon as he looked back, he knew he was mistaken. Sometimes the women looked nothing like her, and his stupidity sent a tremor through him. He had heard about a man struck by a palsy that robbed him of his ability to read playing cards, but affected him in no other wise.

Sir Kenelm considered his wife's face was no less beautiful than it had been, nor older, nor sadder, nor different in any ways that he could discover. It had only lost a certain "this-ness" or *haecceitas* that made it her own. She looked most fair, admirably fair, only she did not look like herself. But where would the subtle Dr. Duns Scotus, author of the concept of self-sameness, have located her *haecceitas*? In which element of her features did it reside?

Kenelm always thought he knew her face so well—until he saw Venetia again after an absence, and her face surpassed all his imaginings. She was the master copy; all other versions of her were clumsy approximations. But now, he felt as if his memory was more accurate than what he saw. What defines a face from any other? A jot, a drop, a tare, a whit, a corn—

how to measure the tiny gradations that define a nose, which give an eye character, which make your lover's well-turned cheek their own?

Kenelm beheld the Queen's ladies preparing for the masque, assembled in the great hall with three dancing masters in attendance. He watched through the wide lattice of the upper chamber, searching for his wife. He could not distinguish her. He felt his brain at work as he scanned the ladies' faces, and the fusiform gyrus of the bilateral extrastriate area of his brain, later identified as the area responsible for face recognition, started to throb, deep behind his ears. It grew warm, and ticked within the pulpy wetness of his *pia mater.* Still he could not see her. The women turned back and forth. He noticed Olive, Lady Vavasour, Lady Finch and little Anne Ogilvy. His fusiform gyrus glowed as he saw them. He recognised them spontaneously, as if they were printed words. He did not read each of their letters in turn—the shape of their nose, the bridge of their brow, the distance between their eyes, the a, e, i, o, u. Instead, he read the whole face. And yet his loved one's face was lost to him. The fusiform gyrus of his bilateral extrastriate area pulsed and whirred with effort.

Perhaps, dreamed Sir Kenelm, he could recognise his wife by means of the application of an Instrument of Measurement, a Theodolitus, a Pantometer, Alhibab, or othersuch Ingeniose Device, which he might use to search and define the contours of her lips and nose, like Archimedes' Burning-Glasses, from a distance. But were his compasses sharp enough? Could he divide her face into 80, 120 vectors? This would be the standard measurement for facial recognition software.

Face-catchers in alleys, byways and palace balconies ought to be equipped with night-vision capability and pre-programed to recognise, for instance, a wife. They would depend upon measurements on a sub-millimetre or "microwave" scale, in order that a face might be rendered as a precise mathematical space. Useful to any husband, he reasoned.

Sir Kenelm wanted to track the changes to her face, to map and model it with callipers every day so he could learn to recognise it again. He would have his own astrolabe for keeping sight of her beauty, and have it always in his pocket—

Venetia interrupted his reverie by waving. Of course, when she blew a kiss to him, or when he heard her voice, or felt her animating spirit, all his doubts fell away, and the ranks of alternative Venetias crowding his brain shrank to nothing. Problems begot problems, but certainty was its own reward.

> "Inigo Jones greatly approved of the paintings, and in order to be able to study them better, threw off his coat, put on his eyeglasses and together with the King began to study them very closely . . . As the King had removed the names of the painters, which I had [affixed] to each picture . . . Inigo Jones boasts of having attributed almost all the paintings correctly."
>
> From a letter by Papal envoy Gregorio Panzani, 1630*s*

Although it was late at night when the paintings arrived at Whitehall, the King came directly, insisting the cases were opened at once, even without calling the Lord Keeper of the Paintings. The King took a candle by which to study them closely, pulling off their wrappings like other men remove women's girdles. After a time alone with the paintings, he sent for Inigo Jones, whom he guessed to be up late working, as usual.

Inigo came hastily, abandoning his half-inked designs for the masque, dressing quickly in his best furs, but shuffling in his slippered feet, as his boy had taken his boots for polishing. The King led Inigo through the long gallery up a winding stair to a small, warm chamber where the new paintings were propped up against the panelling, their wrappers strewn across the floor. "What have we here?" said the King. "Let us play a guessing game."

When Charles dismissed his servants and grooms they stood on the other side of the door, or congregated in corridors, waiting to see if they could be of service. But there was deep silence now, and Inigo sensed they were actually alone. Charles held a candle to the crackle glaze varnish of a black masterwork, which reflected the candle in its gleaming fissures. As he trawled the surface, Jones wondered what Gorgon or beauty the candle would find, until out of the darkness came a hand—long-fingered, accusatory, pale, attached to a smooth blue cape and furred cuff.

"Whose *hand*-iwork is this?" said Charles, smiling.

Inigo did not play for time. "Lorenzo Lotto," he said briskly, accenting the name with brio. "Oft mistook for Titian."

"Hmm." Charles pretended to consider the hand. He moved the candle upwards, catching an almond-shaped eye, and a full Florentine cheek.

"I know so much less than you, but I think this is the work of Andrea del Sarto," said the King.

Inigo was a great draughtsman and scholar, but he could not countenance the idea that the King might be cheating. It would require a leap of cynicism impossible for such a one as Inigo, whose loyalty to the crown was a cornerstone of his faith. Inigo's King was God's representative on earth. When Inigo's King laid his hands on the scrofulous, they were healed.

Looking at the flickering paintings, barely visible by the firelight except as coloured howls in tarry blackness, Inigo began to sweat. As the King's architect, famous for his Italian learning, his knowledge of Palladio, his connoisseurship—he had much at stake. He needed to recognise the next painting illuminated by the King's candle. He would mortgage his soul to get this one right. Out of the darkness came a thick green stalk and a twisted yellow head, densely petalled, against a sun-baked background. The candle revealed a whole cluster of spiky, astonished flowers—twelve apostles blazing in an earthenware pot. Thanks be to God, this was an easy one.

"Van . . . ," said Inigo.

"I agree," exclaimed the King. "The other Van . . ."

"Van Gogh," they said simultaneously.

Inigo Jones had the will to rise in the world; the King was gifted with the opposite quality. But tonight, the King was in control. He moved the candle around, enjoying his power, revealing the backwards curve of a bowed head, painted with great gusto, and a shadowy face beneath it, worried and cracked.

"An old man," said Inigo. "By, by, by . . ."

"Well, sir, I know whom I believe it to be by . . ."

"Your choice, Your Majesty?"

"Andrea del Sarto, again," said the King.

"I disagree," exclaimed Inigo, all his pomposity gathering itself up like a little stormcloud about to be released as a sneeze. "I say this old man's head is painted by Leonardo."

The King was delighted to have beaten Inigo, even though he had contrived to do so. The King loved to be clever, more than almost anything else. In their boyhood, his brother Prince Henry was popular, sportive, playful, strong—but Charles was clever.

When he checked the paintings against the scroll of descriptive inventory, reading them aloud, he was able to disguise his joy completely until he came to the final entry. "Oh dear, Inigo," he said, laughing. "This one you reckoned to be an old man by da Vinci is in truth an old woman by del Sarto. Oh dear me."

The Masque of "Luminalia"

In Which Queen Henrietta-Maria Restores Dawn to the Benighted Kingdom

Expecting to hear the sound of the sea, Sir Kenelm lifted to his ear a shell. Instead he heard battle, Englishman fighting Englishman, bloody outcry, rapine and regicide. Peculiar. This shell gave him a queer feeling, and looking at it as if it had a bad smell, he put it down on his dressing table, and decided not to include it in his costume.

The masque was on tonight. The masque was where they went to dream, communally. It was glamour, enchantment. It made Icons of women and Heroes of men. It was a mirage, which rose and was then extinguished, never re-created. It was the aery, playful sport of the Higher Imagination. It was castles perched upon clouds of air, princesses and darling fauns, and naughty comic dwarves. The masque was Disney. It was the very opposite of the brawling ultra-violence that the public theatre had become, all bloodshed and confusion, incest and people running about with hearts on sticks.

Sir Kenelm wondered if this rift between court and town entertainments, between the country's head and its belly, indicated the kingdom's physiognomy was a healthy one, or no.

Perhaps he should wear the family ruby. It was a twisted heart, asymmetric, and set in a fine enamel representing the Pelican in her Piety, the white bird pecking her breast to feed blood to her family, or rather, the whole nation. It was an old design, fashionable in Elizabeth's day.

That evening's masque had the ingenious theme of Light and Darkness, and during the moments of Darkness, his ruby would glint and glimmer, burning with its own light, the light that all true jewels held within them, be it ever so elusive. The ruby had refused to shine in the dark ever since his father's execution, but Kenelm had seen its rays growing stronger lately. He held it up to the light, breathing on it, polishing and turning its golden setting, trying it out upon his breast, his cap, his collar.

Because it was Mistress Elizabeth's Twelfth Night holiday, Venetia was pacing round the house playing the part of housekeeper for the night, checking no candles were left burning in the upper rooms, that the dogs had been fed, that the boys' breakfast was ready for the morrow: that the bills had been paid, and that the cook had the keys on the Malaga sack barrel, which was no more than half-full, so that the household could get pleasantly yet not injuriously drunk.

Venetia did all this wearing her watchet-silk masqueing gown, hung with wing-like capes upon her shoulders and tied at her wrists, so as she darted into the nursery and kissed the boys as they ate their supper, they thought she was the most exquisite mother-nymph. They were proud of her small waist and her expensive scent, and young Kenelm got up and bowed to her, as he had been taught, and she kissed him, and held him close, but not too close, because he had honey down his shirt-front and she was in her costume.

The river was smooth and silty-white as they went by wherry to Whitehall Stairs, joining a queue of water taxis at the palace jetty, bobbing as they waited to disembark in the last of the winter-afternoon light. All through December, Venetia had been staying at the palace much of the day and sometimes overnight, preparing for the masque, and now she returned as a guest and player. In truth, there had been little rehearsing, but frequent rising and descending in mechanical chariots, in order that the ladies could endure it without too much fear. The actor from the Globe was used to working with male players only, but he was impressed to see that women could project their voices "almost as well as men." He did not wish to tire the ladies out unduly, though, so much time passed with his demonstration of the art of splitting a chestnut in the air with a rapier.

"Enough chain and jewel in my boat tonight to sink her," said a wherryman called Plank.

"I had that Spanish ambassador in my boat once," said his friend John Duckett. "Gondomar. The one they mocked senseless at the Globe. 'Signior-ee-ee,' that one. Not a tipper."

"I had that courtesan in my boat tonight," said Plank. "Mistress Lively. When I cries Oars, Oars, I don't expect 'em to come running. Maybe I'll try crying Rollocks instead."

Across the city, in Fenchurch Street, the Twelfth Night festivities stopped the constant traffic of customers through Choice's premises. With the servants and apprentices off, the place had an unaccustomed silence.

Lancelot Choice leaned back with his hands behind his head. "Ah, my dear," he said to Margaret. "Is this not peace indeed?"

Margaret looked up from the sweaty keel of her cooking pot. "Oh, mightily so," she said pleasantly, out of habit, while wiping down her apron, which was dirty from dismembering rodents, and pushing a foot-pedal, which turned the vipers on their spit.

Her method of preparing the Wine had become more efficient lately, allowing larger batches to be produced quickly, and if a little golden eye or skein of skin fell into the pot, it was unlikely to be removed.

Margaret's illness had not killed her, but it had left her weaker. The skin around the viper's bite was still engorged, shiny-smooth and new, and she limped, and felt the pain of it during thunderstorms. Choice, conversely, had gained a new sleekness and authority as their enterprise prospered.

"Now would be a very good time for us to twist the lancet," he said. "To set our vipers wiggling in a new direction. I conceived of the idea three weeks ago, and yet we have not tried it out."

Margaret sucked her teeth.

"What a nice piece of work you are, waiting till our Twelfth Night holiday to spring this on me—"

"Margaret, we must offer our ladies something more than Viper Wine, before they lose their appetites."

Margaret said they could not try the Experiment tonight, because wax was too low.

"Another candle needs be fetched, then."

With an unforgiving glance at him, she went. Lancelot Choice considered the serum, splattered about the vial, which he had milked yesterday from the fattest adder, holding its head fast and enraging it until it spat its bile with impotent spite into his beaker. Choice was not a sentimental man but he felt a certain male kinship for this lethal beast, shackled from birth, deploying its ultimate defence, which turned into a dribble in his captor's beaker. Still, here was enough poison to kill a man; the immature viper's bite that Margaret had suffered was enough to paralyse her limb for two weeks; thus one tiny tear, one globule—a little bead to sit upon his finger's end—that was plenty for his purpose tonight.

While he was waiting, checking his face in the glass, he thought of his new client, the girl who would not stop talking. She was full of thoughts and questions, and the better part of his nature thought he ought not to treat her, as she was too young. But then he considered what he was for. He was no conjuror, no cunning-man. He could not make a girl beautiful, no more than he could roll back the years. But he could lightly tweak a woman's blood, so she was more luxuriant in all her parts, and woozy with confidence. Thus he found himself helping this Child, making another Customer of her by telling her "*Non semper erit aestas*"—"it will not always be summer." Take precautions while you may.

She carried her vials away, beaming. He considered it a prescription for anxiety.

Margaret's tread was slower than usual on the stairs, and when she came in she sighed heavily at him.

"Be not so, Margaret," he said sternly, sharpening the lancet with a frisking noise.

She grimaced.

"'Tis only a smally-wee incision."

"Will sutures be made?"

"Only if the wound gapes incontinently."

She watched like a slaughter-lamb as he laid out the cloth upon their dinner table carefully, with the pillow at the head's end.

He smiled, and his beauty, the symmetry of his steady gaze, comforted and inspired her.

They prayed, kneeling side by side, and then, according to their plans, he got onto the table and lay down. Margaret covered his neck and shoulders with a dirty, stained towel, so that a new one might not be spoiled with bleeding. She breathed upon the lancet, and wiped it on her apron, before beginning.

He had marked his forehead for incision with a small chalk line.

"Be not too slow, Margaret, but slice with conviction," he said.

"Quiet!"

The blood did not shed much, but pooled thickly under the cut. She fed the serum of adder poison, diluted down with three parts witch hazel, into the wound using the tip of the lancet and pressed it shut. She wiped her finger on the towel before starting on the other side.

When he raised his eyebrows, his skin creased upwards, giving him the two curved wrinkles across his forehead that they called "the Lawyer's Moons" or "Moon-tides." They had planned that Margaret should erase both Moons today, but as she moved around him, with the lancet flashing, he sat up, sharply.

"Enough—'tis well done. I had rather put the risk upon my next patient, for women take their medicines differently to men, and it is Saturn in my stars, so I should not have the full treatment. I shall see how that takes. I must not jeopardise the practice; our business is maintained by my beauty."

The immobility took hold after a few hours. He barely needed a bandage, and as night fell, he began reproaching Margaret for not making him take the treatment on both sides of his face, because at present his brow showed only a Half Moon. One side was stretched and taut, the other traced with care. To be sure, the wounded side had lost something of its animation, but it had gained an uncanny smoothness, very like a side of bacon.

"It is a good rule of my art, which I should remember, that everything must be done with symmetry."

"Should the hiss-pissers have my other ankle too, then?"

"I have a mind to ask for the second dose this instant," replied Choice, looking in the glass. "This is the very thing a Lady needs to finish what the Wine has started. I will take one or two of the Ladies into my confidence, and show them how the example works upon my own skin. This will inspire their admiration, nay their jealousy."

Choice was pacing around.

"It is good commerce, Margaret, to always offer customers more . . ."

"Lie thee down, then," she said, and took up the blade again, so their Twelfth Night revelry might be completed.

In the Palace courtyard the plaster spaniels in the fountain had stopped chasing the mallard around the mechanical clock, their movement stilled by ice, their ears and noses white with frost. The gravel looked sugar-glazed and the sky full of goose-down, as the revellers arrived in their furs and over-mantels, nervous and excited; even the oldest councillors of state, who had been coming to masques for thirty years, had a quickness in their air-hanging breath, wishing well on the occasion. Sir Francis Knollys, Penelope's husband, muttered prayers for the masque's success when he awoke that morning, because this game, this play, this ceremony held the symbolic power of the nation's dignity, and as his thin old black-stocking'd legs stepped into the hall, he felt that if this evening's entertainment fell apart or failed, the state would falter too. The threat of Popish plot or powder made the masque more precious.

They were seated according to precedence—a complex operation overseen by the Earl Marshall. With ambassadors and bishops, the audience had swelled close to four hundred, but the whole show was meant to feel as small and intimate as possible, a private entertainment for the King and his favourites. Thus the set was designed for Him alone, so only His seat, beneath the canopy of State, saw the vanishing point of all perspectives: to Him, each optical illusion was perfectly maintained. Those whom politics had consigned to side-seats could see string-pullers, sea-tossers, lantern carriers. They saw the man who made the moon rise, climbing his rope-ladder into the starry black-clothed heavens. When Venus—Henrietta-Maria, of course—rose like a (fully-clothed) goddess from the waves in a huge scallop shell in Neptune's Triumph, they saw the stagehands cranking the waves about her; the King saw only sea. They saw the workings of the clock; he saw only the time.

Kenelm was waiting in the audience, bantering with his fellow gentlemen of the Bedchamber, but he was nervous for Venetia, playing with his gloves, turning them back and forth. He wanted her to perform well, of course, but more than anything, he wanted her to be happy with how it had all gone; he felt so powerless as he sat there in the eternal predicament of the watching spouse.

Inigo Jones had presented two masques every year for the last eighteen years, but his blind mother had never attended. Tonight, instead of standing in the wings, watching anxiously and pacing like a revenant, Inigo was sitting with his mother in the audience, holding her hand, and describing to her the masque.

"There is a rich curtain, overlaid with the word 'Luminalia,' the title of our piece. In front of the curtain is a tableau of naughty cherubim—sons and daughters of the court—in antic postures. Little Lord Maltravers is riding a model snail. Another boy is shooting toy arrows, another blowing a writhen trumpet, making that confused sound. Lady Hutchinson's daughter is asleep inside a pumpkin flower. Another is drawing with a vast pencil, quite as big as she is. Another is hardening darts in a candle. Oh, it is excellently done. And—now we stand, Mother."

The cornets proclaimed the arrival of His Majesty, unconstitutional king, who would not deign to deal with parliament, but preferred to sit with nymphs and zephyrs. When he was in his seat—or rather, upon his throne—Inigo's commentary began again. "Every candle in the place has been extinguished, abruptly." The half-alarmed gasp of the audience led him to reassure his mother—"It is done by direction thus. Now the curtain rises, discovering a scene of darkness. Countryside and woods, and further off, a calm river, lit by nothing but a Harvest moon. It is reflected in the river below, this being achieved by a concealed mirror."

The Hall was left in darkness and silent contemplation, admiring this night-time vista, until a barn owl's long, low call came, gently upon a flute.

"Ah," admired Inigo's mother, and clasped his hand tighter.

Then a long-eared owl's shriek startled the audience, and the night seemed to take on depth and breadth, as if mice were being hunted in the forest, and the trees rustled on cue.

A nightingale's liquid song poured out of the darkness, and then a frisson passed through the audience. "A bat has flown across the moon," whispered Inigo, "by means of wire."

"And now from the hollow cavern under the stage, a chariot rises, drawn by two great owls. They are the sons of the Lord Devereux. Their feathers are given by the King's kestrels. In the chariot sits a matron dressed in purple, stars of gold upon her dark hair, over her face a veil of russet cyprus. She is a singer from the Queen's company called Mistress Streisand. Her lips are purple coloured. She rises—"

"Night!" said Mrs. Jones.

"Aye, she is Night, and she wears two black wings, which are pigeon feathers dyed. Her chariot rests in the air a moment, so all may see it. She is lit with a very blue flame only, a compound of chymistry given me by Kenelm Digby; all else is darkness yet."

"Why dreadful queen dost thou appear / So early in this hemisphere?" asked the chorus.

Mistress Streisand's reply filled the hall with vibrations of Night. Venetia watched from the wings, rapt with delight as darkness spiralled out of Night's mouth, rising up from her lungs. The singer was so certain of her art, it came as naturally as if she were talking. When the aria paused, she closed her lips momentarily, as if tasting the music, before soaring into a new, more anxious key, like a sky turning from blue to indigo. The King pointed his staff at her, and she paused.

Pause.

Her mouth stayed open as if gargling one enormously long note; her purple cyprus veil was suspended mid-air.

The King revolved his staff of state.

Rewind!

Her lips closed momentarily, as if tasting the music, before soaring into a new, more anxious key, like a sky turning from blue to indigo. The King watched, smiling dispassionately. He considered rewinding that moment again, but did not. The song and the singer raced each other on towards their apogee, and as she reached the highest note, the great curtain covering one of the windows in the hall was rent down, as if by her singing, and the darkness she had brought with her across the world outside was revealed, to fulsome applause.

"Now Night's attendants appear," whispered Inigo. "The first Vigil is in blue with a bat upon her head. The second is in black, and wears a screech owl. The third wears a dormouse, and she is laced in silver dew. Now they dance with the figures of Sleep."

Sweet music crept across the audience, and the Vigils of Sleep danced a stately saraband, while Inigo spoke quietly in his mother's ear.

"There's Oblivion, a knave who always missed his rehearsals. There's Silence, an old pantaloon with a garland of peach-tree upon his head. And there's Sleep himself, a fat man in black. Sleep looks very like Ben Jonson, but I do not think Ben Jonson moves fast enough to represent Sleep."

By the heavy sigh of fabric and the sound of relaxation in the audience, Inigo's mother knew the curtain had fallen. A night-watchman's bell rang from the back of the hall.

"Here is the anti-masque, mother—nothing but foolish knavery. I must to the Queen."

Inigo slipped out between the rows, while two thieves ran through the hall, carrying clanking bags of plate and alarming the audience for a moment, until it became clear it was a mock-disturbance staged by actors, and the thieves were pursued by two night-watchmen, wearing false bellies and crying fury.

Next came Groucho Marx, dressed as a cook, with a tray of popcorn cornets.

"This is my room and region, the Banqueting House. Nothing is to be presented here without my acquaintance and allowance to it." He handed out popcorn to the audience, giving it to those who did not want it, telling others that they did not deserve it, and extemporising as only he could. He called out for his fellow cook, who thickened sauces with sulphur and made custards of Mercury. "Have you got a Philosopher's Egg—I want to make an omelette . . ."

Kenelm laughed loudest of all, because he knew the words were directed at him. His hair tumbled down his collar lank and golden. He was worried Venetia had not yet appeared.

"Now," shouted Groucho, "who is for the pot?"

An apprentice cook came pulling into the hall two dwarves, Jeffrey Hudson, the Queen's Lord Minimus, and Archibald Armstrong, the King's dwarf, strung together with ropes around their necks like partridges.

"A brace of dwarves, Master cook!" shouted the apprentice. "Delicate birds."

"Very good, so in we go," said the dwarves climbing up a ladder, bowing to the audience, and jumping into the pot.

"It looks warm in there," said Groucho Marx, puffing on his cigar. One of the dwarves escaped out of the false bottom of the pot, and Groucho chased after him.

"The ingredients are escaping—that's a recipe for disaster."

In the wings, the Queen and her ladies were peeping through the curtain, and laughing and shaking with delight at the spectacle.

After the waggish anti-masque, a new mood of serenity prevailed, as the curtain rose.

"Another setting, Mother—the City of Sleep. Gold towers, windmills, and other extravagant edifices."

"Scenery, all?"

"Aye, but so well-made, Mother. Out of the Palace of Morpheus come five nobles, dressed in white and wearing garlands of grapes."

The King stood, and raised his staff of state . . .

Fast Forward!

The nobles moved with exaggerated, knee-gnashing speed, Thomas Howard the Earl of Arundel, Master Denny, Master Hay, the Lords Lennox and Devereux, processed out of the Palace and marched at the double around the cloud-capp'd tower and down to the front of the stage, as fast as toy soldiers, while the music played at triple speed.

"And now here come five other nobles, sentinels of the Ivory Gate, whence come only truthful dreams," said Inigo, speaking very fast. "Lies-and-false-imaginings-come-through-the-Horned-Gate," he said, double-quick.

"Andnowtheybow," he added, high and squeaky.

Their little troupe raced to the front of the stage, where they became stuck in the middle of a bow, as the King revolved his staff of state backwards and kept them on slow speed, so that their obeisance took a satisfyingly long time, and their eyelids drooped and their arms made stuttering tracks through the air, so they appeared to have fifteen hands apiece, until he put them onto double speed again.

In the audience, sitting beside the King, the Earl of Strafford clapped powerfully, although his low forehead was contorted into a deep frown. He privately wished the King would not exercise his divine authority thus. It was not politic to play with his nobles, now there was no parliament.

The whole masque remained on Fast Forward as the Sons of Night appeared out of a cave: Endymion Porter, wearing a white sheet and laurel wreath, representing Phantaste, the Spirit of Anything that Can Be Imagined. Endymion played the part with relish, although he could not act, and never would be able to.

Faster!

Then the dawn began to rise, as a hundred little flames, and then another hundred, were lit on cue, their pink glass candleshields turning to create the effect of rosy light.

The King knew the Queen was about to enter, and so he pointed his staff of state respectfully at the scene on stage.

Play.

"The heavens begin to be enlightened," whispered Inigo to his mother. "It is a delicious prospect. The scenery turns on its axis—it is made of many triangular posts, which revolve in unison, revealing different scenes."

"Your clever notions!" said Mrs. Jones.

"No, it is only copied from the Greeks. They are called periaktoi. This way they turn, and turn, giving a painted vision of rows of trees, fountains, statues, arbours, grottoes, walks and all such things as might express the garden of Brittannides."

Happy King, to rule over such a country! Such a pleasant land of grotts and groves, where every subject might walk about his arbours and fountains, without worrying that the land was falling into two factions, whose disagreement would rend the nation's heart with steel.

The chorus sang: "The bright perpetual traveller / Doth now too long the day defer," which was the cue for the Queen, hiding in the wings, to make herself ready to mount her golden chariot without any back, and she and her ladies prepared for their entrance.

But first, Phosphorus the Morning Star came to light her way.

"Out of the pale sky, Mother, descends a fiery white bark, sailing across the clouds, bearing the brightest mirror-lamp I could design."

The audience sighed with rapture at the tiny white boat. Sitting in the prow of the boat were two figures: Lord Mountfitchet, dressed in white silk, paired with Lettice, who was wearing a gown that shone like a sapphire, or kingfisher's wing. The spitting phosphorus lantern disclosed their smiling childish faces as they played a game of handy-dandy, their palms raised to one another in idle slaps.

Fond applause sounded like summer rain in the hall.

"The twins of Phosphorus have been chosen to represent the loving unison of the King and Queen," said Inigo to his mother, as Lady Darnley stood in the centre of the stage and spoke her lines, clearly and with a sense of irony, even though she was a woman:

"Their minds within / And bodies make but Hymen's twin—"

"A woman?" asked Inigo's mother. "Speaking?"

"Aye, Mother," said Inigo, squeezing her hand, to indicate she should shew no alarm.

Backstage in the semi-darkness, two sweaty stagehands, Lubber and Vogg, turned the crank that made the Morning Star descend.

"Ten more?"

"Ten more and then we move to bring the dawn."

"Heave six."

"Heave seven."

"Think of the King."

"Heave nine."

"Ten for a job well done."

"There she goes," said Lubber, nodding his head to the Queen's satin slippers, which he saw at eye-level through a chink in the wooden stage structure as she traversed the upper gallery. They were white and sewn with pearls, and Vogg raised his cap to the slippers, although their wearer would never see this act of veneration.

"I feel towards her as if she's my own daughter, but then my wife says that's because I'm so often carpenter for her wooden boards and foot-rests, so it stands to reason."

The music swelled. The architect did not know it, but the velvet black eye mask that his mother wore to hide her cataracts was damp with tears. In her mind's eye the spectacle was unbearably rich. "And now the Queen enters," he whispered, getting to his feet, and taking his mother's arm to help her up, as the royal trumpeters sounded her entrance.

"She descends from the upper part, in a chariot heightened by gold. Reflectors set all about the hall redouble every candle's light, which in turn reflexes onto the masquers, their silvery habits. The Queen's majesty is highest, and several of her ladies are with her, seated somewhat lower. She wears a heavenly crown, ha. She cannot wear the crown of England, because of her religion, so the costume is chosen to make a point. About the Queen's person are rays of sunlight, somewhat like the Madonna at St. Sulpice. She smiles. The sky grows lighter, and more pink. This rare effect is created by reflectors being turned inwards, towards diaphanall glasses, filled with water that shews like the ruby stone of the orient. The habit of the masquers is close bodices, and their colour is Aurora, embroidered with silver. Diadems of jewels lie atop each head, and falls of white feathers, and tiny round metal discs, which we call 'Oos,' reflect the light—"

"Too much detail," said Inigo's mother. "Tell me something interesting."

He could not speak at all being, for a moment, too hurt.

"Each costume costs about thirty pounds," he said.

Having descended almost to earth, Aurora was now entertained in mid-air by a cloud of zephyrs, which ascended from the stage in the chariot that used to belong to Night.

"Hup two," said Lubber.

"Hup three," said Vogg.

"Oh, these zephyrs."

"Keep them cranking."

"Are they made o' lead?"

"Think of the tankard."

"Aye, think of the ale."

"Turn this thrice and we'll be done."

"Twice and we will o'ercome."

The last turn of the wheel was always the hardest.

"But look, there she sits amongst the clouds!" said Lubber, peeping through the scenery at the Queen on stage, his whole aching body covered in goosebumps of awe.

"Is she not a flying thing of wonder!" marvelled Vogg.

Venetia was chiefest amongst the zephyrs, and she sat highest upon their chariot, reclining in luxuriant pose, her head inclined backwards and her white neck and shoulders exposed by a gown that threatened to slip from her shoulders at any moment, while the two younger zephyrs waved large silk fans and pretended to play their paper harps, plucking, as the musicians below them made their real harps vibrate with fine appeasing melodies and glissandos.

Venetia's chariot paused mid-air, and realising she was half in shadow, she found her light by leaning forward. With a whip in her hand like Boudicca, she fixed the audience with her arch and glistering eye, as supercelestially camp as any priestess or diva, before or since. She spoke:

"Thy journeys never can be past
But must forever last
Tis not limited how far
Because it still is circular—the audience rippled with laughter, as was her design—
Thy universal beams cannot grow cold
Nor mortally wax old
Nor will they ever tire
Fed with immaterial fire."

Applause powered her silver-gleaming chariot higher, so she seemed to levitate upon the goodwill of the audience, their admiration plumping her skin, till she shone like a creature of phantasy. She felt herself gathering, rising, filled full of honey fame, which overflowed into her cracks and privities, as she flew upwards like no earthly dame, her eyes ecstatic, her hair curling with pleasure.

Sir Kenelm forgot to be nervous for her. She was here, his water nymph from Enstone House—

The King jabbed his staff of state at her—

Pause.

Not a cell divided, not a hair greyed, not a mole darkened, not a line deepened, and the plaster spaniels no longer chased the mallard round the fountain of Whitehall Palace.

In 1584 a government decision was made that Queen Elizabeth's beauty was to be maintained in portraiture, and she did not age from that time forward.

The zephyrs' light fabrics were caught in mid-air, their cheeks mid-smile.

Venetia ran outside into the night air, to cool her skin, which flamed with happiness. She was cured of her own mortality, and like someone freed from long confinement she ran into the darkness, and panting at the edge of the muscled, tossing Thames, and she gasped as she saw that even the river had paused.

It was stiff as beaten egg-white.

She would never age, but always be beautiful.

The pause had killed the river's flow, and reduced it to a representation of a river; the pause had killed the soft redoubled light that played around the Banqueting Hall, and the smell of the candles, and the slight wobble of the chariot. The pause had killed the moment, and the moment lay there dead and ready for the taking, glossy and permanent.

The King hummed, scratched his royal head. He picked the moment up, and put it in his pocket, intending to look at it again later.

He revolved his staff of state.

Rewind.

He wanted to make the candles in the hall burn backwards, and the zephyrs' fans suck up the air they had dispersed, and their fingers to unpluck their harps, and Venetia to retract her smile. But he could not make it happen.

Queen Elizabeth never looked in the mirror after 1584, and her courtiers were so certain of this that the ladies of her bedchamber once daubed her nose with cochineal, or so Ben Jonson said.

Venetia realised the River Thames had not paused, only frozen.

It was the cold, making her confused, and the vipers in her blood were tricking her imagination, so in her vanity she believed she had arrested time. For the last few days the river had been viscous and becalmed, and now it was a massy solid, and presently there would be skating on it, and bowls. She heard the hubbub of voices inside the masque and she knew she must go inside.

The King rotated his staff impatiently.

Rewind was stuck. He could make a singer repeat her line as many times as he liked, but he could not make the candles unburn, nor could he make the Thames flow backwards, nor could he put a grown smile into bud again.

Even he, the King, divinely entitled to rule as God's representative on earth, could not achieve this simple thing.

It was hard being King.

Play, play, play, play—let us dance and sing, for tomorrow we die. Handy-dandy, whirlabout. The performance was over, and a new game had begun, the courante starting up, calling the dancers to the floor. The masquers quitting their chariots and clouds, stumbled in their haste to join the dance, still wearing their diadems and falls of feathers, so that the masque continued, in the form of dancing. The masquers and their audience joined and mingled, hot atoms seething amongst the cold, turning formally between each other, hands raised in a courtly contretemps, heads bowing in obeisance, heels tapping out a demi-chasse.

And as the dance brought faces closer and then carried them away, like tides in a stately sea, Kenelm looked for his wife, overfilled with pride and anxious to praise her with kisses, but he could not see her. Perhaps it was the rapture of the dance, and the enravishment of the masque, or the work of a nimble apothecary, but he could not find his wife.

Confused, entranced, he saw echoes of her in other women. Aletheia Howard had the set of her eye; Mistress Whisk the pallor of her brow. Belinda, Lady Finch, had something of Venetia's new glowing serenity; none of them frowned, or seemed capable of displeasure. Even Lady Vavasour was dancing, as if she wished to make a show of herself, though she had not disported at court for ten years or more. What epidemic of beauty was this? Was Venetia's beauty catching, like a virtuous plague? All the ladies had lost their cracks and wrinkles, their scorched lead faces. There was a proud communal bloom to them, like a richly cultivated bed of roses.

He thought he caught a glimpse of her, but a mole on the upper lip told him it was Olive, Lady Porter.

Guide me, spot of beauty, to my Venice, like the morning star, muttered Kenelm, reaching out, blind, somnambulant.

Then he saw Lady Porter's double, but he realised it was Anne Ogilvy.

No, here was Venetia, flashing azure in her famous dress. He had found her. Kenelm reached to twirl her, but then he recoiled, repulsed because it was not Venetia, only Lettice, blazing in Ultramarine: Lettice as her living likeness from their courtship, years ago.

He let the dance carry him onwards, into the figure of four the dancing master called "shining star."

They all raised their left hands, and he saw the far point of the star was Venetia, but then he turned and found another Venetia at his left, and still another at his right.

"Did you see me?" shouted Endymion. "I was the Spirit of Everything that Can Be Imagined!"

Edward Sackville was showing off also, turning his ankles for the ladies. He was incorrigible. Whenever Kenelm wanted to hurt himself, like holding his finger over a candle, he considered how Sackville had sought to sleep within Venetia's encircling arms.

Uplifted by the dance and cuffed about the head by wine, Kenelm looked wildly about for Venetia, but he could not see her. He had lost the art to know his true Una from the many false Duessas, his original from the multiplying counterfeits.

Kenelm turned round and about, thinking of those early days, when so many faked copies of Venetia's portrait came, unlicensed, from the limners, and each copy's copy degraded a degree, a minim too heavy in the chin, a jot too wide about the eyes, until the only thing about the portrait that was hers was the name engraved below.

His head wheeled, but his legs were carried onwards by the dance. Sweat made his blond quiff stand up like a staff.

There was a great cry and the crack and clatter of silver and glass, and Kenelm guessed the banqueting table had been turned over at the far side of the hall. It must be midnight already.

He saw a foreign ambassador run out to try to put right the damage to the banquet, and laughed at him for not knowing the midnight tradition of turning over the table. The feast was always overturned, for sport's sake. At the crack of the table a new galliard struck up, faster and louder than before, and the crowd leaped to the music.

Venetia was revealed, strobe-lit, in the midst of it all, moving, yet not out of breath, smiling like the goddess of the dance. Behind the serene mask, her thoughts were tumbling: the child Lettice wears my dress, my Ultramarine that Edward Sackville called the colour of Jerusalem's sky. I never gave it to her. I brought it for the Queen, not for her. Now she dances with my husband, and leads the masque as the Morning Star. She usurps and supersedes me. If this is the natural order of things, henceforth nothing in me is natural. Bring me to drink the gaudy immortal. Let me become super-natural.

The drums beat out a new tune: "Love Will Tear Us Apart."

Venetia was thrown opposite a young blood called Wharton, who was dressed as a shepherd, in a rich silken cape, ringlets and Arcadian sandals. His hair was bright blue. "Madam," he bowed deeply. "I adore your daughter Lettice."

Kenelm stamped with the music, feeling the terrible, preordained joy of it, the heartbreak, tearing us apart.

"Again."

The song made him feel like a link in the endless chain of human longing, as he flicked the sweat off his blond quiff, he danced with every sinew of his body, the music animating him like a spirit-wound clockwork man.

Here she was. As he came close, he leaped and kissed Venetia once, which was all the steps would allow. The dance could not be interrupted by any one couple. The dance was bigger than the dancers. Everyone was intertwined, like a living weave. Moving back and forward, around and about, with steps their bodies knew so well their heads could forget them, and caught in the automatic bliss of repetition they turned to and fro, surging and stamping, dancing together in mutual regard and Kenelm rose, jumping, ecstatic, amongst a vast crowd of moshers, waltzers, pipers, ravers, tranceheads, and Pan himself was calling the tune.

Lenten Scars

Three Months Later

> "I can calculate the motion of heavenly bodies, but not the madness of people."
>
> Isaac Newton

Venetia was sitting at her dressing table in the grey morning light, peeling the night-bandages from her face. She heard her son Kenelm's quick footfalls approach her door, and did not stir to let him in. He rattled the doorhandle, and she ignored it. Let him think she was still sleeping. She wanted nothing more than to let him crawl into her bed, to cuddle his hot little body, but she could not let him see her before she had applied her paint. He would judge her wounded, or in pain. He would cry out in alarm, perhaps, the first time he saw his mother's scabs. So she must wait till she was made up for the day before she greeted him. His morning kisses, his closeness, was the very thing she must deny herself if she was to keep his love.

Over the months following the masque, Venetia had lost her taste for sleep. She went through the motions of sleeping, drawing her curtains, putting on her nightgown, larding and binding her face and resting for a few hours, when she slept more than she realised, but lightly. To her it seemed that most of the night she lay seething, waiting for the dawn.

She awoke before her fire was made, and she was at her dressing table when Mistress Elizabeth brought her morning posset. As soon as Mistress

Elizabeth was gone, and sometimes a little before, she unlocked her cabinet and emptied a new vial into her drink, making a curdled pink bowlful, her first Viper brew of the day, which she sipped quickly, whispering Lenten psalms. Then she performed her daily tractations. It required time and care to bring her scabs and stiffness off.

She sent for a bowl of scalding water, which she poured on pot-pourri and hooded herself over, and when the rising velvet vapours of hot rind and valerian root had softened her mood and steadied her breathing, she began to palpate her face, starting with her temples: fifteen circles of the left, fifteen circles of the right; and back again. Her fingertips were the best method, she found; she had no use for the little jet beads Choice had sold her for the purpose. Next she worked across her brow, first rubbing her fingers in myrrh-grease, the better to soften the crusts and serrations that formed overnight. Perhaps that was why she could no longer sleep: she could feel her skin thickening over, like water frosting or custard blistering. It was wonderful to sense how fast she reacted to the treatment; that prickling sensation of new scabs forming was the opposite of slippage, wastage and decay. Instead of slackening, she was tighter by the hour.

Because it was Lent, the pain was particularly appropriate; she considered her tractations almost an Observance. Not quite the Stations of the Cross, which Henrietta-Maria undertook with such piety. Venetia had attended such a pilgrimage around the gardens of the Queen's villa in Greenwich, when they toured the seven improvised shrines barefoot, Venetia maintaining a displeased silence all the while. She preferred to purify her flesh at home. Venetia slapped her face a dozen times with a cold cloth, to feel the blood tingle in her cheeks.

When they sent a body up for anatomy, the doctor's men held their torches near the dissection table, and lutes played: the same three chords, and an arpeggio. Kenelm had told her all about the anatomies at Amen Corner. They read aloud the history of the deceased; a sailor, hanged for theft; a woman of no virtue, nursed through her agonies at Bartholomew's. Ever a different story, ever the same ending. Then the thorax, the parlour of the body, cut open with a razor; the heart, revealed to tell its story.

She had grown up believing that the heart was the font of all affection and kindness; that usurers and villains whose cadavers were opened were found to have no heart; that heartache was real, not a figure of speech; and that all one's deeds were inscribed on the heart, so that when the body died, the heart was taken into the House of Judgement to be read, like a book, by God. Now she was told that her heart was a two-chambered pump, which pounded like a brewery or a city system of locks and canals, pressurised, efficient. Previously the blood was quickness and life, and the heart was hope and care and tenderness, but now the blood fetched and carried, and the heart was two pistons and a plunger. She was a mechanical being, then, so why not mend her?

How she missed Kenelm, now he was away at sea again. She longed for him, fearing for his safety, and yet she had taken full advantage of his absence. She went to Choice directly Kenelm sent word he was at Dover. She must be cut open quickly, so she had time to heal before he was back. She tensed every time she heard the Mercury letter-boy's bell, in case it was a note from him saying he was come home early, although she knew by experience that Kenelm never came home early. He was too enraptured with the world for that. He was gone to sail across the Bosphorus on the wings of a mechanical eagle—or if not, then he was witnessing a new city built upon marshes and artificial islands. No, wait; he was gone to see a clock that kept its time by the sun-magnetised seed of a sunflower, owned by a Jesuit from Westphalia. He had talked of all these ventures, and the desire to travel had overtaken him, as it did periodically, so that his will to be gone was stronger than his motivation for going. When he wanted to leave he was caged and fretful until he went. His library building had overspent him for a year, and she gave him some of her private monies—her gambling fund—to send him on his way.

She had rehearsed the Procedure in her head so many times, but when it came to it, she put forth no more than a track of ruby tears across her forehead and down each cheek; afterwards, she produced only small degrees of pus. She barely noticed the pain. The elation of her new endeavour carried her onwards. It was the most advanced treatment possible, practised by her trusted Physician. The tiny quantity of Viperish serum he introduced into her wounds was enough to sweetly paralyse, but not to harm. She knew it was poison, but everything worth having is a poison.

Since the Queen's Twelfth Night Masque, she had never been at a loss for direction; she had not felt alone, but always accompanied by her mania. Whether she was playing with baby John or directing the household, the mania expressed itself in one word, which like an incantation she heard repeated in her head: "*younger*." It was an imperative, to herself, to Choice, and it summed up her new purpose. She said it through tight lips, like a curse, a profanity, or she smiled it with the impatient glee of a girl. "Younger, younger." It had no answer, no context. One simply repeated the command.

She could hear the boys running about the corridor, trying to get her attention. Her little loves! She visited young Kenelm at his military practice in Bunhill Fields the other week, turning up in her white veil, interrupting the marching song, and telling the lieutenant soldier she was taking him home. She wanted to spoil him for his saint's day, so they could be alone together again for the afternoon, as they always had been, playing Rise Pig and Go, or Fox i'the Hole. But when they were home, and he would not drink his beaker of ale, she realised he was not happy, and he told her in a stiff little voice that she was the only mother to come to the artillery field, and that she should not do it again.

With Kenelm away, she wore soft clothes about the house, and took porridge for supper, and relaxed all her habits. It was a comfortable, drab life, enlivened by the riveting project of her Improvement.

Her morning face-palpations took about an hour. It was necessary work; one treatment led to another, as calf to kine. She heard the clatter of the cattle going willingly to the market down Cowcross Street to Smithfield, and she looked at herself in the mirror with the wide eyes of a milk-calf. She laughed, and a scab in her cheek lifted, stinging her back to piety.

She blotted, fanned, pressed her face with cold linseed water, painted with ceruse so the redness and the serrations were covered, and she was ready to begin her exercises. Chater came up to help with these; he was such a kind friend to her these days. He understood everything, without needing to be told. Ever since she started her course of Viperish Infusions, he had taken such care of her, never reproaching her and bringing broth to her on the days she was bleeding or bruised and needed to stay closeted from the household. He was her confidante again, although they never spoke of her Improvements—he only responded tacitly to her needs, with an officious air that she found comforting.

First they prayed together, and then he got up and took off his wide black hat and cracked his knuckles in preparation, forgetting that Venetia had forbidden him to do so. He took the daily practice of her Exercises with high ceremony. Rubbing her back with his fists, Chater could feel her vertebrae, perhaps because of how much thinner she was grown, or because something in the Viper Wine leached the goodness out of her. He held her arms behind her while she leaned forwards; he helped rotate her arms in their sockets, as a means to suppleness. They both bent their heads to one side; then the other, fifteen times. Their movements were based on the fencing exercises of Jacob de Gheyn, which so many men followed as a morning drill. Venetia had seen the book. Except her aim was not to thrust and kill, only to move more smoothly, and carry herself with her old, sweet, flowing locomotion.

As the exercises sent her blood pounding, through her formerly feeling heart, it gifted one word to every vein and corpuscle: younger. *Younger.*

When the physicians had no more bodies, they anatomised living creatures, rats or dogs, which demonstrated briefly the final workings of their flapping hearts. Life was the secret that could not stand to be known, and concealed itself at the very moment of its uncovering. Kenelm's friend, a Kentish man called William Harvey, was the chief anatomist. When they were crossing the Thames together a waterman stopped Harvey and gave him a transparent shrimp, for which Kenelm was surprised to see Harvey pay a crown. He showed Kenelm the repetitive pulsing movement of the organs visible beneath the shell. Younger, younger.

"*Vindica te tibi,*" she muttered to herself. It was their motto, and she followed it every day, through the thrilling agency of her own progress. "You must change your life!"

She tried a smile, with some success, barely even wincing, although the blister on the curve of her smile put forth a little water as she moved her cheek. She dabbed it, and repainted. She looked in the glass, sideways, the better to see her newly smooth outline. She was so lucky, she considered, to live in this Age, at this rolling edge and frontier of time, where there was such advanced Understanding, and such cosmetic treatments were possible.

The sound of urgent blades cutting the air brought the Queen and her ladies-in-waiting out of their rooms. Squinting at the sky and shielding their faces, they held their skirts against the unnatural wind. The Thames was marked with concentric ripples, and a huge circle of grass in the Palace's east lawn was flattened by the breath of this great, whirring gnat as it prepared to land.

Behind its eyes sat Kenelm and Endymion, wearing earphones. They had been charged with delivering the precious cargo to the Queen quickly and so here it was, because she could not wait another week. Too many of her treasures arrived spoiled, or were confiscated on the way—the Christ she commissioned from Guido Reni never left Rome, censored by a Cardinal. She had implored Endymion, twisting his name with her tongue ("Hen-day-may-on") to fetch her painted altarpiece safely. Rubens had never made her anything of her own before.

The machine shut down and before the blades slowed to a still, the hatch was already open and the parcel conveyed across the lawn, wrapped in brown sisal and bulky yet invested with so much glamour it was as if it had come vaulting out of the sky.

In the long gallery the altarpiece was shrouded and propped against a wall, so that the Queen might enjoy the drama of its unveiling; her singers were gathered to raise a jubilate. As she and her ladies knelt, the soft volumes of their dresses gradually sinking around them, a shaft of bright light on the other side of the room gave the scene a reflected glow. Endymion perceived this would glare upon the painting, and he pulled the window-covering half across, making a softer gloom. Endymion asked George Gage to remove the wrapping, who asked the Groom of the Gallery, who told his boy to do it. Endymion had already checked the painting for flaws.

The winding sheet would not come off the highest corner, and a stick was procured to fetch it down. When it fell, the canticle reached a height, the singers raising their voices in a sweet discord, and the Queen looked up.

Christ's beloved body was raised above her, so towering and foreshortened, she felt she knelt at the foot of the cross. His body was waxen-white, yet still living, and His muscles rippling, as if He were lifting a great weight to the sky, not suffering to death on the cross, but raising the roof of the world. About him, two soldiers carved the air with lash-whips, their bodies so muscular they were almost deformed. Poor Simon of Cyrene was nearly crushed beneath the cross, while in the midst of them, bone-white in the gloom, Christ shone so He made Henrietta-Maria's eyes burn. Another soldier tried His flesh with a pike, and the blood and water fell thickly—the sacrifice that must be made to renew the world. Christ's little beard was pointed and his eyes were so familiar they pulled Henrietta-Maria's soul out of her skin. His body moved her as if it were her own husband's body, prophetically sacrificed before her eyes. He was the son of a King, how could they kill him?

The Queen was easily revived with swooning-water. Lucy Hay carried sal volatile always with her, as Henrietta-Maria had frequent need of it lately. Everyone at court presumed she was with child again. The musicians broke off in sympathy, and when it was ascertained she had only fainted, resumed at a tactfully soft pitch. As she came round, the Queen babbled half in French, half English about her attempts to convert the King. "He comes to Rome, *chaque jour*, he falls . . ." The ladies pretended not to hear.

Endymion was also moved by this painting. It depicted the actual moment of Christ's death, in full colour—pious *and* spectacular. To look upon this Rubens was to develop a second sight, to enter a moving world. Actions and their consequences were both contained in the same painting: the spear piercing and the blood spurting, the eyes of Christ illuminated by the thunderbolt, the changing darkness of the sky, the momentary eclipse of the sun, the hysterical feathers of the frightened birds . . . Everything was in motion, and yet painting was a static art—this was the fascination of the thing. It was the paradox that made the painting rise to meet the Miracle. The peacock at the foot of the cross, symbol of early Christians—that was very Rubens. He must have had that mouldy peacock hanging around his studio, left over from *The Judgement of Paris*. I give you Christ's Passion, with a peacock at no extra charge . . .

Henrietta-Maria and her ladies left the gallery to take some air. She walked away light-headed, supported by her ladies, but pleased beyond measure with the proof she had given herself—and everyone present—of her spiritual and artistic capacity to be moved. The painting's value could not now be doubted. Endymion fancied that the Italian ambassador would already be noting this incident down in his dispatches.

On the sunlit side of Whitehall, William Laud, dean of the chapel royal, and de facto Archbishop, was giving communion to the King and his men. "The Lord bless you and keep you." The King and his gentlemen knelt at the top of three steps, before an altar guarded by a rail: this was how Laud believed communion should be taken, and this was how it would soon be administered, across the whole country. High and low would have to respect this. Laud was moving along the line of men, giving the Protestant sacrament to Kenelm with particular joy, when a Groom of the Bedchamber discreetly approached the altar and whispered in the King's ear.

Laud heard something about the Queen and guessed it was to do with her health. He turned back to the high cross, and focused his mind on communion. Laud closed his mind to the Popery the Queen practised in her chapel. It was one of the inevitabilities of serving royalty: the King had to have a dynastic marriage, and it was only unfortunate that his bride would not come over to the established Church. Laud hoped she would, for the sake of her soul and his ministry. Last week, he dreamed that the Queen had made a gargoyle face at him, before slamming a door. He wished his dreams would not make such affairs of state personal, but this was ever his burden. He had nine older brothers and sisters, and his mother always said: as the tenth, he was paid to the Church.

The King crossed himself and rose to go to the Queen while Laud continued to dispense communion. He suspected the King had gone to see the new painting. Laud longed to see it too. It was his will to reconcile the established Church to beauty. Paintings and altarpieces; holy chalices and vestments for priests. Altars set away from the congregation, pulpits for the authority of the priest. No more Puritan altars in the middle of the church, mimicking the Last Supper. No more gadding to hear Puritan sermons in other parishes, no iconoclasm, no hairshirt whitewashing of church frescoes. Carved pews, decorated ceilings, even sculptures of fatted cherubim and paintings of Christ—these were more than permissible, these were to the greater good of God. All must beautify and glorify His name. To glorify we beautify. Amen.

Mary Tree: 252 Miles Travelled

THE GODLY MEN and women of Childe Biddeford made me so welcome, that although I only intended to pass one night here, on my way from Gayhurst to London, I have now stayed two months almost, and yesterday I clean forgot my own name. The reason being that everyone here calls each other by Virtues, that they might be minded to follow the Lord more closely every time they call and reply. I cannot tell you what my new name is, just for the moment, because it may bring me to laughter, and laughter is one of the cracks wherein depravity enters, so I will talk no more of my name, and continue plaiting these rush mats, as Mistress Be-Busy bid me.

I forgot, I should call her "Be-Busy" only, as she holds not with titles.

As soon as I showed my face here, walking into this valley one spring-like day, the men and women made out they recognised me, waving and telling me "welcome home." It was odd, but I gave myself over to this false homecoming. I suppose it was a dream I have long held of belonging. I told them I must be about my master's business, meaning Richard Pickett, but they said I must be about my Father's business, meaning Our Lord. I found it difficult to answer that one. I have almost enjoyed my time here, eating only beans and plain foods, and seeing all the preachers as they pass by. Last week we had a calm and quiet minister who talked of Providence, and the universal purpose of portents, which made me wonder what purpose my Mark portended. Then this week a full-passionate preacher spoke out against the King's Archbishop, and his idolatry, and men wearing what they call "lovelocks," and his condemnation was so stirring that it made everyone rise to their feet, glad almost to tears.

The people here perceived I was lost and they wished to claim me as their own, and yet belonging is not such an easy matter as that. Being tucked under a shepherd's arm is not enough to bring us to a flock. Zealous Goodenough is the father to this congregation, and kind as he is, I do not feel he is my father. I do not wake every morning praising the Lord—some of the women here say psalms in their sleep, I swear—and fasting does not agree with me. I do not wish to wear a bonnet always, as I think there is nothing sinful about my hair. But on these matters there is such agreement here, it is as if they are an army waiting to do battle, valiant and full of righteous hope. Often they speak of raising banners, marching, and making ready their weapons of faith. I was relieved to hear that by "weapons of faith" they usually mean their tongues, to talk Scripture.

Which brings me to my name—oh my name! It is Crush-Evil-'Neath-Your-Toe. I am glad Annie Braxton is not here for she would laugh until she shook. I was given the name at prayer circle the evening I was received into Communion. I support the crushing of evil, only it is not pleasing to find oneself replying to the name of "Toe."

At prayer meeting yesterday Zealous Goodenough declared that godly men and women shunned beauty, as a false witness, a lure, a trap and a trick to send us mad, and then as he was talking he came over and smiled at me and put his hand on my shoulder, as if to say: Look at this unbeautiful one we welcomed in. Then he asked around the room in turn, Do ye shun beauty, do ye shun beauty? But they never asked me, because it would be like asking a cripple if they shun walking. Perhaps it was as well they did not ask me, because I do not shun beauty. I long to catch a glimpse of beauty, to grasp its trace in every living thing. I see it in the hedgerow and the brook. I see it in the clouds. I thirst for beauty as much as any other girl who never owned a pretty kerchief nor a gay garter.

My name is not "Only By Marriage," nor "Crush-Evil-'Neath-Your-Toe," I said to myself, as I tiptoed out of the lodge last night with my pack at my back. My name is Mary Tree. The white owl beckoned me with her call, and I feared it was Sir Richard's spirit. At least I have weathered out the worst of the winter here, although it was not so warm yet that I was minded to rest, but I kept marching all night, till I walked into dawn, with Richard's shard always at my back.

As it began to be sunny, I came upon some milkmaids with their pails full for skimming, and it pleased me so much to learn none of them were called Here-Be-Zion nor Have-Faith-In-Him, but only Jane and Susan. I thought I must have been brain-sick to linger so long with those Puritans, and yet I met many more Brothers and Sisters along the way as I trod the green paths onwards.

Adulterated Candies

At the silver Thistle, a dirty apothecary's on Shining Lane, the stock was being despoiled, the Cures and Healing Tinctures shaken out of their stock-jars so they collected on the floor in great powdery pyramids, sherbet-coloured ground coral mingling with verdigris and sparkling talc. Clouds of marbled dust swirled in patterns unknowable in the light from the little round window. The proprietor of the shop had buried her face, refusing to witness the waste of her goods, and crying silently into a huge grey napkin. The doors to the premises were locked; one boy was searching the back room, while another climbed the ladder, upending the jars one by one. The College of Physicians was making a raid.

The Censor stood with his hands folded, a tall figure in his royal purple gown, making his customary speech.

"We, being informed that your practice was a low operation no better than a quack-salver's, and your co-conspirator, Thomas Leake, an unskilled glyster-pipe pusher, specialising in powdered pigs' bones, and you a medicastra, or that is to say, a base and female Empiric—"

"Ay me." She shook her head.

"Who learned all she knows of Physick under a country hedge—"

"Nature's cures are my cures," she interjected, looking at the Censor with one pale blue eye, and another clouded by cataract.

"And so, Madam Garley—"

"Gurley," she said. "Begg Gurley."

"If you will. Madam, we find cause to censure your trade in the strongest terms, and investigate your operations."

"Can't it wait, sir?" she said in a soothing voice, like a big pigeon. "Master Leake's coming back within the day. He's gone up Islington way, to do some fishing. It's the Lord's Day, isn't it?"

She was attempting to cast a spell on him with her gentle voice, and her pale eyes, and he would not look at her in case he gave in.

"We have tested your wares with our expertise, our physician's assay, and thus we learn"—he pointed with his wand at the heap of shimmering powders—"that your Gold contains no Gold but Fool's Gold, that your Frankincense is two parts lavender, and that your Tincture of Coral is chalk stained with cherry juice."

Begg made a gesture close to a shrug and turned her face away.

"All your wares must be impounded. None can be trusted. What further miseries must you cause the sick, the needy, by selling them these adulterated candies, when you could be treating them honestly by bloodletting them at the right time of the moon . . ." The Master was about to expatiate on the importance of astral timing, when he caught sight of a mouldy box behind the counter marked "Begg's Cabinett of Egsquisite Rarity."

"And what further criminal dissembling do we find here? Myrrh that is nothing but your own perfumed ear wax, perhaps? Ah, the favourite Unicorn's Horn—"

"Now leave that be, for that *is* the real thing," cried Begg, standing up heavily. "I paid a pretty pound for it. A king's ransom, that was."

The Physician Censor shook his head gravely. He popped the lid off the small box, sniffed the white ground.

"Where did this come from?"

"From a unicorn's forehead, of course."

"Begg Gurley, I tell you: the True Horn is so powerful you would never afford it. No physician can, come to that. If they could then London would be a healthful place indeed."

He tipped the box upside down, creating a small snowfall of valuable scurf. Begg Gurley yelped, seizing her fist in the air, her tongue vainly protuberant.

"Now we will sweep up and soon be gone, and your fines will be charged accordingly."

Just at that moment one of the boys came in from the back room carrying a box and some scales. He said something in the ear of the Censor, who suppressed any satisfaction as he made his final pronouncement: "And on top of everything, your weights are off, so I am confiscating these as well."

Aware, in theory, of the College of Physicians' raids, but unaware that one was being visited so thoroughly upon his fellow apothecary a few streets away, Master Choice continued, unperturbed, to welcome his best customer. He had not seen Venetia for almost a month, and he was interested to see the results of his labours.

"Well, what do you say?" asked Venetia, stepping into the light and revealing a half-healed face to her Creator.

Master Choice looked at her steadily, and did not speak.

Choice's premises had expanded, so he commanded a full house on Fenchurch Street. Upstairs was kept clean and dainty, draped with fashionable flame-cloth hangings, while downstairs was given over to the ever-expanding pits, the furnaces, the vats and racks. To contain the problem of splatter, there was even—of this Master Choice was particularly proud—a dedicated disembowelling closet.

Choice usually came closer, so Venetia could feel him breathe upon her, but this time he moved away, as if he were trying to see the whole picture rather than the brushwork. He still did not speak, and he frowned as his eyes roved across what he had done.

Most customers were now scheduled to strict half-hour appointments. Some were more trying than others. Little Lettice spent so long expressing her thoughts on the war in Saxony, the use of the colour red in the clothing of unmarried women, and, in order to explain the Wine's effect upon her, the usual hues and clarities of her chamber pot, that Choice wondered if she was unhinged by the Wine, or if she were always a babbler. When her allotted time was over, he turned away to the wall and started humming to himself while he wrote up his Observations, made a note of the astrological position, and tidied away his Instruments. Lettice did not infer the significance of these actions. She talked on without ceasing. He also needed to stand, and open the door for her, before she would leave.

In his innermost heart, Choice looked at Venetia's face, and asked himself, *Ye gods, what have I accomplished?*

To his customer, he spoke thus:

"Well, madam, I have delivered six Viperish Infusions to my lady's face, in symmetrical manner, across the forehead, in the crucible of the frown—which is between the eyebrows—around the eyes, and in the crease twixt nose and lips. The fruits of my labour are now before me."

And, he might have added, all around him: two of Venetia's infusions had paid for a portrait of Master Choice, which now hung above the sign of the star; two had gone towards the rent; and the last two, prescribed belatedly, eased the pressing cumulative deficit of his coffers, and allowed Margaret Choice a new mattress.

Aletheia Howard's patronage was a great financial blessing, although she had warned him most peremptorily that she was *una Contessa*, but she would not pay *una Contessa*'s fee, so he must charge her *uno prezzo giusto*—a fair price. He laughed as if she were an ill-informed woman and said that prices varied according to the season, the availability of vipers, the composition of the Wine . . . Aletheia looked hard at him and said she had great experience of the antiquities merchants of Naples, and that she would pay what her friend Olive paid.

Lancelot Choice still had not replied to Venetia's question. He swallowed.

"I see before me a forehead that has no creasing upon it, and no trenches. I see eyes that are free from crow's feet, a little swollen, but not so much that my lady's eyesight is impaired, no?"

"I retain my perfect sight, thank you."

"And as for the cheeks, well, they are fuller than they were. Time and palpations will bring them into shape a little more. Now, I need to see the motion of your notions. Is it that time of the moon with you that you might give me a wee smile, my lady?"

Venetia smiled without emotion, like a string puppet.

Olive was now in the habit of sending Choice scrawled billets-doux, in exchange for his vials of Viper's Wine. Of course, she paid for her Wine, but she had started to feel that it was cruel to acknowledge his matchless weekly offerings with money alone. So she wrote back with thanks, observations on her health and kind solicitations. Every week he replied with more wine, and their phantom correspondence kindled Olive's desires to ever stronger heat.

Endymion was home again, loving-stern, full of expectation and demand. He wrote to her from Le Havre, telling her to "make much of herself" before his return. She put on her new stomacher of incarnadine satin, laced about with silver, and her petticoat of tabby rose, little thinking that when he saw her he would set about her with a horse's bit, a metalwork contraption from Vienna, designed not for breaking in beasts but for men's gratification. She refused to wear it, but she let him prick her sides and rump with his toy whip, which sent him faster into tilt, as he shouted old jousting cries and battle oaths. His roughness made Olive's fantasies the sweeter; how she longed to condescend to Choice, to lavish herself upon his surprised and grateful person.

When he saw Venetia's smile, Choice felt a cold stone on his heart: this will do for me.

Her face was still her own, give or take a lumpy, swollen aspect, not unlike a water-corpse. The puffery looked unfortunate, though it served to eliminate her runckles. But he had gone too far, and the movement of her smile was stiff and uneven, like warped parchment, tighter on one side of the face than the other.

"Thank you, my lady. Hear what I say to you now: there's no cause for concern. With time and palpations . . ."

Venetia turned her back on Choice and strode towards his mirror, his new bevelled mirror. He chid himself for speaking amiss: whenever people are told there is no cause for concern they always cry panic.

"Good Choice," she said in a small voice, which he dreaded would become shrill, a scream as she looked in the mirror. But the low purr continued. "*Dear* Choice, thou art a Daedalus, a fabulous artificer." In the mirror, she turned her face this way and that, like a lady trying on an invisible hat. He wondered if it was a distorting mirror, a scrying glass, to show her such a different image than the one he saw. "Your art is beyond my happiest imaginings. I am only sorry we did not do this sooner. I think a little more, here and there, and I will almost be ready."

"Indeed, my lady," swallowed Choice. Ready for what?

"Although, of course, like the painter, you will find your work is never finished. Titian used to sign his work *Titianus Pinxit*—Titian was painting this. You should use the continuous verb as well. You will always be needed by me, Choice. Continually! If I must to the country, you shall thence as well."

She turned and beamed at him, and seeing her left cheek stretch taut as calfskin, he recoiled, stepping backwards, until he was up against the closet. He could see himself in the mirror now, trapped behind her, pale and surprised, his fake, customer-soothing smile still garnishing his face.

Choice had intended to create a dependency in his customer but now that ambition had so manifestly been achieved, he needed a few moments to understand his own startling success. Her attitude was surprising, and even senseless, given the condition of her appearance, and he blinked as he tried to believe she was truthfully happy, not firing some ironical barb, nor prating distractedly. But she was genuinely satisfied. And she was no mad lady. It was a sideways slip-slide of her brain, he supposed. About the nature of our own bodies, we can be mightily self-deceived. He remembered the Abbot at Westchester who ate himself to death. Oh lucky Choice, to have such another as his customer! This goldmine could run deep.

Her reason was strong, but her appetites were stronger—for love, for cards, for Wine, and eventually, for beauty. Choice perceived this, and played upon it. In that dark January when Choice persuaded Lady Digby to try his Viperish Infusions, he tempted her with all the skills of his quick tongue: flattery, accompanied with a little denigration, designed to make her doubt herself. ("You are radiant, my lady, but you are runckled, and there is nothing worse than runckles, for they multiply . . .") Then he explained the latest cosmetic Infusions practised in Italy, with diagrammatic explications and the like—for he knew her soul was Considerate, prone to cognition, rather than feeling. She was discriminating. She preferred to survey a topos from many angles before proceeding. In this respect she was somewhat like a man. All the while Choice managed to maintain—and in this he was most sly—the air of someone who did not want to give his expertise away lightly. He did not press the Infusions on her but kept them back, carefully concealed, like a valuable miniature in a kid-skin pouch. He made her suspect he might be guarding it for another, more deserving customer. He played upon her vanity and ambition like a flute.

"Next, Choice, I would like you to work your Ingenuity, your marvellous skill, upon my lips. 'Rubious portals of pearls' that they once were, to Ben Jonson. Or—this was Wat Montagu, I think—

"'From cupid's hallowed gates, let fly
The words of love I lay my glory by.
Thy lips all bounties give, all peace supply . . .'"

She sang the words, letting the notes float loudly across the room, putting on a show for him, twisting her wrists sinuously, like a mad Courtesan. It must have been a sport she learned a time ago at court.

"'Or Venus, mistress, let me die . . .'"

The music that she heard in her head took her a final twirl, before she sank before him in a smiling curtsey.

Choice clapped, out of embarrassment, because he wanted to make it stop. And yet he had to admit, she was magnificent, in her bravado. It was commonly said that women had no Character at all, but that seemed not to be the case with the women that came to his shop of beauty. If anything, they had too much.

He could see that her lips were still well-formed, and yet the pigmentation of her cupid's bow had become less distinct with time, and the out-size puffery of her cheeks made her lips seem less full, so they had become lost in the overall design of her face. He wondered how he could possibly accentuate them. He had never treated lips before. He paused, choosing his words daintily, as ever. Since he was a boy his eloquence had worked for his own protection and promotion. How could it be otherwise, with six brothers and no way of getting his mother for himself?

"Until Saturn is out of its retrograde, you will do harm by moving your face. The Viperish Infusions are working, and for the sake of their, ahem, continued success, you should guard your face and rest it quiet."

Choice hoped this would keep her from showing herself abroad too much, and frightening the clientele.

He could see by Venetia's face that she did not think much of his suggestion. She was always being told to stay in bed, safely away from view, until she was ready for churching after childbirth, or her husband was home, or the pox was no longer abroad. Well, she would not stay closeted. Not this time. Besides, she was going to mass with the Queen at Whitehall on the morrow.

"And my lips? When will you bring them to that pitch of beauty I require?"

There was such trust, such dependence, in her voice, that Choice's tongue flickered with pleasure, as he marvelled at how this knot he had tied could grow tight, and tighter still.

"O lady, worry ye not, we will bless your lips with venom."

A Letter from the Mouth of Hell

To my dearest Son, Kenelme Digby Esquire,
I write thee now from the side of a great beast. The beast's colicky stomach rumbles all night long (as yours did once, when you were newly born) yet I can sleep well enough, because I am of that strong Digbean constitution, which you are too. What a blessing we both have in that. The beast snores even now as I write, and light rocks are sent bouncing around your father's head and the ground trembles a little. The beast, as I tell you now, in manly confidence (please be sure your mother does not take this letter, and read it) is a tall and glowering mountain. I am about two-thirds up.

I set out accompanied with a strong cohort of local Cicerones, which is to say guides, tho. their number has diminished as the climb has become perilous, the air thicker and so on, and now I am left with one good man [there was some crossing out which young Kenelm could not read]. *It seems, dear son, that in the last hour or so my one remaining guide has left me and taken with him the cooking-pot. Perhaps it was the darkness which is lately seen in the sky at noon which offence'd him. All is well, at any rate, as he leaves me to my profound Observations uninterrupted.*

Many Unnatural Disturbances beset this country as we approached the beast. Inland basins were all dry or suck'd up as if the land thirsted for water. At Castellammare di Stabia the sea began to boil and churn. At Santa Maria di Pugliana great rocks were hurled down upon the village, and the church bell rang of its own accord. On Sunday the sea tide turned sharply, leaving fishermen's boats stranded and dancing fish exposed along the shore. Then the wave was thrown back at the land with great vehemence. None can say what this indicates, although there is a belief amongst the populace that the local landowner, absentee, and reviled for stopping up one of the public wells, is rebuk'd by this action of nature.

Strangest of all to relate was the profane hush which settled over everything: the sweet wind, foamy sea, racing sky—all these were mysteriously suppressed, or suspended, so that the World itself seemed not to turn. No birds sang, flies vanished and horses were as amaz'd as men. This was, they say, the final Sign or Import of some great Violence to come. This came to pass on Tuesday. Today is Friday. Please to keep this letter safely in case the beast wakes and my notebooks are destroyed—

Kenelm was interrupted here, because his lantern was extinguished, although he could not discern why. A gust of sulphurous wind had dowsed the wick perhaps? Feeling slow on his feet, Kenelm stepped outside his little pavilion made of Ottoman rugs and elegant pilasters, pitched upon the rocky mountain-slope, and now sorely asquint, but still standing. He strode a healthy distance from his camp, to a promontory where he could breathe better, and he looked across the tranquil moonlit bay towards Ischia, where the sea doubled the luminescence of the moon, and he recognised God's benediction.

It began to rain—he could hear the noise of the raindrops falling all around him. And yet the pitter-pat was too sharp, too biting, and he realised the sky was sending down not rain but tiny particles of stone. They hit his head like miniature agassi or hailstones, bouncing off his shoulders. He went back inside his pavilion, and cradled his head within his arms, until he fell into pleasant dreams of standing atop this ill-mannered mountain.

A spring morning dawned, shared by all those who happened to be alive at the same time as one another, that unwitting complicity that means everything and nothing, and goes un-noticed, or glimpsed by historians or curious novelists. In Italy, Kenelm woke with a start on the side of his mountain. In Rome, Athanasius Kircher was up early, working on his Polygraphia Nova, a universal artificial language that was not yet a failure. In Amsterdam, Rembrandt felt the heavy coin of his first princely commission, and knew it would be enough for him to offer marriage. In Fleet Street, Samuel Pepys was kissed and held aloft in his swaddling by his father, for he was one month old that day, according to his wet-nurse Goody Lawrence. In Cambridgeshire, Oliver Cromwell, newly married, taking his morning contemplation in the Fens, heard God's voice in the croaking of a bullfrog: "Repent, repent."

In the Whitehall Palace gardens, Venetia was tiptoeing along the Avenue of Limes, playing hide-and-seek with Queen Henrietta-Maria. The early golden sunshine and the shadows of the trees striated the path, and in the deep shadow, she noticed a gardener was hiding with a rake and a wheelbarrow behind a tree, not as part of the game but out of deference to it. She could not bestow a smile on him, or her face might break from its tightness.

Before her, up the path, she heard a giggle from behind a tree and saw a flash of the Queen's holy body darting away, towards the parterre. Venetia gave chase, tripping daintily in her cork-soled platform shoes over the gravel, elated to have been chosen by the Queen to join her after mass as a sportful companion for her recreations. She only chose pretty companions.

Today Venetia had shown herself unveiled in the Great Hall for the first time since her Infusions. Lucy Bright kept away, on the other side of the hall, even though she must have seen her. Venetia tried not to think about what this meant. Ben Jonson was another one whose gaze she feared; his Discriminating Eye. He made it his business to know about all the minutiae of life, alchemists' receipts, and shopkeepers' books, and soldiers' slang, and he took a particular interest in great ladies' Improvements, and she was half expecting him to re-work one of his old satiric poems for her—

"Ah, Venetia, here she is, busy distilling her husband's land / Into decoctions, and in her chamber manned / By ten Physicians, lying about the spirit of amber, oyle of talc . . ."

But instead of teasing her, he fell quiet and stared at her, taking in the new uneven puffery of her face and eyes, the stiffness of it. "The ambitious faces of the time . . ." he muttered, quoting himself as usual. "The more they paint, are the less themselves." The beauty he had so long ago desired—loved without hope—had now destroyed itself. He always thought her so royally assured of her own perfections, but he saw in her wounded face how vulnerable she had become.

It would be kind to flatter her, and more than that, it was expedient. The venality in his soul stirred as he saw an opportunity. Sir Kenelm was master of three thousand a year.

"I shall write a poem celebrating your new blooming beauty, lady, which has a turn of the Orient about it, I believe. 'Matchless, Unusual, Oriental Shee . . .' "

So pleased by this was Venetia, so keen to take it as her due, she forgot to consider the fact that, since the fire that consumed his house, Ben was almost destitute, with a dwindling list of patrons. Before they parted, he lowered his black-clad bulk towards her, whispered "Matchless" in her ear, and puckered his slack lips, depositing upon her cheek a Judas kiss.

As she tiptoed along the gravel of the Queen's garden, in and out of the sunshine, she cried out with surprise as a warlike tot ambushed her from the laurel bushes, growling, "Avast!"

It was Jeffery Hudson, Lord Minimus so-called, his toy rapier glinting in the sunshine.

"Pass ye not this way, Her Majesty goes!"

He was out of breath and his voice was penetratingly pitched, low and high at once. The feathers of his hat, perched on his head, were about level with Venetia's waist. He pretended to regret his fierce approach, and mimed sheathing his sword with decorous chivalry.

"I do not mean to alarm you with my swordplay, lady," he said, bowing. "I have but lately been released from the clutches of Pirates in the Channel, so my manners are grown rough, rough, hee hee!"

Everything about Jeffrey Hudson's manner was contrived, as if he were constantly acting. He made his anger and his griefs or longings especially funny, and he knew it; he played his passions for his public. His mode of address was always mock heroic. When he spoke of Pirates, he was not lying. When the Queen was first with child he was sent, along with others of her retinue, to fetch her favourite nurse and midwife; the party was detained on its way home by Corsairs, and the Queen had all her retinue wear black until their safe return. Jeffrey Hudson was the Queen's favourite curiosity, and his archness was the making of him, and yet, since he lost so much of his soul withal, it was also his undoing.

"Shall we onwards together, my lady, and I protect ye along the way?"

Trotting over the lawn in pursuit of the Queen, the pair of them came upon a stone pilaster, topped with a curious beast. Sitting on its haunches cleaning its tail, shivering gently and chattering to itself, was Pug, the Queen's monkey. Venetia had heard of this creature but never seen it. She noticed it was balding in places, and as it looked at her with comprehending wet black eyes, she thought it was the loneliest-looking creature she had ever seen.

"There, there," she said, reaching to stroke its pink and sable head.

Pug tried to bite her but all his teeth had been filed, so he only clamped her hand pathetically.

"Naughty ape! You spiteful *singe*!" Jeffrey Hudson tried to discipline him, but Pug was just above his reach, and he made a show of swiping vainly.

Pug scratched his head and then climbed into Venetia's arms and buried himself under her throw, trembling.

The three of them moved on towards the Orangery, their shadows exaggerated over the grass. The vast baroque fountain, which the Queen had lately had shipped from France, gurgled merrily, calling them across the garden, and feeling the compulsion, the necessity to be playful, Venetia, the monkey and the dwarf darted around opposite sides of it, the better to surprise the Queen. The low sun caressed the curves of the Nereids in the fountain, and turned the grotesque sea-monsters around them into even more frightful creatures; the rough-sculpted rocks rose out of the waters, pitted and misshapen, while the Nereids posed upon them, waxy-smooth and wave-tressed.

Gargoyled by the cruel sunlight, Venetia peeped out from her hiding spot beside the fountain, looking for the Queen, whom she thought must be behind the box-tree hedge. Setting Pug free to dance around her in circles, she tottered forward in her platforms. Jeffrey Hudson followed, roaring and waving his cutlass. Their shadows stretched like caricatures across the grass. A giant man, the Welsh porter new to the Queen's retinue, stood up to join them from behind a box hedge, and stepped right over it, as easily as if it had been a doorstop.

"What merry company," laughed the Queen, when she and her pale blonde lady-in-waiting Lily Hutchinson had finally been caught, squealing, at the centre of the box-hedge maze. "I wish the King could see us."

"I was quite afraid!" said Lily.

Just then, a court deputation appeared in the middle distance, coming out of a little door in the wall by the Orangery. English Chancellors in black, stockinged and spider-like, bearing papers and writing boxes, contended with a delegation of French Seneschals also moving along the narrow path. The Queen was trying to arrange Pug in the arms of Jeffrey Hudson, and Jeffrey Hudson in the arms of the giant, so they might make a teasing tableau, before she was interrupted by Sir Francis Knollys.

"Your Majesty's name has been bestowed upon a territory in the New World—it is to be known as"—he referred to his parchment—"That is to say, the King has decreed that territory is to be known as 'Maryland.' "

The Queen clasped her hands together with delight, and made a gracious curtsey.

She is a Medici princess, and one of Anjou too, and yet she is pleased that a portion of lawless wild-scrub far away is named for her? Venetia was unimpressed. She saw a familiar figure lingering at the back of Sir Francis's deputation: Penelope Knollys, wearing a neat white cap and collar, squinting in the sunshine, ill-at-ease in the Queen's private gardens. Penelope would rather be at the gaming table, though no one knew it but Venetia. She made a curt sign to Venetia that indicated, with the eloquence of a well-used face, that she had seen her, that they would speak when they were able, and that relations between them were good enough, although they might have been better.

A child with a posy for the Queen looked at Venetia too, but looking did not lead to liking. Crumpling its face, the child hid in Penelope's skirts. It peeped out again with a fearful expression, to see if Venetia was still there. Its rosebud face bore the honest dismay everyone else concealed. Venetia only thought: What a badly brought-up little tenderling.

When Venetia came close to them, after the Queen was taken in to sign papers, the child would not stop staring. Her little chin began to wobble, and when Venetia blew her a kiss, she panicked, and tried to run away. Penelope needed to send the child off with a nursemaid, for everyone's sake.

"Art well-tempered, dear?" said Penelope, when the child was gone. She did not meet Venetia's eyes, quite, but preferred to drop her gaze beyond her, avoiding looking her full in the face. Venetia put her unease down to the fact that they had not spoken for months—since their meeting in the Bourse.

"I am full of delight, darling—I have been playing with the Queen and her intimates."

Penelope gave a little grimace. "Indeed."

As they talked of that and this and the other, the morning light reflected off the honey stone showed Venetia that Penelope's complexion, though waffled by pox, was not bad at all. Penelope had not even attempted to hide it with paint; her self was its own sufficiency. Attracted to this solid quality that she so lacked, Venetia remembered, on the instant, that she still loved Penelope. Venetia offered her arm, and Penelope took it.

"So you know that dear dog Standon who belongs to Edward Sackville—the piebald terrier."

Here we go, thought Venetia—Penelope's confidences begin again. "Yes," she said wearily, and yet pleased to see her, and to talk inconsequentially. Besides, she remembered Standon, from the days when the Sackville brothers courted her—Standon with his rough pink tongue, constantly panting at her, flirting with her every bit as much as his master. He must be an old dog now.

"To preserve his inheritance, he's lately pupped with a bitch of good breeding. And do you know who was sent the best whelp of the litter? Only little Lettice."

"What?"

"Well, he's a black-and-white brave boy with a good stern on him."

"And why should Dorset send such a one to Lettice?"

"He's courting her for marriage, I believe. Ever since the Queen's masque where he was taken with her dancing."

"She did no dancing! Not on stage."

"Ever since then he comes to walk and talk with her daily. I've played the part of matron with them."

"He does not mind her prattle? He's noticed she's a bagpipe and a gabbler?"

"He says her fresh ways have given him new life. He loves to hear her prating on, and laughs all the while, and strokes his beard. He says Lettice is the wittiest She in London. Talk of their marriage is not generally heard yet, but—I tell you in confidence—Lettice's father has had word from Dorset."

The tightness in Venetia's cheeks stung like lemon. She became aware, abruptly, of a sourness brewing in her mouth. The day's bright light, and the crispness of the palace gardens, seemed to take on a hurtful edge. Venetia spoke in a low, jocund voice that did not become her: "It's a sinful match, and sure to be barren, for Lettice's mother was well-acquainted once with Dorset," she said.

Penelope stopped where she stood, and disengaged her arm from Venetia's.

"Venice, that is vile gossip, and slander, and it is beneath you to repeat it."

Venetia knew that what she intimated was not true, and she also knew that there was enough reason in it to make it dangerous gossip: Lettice's mother, Arabella, had been admired by Dorset. That was the end of the matter. But if it became the thing on everyone's lips, it might be enough to stop the marriage, or at least put it in doubt. She looked at Pen with a naughty expression, trying to charm her out of being too cross.

"I know I am bad, Pen, but you love me when I am bad."

"D'you know, I am dismayed by you, Venetia. A change has come upon you that I did not like to speak of, but since you begin this muckworm talk, I will tell it to you plainly, so I shall." Penelope was more angry than Venetia had expected. She was not given to shouting, and her speech had a quavering, pent-up quality, which Venetia had never seen in her before, except once, at the table, when Penelope was called for passing off a Tom and two Tibs as a Gleek, and she was indignantly innocent.

"First, you have meddled with your face. I know not with what nor how, but you are now so far from the beauty you were born with, you are become one of the Queen's menagerie of freaks—a grotesque. Yes. I saw you there today: the dwarf, the giant, the blackamoor, the monkey—and yourself, skipping for the Queen, as tame frights to set her beauty off—"

"There was no blackamoor."

"I have not finished. She does not have you with her for love, but for sport. I tell you this as a friend: you do not look well. You are like a spiny fish before it squirts its poison, all puff'd up. And you are not sound." Penelope tapped her forehead. "Some quack has robbed you of yourself. Some youth-salve or unguent has filled you with bitter gall or malice, and it has begun to seep out of you, so the look of it is upon your face. I'll say no more, for I do not wish to be merciless, but I tell you, you must mend yourself."

Penelope turned her back, and walked off down the cloister, towards the north of the palace. Venetia was too surprised to do anything else but watch her all the way she went, the stiff grey twill of her gown, the slight hobble in her walk. She gazed still, as she receded, and a group of court minstrels and musicians got in the way of her, playing a vulgar jig, and Venetia strained so she might see the last of her dear old Pen, and even as she turned the corridor, Venetia still hoped she might turn around and wave, or show some sign of forgiveness or retraction, before she was lost to her sight, and Venetia was left alone, cold and naked with self-knowledge.

On the slope of the beast, Sir Kenelm took advantage of a slight sea-breeze to begin his ascent. It was early afternoon, and yet the sky was already growing dark, thickening with dust. A beetle ran to him over the shale and waved its pincers, begging for help, or raising alarm. Perhaps in consequence of solitude, Kenelm had taken to talking to himself of late, as he climbed: "Here's a rooftile. There's another. There were habitations here once, in the fertile valley below this mountain, but they are long gone, consumed by some violent force—the Magneticall Effluvium of Time itself, perhaps . . . There's a flip-flop. A canister called 'Kodak.' Here's an ice-cream wrapper." He studied its faded writing nostalgically, reverentially. "Detritus from another age becomes precious. Displaced matter is dirt, but it is also treasure . . ." He looked at the Cornetto wrapper, which after serving such a short and melting purpose had endured so many years in rewind.

"Calypso Ice Cream—they have named it for the witch who trapped Odysseus and ravished him in a cave on Ogygia for seven years . . ."

Beneath him, under centuries of ash, the private libraries, the faun-fountains, the frescoed villas—all were safely packed beneath the sod; unknown, but not undreamed of. The graffiti howled, the asphyxiated dogs rattled their chains, the people ran for their lives; the buried silence of the past deafened Sir Kenelm.

He sighed and continued climbing the spine of this incalcitrant, growling mountain. As he rose higher, he seemed to provoke an even greater lowing in the belly of the ground beneath him. He had never climbed a mountain before—to do so was not yet fashionable—but one thing he had not expected was that it would be so loud.

Venetia wrote a brief note to Choice saying that she renounced his services, and thanking him for his Compleat Discretion. She paused, breathed, ripped the letter up and rewrote it. She said she renounced his services *for a time.* Then she sent the note.

Chater's eyes stretched when Venetia told him she would need his help. He placed his hand faithfully across his chest, delighted to serve her. Since Sir Kenelm was gone abroad again, and Father Dell'Mascere had become so devoted to the choir, he was hers entirely, and he was inwardly agog to know what new barbarity or self-punishment she was planning, and what role he could possibly play in it.

And yet all she seemed to want was the promise of his company. She told him she was taking to bed for thirty days and thirty nights, and she wanted him to read to her every day, and to have charge of the boys at their meal-times. He was to let no visitors nor correspondence pass into her chamber, and to see that thin potage and manchet bread were sent up, as they were all she would sup.

"And a little brandy posset, I may have need of that."

At first Sir Kenelm thought it was another Expedition ahead of him, lighting fires. He called out "Hallooo" and then remembered he was in Naples. "*Buon giornooooo . . .*"

There was no reply but a hot and salty gust of sulphur, which hit him like a whip, and he realised the fires were globules of burning matter, spontaneously generated by the wind and rocks. No wonder the heat was growing more intense. This was a journey of some fascination. He felt as if he were observing a vast alchemical Work performed by God—the moment when the dragon's sister puts forth her flux. He had drunk the last of his flasks, but what of it—onwards was the only way. He felt the mountain grumble its assent.

Venetia paced around her chamber like Sackerson, the tethered bear at Southwark. She expected that the lack of Wine would leave her enervated and supine, but no, she could not pass a moment's stillness. As soon as she stood up, she wished to stand no more; as soon as she reclined, she wished to stand. She was like an ant on a fire-griddle. Her legs carried her back and forth, but her will, her whole soul, was contrary and dissatisfied with every proposition. She tried to read her Bible while she walked about, and this helped for a time, as she leafed through the pages, although her mind was soon too restless to finish any sentence, any thought. She itched all over her body, a phantom prickle that moved onwards as soon as she pursued it. It was only after some time that she realised she ought not to be using the heavy, rough edge of her Bible to scratch herself. She kissed the Bible and put it away with a trembling hand. What was the point of this torment, if not to become Good?

A vast belch of smoke and gas from the top of the mountain threw Sir Kenelm backwards. As he righted himself he saw melted ore dribble down the side of the steaming mountain as if from a smithy's pot. It poured with a sensuous power, setting into furrows and dollops that blackened as he watched. This orange quickening, this incandescent flow, held him fascinated as he sat on a rock, covered in pumice dust, sweat, and shirtless, from the heat. So Vulcan's mountains did exist, and more than that, the mountain he had three-quarters climbed was one of them: a volcano.

It had erupted before, he knew, and it would again, and it was humanity's curse to be continually surprised by it. Communal memory had forgotten the Roman towns below the sod, as it would remember and forget them again. His skin was cracking because he had removed his clanking armour, his bio-suit, his gas-mask. He smelled the bitumen that sealed up Herculaneum, and he choked on the dust that re-covered its charred treasures a thousand years later, silting up the runways, the resorts, the roundabouts. He felt the feather-light stones of many eruptions simultaneously.

> Akathisia—(from the Greek "inability to sit still") a profoundly uncomfortable feeling of inner restlessness. A symptom of opioid withdrawal.

Venetia could contain herself no longer. She left her chamber and headed for Sir Kenelm's study. As soon as she began walking downstairs, her body ached to be at rest, and as soon as she paused, she wished to walk again. She flung Chater out of the way with a look when he tried to stop her going into the study. He watched grimly, afraid she was going to do something desperate. He believed she was missing some drug that Kenelm usually gave her and he worried that she might eat antimony, or swallow one of his telluric compounds.

She bent to unlock the door and caught a glimpse of herself, puff-faced and desperate, distorted by the brass doorhandle. She pushed aside Kenelm's stacks of books, and stumbled towards his laboratory table. As she stepped nearer she swerved towards her goal. From the back of his chair she seized the sheepskin he wore on his cold nights' work, and buried her face in it, catching the scent of him, and shuddering into it for comfort.

Lo, the walkers approach the fiery furnace, Shadrach, Meshach and Abednego, and yet they withstand the heat . . .

A wet mirage danced ahead of him, watermarking the sky, and Sir Kenelm trod towards it, his hair crisped by the heat, his mouth parched, his curiosity infinite.

He longed to look inside the Crater, thinking he would see visions from Dante's *Inferno*: alchemists degraded in the tenth chasm of hell, or the dreadful procession of sinners with their heads on backwards, their tears falling down their buttocks. Every step took him closer to his father, whom he would surely find in the circle reserved for plotters, holding his own heart aloft and calling, "Thou liest!"

He could not tell if he was crying because he approached a great theological mystery, or if the hot sulphur in the air was making his eyes run rheum.

> "I thought I beheld the habitation of Hell, wherein nothing seemed to be much wanting besides the horrid phantasms and apparitions of Devils . . ."
>
> Athanasius Kircher, the Jesuit polymath, on climbing Vesuvius to look in the crater in 1638

She was twice a mother, monthly cursed, inured to routine aches and torments, which she knew so intimately, they became part of herself. Pain was nothing to her. It was constant, a tame companion. What she was suffering now was different—it seemed to have no source, but traversed her whole person and her mind. She vomited and perspired and shook. She scrabbled to look in her scrying glass, expecting to see that without the Wine, she had aged a lifetime already. All she could see in the glass was her young self, tempting and taunting her.

A thunderclap and torrents of rain would have cooled Sir Kenelm, only the rain fell hot, almost scalding, and it carried streaks of ashes down his torso. He shielded his face with a bandage improvised from his garter. Looking up, he saw a rolling wave of red-hot molten lava cascading over the lip of a distant peak, spooling downwards, gloopy, implacable. He let the image burn upon his inner eye, so he could be sure of his own understanding when he told this tale again.

Then he saw the red chargers foaming towards him, and he turned on his heels, and with the heat bellowing at his back, he ran.

Would she do well to die here? A chill calm settled upon her, and morbid presentiments passed swiftly before her eyes, like black shadows under a boat, indistinctly glimpsed through blood-warm waters.

He ran over the pumice, sliding with heavy speed downwards after so long ascending.

Another rumble announced a great vomit from this beast's belly—HERE IT COMES! He ducked, and as the words came to him, it arrived: the pyroclastic surge.

Panting, he came to the site of his old camp, but there was nothing but the highest pennant of his pavilion sticking out of a great ash-slide. His notebooks, his books and baggage—gone. He felt this was a signal that he should continue downwards with all haste. He realised for the first time the recklessness of his endeavour. He thought of Virgil—"*Facilis descensus Averno*"—It is easy to descend into Hell. The difficulty is coming back.

Venetia fell at last into a lucid sleep, tossing and thrashing as the poison left her body. If it was true that snakes soaked up all the putrid qualities of the earth, no wonder she had been so deformed by their moral poisons. And yet she would do it all again, in a heartbeat. *Il faut souffrir pour être belle.*

Kenelm longed to return directly to his love, his boys, his home. As he clambered over the lower crags of the summit, he felt the blessing of the sea-winds on his face, cooling and reassuring him. No one would believe his tale of climbing the vulcan's mount. He would do better to regale the Tribe of Ben with stories of how he had been caught between Scylla and Charybdis, or how sirens had sung to his ship.

In Naples, he had no hero's greeting, for most of the townsfolk had gone to safer ground, and at his lodgings there was only an old dog lying in the shadows, who barely looked at him. He slept for a long time, disorientated by the quiet of the lodging house, waking only to drink with the thirst of a shipwrecked man. Finally one afternoon his body decided he was fit to rise, and when he was clean and steady enough to walk abroad, he lit fifty candles before the Virgin, and bought Venetia a set of pearls, earrings and necklace, at great price. The pearl trader should have been pleased to find a customer but when he saw Kenelm, he instantly perceived his love, his wealth and his homesickness, and Kenelm could do nothing about this, as he could not hide what he was. He felt the pearls glowing with their own luminescence, even in the dark drawstring purse next to his heart.

Venetia slept heavily. Chater tiptoed about her room, drawing the curtains, opening the windows. The household was beginning to fear for her, and so was he. It was not even Lent any more, and yet she remained in her chamber day and night, taking only gruel and brandy posset. On the far side of the bed were two stale pots that Mary had missed. He studied Venetia's slumped body, and he went, quickly, to fetch from his chest his priestly articles, his unguent, his Bible, his bell.

"May the Lord make haste to save thee," he whispered, panting, making a sign of absolution over her sleeping body and ringing the tinkling bell, getting his pot of salve ready to administer extreme unction.

"Oh, Chater," she replied, in a thick, crabbed voice. "Leave me alone and let me be."

"I do not wear a rug. My hair is 100 per cent mine."

Donald Trump, 2004

JING, JANGLE: THE new bright brass bell above Choice's door sounded more strongly than usual. The customer upon the doorstep was a gentleman, well dressed, in late middle age, with a bluff countenance and broken veins across his nose. He sniffed deeply as he took off one tough leather glove, then another, and thwacked them upon his knee as he sat down opposite Choice. He was surely known to the court, from his dress, and there was a heaviness to all his motions, a roughness, which was somehow sensual. He seemed loath to say for what he had come, and he looked around the room a few times before beginning.

"I hear your trade multiplieth."

"Indeed, sir. May I ask your name, for my book?"

"Don't put it in the book. Between ourselves, my name is Endymion Porter."

Choice coughed. He knew that those love letters from Olive promised no good. He only hoped her husband was not here to demand a duel. He would not pull pistol for that doxy.

"I'll tell you straight. I'm used to passing time with Continental physicians, so I am well acquainted with their practices, their Methods and their Manners. Your trade holds no secrets for me, Choice."

Choice could not help observing that Endymion Porter carried an oversized sword. He had the look of a man who was not afraid to knuckle-fight, either; a gentleman who was not always gentle. He spent his time buying art, Choice knew, and he supposed he drove hard bargains. Choice was reassured by the nearness of his lancet, in a drawer in his desk. He knew it was there; he could have it in his hand in two quick movements.

"Now, I'm not a handsome man, but I have a certain look to me. I'm frequently about affairs of state abroad, and I find a swarthy, weather-worn complexion does follow after time spent in the sun. I've Spanish blood. It's on my mother's side. It's from the mother that the dermis comes, they say. The fleshy parts are generally bequeathed by the softer sex. I read it once, in Fludd's great book—" He broke off. "You fellows do work upon a man, you do. With your silence! Ah, me. So let us to it . . ."

Endymion slapped his glove across his thigh again. Choice was beginning to perceive gratefully that the former ambassador to Spain was not here to avenge his wife's honour.

But just as Endymion was about to tell Choice what it was he wanted, he got up and distractedly perused the monkey skull that Choice displayed in a small cabinet of wonders, a new acquisition that he kept above his desk, flanked by fashionable flame-drapes.

"What the goodyear is this? It's never a child's, I hope . . . ?"

Choice was used to prevaricators. "What's my duty for you, sir?"

"Well, I'll tell you what it is. I'm a man of action. I travel for my employ. I'm often painted by great artists. I sit to them at great length. The paintings are passed around, from court to palace. I must play the man I am, d'you see? I must improve my aspect. At present, I am great. I do not resemble greatness."

"I think I see, sir," said Choice. "You would be pleased to benefit from my drink of beauty."

"That's it!"

"In order to improve your complexion."

"Yes. Yes. Yes." Endymion smote his fist upon the table. "It's too much swagged and bagged; it's too ruddy. It needs attention."

Choice stood up and stepped closer, looking across Endymion's face. "Too coarse, too rubicund, too jowly," said Choice, peering at him. "Too scarred and stubbled . . ."

"Well, steady, sir, let us not kill the cat with kindness." Endymion pretended to laugh, raising a hand defensively in the air. It was clear his pride was pricked by Choice's words. Choice had not treated a man's complexion before, and he saw he was going to have to exercise more tact.

"Beside the pallor of the Stuart house, my face is like . . ."

Choice declined to suggest "an old walnut shell" or "a crack'd barque's bottom."

"My face is like a man's, sir, a man's. Hearty and oaken. But I am the procurer of the King's paintings, and it does not become me to resemble a man of war. Maecenas was no knocker, but he has the benefit of being rendered in marble. I cannot resemble Apollo, who is the god of sculpture, but I should look a little more like a lover to my good wife."

Tempting as it was to Choice to become the physician in a farce, and treat the amorous wife on one side of the door and her proud husband on the other, taking money and favours from both, while feeding them up on the same decoction—yet he was more prudent than that. He knew how farces ended: with a tradesman carted off to the stocks or worse.

"Nothing would give me greater honour, sir, and I can offer you an infallible tonic for the gout, or the stone. I can give you a powder that will turn your hair white as chalk overnight. I can offer you a honey poultice for a sore thumb. I give ladies a drink that helps them through their moon-times. But for the delicate matter of which you speak, I have no Cures or Simples that are guaranteed . . ."

With care, Choice wriggled, and span, and got himself out of the job. It hurt, to let such a customer go, and after the loss of Venetia too. But he preferred a customer who held no public office; who had no recourse to lawyers; who had no standing with the sheriffs, guildsmen or magisters; who could write a love-note but not a legal writ; and who was, above all, anxious to protect the precious egg of a virtuous reputation. In short, Choice preferred his customers to be female.

Venetia had never visited St. Bartholomew's before, and now she knew why. Although she lived six minutes from its poxy portals, she could not stomach it. It was too much for any healthful person to bear; as she stood here, with the saintly Sister, she had to fight the impulse that told her, Get out, get out, and save yourself.

The ear was offended first. The groans and occasional cries could be heard all along the cloister. Then, upon nearing the sick room, the stench, and the stickiness underfoot, which no amount of rushes could disguise. Venetia could hardly bear to look at the men, semi-clad, covered in pustules, or with swollen tongues lolling. She knew they must feel envy, or longing, as they saw her standing there, covering her little nose with her lavender kerchief, but they only stared into the distance with a sick, blank acceptance. Surely these were the worst cases, displayed to her by the Sister thus to play upon her feelings, like any Shiver-Jack begging in the street?

"These are the Hopefuls, waiting to be seen," said the Sister. "We call them Hopefuls because we hope the physicians will find their cases of interest, and if they do not, we feed them, keep them warm, send them hither upwards or beyond."

A woman crouched in the corner looked blessedly whole, until she turned her head to one side revealing a goitre on her neck, blue-black and stiff as a fungus on an oak tree.

She was here because she was become Good. She had made over £100 of her gaming monies to Bartholomew's, which was the work of a very Good woman, not to say an excellent gambler. At their game of cards later that day, she would tell Penelope all she had seen, so she must not forget the details—the woman's purple goitre. That man without limbs. With her presence here and her donation, she had atoned. For what crime, she could not exactly remember, but she knew Penelope was cross with her.

Thank God in His Mercy she had brought a basket of bread and cake. The Sister was talking about bloodletting and stools and Venetia could not endure to hear any more.

"Sister, please you take this present from the Digby household, and make a note that I, Lady Digby, was here to give my peaceful good wishes," she said, offering the basket to the Sister with a generous motion that allowed her to turn on her heel and, nodding at the patients right and left with due seemliness, which disguised her haste, she sashayed out into the cloister, and the fresh, foul world beyond.

In Which She Loses at Cards

"IS LETTICE MARRIED yet?" asked Venetia, adding, a little too graciously, "I do hope they will be happy."

She was wearing her new plain grey dress, twice as expensive as a gaudy one, and yet infinitely suitable, she thought, for someone who had gained wisdom through suffering.

Olive threw a glance at Pen, who caught it.

The cards made secret fans in their hands. Pen put down a ten and a Tib with a smack of the thumb.

"They were married at midnight last Saturday. To preserve her estate since her father's demise it was done withal speed," she said.

"Well, I do rejoice!" said Venetia. "I pray they will be happy despite everything."

"Despite everything . . . ?" queried Olive.

"Oh, you understand me," said Venetia, and although she wanted very much to add more, she did not. She was Good now, was she not? She played a six, with an indifferent pout. "I wish them every earthly joy."

"I think your face is gaining its old sweetness," said Pen gently.

"You are so much more whole," agreed Olive. "No little girls would now be affrighted by you; no, not at all."

The story of the incident in the Queen's garden, when the Earl of Newcastle's tot ran crying from Venetia, had clearly been doing the rounds.

"I thought we'd have some China Oranges," said Pen, changing the subject. "To look at, of course, not to eat. They're such bright worlds, I fancy they dress a table."

"Some silly girls do be dancing and fidgeting. It is the way of children," said Venetia. She was becoming used to her new attitude of forbearance.

If she carried on like this, she would grow almost saintly. It was only a pity that the Wine would not leave her alone. She was free from it, and had not drunk it for a month and ten days, and yet it came into her mind unbidden, moving discreetly, like a scent, or a distant memory, or a tune she could not quite hear, so stealthily that it seemed to gain admittance without knocking, until there it was, beside her, pawing her shoulder, mewing for attention.

"And so you have me," said Olive, laying down a Knave, King, Queen.

Venetia paid with the last of her coin.

"The rest of my pot has gone to the lazars at Bartholomew's," she announced. "I think when you have won so much gold at the table as I have, you ought to think of those less fortunate, who have no arms or legs, or who have great goitres at their throats the size of, oh, at least a double fist. The last occasion I was there I saw one growing on a poor woman, fair in other wise."

The other ladies turned slowly to look at her incredulously, as if they had never seen her before. Penelope stopped with her posset cup halfway to her lips. But Venetia did not notice. She had thought about the woman a good deal that day. She was not so very far away from going back to see if she could pay for a physician to remove the putrid growth. It would be such an easy thing to accomplish. She knew now what the lancet could do.

She had been so long concerned with being seen that she had not seen at all; she had suffered a physician to cut her, though she was sound in body. It was a miracle she had been delivered from this folly; it was a miracle that Kenelm had cherished her since he came home, without seeming to notice the small puffiness, the tiny symmetrical scars she bore.

She looked at her friends, with tears brimming.

"Forgive me, ladies, I am grown conscionable at last!" And she pressed her kerchief over her eyes.

"Venetia, darling . . ." Olive put her arms around her. "You lost today but you are still the best player of us all, the best I have ever encountered."

"Come, come," said Pen. "She is moved not by her loss but with higher thoughts. Let her have a moment with her spirit. Then we will plan our May Day tournament. We shall visit the King's park, where there is a new pavilion for sports. Will Kenelm come?"

"No," sniffed Venetia. "I do not like him to see me at the gaming table, it shows too much cunning in me."

"I'faith," said Pen, "I think he knows the cunning in you and loves you for it."

"We all do," said Olive, and they embraced across the table in a thrice-fair hug, something like the Graces, before they set about beating one another in one final, ruthless game.

"One Small Step for Man . . ."

Kenelm was back in his library.

Clouds of inspiration scudded across the ceiling; cherries of virtue swagged the stained-glass windows, so well done it was a wonder birds did not shatter them with pecking. The door of the library locked with a willing click, and he was at last at home in his own mind. Through the windows he could glimpse his green thought-garden, where Van Dyck's tall and prickly sunflower grew ever higher, glowing with its own fierce brightness, like a nuclear daisy.

He might read while he leaned against any shelf, or at his desk hidden in a little scriptorium at the rear of the library. He could rise from his reading with some deep question, stroll to the pertinent section, put his finger upon the book he wanted, and browse onwards from there, ranging over his shelves, like a honeybee across a wildflower meadow.

This library was his very soul made visible.

There were, admittedly, one or two problems.

Overspill was stacked against the far wall, and in front of every section—as, Greek, French, Americas—a little pile of extras that did not fit upon the shelves was propped upon the floor. He must have been too conservative in his initial estimations; moreover, during the time it took to build the library, he had, inevitably, acquired more—bagfuls from Naples and Genoa.

The library was so over-filled that it would take twice his life to read everything it contained, and still the library was incomplete. A glaring white hole remained on the far wall: their Van Dyck painting was not yet in situ, and he felt an unanswerable need for it. That emblem of their union, of their blessed equity and love, was the very thing he wished to have presiding over his library, and yet it was absent. Having been away, he needed his props, his paintings, to tell him who he was, and how happily he was married, just as the Great Cross at Cheapside told him he was almost home again.

As a favour to Van Dyck, Kenelm had agreed to forgo his painting for a short while, allowing the artist to display it at his studio at Blackfriars, to beguile and inspire visiting patrons. They came for a solo portrait, then they saw the Digbys' panoramic grouping, and lo, the whole family was signed up.

Van Dyck had offered him a copy, but he did not wish for a copy, only for his friend's own work. The portrait was mightily well done, capturing such grace in his Venetia, and some sort of courage in himself, he supposed. It was a world away from the flat, stiff likenesses of his forebears, who always seemed propped against the dark. Instead, this was utterly of the moment. Their health was unsurpassed; they seemed to breathe, to sit comfortably in their chairs. Venetia's expression had a wisdom, a glowing forbearance, to which people were much attracted.

And yet in truth she was more tense than ever since he was come home. She turned her head away from him, like a sick heliotrope. Was the taste of her lips different? Was her climacteric come early? What was the unusual heat in her kiss, and the coldness in her limbs? He wished he had the portrait, to help him to see her better.

Every gent and lady who aspired to immortality, or fashion, or merely the epithet "fine," passed through the Blackfriars studio, and all of them saw the Digbys' portrait. They came up the water-stairs and into the grand salon, where the painting commanded the light from the river. Many of the studio visitors exclaimed to see the Digbys, greeting their portrait, and babbling as they took it in.

"But so it is, when you are born a true beauty," sighed Mistress Daubigny.

"Age cannot wither her," said Belinda Finch, peevishly.

"D'you think I should wear more blue?"

"Venetia Stanley, is it?" said the husband of the first. "She's one they say is altogether"—he whistled and drew curves in the air—"*bona roba.*"

Both ladies nudged him with embarrassment, as if the painting could hear.

"Oh gee!" said Andy Warhol. "She looks so unhappy. It really suits her. It gives her an expensive aura. I bet she folds her money lengthways. I met a Rothschild who kept her money folded in a little Scotch purse with a pom-pom . . ."

Sir Kenelm frowned at this silver-haired changeling and asked him what his business was. "Just teaching Van Dyck some tricks. I told him never to include a pimple in a painting, because a pimple is a temporary distraction. I shan't stay long, though—I'm too insecure to talk to strangers."

The editor of *Vogue* passed through, too, gazing at Venetia briefly, nodding dispassionate approval. This was perfect. Venetia would sell; she was a cover. Anything could have happened to her in life, too much Botox, or too much drink, or a botched lip job—none of it showed once her image was up here, tweaked and manipulated. Van Dyck could always be counted upon. Any second-rate artist could create a generic beauty. The point was to make the beauty particular—ideally, recognisable.

When Edward Sackville saw the painting of Venetia, he genuflected, or so it was reported. It became common for gentlemen Kenelm scarcely knew to say, "Oh sir, your wife is looking so well," or, "Your beautiful Lady, what a fine pairing you make," which gave Kenelm an instant's confusion, before he realised these strangers had seen their portrait, and thus the familiarity they felt for him and his wife was an illusion, maintained by a trick of oil and brushwork, as one illusion begets another.

And like an abysm of mirrors, the illusions carried on, so that it was declared at court that Venetia had never looked more gracious, never commanded such noble charm. The cleverness of the portrait was that Van Dyck had not overstated his case, but given her an aura of tired elegance, a mildly enervated wanness, and—most clever of all—she looked very like the Queen. Even though the Queen was ten years younger.

Venetia's likeness went out into the world, on billboards, on a big screen, displayed, retouched, elongated, a fantasy, a capriccio of perfection, and it barely mattered what her own self had become. The images were so much more powerful than she.

Which sculptor could make a King's likeness without ever looking on him? Better to ask which working sculptor could not do such a thing. Images are made of reputation; likeness follows scurrying after. Bernini kept a Van Dyck study of Charles I in his studio, then sent a marble bust in its image over from Rome. It was widely agreed that the bust captured perfectly the King's divine soul and earthly physiognomy. The court viewed the bust as more wondrous because of its tele-production. It was said that as the King turned to Catholicism, the hairline cracks in the marble forked and spread.

In churches all over England, paintings were coming into bloom. Under Archbishop Laud, icons and statues and carvings were permitted again, brought out from their safe-houses, unwrapped and dusted down. Steeple-crosses, bench-ends, misericords: all the symbolic prettinesses of a church appeared, and the Puritans shut their eyes to these distractions, these superstitions; and when they could not shut their eyes they shook their heads, inwardly revolted, their silence building up, with mounting pressure, against the wrongful tyranny of the screen, the stage, the lie of painting.

Kenelm did not mind that his own hairline, according to their portrait, appeared to have receded a little, shewing a glint of shiny scalp. He believed, with Dr. Fludd, that baldness was a sign of astuteness, and a subtle mind. Van Dyck knew this, or else he would have given him more hair. He was not only a great artist; he also knew how to please.

It was pleasant for Kenelm to hear, several times a day, how beautiful his wife was looking. He could not help but believe it, by repetition. And yet a part of him knew that since he came back from Naples she was somehow changed, scarred and distorted, and he wondered if his eyesight had declined of late, and when he was at work reading a small script or reedy cipher in his private library he used spectacles—but he would never have worn these to read his wife's face. That would have been cruel. He was more careful of her than that.

It saddened him to feel her detail slipping from him, as a fern, which he loved to regard in its furled intricacy, might become a curved prow of green; the Natural Philosopher in him longed to perceive her through a magnifying glass. But the Alchemical Philosopher in him knew that now his sight of her was softened, he was closer to perceiving her as she was in his heart. If the Stone were in a different guise or obscured with clouds of Sulphurick vapour, he was yet nearer to the truth of the Stone, by understanding its qualities rather than its appearance. One does not see only with the eyes.

He never liked to riddle thus about Venetia; his tendency towards her had always been instinctive, sure and true, not thought, or scrupled, like a scholar's disputation. But now he felt as if he could not quite reach her. And so he decided not to put his mind to it, but to go and kiss her. He trod the stairs with vigour, a husband on the tarmac, in the taxi, on the doorstep.

Perhaps after they had been good lovers to one another he would give her the Naples pearls, which he had bought for her in a fit of homesickness, but now doubted, and had not given to her yet out of some little embarrassment. What if she asked how much they cost?

He found her door was locked, and he had to pause outside while she moved around the room, begging his patience in a high, guilty voice. What was she performing? One of those arcane female procedures, about which he did not wish to ask. He waited, counting the lines on the palm of his left hand.

On the other side of the door she took a final, decisive gulp, and hid and locked the empty vial in her closet. Well, what of it? She could do what she liked. She was now Good. She visited Bartholomew's, and gave her money to the poor, and she did not drink the Viper Wine any more, so what harm could it do to sup one last time? She had forgotten what it tasted like. She was Saved.

Then the messenger boy had come before her with a May Day basket. She had received several of these already, from friends and neighbours, but this one looked different. It was set with snakeweed and little scarlet pimpernels, and shaped so she dared to hope it might contain a vial, and as she unfolded the wrapper she saw her heart's wish, red and shameless, cloudy like a sandstorm, and just as heavy as a vial of Viper Wine should be. Across the inside wrapper in his sinuous writing, Choice expressed a few carefully chosen words of obsequious address, and wished her a "fair and beauty-filled" first of May.

She nearly sent it back directly, but all the messengers of her house were busy, and she hid it in her closet instead. There it throbbed and tick-tocked the whole day through, pulsing like a living heart. She tried to close her ears to its noise, but even when she was upstairs, with the boys, or looking at the new editions of *A Mirrour for a Modest Wife*, or talking with the cook about their May Day dinner, she heard it. At some point in the afternoon it became clear to her that there was one easy, elegant solution to the Wine's disquieting presence in her closet.

The taste of it was stronger than she remembered: bitter as witch's spittle. She swallowed the first half and lay on her back, laughing, dizzy. She began to cough, throatily. Choking, she tried to sit up, but carefully: at all costs she must not spill the second half of the draught. She was gazing into the vial's red whirlpool, trying to decide whether she should drink the rest now or tomorrow, when she heard Kenelm's knock at her door.

When she let him in, the Wine and his hot blond kisses acted together, like a love-charm. She was giddy with longing. As Kenelm touched her and she closed her lids, she saw before her eyes pink worms dissolving into burnished gold, turning into the forked tails of the ribbons on the Maypole on the Strand, flying into the red-dark depths of the stained glass in Oxford. But she had not been to Oxford these ten years. She giggled aloud, and Kenelm thought it was because he was tickling her, and he tried to tickle her more. She gasped, because she felt his fingertips brush her scarring. She turned her face away.

They were usually gentle lovers to one another, unlike Olive and Endymion and their chilli-pepper pleasures. Yet this time she felt a will to bite, to pinch, to punish him for being so kind to her, so blind. She did not like the foolish happiness in his smile. She showed him her back, inviting him to mount her like a jade in a stable, arching her back, putting her tail in the air, knowing he would be thinking of the Skyrian horses in the *Iliad*, waiting for Zephyros, the West Wind, to fill them with foals that would run fast as the wind. He was so quick she had only a brief, blood-pumping pleasure in it, and as they embraced afterwards she put her back to him again, flinching and removing his hand when he tried to stroke her cheek.

Yearning to be understood, she asked him if he ever wished for his youth again.

"Oh, plenty times, my darling. To put all one's strength and urgency into games of mud, and hunts for birds' nests. To shoot the cannon of dried peas. To be admiral of a toy boat. To see the world in a hazelnut shell, a squirrel's goblet . . ."

She let the wind whistle through the gulf in their understanding of one another, as he talked of Gayhurst and childhood, and for the hundredth time he said she broke his toy horse when they played together as toddlers, and she replied she did no such thing. She put on her nightcap to preserve her curls and before they fell asleep, she asked him for a story: how when he was a lad of eleven he was taken by cart across the county to meet Shakespeare, and Shakespeare bid him—what was it? But Kenelm was already twitching with the first jerks of sleep and he said he would tell her the whole story in the morning, with the boys.

The cries of the second watch of the night woke Kenelm, and he left Venetia where she was sleeping and trod gently to the window. He had been dreaming, as to his shame he sometimes did, of other women, dildo-toting drabs with unlaced gaiters, and he exhaled with happiness and relief to wake and find her sleeping next to him. From lust and madness she was his salvation, his best beloved. He wished she would take less of the bedclothes. She could be selfish in this respect. He groped for the cold ceramic pot and urinated into it—or nearby, it was all one—staring beyond the half-drawn curtain into the midnight empyrean, the soundless indigo. A dog barked, but no friendly dawn showed yet, and all of London seemed abed, only a strange visitation streaked across the darkness: a most curious cloud.

Kenelm moved towards the window.

The cloud, like a pale apparition, stretched out across the sky in a shining, shifting drift, which glowed yellow-pink. As Kenelm looked closer, he saw the cloud had a nacreous quality, pearlescent and particoloured, like the inside of an oyster shell.

It seemed to glow of its own sweetness. Kenelm could see no braziers or beacons flaming in the city beneath—the cloud, he judged, was not the reflection of light but the source of it.

"A noctilucent cloud," said Kenelm, trying the words out.

It reminded him of the Philosopher's Stone, when, cradled in its aludel, it developed its rainbow sheen, after the third crisis of the Great Work had passed, and the hermetic corpse began its exquisite putrefaction.

He pulled the window-drapes apart and hastened to wake Venetia. The bed and its white hangings were changed by the coloured light, dimming from saffron to sulphur, and thence to palest green. Green was the colour of the lion in alchemy, corrosive and devouring.

"Look," he said, excited as a child to show her his discovery, "a shining night-cloud . . ."

But she was sound asleep, and would not stir, though the cloud was softly breaking into new colours. Was this sorcery or merely radiation? Was it light pollution from an undiscovered country? Or the gorgeous smoke-puff of a future disaster, drifting silently through his mind like a ghost ship through the sea?

Was this the long-awaited star, the satellite of love?

"Oh, oh, oh," he sang gently, "Satellite of Love."

He sought to rouse Venetia but she would not let go of the coverlet.

"Come, come," he coaxed her, trying to pull it out of her hands, though they would not give. "Of what does this cloud foretell, darling? What does it signify? Every portent has its meaning."

Venetia lay pale and inert.

He knew the cloud was warning him of something, but he did not know what, and his ever-postulating mind went straight to the political, foretelling the revolt of Parliament, or the failure of the Exchequer, or a sickness in the body politic. Perhaps they would be drawn into the war on the Continent. Or perhaps the Godly ones would have no more of Papistry, and rise to drive them out. Tomorrow was the first of May; perhaps the cloud was a May Day token, come to wake him to bring in the spring.

The aurora borealis, which men called streamers, petty dancers, or goat-dancers, had burned so brightly red under Tiberius that people believed it presaged fire.

Tycho Brahe believed the streamers brought on infectious diseases.

Elizabeth I saw the firedog playing with fire, and called John Dee to explain its portent.

He gazed at the cloud, as Venetia's calm body lay beside him, and he tuned into twenty-first-century voices arguing in his head about "the recent phenomena only just observed in the sky, which scientists have agreed to call 'acid clouds.' They are made up of tiny reflective acid crystals, so they shine like mother-of-pearl, but their source and their significance is still a mystery. Some say they are a sign of global warming." They were a tenuous phenomenon, vaguely understood, but thought to be symptoms of—the voice grew ominous—"climate change." The voice brightened. "Now for the shipping forecast," and the signal faded out, as the cloud drifted gently over the horizon, and the first light of day showed in the sky.

He tiptoed out of the bedroom, and in the grey dawn he consulted his books on shadows and eclipses, and his tracts on heavenly bodies, hoping that he would find amongst them some recognition or explanation, until, still turning the pages in his mind, he fell asleep in his hammock.

> "When the shrill and baleful voice expressing her heavy plight strook my eares . . . in an instant my fansie ranne over more space than is between heaven and earth. I presently grew as senseless almost as the body that I had in my armes. Amazement, upon such occasions, for a while supplieth the room of sorrow."
>
> Letter from Sir Kenelm Digby to his brother John, 1633

May Day morning, 1633, and the city was up early, excited, noisy. The great Maypole on the Strand was already strung with ribbons and in imitation every city green was raising its own with shouts and heave-hoes. At Charterhouse crowds had gathered to see the boy singers of Sutton's Hospital performing from the church tower like so many skylarks and warblers, their little mouths wide with song. A soloist was chosen, though he was one of the youngest, and in his nerves he reached an even higher peak of clarity, and his song carried through the green town square and beyond, mingling with the shouts of the men setting up archery butts, and rolling beer kegs, and building bonfires, so that the pious men and women who had come to hear the choir's singing threw stalks and leaves at them and shouted down the noise-makers in an angry chorus.

Kenelm was roused from his hammock by a frantic pounding at his study door. The birds in the green garden outside his window did not cease their singing as he ran upstairs, following the screaming of Mistress Elizabeth, who was on the threshold of Venetia's chamber. The sun smiled through the bed-drapes, and on the serene image of Venetia, lying in her bed, elegantly pale, at rest, and yet more profoundly at rest than she should be, so that her body lay too heavily upon the pillows, and her dark head hung backwards, like a flower on a broken stalk, as he grabbed her to his chest.

Cries of joy echoed up from the street across the Digbys' garden as the maidens came a-maying, to take their places on the green, and the ladies in the crowd waved their ribbons and flowers, and boys hawking posies shouted "Meadowsweet and sage! Hyssop and clary-wort!" as Sir Kenelm uncurled Venetia's cold white fingertips, gracefully curved, and stiffening with every moment. The May maidens called to one another and waved their ribbons. Sir Kenelm shook her, and like a lovely dancer, she moved willingly in his arms. He wailed to heaven, as in the street outside a hurdy-gurdy struck up a May Day jig.

He found her scrying mirror, slipped it from its velvet drawstring, and held its polished surface to her lips, her nose. The mirror stayed inert as steel, with no kind bloom upon it. Even its most sensitive wet-black screen could not find a trace of presence, a ghost of breath. He cursed the mirror for telling him the truth. The crowd outside cheered as a man already drunk and abusive was ear-yanked away by the aldermen's men. A girl who was too young to be in the procession cried, and those who were glad were innocently so, without knowing their good fortune, and buds bloomed, and magpies cackled, while at the corner of the canvas, unnoticed by the ploughman pushing his oxen across his cliff-top field,

Icarus fell out of the clouds like a sycamore seed, spinning, and plunged into the drown-deep sea. Only a farmhand gaped at the boy streaking through the sky.

In catacombs, in mortuaries, in pits barely covered by seed-grass, the bodies of those who died of plague were quickly laid, too distempered to touch, too putrid to look upon. Death had undone them, so they were unrecognisable, yet Venetia was pallid-perfect so it seemed, like Juliet, she might wake at any moment. Kenelm, kneeling before her staring, tried to fix in his mind every line, every dear pigment.

When Dr. Donne prepared for death, he had charcoal fires lit in his room, and a carpenter come to build him a wooden urn and resting board, and he rose from his sickbed, wrapped himself in his winding sheet, and stood inside the urn, wherein there was room for his feet withal, and in this pose of eternity he had a sculptor take his living portrait, for his death's monument. His shroud was knotted top and bottom, and peeping through was his lean and death-like face, eyes closed, and turned to the east, towards the Second Coming of our Saviour.

Sir Kenelm gasped with inspiration. Van Dyck should come and paint Venetia. He reached for the telephone, but it was not there. He grasped for a text, a keyboard, pager, telegram. Pay-as-you-go. Hologram. Loudspeaker. He found a piece of paper and quill at her bedside, and scribbled words upon it, as fast and clear as he was able, through his distorting tears. When the letter reached Van Dyck at Blackfriars, where he was at his easel, he fell upon his knees and crossed himself, and it was only afterwards that he marvelled at how the letter had reached him, even though his name and lodgings were written in backwards mirror-writing.

News of her death was spreading abroad, called out by the crier to the May Day revellers, above the din of "Ninny-heigh No" and the thunk of arrows into the butts, and there was a compelling fitness to the salt of tragedy on that sweet May morning, so that talk formed on hasty lips between sips of ale.

"Dead by a mystery no man can answer."

"Dead by her own good heart—she was tending the lazars at Bartholomew's lately."

"Dead by an ague come up from the marshes."

"Brought to bed early of a babe, no doubt."

"The best do always fly the fastest off."

And tastiest of all, confidentially, between bites of crumble pie and sweet-pud:

"Her husband was forever mixing potent drugs and pharmacies, which he did give her to drink, nightly."

When Mistress Elizabeth came into the room, Kenelm turned to look guiltily at her, as if she had surprised him in a covert act. He was leaning over the body, holding Venetia's weighty head upon one side, as he fixed an earring to her still-perfect ear. It was a huge pearl, and he opened his hand so that he might show Mistress Elizabeth the other pearl, which he had yet to fasten. Mistress Elizabeth averted her gaze with her usual deference, but she wondered if he was losing his senses. His face was coursed with tears and snot, which he wiped upon the cuff of his shirt. "Oh, that's fine, my darling!" he said appreciatively, looking at how the pearls suited Venetia. "That's fine indeed!"

Mistress Elizabeth bid the King's physician, Sir Theodore de Mayerne, come into the bedroom—his boy was made to wait downstairs, with the weeping Chater, Olive and Pen. Sir Theodore had been summoned from a patron's house, where he was about to eat a May Day marchpane pie, and under his cloak he still had his napkin tucked into his doublet, and a hungry look about him.

"My darling," said Kenelm to his inobservant wife, "I should have given these to you before—presents which I brought for you from Naples." He spoke almost flirtatiously, tucking his blond hair behind his ears.

Theodore de Mayerne recognised this behaviour. He had been in attendance in 1612 when Prince Henry, England's golden hope, died aged eighteen of a fever. He had shaken King James to stop him babbling like a brook. He knew grief; oh yes.

"Come, sir, step aside and let me see her," he said firmly.

"LEAVE US BE," roared Kenelm, pushing Mayerne away. "You are dressed to go a-maying, I can see your gaudy doublet. And you have forgot your muckender, which is still tucked under your fat French chin."

Mayerne had heard it all before. Scurvied children tried to bite him and women cried shit and damnation on his head during their childbirths. He bore Kenelm no ill will; besides, he liked his own stately girth. "An evil soul rarely dwells in a fat body," was his habitual remark.

Kenelm turned his back on Mayerne and tenderly fastened the rope of pearls around Venetia's neck. "She shall have her present for a May morning. There, how lovely she is."

Kenelm remembered how he had spoken to his boys in their mother's womb as they kicked and quickened; how he laid his hand upon them and felt their souls a-bud. Talking to Venetia now was similar. There was the trace of her, the shape of her, just beyond his reach. He could not think of the word purgatory. He would rather sing her an old song of their courtship, marking time upon her counterpane with his fingers: "Under the greenwood and round again."

Or perhaps—"Love Will Tear Us Apart."

When Mayerne splashed cold water in his face, Kenelm came to his senses, and stood aside to let Mayerne make his examination. Kenelm could not bear to watch the indignity of it, and after telling Mayerne to leave her face and hands unmarked, he left her bedroom, and stepped into a new world of grief; the familiar hall, the dining room and library, all the same, yet changed beyond measure, so it felt like an empty simulacrum of the house in which he used to live.

The boys were still in their nightshirts, much distressed, with cold little feet, which Kenelm rubbed as he spoke to them. They could not see their mother, no, but their granddam was a great good lady, and she would care for them while the house was all unresting, until their mother was well again—

They peered at their father's wretched head, as he turned away and sobbed violently, having told a lie that none of them believed. The boys rattled into the country with their nurses sitting at the rear of their coach and their bags of treasures badly packed and flung together. The godly would not let them pass through Highgate, as they were protecting the village, keeping it pure from May Day celebrations, and after a detour, their coach passed at last into open country, where they saw whole villages out a-maying, waving blossom boughs and singing and raising tankards at their coach, and calling them "cuckoo," and being children, they called "cuckoo" back, and waved, and laughed.

In years to come the memory of this would grieve them, and they each kept it secret from the other, ashamed and questioning: why did no one help them to be better?

At three, Kenelm tried to pull the bell out of their clock in the hall so that it might not ring any more, because time should not go on so blithely without her. He went into his study expecting it to be destroyed, and all his bottles broken and notebooks burned, but it was as neat and familiar as when he left it, only the blankets on his hammock were disarrayed, where he had left them when he first heard the terrible pounding on his door. He decreed they should never be folded but always left in that stricken attitude. He was comforted by this, and drank a little Rhenish wine which he was given, although he could not eat. When he went back into his study, the maid had already folded the blankets away.

He felt betrayed by his clock, and the fountain in the town square, and the spigot in the stable-yard, because all of them flowed, and had not stopped at the moment of calamity. But when he drew the curtain to his study, he saw that the great sunflower's head was newly drooped at an angle of despair, as if the world had gone to darkness, and there was no bright sun to turn its head to follow. This gave him comfort: this most Sympatheticall of plants.

> "Scientists have discovered that sunflowers can pull radioactive contaminants out of the soil. Researchers cleaning up the Fukushima site in Japan are putting the flowers to the test."
>
> *Japan Today*, 2011

> "We plant sunflowers, field mustard, amaranthus and cockscomb, which are all believed to absorb radiation," said the monk [Koyu Abe]. "So far we have grown at least 200,000 [And] at least eight million sunflowers blooming in Fukushima originated from here."
>
> Reuters, 2011

And yet Sir Kenelm knew, with the heavy physical knowledge that accompanies heartbreak, that the sunflowers planted in Fukushima were proven not to be effective in dissipating radiation, reducing caesium in the topsoil by a negligible amount. Even their famous heliotropism was misconceived. Sunflower buds revolve with the sun. The mature flowers are only east-facing, like any others. Sir Kenelm looked at the grizzled plant, its tortured optimism, its petals rendered in a thick impasto. It had not saved Van Gogh either. Poor flower. It was condemned to brightness, though about itself, it was thoroughly disillusioned: that he recognised.

The Deathbed Portrait

"It's a kind of dance of death. But it's her life force I was responding to. I hope to put a little bit of life into charcoal. Whether [the work] is of someone dead or alive is irrelevant."

Artist Maggi Hambling on drawing a series of deathbed sketches of her lover Henrietta Moraes, 2002

"When we came in, we found her almost cold and stiffe; yet the blood was not so settled but that our rubbing of her face brought a little seeming colour into her pale cheeks, which Sir Anthony Van Dyck hath expressed excellently well in his picture . . . A rose lying upon the heme of the sheet, whose leaves being pulled from the stalk in the full beauty of it and seeming to wither apace even whiles you look upon it, is a fit emblem to expresse the state her body then was in."

Letter from Sir Kenelm Digby, 1633

By candlelight, and dawn, and daylight, as it filtered through the bed-drapes, Van Dyck worked constantly. The sorrow all around him, the sobbing in the hall where Chater held vigil, the distracted presence of Kenelm coming and going from her bedside, and the disorder in the household, did not seem to penetrate him; his lean moustaches were fixed in a placid expression of concentration, as he painted, so any common observer might think he was unmoved, when in fact all the sensitivities of his soul, and his precise brush, were working to transmute Grief into Comfort.

Tin-lead yellow, Bismuth white, orpiment. By continuous circulation they may be sublimed and fixed together and lastly by coagulation, become immutable. Thus is the painter like the alchemist. This vision of cruelty and despair, this horrid, unwonted scene, this death's head, about to putrefy, sighing as its cavities gave up their air—he would, by his Art, render this into a vision of serenity and calm; his most Intimate work, tender and careful. Her pale form, enclosed by dark blue drapes, like a pearl in a velvet setting. Her nightdress and cap, clean and shining white; her face, set in an attitude of sleepy contentment; her eyes, caught between opening and closing.

Van Dyck almost smiled as he worked. It was a beautiful sight, if you but had the fortitude to see it so, and did not let the fear of your own demise cloud your vision. His art could transmute the awful question, the why that howled above her head, into a serene certainty: we all must come to this long sleep. Tin-lead, smalt blue, azurite. By his manipulation these base metals and tinctures would become Higher. This brief interlude between death and decay would, by his painter's alchemy, become lasting. Van Dyck always hesitated to use the word eternal, even in his private thoughts; he was not to know it would be carved upon his own tomb by his English admirers.

"The pearls are not very lucid," said Sir Kenelm, standing at Van Dyck's shoulder, looking at his work in progress.

Van Dyck wanted to shout at Kenelm, but remained silent.

The body in front of them let forth a noise, which sounded like a plaintive snore, and startled Kenelm, so he ran to her body, and clasped it in his arms, desperate to take the noise as a sign of life.

Van Dyck was about to call out to Kenelm to bid him stop deranging his sitter—she would take some putting right—but he contained himself, breathed, and continued painting. There was not much time left.

He had painted posthumous portraits before. In Antwerp, his tutor Rubens sent for him in the middle of the night, and Van Dyck found him kneeling over his wife Isabella in her open coffin. Now that was a task to paint. No sleep, all night; the children wailing, the bell tolling and the priest imploring them to go to church to bury her. And Rubens, weeping, and ordering him about at the same time—suggesting a better light, a

Venetia, Lady Digby, on her Deathbed
by Anthony Van Dyck, 1633

more dramatic composition, and so forth. All he produced was a poor copy of Rubens' style—a stiff tableau of death. But that was seven years ago, and since then he had gained so much in confidence, that he now worked within his own preoccupations. Every day, he painted portraits capturing his sitters' steady, living breath, and this was very like, except this portrait caught the final whisper of breath that a body exhaled.

That breath was deemed precious, because it contained the essence of the spirit departing the body. Vasari related that Francis I was present at the moment of Leonardo da Vinci's death, clasping him in his arms as he died, sucking from his lips his last exhalation, to make it his own inspiration.

Sir Kenelm clutched the counterpane, imagining he could feel Venetia's breath upon his cheek. He hovered closer, searching for the phantom of her sleep-sigh, her departing pneuma. He wished he could have caught and captured it. A glass bulb would have sufficed to catch her spirit in, the filament crackling with her presence.

Kenelm—whose mind was then unmoored and skittering through time—remembered that when Thomas Edison died in 1931, his last breath was captured in a test tube by his son Charles, kneeling at his bedside. Edison's great admirer, Henry Ford, the alchemist of speed and metal, displayed that empty test tube at the Ford Museum, outside Detroit, where on a small plinth the glass performed the high service of making the invisible visible. The inventor of the light bulb's breath was a worthy catch, but how much sweeter, how much more useful for his Great Work, would his own wife's breath have been?

But though he dragged a net through the heavens, he would never find any of her vitality. He shuddered as he felt the flames that would, in 1666, consume their double tomb, raging around their grave like a furnace, blowing the windows of Christ Church Newgate, blackening her gilt memorial, and turning their ashes loose across the smoking rubble so they mixed together in the wind.

The calcium of bones, the keratin of eyelashes, the exhalations of our bodies—all these are reconstituted as carbon atoms, used to make the world anew: the earth, the lilies of the field, the ink of this book. What is can never cease to be. Kenelm found comfort in these alchemists' precepts, touching them again and again like rosary beads. We are all stars, and to the stars we return.

Tin, lead-white, bismuth. Van Dyck's brush moved with gentle care. His portrait listened so closely to Venetia; all the closer, because she would never now have anything more to say. In life, a portrait of this intimacy, with the sitter in her nightgown, framed by bed-drapes, would have been outrageous. But she was safe, now, from any ill remark, scandal or unwonted action. She had become a monument. She had always sought to preserve herself so that on future occasions she would not be found wanting, but now, at last, she was ready.

The woman is perfected
Her dead

Body wears the smile of accomplishment,
The illusion of a Greek necessity

Flows in the scrolls of her toga
Her bare

Feet seem to be saying:
We have come so far, it is over.

Sylvia Plath,
from "Edge," 1963

Van Dyck finished this painting himself, without delegation. He applied the final white gleam to her pearls, her one, half-open eye. One eye symbolised occult knowledge: there was no accident in Van Dyck's art. He worked softly, stealthily, so that nothing might jar the peacefulness of his creation, and all the murmurs that he had ever heard resonated through his brush. He saw her with the artist's double vision. And if, onto the dark expanse of her counterpane, he threw a snake, twisting first into the form of a blanket's gold-enamelled hem, and then into the guise of a viper's scaly back, it was only because artists cannot help themselves.

Let Me Speake!

GRIEF MADE KENELM'S mind turn over, like a boat, and—

Let me speake!

Those who would protect him told him he ought to put his mind upon a different subject. He could not sleep, or eat, but existed in a heightened state of consciousness—

Oh, is't so indeed?

His beard grew untended, his hair unshorn—

Enough from you, who hath spoke so long! Let me have the reins awhile.

Note—The following is taken from Sir Kenelm Digby's correspondence, including a long letter to his sons, written in the weeks after his wife's death, 1633:

I can have no intermission, but continually my fever rageth. Even whiles I am writing this to you, the minute is fled, is flown away, never to be caught again.

I have a corrosive masse of sorrow lying att my hart which will not be worn away until it have worne me out.

Not only while I felt the first violence and heate of a passionate and extreme love; but even to her dying day, when I had time enough to observe her and to know her thoroughly, and that almost ten years had converted that which might be thought desire and passion into a solide vigorous and peacefull friendship which (believe me, my children) is the happiest condition and the greatest blessing of this life.

In a word shee was my dearest and excellent wife that loved me incomparably.

Many times she received very hard measure from others, as is often the fortune of those women who exceed others in beauty and goodness.

Although it be not the custom with us in England to have the husbands all the while present att their wives labours, yet she understanding that it was warranted by practise of most other countries—a mann's strength as well as counsel being in these cases often times necessary—she would never permit me to be absent. She had so excellent and tender a love towards me that she thought my presence, or my holding her by the hand did abate a great part of her paines.

What she won at play furnished her with a certain large revenue, which she gave for the poor. Before she died she disposed of £100 in one lump, to be prayed for.

Whiles she did play, one could observe neither eagerness nor passion in her; no stander-by could have guessed by her countenance whether she won or lost.

Her presence and comportment was beyond all that I ever saw; it would strike reverence and love in any man at the first sight. Her cheeks grew pink through exercise . . . Her blue veins shewed in her forehead . . . Her face could not be expressed upon a flatt board or cloth, where lights and shadows determine every part. Even a little motion in so exact and even a face gave her a new countenance, the life and spirits of which no art could imitate.

[She lost some of her hair] with the birth of one of you boys. Nothing can be imagined subtiler than hers was [her hair]. I have often had a handful of it in my hand and have scarce perceived I touched anything. It was many degrees softer than the softest that I ever saw, which hath often brought to my consideration that [one] may judge the mildness and the gentleness of the disposition by the softness and fineness of one's hair.

Her hands were such a shape, colour and beauty as one would scarce believe they were natural, but made of wax and brought to pass with long and tedious corrections.

Now towards her latter time she grew fatte, yet so that it disgraced nothing of her shape.

When she had been dead almost two days I caused her face and hands to be moulded by an excellent Master, and cast in metal. Only wanness had defloured the sprightliness of her beauty but not sinking or smelling or contortion or falling of the lips appeared in her face to the very last. The last day, her bodie began somewhat to swell up . . . which ye chirugions said they wondered she did not more, and sooner, being so fatt as upon opening up she appeared to be, and lying in so warm a room.

When she was opened—

Are you sure this is suitable for your readers—your little sons?

When she was opened, her heart was found perfect and sound, a fit seat for such a courage as she had when she lived. In her gall was found a great stone bigger than a pigeon's egg. In her spleen, two cartiledges, quite extraordinary. There were severall of the most eminent doctors and surgeons of London at the opening of the body. There was but little brain left—

An autopsy such as this was unusual, reserved for deaths which were suspicious or unexplained.

—and this was thought to have caused her the most sudden and least painful death that ever happened.

A cerebral haemorrhage. It is also said she drank a preparation known as Viper Wine.

For to impute any cause of her death to Viper Wine is without any grounde at all . . . Of late she looked better and fresher than she had done in seven years before.

How old was she?

She was born on St. Venetia's day, 19th December 1600. She was designed for my salvation. And if here she was so faire, what will she be hereafter?

Come, sir. Crying will not help her now. Would it comfort you to speak a little more of times you passed together at Gayhurst? Have you returned there yet?

As I rode along, at every step some new object appeared to whett and sharpen my sorrow for they called into my memory a multitude of severall circumstances that had bin between my wife and me in that time which I may truly say was the happiest I ever enjoyed. A tree we sheltered under against a shower of rain. When we were hawking, retrieving of a partridge, I remembered how with admir-able agility and without the help of any body she leaped from her horse to save the hawk from a dogg that else had killed her as she sat pluming the quarry in her foote. By heaven, I never saw anything so lovely as she looked then.

For of all the women that ere I knew (and I will except few men) she was most capable of true friendship. Now my mother, who was ever most averse to her in life, can say as much. If my wife had lived, they two had bin upon good terms by this time, for my mother was overcome by my wife's goodness and had resolved att her next coming to London to have expressed it.

And her funeral?

The funeral was held by night, to enhance sorrow.

At midnight, the bell of Christ Church Newgate tolled the arrival of her bier, dressed with violets. Her black marble tomb was inscribed with copper gilt and set with a bust of her head and shoulders, a good likeness taken from her deathbed, that her beauty might be kept eternally in the mind of the living. The path to the door of the church was lit by flaming torches. Inside, the church was candlelit.

Many hundreds viewed and kissed her corpse. Never was a woman more lamented. Many observed they had never seen so much company. Most came of their owne free motion, for neither the shortness of the time nor the extremity of my passion admitted me to invite any. So many carriages came, Charterhouse was full. Guests included the Prince's governess, secretaries of state, privy councillors, Aldermen and Sheriffs of London. She was given a Protestant burial.

The only way to have her funeral made public was to make it Protestant, although it meant that Chater was not able to attend, but stayed crying in the churchyard throughout. Amongst the elevated throng in the church, were there many strangers? Those who never knew her, but whose habit was always to go to notable funerals, where they never failed to shed a tear. Those who had waited, years ago, to see her carriage pass, cheering and waving to catch sight of her; those who were convinced of her goodness and kindness to the poor, her virtue as the author of *A Mirrour for a Modest Wife*.

And what of those who had done her harm? Was there, at the back of Christ Church, Newgate, behind a rotund Norman pillar, a familiar figure, soft and massive, one medicastra by the name of Begg Gurley? For she considered herself a rightful mourner. She was accompanied by her common-law spouse Thomas Leake, he as thin as she was plumpy, as if they had only a certain amount of flesh between them. Her shoulders were heaving as she cried for the loss of her Great Patron, and yet she was grateful that, during her life, she had at least been able to help her more than once.

In the front pews, Olive, crying; Penelope, grim-faced, looking older than the week before; Aletheia, in her high mourning hat and cloak, with pale blue veins delicately painted in oil of Turpentine upon her forehead; Lucy Bright, veiled, her head bowed. The doctors' account of the brain-spill, the blood-flux in Venetia's mind which killed her, left some convinced, and others suspicious and uncertain. But all her friends were conscious of an inevitability, a just and fitting drama to her death. It had a certain flourish. To die so elegantly, leaving a husband distraught, a city talking; to die overnight, without blemish or ague; to sit to Van Dyck, after death: if anyone in their little set could pull this off, it would be Venetia. The women mourned and their cheeks were coursed with tears and all, except Penelope, were plumped and dark-eyed from that day's Drink.

The chief mourner was, by tradition, a woman judged to be of roughly the same age and distinction as the deceased. She walked behind Venetia's coffin, decked in violets. Her eyes darted and she opened her mouth frequently, as she looked at the mourners around her, as if she was pleased to recognise them and wished to speak to them. One would almost have thought she was enjoying her role, were that not such a regrettable idea. But Venetia could not have wished for a younger or more elevated woman to follow her coffin, for this was Lettice, newly Countess of Dorset.

Ben Jonson took up half a pew with his great bulk. He presented Kenelm with the manuscript of his new poem "In Praise of Venetia," except the first part was not about Venetia, but swiped instead at Van Dyck, repeating that he, Jonson, was a worthier witness than any painter:

Not that your arte I do refuse
But here I may no colours use
Beside your hand will never hitt
To draw the thing that cannot sit—

By this last line he meant "the mind." He found his stride later in the poem:

It were time that I dy'd too now shee is dead
Who was my Muse and life of all I seyd
The Spirit that I wrote with and conceived!
All that was good or great in me shee wean'd
And sett it forth! The rest were Copwebs fine
Spun out in the name of some of the old Nine . . .

So sweetly taken to the court of Blisse
As spiritts had stolen her Spiritt in a kiss
From off her pillow and deluded bed
And left her lovely body unthought dead . . .

For this so lofty form so straight
So polish't perfect, round and even
As it slyd moulded off from heaven . . .

They were his old familiar rhymes, reheated for the purpose—and the one person who would have spotted the paucity of his invention, and teased him for it, was gone.

Kenelm gave a brief, half-mad funeral address.

Three weeks after her burial, my thoughts tumbled every corner of her grave where her face is covered over with slyme and wormes, or her hart has some presumptuous worme feeding upon it. I wake all bedewed with fears, womanish with weakness. I eat a miserable little pittance and scarcely gett an hour's sleepe a night.

And the rest of the household—tell us, how does Chater take the loss?

As I sate this morning meditating deeply on my blessed wife's death (which I do in particular manner every Wednesday) her old servant brought in her picture and sett it downe before me, going immediately out againe without speaking one word; which I perceived his teares that ran trickling downe his cheekes would not permit him to do.

Van Dyck's painting is in your arms even now?

This is the onely constant companion I now have . . . It standeth all day over against my chaire and table, where I sit writing or reading or thinking, God knoweth, little to the purpose; and att night when I goe into my chamber I sett it close to my bed's side and methinks I see her dead indeed; for that maketh painted colours look more pale and ghastly then they doe by daylight. I see her, and I talke to her, until I see it is but vain shadows.

Your children are still with their grandmother?

God knoweth it so fareth with me as I am not able to raise any in myself, much lesse to administer unto an other. As it fareth now, I am fitt not for society or relations of others to me.

You are to move house, I hear.

There is such desolation, loneliness and silence in the house where I have had so much company, so many entertainments, so much jollity.

My mother advises me "to put a bridle" on my grief, as we should "not sett our hearts over much upon a fading subject." Many of my discreetest friends advise me rather to seek all meanes to divert my botelesse thoughts from this sad object that can never be recovered; and they chide me because I do otherwise. But for my part I am resolved I will never beguile sorrow if I cannot master it: I will look death, and it, in the face; and peradventure when we are growned better acquainted and more familiar, we shall be good frendes and dwell quietly together.

I conclude from my premises that the golden chain of causes which by severall links reacheth from heaven to earth, beginning with God and passing through the Angels, the orbs of heaven and the planets, downe to the lowest elements, knitting together the intellectual, celestial and materiall worlds, and lapping in eternal providence and her two handmaids, chance and fortune, did bind together my wife's and my handes, hartes and soules, which death cannot lose, but rather will ferry us over the tempestuous sea of this world to enjoy our friendship in tranquillity and aeternall security where the first knot of it was tied and where the first link of the chain was fastened.

For the first few months my soule has been oppressed with strange agonies. But now I lye quietly, and it lyeth gently upon me.

Sir Kenelm began the dissolution of his library by packing away the Americas.

He turned the pages of his pharmacopoeias, his uroscopies, his prognostics, his *Terrestrial Paradise of John Parkinson*, and the pleasure he used to take in their engravings was like ashes in his mouth. The seascape murals above him were flat and tawdry, the busts of the Great Authors were plaster bodges looking down on him. There were no Atomes dancing in any sunbeams here. The spirit of Mercurius was no longer in this house.

He packed away his Atlases and rolled his Mappes, although he barely had the strength to lift them.

The treasures he brought back from Florence—no, Siena—when he was seventeen stirred nothing but weariness in him. The perfume of their vellum was too rich for his senses. Livy's *Punic Wars*, Cicero, Seneca's tragedies, Petrarch's sonnets: without any sentiment, without even a fond glance over his juvenile annotations, he thrust these in the box. They were going to a better place.

Through the painted glass he saw his Peruvian marigold, bent and blowsy, sorrowing in the garden. And yet the chattels in the house retained their freshness, pert and serviceable. He rebuked their callousness, their durability. Her possessions showed no Sympathy, her boots had kept their shape and her playing cards were impervious and bright, though she had been dead four weeks.

His vainglorious library, with its ceiling of clouds, its lovers' motifs, its sententious aphorisms engraved across the walls: its whole conception and ethos was lost to him. He could not comprehend the babyish happiness he must have enjoyed in order to commission such a den.

There was but one remaining fixture of the library: his armillary sphere, sitting on the edge of his desk, brassy emblem of his former certainty, his mechanical universe. He ran his finger over it so its spheres spun around his little earth, cosseted at the centre of the sky. This model of the universe he now rejected. Galileo the Starry Messenger had sought to destroy his faith in it with reasoning; now life had done that job instead. He lifted the delicate mechanism above his head and slammed it onto the library floor, where one of the soldered brass hoops split resonantly. He scooped up this cracked ribcage of the heavens, to keep as his only trophy, emblem of his broken state.

He shut the door with easy finality, knowing he could always return in his mind.

> "Sir Kenelm donated fifteen trunks of books, comprising 233 codices, five rolls and a catalogue, to the library of Sir Thomas Bodley . . . He also gave 'fifty good oaks' from Gayhurst [for the provision of shelving]."
>
> *The Index of Middle English Prose Handlist*, 2007

Although the journey across the city seemed an impossible undertaking, with his groom's help Sir Kenelm went down by carriage from Charterhouse to Van Dyck's studio in Blackfriars. Kenelm's groom turned the coach round while his servitor left him on the doorstep of the studio, with his potted sunflower and his smashed armillary sphere boxed up beside him. When the studio boy opened the door to the unkempt man in black waiting on the doorstep, he took him for a beggar.

"If a man can poison his wife with impunity . . ."

Van Dyck ran through all the possible backdrops: distant mountains, broken columns, rich curtains, garden views, imperial arches . . . Sir Kenelm motioned to his preference, which was a putty-brown drape of cheap material.

"If a born Catholic can use his improper knowledge of plants and herbs to plot the downfall of his own wife, what harm might he do our country and our King?"

Sir Kenelm barely spoke during their session. Van Dyck imagined him as Harpocrates, except instead of depicting him with the index finger of silence held to his lips, Van Dyck showed how the tendrils of his beard grew almost over his lips, like ivy sealing up a gate.

"As a wife she was hardly spotless—you can imagine he might do it in a jealous rage. Naming no names ;)"

Kenelm lay his right hand upon his heart, spontaneously, and Van Dyck saw he rested easily in this position of defensive sincerity, and asked him to remain thus.

"They put poison in their bejewelled rings, see. And then they unclasp, flip and tip it into the wine-cup of anyone they wish to do away with."

One finger on Kenelm's right hand was trapped inside his black garb—his little finger. It was a natural detail, infinitely casual, and yet to anyone schooled in Hermetic wisdom, it showed that Kenelm's powers were in abeyance, his riches lost, and his strength in decline. The little finger was the finger of Mercury.

"I gave prophecy this marriage would come to no good ends, Lascivious Shee and Whoreson Hee, spawn of a plotter's loin!"

Van Dyck talked as he painted. "So you know about the *Sidereus Nuncius?*"

Kenelm regarded him balefully.

"Sentenced by the Papal Inquisition. He is under house arrest. He abjures, curses and detests his theories. In order to live, he has recanted heliocentrism."

There was silence, except for the gluey sound of Van Dyck's brush moving, its heavy swirl in the oil pot, and the bright tap of its shaft on glass.

"She must have suffered the whole night through—just at the very going out of April and the coming in of May . . ."

The all-seeing sunflower knew that both the men were in the Catholic faith. Since his wife's death, Kenelm had taken the sacrament from Chater, relapsing to the automatic faith of his childhood, the comforting folds of the Marian blue cloth, the heart's-ease of the Miserere Psalm. Only the Catholic liturgy made sense to him. He would, in time, publicly confess his relapse, his homecoming. Not yet.

Sir Kenelm Digby, by Anthony Van Dyck, 1633

In the painting, Van Dyck made Kenelm's face composed and sanguine, as decency demanded, but he let the sunflower next to him howl and weep, its petals shrivelled by an unseen blight.

Ovid wrote of Clytie, abandoned by her lover the sun-god Apollo, sitting naked and unkempt upon the ground, turning her face to watch the sun as it passed by. In time her legs became roots, her arms tendrils, her yellow hair was torn into petals, and she was transformed into a bloodless plant, a sunflower.

"He's said to be a broken man, but where is he? Has he been seen abroad in mourning clothes? Has he given out alms in her name, or set up any town monuments in her honour, or done penance beside her grave?"

Sir Kenelm's mourning portrait was finished, copied, passed around. Its profundity and novelty were noted. It was not a memento mori; it contained no traditional mourning emblems. It was a problem painting. What shall he do now? What should be done with him?

"We shall see many more cases like, unless this is brought to trial. And yet the Lord Chamberlain, the Master of the Rolls, the Archbishop himself, none do lift a finger against their friend Digby . . ."

It was high summer, and long days of thirsty drinking gave way to pale blue evenings, by which to wreak rough justice. The whisperings about Venetia's death had built into a consensus, and the mob found itself with a righteous purpose. Where justice was perceived to have failed, savagery crept in. The mob smashed John Dee's custom-made laboratory instruments in Mortlake in 1583, and drowned his devil books in the well. The mob hunted the astrologer John Lambe in 1628, hurling pebbles till he was blinded, and when he hid, cornered, it waited outside the door to complete its work when he crept out at dawn.

When angry men came to Sir Kenelm's home, they stood on Charterhouse green bearing torches, stones and whips, chanting for justice to be done, for his Catholic books to be burned, and for his life-taking conjurations to cease. A local woman who did the Digbys' washing shouted at them, as she hurried by, that they should feel compassion, but to the mob, Sir Kenelm's misfortune was a stain, a sign of guilt.

When nightfall brought anonymity, the mob became stronger and more brutal than any of its members. It rammed down the back door with picks and shoulders, and ran into his courtyard, shouting to frighten off the bad spirits working in the service of Sir Kenelm, fearful that he—a murderer already—might wield a musket at them in the dark, or worse, operate his unseen instruments of sorcery. But they had no sport there, for the Digby library was already packed up, the household dispersed, all contents sold, all wishes spent and dreams departed, and Sir Kenelm gone.

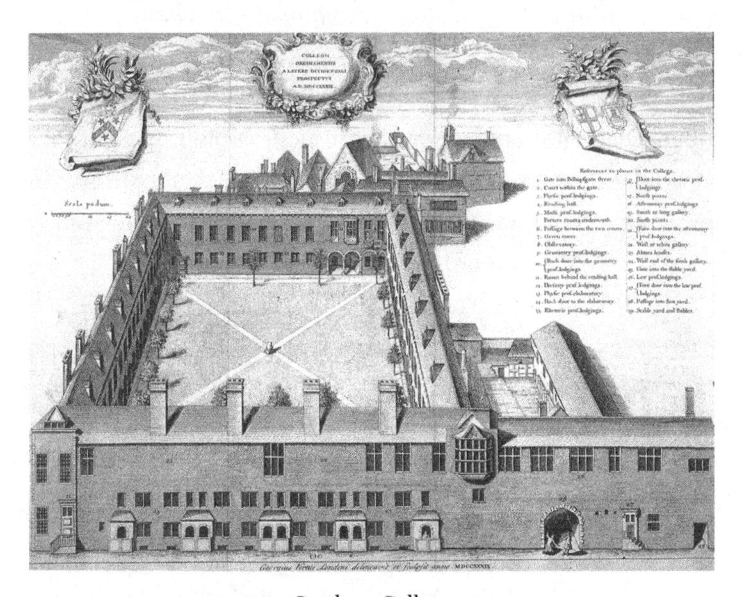

Gresham College

> "Gresham College is an institution of higher learning founded in 1597 under the will of Sir Thomas Gresham and today it hosts over 140 free public lectures every year within the City of London. Its original site in Bishopsgate is now occupied by Tower 42."
>
> Gresham College website, 2013

At Gresham College, that exalted seat of learning, the porters maintained a jovially paternal attitude to their charges, the professors. The college was founded in Elizabeth's reign with provision for seven professors, a pleiades of experts in Rhetoric, Divinity, Music, Astronomy, Geometry, Medicine and Law, all supported by stipends and sheltered from the world that they might perfect it. Witnesses to the unseen Microcosmographies of life these gentlemen were, and masters of the circle and the square, with often two degrees from the Universities apiece—and yet between them they gave rise to so many crises, by forgetting to take their meals, losing their keys, exploding their laboratory furnaces, accruing debts mistakenly or falling a-prey to Abraham men and the like, that the only way for a porter to handle a professor was with firm and amused patience.

It was a rich foundation, newly built and endowed, and its gables shone very clean, painted against the ubiquitous coal dust, so it was white, whiter than any other building in the City. For all its eccentricities, it hummed with prestige. Gresham College was established in order to advance commercial interests, and it was far and away from the rowdy Universities. It was a rarefied laboratory of the future. Here, the acuity of human vision redoubled every two years—reaching outwards to the heavens and inward to the dust. The stars were becoming places, not five-cornered specks, and fleas were about to be revealed by Hooke as armour-plated, bristling monsters. The sound of the grinding of lenses, simple and compound, which echoed around the quad on Tuesdays, was the sound of the perimeters of the world extending, coming into focus.

What went on behind the closely guarded stone facade of Gresham College was, to the busy city street of Bishopsgate, uncertain, but occasionally signs of arcane experiments were visible. Small and large transparent spheres of wobbling soap came rising with serene iridescence over the gables of the college, before expiring into a single teardrop on the breeze. Sometimes the chimneys belched yellow smoke, or clouds of turpentine blue, or stank of sulphur. For half a term, the sound of cats wailing in concert emanated from the rooms of the Professor of Music; for years, the clanking of a heavy metal chain could be heard around the college, day and night, while Professor Gunter perfected his Instrument of Dimensurement. This was a favourite with the porters, who loved to recall how this massy great chain had been set up like a hazardous trapfall all around college, which no one was permitted to move, only step across—and how, after long attempts at its perfection it had made the gentleman's fortune many times over, being the best tool for surveying distance and calculating land-mass ever yet invented, as well as a sure-fire way to break your neck on a stairway.

Into the college, under the stone-carved grasshopper, which was the founder Thomas Gresham's insignia, were conveyed many pieces of equipment: empty barrels, used to prove the spontaneous generation of mice out of the air; complicated pieces of blown glasswork, made to order, so that a glass beehive might be constructed, a furtive bee-peeper's dream (unrealised until Christopher Wren's residency, twenty-four years later); ores and heavy metals, to be used as medicines.

A file of inkhorns, intellectualists, tech nerds and business speculators waited by the back gate to attend the public lectures once a month. Otherwise, the college was private, hermetic. Professors who passed under the stone grasshopper into the college might spend a dozen years safely inside, shifting the heaviest presumptions with their minds, or blowing thought-bubbles.

In their well-swept rooms beside the green quadrangle they tasted *caput mortuum* and sniffed mercurial fumes until their skin turned grey. They spun quantities of numbers into logarithms and trigonometry, and cooked up new hypotheses on their retorts and alembics. At night in their cots they dreamed of binary code, and genetic therapies, bandages that glowed when they harboured poison, and magnetic devices that told where bullets lodged in breasts. They sleeptalked across the quad to one another of *Voyagers* 1 and 2, already bound for other planets, and babies generated out of dishes. With their half-awakened minds, in the grey dawn, they saw their quadrangle and their dining hall on Bishopsgate become, in time, the footprint of one of the soaring towers of the City, built of calculus, and topped with a constantly flashing light, to warn off angels.

One Sunday afternoon, when the daylight was so flat and uniform it seemed as if there was no source of light behind the clouds at all, the college's peace was broken by a determined knocking. The duty porter rammed open the wooden window in the lodge's great door, to discover there was nothing there except the top of the head of a girl.

"Washermaid?" he asked.

"No, sir, I am Mary Tree," she said, stepping backwards so she might look the porter in the face. Conscious of her Mark, as usual, she was relieved when the porter managed to find it in his heart not to look at her too strangely.

The porter looked down and saw a fresh-faced maid without much to distinguish her from any other.

Mary swallowed. This was the last time, perhaps, that she would need to announce herself and her odd quest to a stranger. She began: "I have some business with Sir Kellem Digbaine—"

She broke off and tried again, more slowly. "I mean, Sir Kenelm Digby. Is he known to you here?"

"Well," said the porter, with savour that presaged a long and equivocatory discourse. "If you mean the gentleman whose hair is long as an hermit's, who never removes his black mantle, and rarely speaks a word, except to friends, and moreover, demands large quantities of crayfishes for calcification, then perhaps we have an understanding. But as you probably mean only to be meddling with his business of grief, then stay away."

When you have been travelling for many months with one object in mind, and you come near to that object, almost within touching distance, small frustrations can be unduly discouraging. Mary Tree heard that tightening hum inside her head that told her she was close to crying.

Mary had already been forced to mourn her long-cherished idea of Venetia, and given up for ever her private fantasy of becoming her lady's maid. Now her whole quest, her long ordeal, was being disparaged by this St. Peter, this gatekeeper.

"Is he here or not?" she said in a voice that was more high-pitched than she wished it to be.

"If you mean, is he present or absent, I can tell you that he's not quite neither, since he's so distracted by his loss, he's liable not to hear you, or if he hears you, he may not see you, unless you be a crayfish, in which case he would have you calcified as soon as not." The porter looked at her sternly. "There are those who would prosecute him for his loss, and drag him through town for a business about which they know nothing, and if you've been put up to this by the Lord Chamberlain, and wish to get a false confession out of him, again I say, stay away."

Mary Tree summoned the last of her strength. She knew she presented a poor spectacle of a girl: weary, with clothes grown shabby from journeying. She was stained across her face, and she could not read or write, but although she had no family, she was friends with all the world. She said with dignity: "I find your words an insult, sir. I'm here because he is the Keeper of the Powder of Sympathy, which is the only remedy to heal my kinsman, Richard Pickett."

The porter's hatch rammed closed in her face, and she thought her pride had ruined her whole enterprise, until the visitors' door within the door clicked open, and the porter showed her in.

> "To avoid envy and scandal . . . he [Digby] retired into Gresham-colledge, where he diverted himself with his Chymistry and the Professors' good conversation. He wore there a long mourning cloak, a high-crowned hat, his head unshorn . . . as signs of sorrow for his beloved wife."
>
> *John Aubrey's Brief Lives,* 1669–96

Mary Tree sat on a step within the quiet embrace of Gresham College, clasping the bound and blackened shard of glass.

The college struck her as somewhere between an almshouse for the insane, and one of the old friaries. A man brushed past her, engrossed in a book that he held up to his face, reading as he walked, pigeon-toed, across the quadrangle. She held the cruel shard to her chest and considered its pathetic bandage, grown brown with dirt. This was the last of her many waits, and it was not a long wait, although it had a semblance of eternity as the light began to be lost from the quadrangle.

Sir Kenelm came moving quickly across the flagstones, his black garments clinging to his body, now so much leaner that he seemed taller. He was carrying the Powder in one hand, and a basin slopping with water.

He barely looked at the girl, but he registered that her eyes were sincere.

"We shall perform the ceremony on the grass here, so that the healing Atomes may be carried through the air to your—your father, is it? What is his name?"

"He is my kinsman—but only by marriage," said Mary, before clasping her mouth as people do when they wish to take their words back. "I mean, he is as much my father as any man in this world. His name is Richard Pickett."

Sir Kenelm paused. He stopped his hand.

"Oh, my dear," he said. "I have received word of him last month. I knew of him a little for his learning of the Caesars. I had a letter which told me of your journey, and—would you like to see the letter?"

Mary Tree nodded first, and then shook her head.

"I cannot read, so you best tell me."

Sir Kenelm sat down with her quietly on the cloister wall. He noticed that she must once have had a mulberry stain upon her cheek, which was now as faint as the moon in the afternoon sky.

"The letter that came, from Devon, I think, from one calling themself a neighbour of the household, makes me think we shall never send forth enough healing Atomes to help him now, for his mechanical physiognomy is beyond our reach."

"Has he gone to France?" said Mary keenly, rising up.

"No," said Kenelm. "No, it is further than that he has gone. The letter bid me tell you that he would never rise again, being sick of his wound unto death."

Mary Tree considered the grey pall that coloured the sky, and shivered.

"He made a good end of it, passing quickly with a hot distemper upon his heart," said Kenelm, who had been moved by the letter.

Mary Tree seemed to be muttering to herself.

"I should have been faster on my journey," she said, more to herself than Kenelm; then, "I have let him down."

Sir Kenelm did not appear to have heard her, or if he had, he did not seem to know what to say. Mourning had clogged that quick facility he always had for talking. But with an effort of will it began to return.

"If the wound was so penetrating as it sounds to have been, the Cure would not have helped him," he said. "It treats infection following on from wounds, not the injuries themselves. So your journey might have taken, oh, months, and he would have been no more saved."

She wiped away a snot-smear.

"Does the letter speak of a dog called Asparagus?" asked Mary.

"I think no, but I will have another look betimes. We shall find you a place here tonight so you can rest a-while and take some sustenance," said Kenelm. "There are many rooms here in this college, wherein all my world is now. It is a Sympatheticall place. There are sizars and servants here, though there are not many who are as yourself, which is to say, women—but you will find that Goodwife Faldo who runs the household will look after you."

He saw that this cheered Mary Tree, and he smiled at her with his new, uncanny, counterfeit smile, and whispered, less to her than to the cold and darkling night itself: "I have many pertinent designs for the Divine Regeneration of Beings."

The college quad caught and magnified the whisper, so that it reverberated as clearly as if he had spoken the words in the great amphitheatre at Ephesus.

After achieving sleep for a few hours, Kenelm woke and bid good morrow to his wife. He fancied she was as pale as ever, although, in keeping with his new habit, he moved the painting into the daylight with him when he rose out of bed, holding it to the window to check she had not developed overnight a blue pall, nor any other distemper of the grave.

As she was making up Sir Kenelm's fire, Mary Tree made a resolution that when Asparagus was conveyed to London, he would be Sir Kenelm's constant companion. The morning needs of a wolfhound, however base, would be preferable to this daily practice of picture-gazing, which she could not help but consider morbid. In his empty rooms there was precious little else to look on. He would be so much the better when he had that grey-whiskered muzzle to gaze upon every morning.

Kenelm's bookshelves were bare, and in need of dusting. Mary was surprised that so great a scholar as Sir Kenelm possessed no books. She, Mary Tree, loved to hold the three books she owned, and when he found her looking at her small volume of flower remedies, he took it from her, and then returned it to her instantly, as if it burned his hand.

At the sunlit breakfast table of Gresham College's great hall, Sir Kenelm instigated a conversation about the custom of the farmers of Saxony, where families who are struggling to feed themselves through a hard winter first toast their grandparents with Meth or Hydromel, then inter them into coffins laid in the ice, where the old people remain frozen until the arrival of more abundant food in spring, when they are disinterred and revived again with more strong drink. The Professor of Astronomy, who was morose after a long night waiting for clouds to part, thought this sounded like an errant foolery. The Professor of Divinity chewed his bacon collops, and did not speak; but when Kenelm used the word "resurrection," he stopped chewing momentarily, showing a face that was highly discouraging.

None of the other professors would sit by Sir Kenelm, as they had developed a prejudice against him for the pungent smell about the east side of the college, caused by his experiments with crayfish. This was the first reason that they kept their distance. The second reason was the common belief that he had murdered his wife. These two offences combined extremely effectively, even in the mind of the Professor of Logic.

Most mornings, Sir Kenelm sat with Mary Tree, reading aloud from Discorides' book of medicine, while Mary Tree followed another copy with her eyes. Since he had no books now, he had been obliged to borrow both of them from fellow Greshamites. He handled the book he read from carefully, as if it were the first he had ever seen, and he spoke slowly, taking care to see that she had the right place, so that with time she would be able to read for herself, he hoped.

Later, while the morning sun was still golden, Mary Tree went down to the banks of the Fleet where Sir Kenelm sent her looking for nettles, cuckoo-flower or sweet william. "They must be fresh and fair, for my purpose," he told her. "Both buds and flowers withal." She carried with her a basket and wore Sir Kenelm's hawking gloves.

Kenelm sat cross-legged before the fire, meditating upon the meaning of "metempsychosis."

At noon, Mary Tree spent an hour in conversation with Chater when he came to Gresham to get his washing done and collect his stipend. She perceived instantly, by his walk, by the sit of his hat, by the cast of his eyes, that he was a Catholic, though he wore no illicit garments. But she was not afraid to talk to him, nor he to her, it seemed. He was the type who found her Mark more fascinating than repellent, she supposed, and he hung about her as she performed her tasks, looking moody and uninterested but, as she perceived, taking solace from their conversation, which was necessary for his uneasy soul. Although Mary Tree was loath to show too much prurient interest in talking about Venetia . . .

"Ommmm . . ." said Kenelm, meditating. "Pherecydes of Syros taught Pythagoras who taught Plato that souls migrate, by metempsychosis, into other bodies. Orpheus turned into a swan; Thamyrias a nightingale; tame beasts were reborn as wild creatures, and musical birds in the bodies of men . . ."

. . . Chater wished to talk of nothing else: Venetia's illness, how he had tended her, and his fears for her, which were rebuffed by her constant affirmation that she was perfectly well. Mary Tree expected him to talk of how dignified and gentle she was, and how she gave to charity, but none of these topics seemed to move Chater; he did not expound on her sweet nature.

"Oh, to make her wait was foolish, such impatience she had!" he said. "Sometimes she was taken by choleric moods, when she would suffer to have no one with her but her Chater." His lower lip was beginning to quaver with fond remembrance. "In those moods she could put lightning up me just by looking." Tears were welling in the undersills of his eye. "I would jump to serve her, and she would tolerate me only, letting me know of my foolishness with the tilt of an eyebrow."

"She was so unkind?" asked Mary Tree.

"She was so magnificent," said Chater. "Such a one as her leaves this life's little stage empty. She had a mirror placed high in the alcove of her withdrawing salon," he said almost to himself, smiling.

"So she could regard herself secretly?" said Mary Tree, who thought she was beginning to understand Venetia's character.

"Ha! No, not for such seeming shallowness. She was not vain, you understand. She merely had splendour to maintain. No, she fixed the mirror there because she used it to secretly view the cards her friends held, I fancy. Winning was everything to her. To take money from other gamblers—this was her best delight."

Mary pondered this. "Even from her friends?"

"Oh, more from her friends than anyone."

That these words came from a priest made them even more confounding.

"She loved Sir Kenelm?"

"Oh, unto death. She thought he was growing maggot-brained, and she used to say she despaired of him, and she thought no one else would have him, except her. When he went away she declined like a plant without the light. She would rather go hungry than appear before Sir Kenelm without her face painted and her eyes coloured, except when she was in the mood for candour, when they would spend all day at home together in their bedchamber . . . I brought them sweet sack and figs and books. I was their trusted one."

When he spoke of her illness, Chater referred darkly to "the drink incarnadine" or "the ruby wine." He never said that this drink was to blame for her death, and yet he came always to the brink of saying this, and would then go no further, switching instead to the theme of his loyalty to Sir Kenelm, and asking moon-eyed questions about Sir Kenelm's health and vigour, and once even enquiring if the shape of his calf held up, which was a question Mary could not answer.

"Ommmm . . . We must all be reborn, says Plato, because there are a fixed number of souls, and many bodies constantly being born, so each soul must play its part again, and again . . ."

It seemed to Mary Tree, as she banked Sir Kenelm's fire, while he sat muttering in front of it, that no one would have any peace until they had a better understanding of why Venetia had died, but then Mary had to go and put the ashes out by the kitchen garden, and service the water butt, and clean the swilling-house floor, before it was time to turn the maslin bread, and at last, to sit silently at the servants' table. Here, she discerned that the others, in imitation of their professors, held away from her, putting up a discreet barrier of indifference, as if she, too, smelled of crayfishes and slander.

When she made Kenelm's bed, Mary was frightened by a cold hand which she clasped under the pillow. It was so heavy it felt as if it were drawing her down, and made her start, but she quickly realised that it was a bronze made from a cast taken of Venetia's hand, and Mary understood why Kenelm would wish to hold it close to him. She propped it up on the counterpane, but it looked amiss, almost as if it were waving, so she tucked it under his pillow again.

"Ommm . . ." His concentration slipped, and . . . Ping! Celestial spam arrived in the brain of Sir Kenelm.

"Private cord blood storage facility—insure the future health of your loved ones by preserving their precious stem cells."

Sir Kenelm accepted this enticing premise. "Umbilical cord blood and tissue is one of the richest sources of stem cells in the body with even better regenerative potential than bone marrow . . . We use cryopreservatives, which are easy to remove post-thawing. Storage facilities are monitored with twenty-four-hour security. From £2,000 with additional phlebotomy costs."

The Buckinghamshire radio mast was becoming less discriminating in the messages it sent to him. Previously it had blocked requests for money.

"Cord blood can be used for treating: juvenile chronic leukaemia, Diamond-Blackfan anaemia, Neuroblastoma, Sudden Death Syndrome, autoimmune disorders including Omenn's disease . . ."

Too late, too late, sighed Kenelm, and the message disappeared. He could feel himself becoming, for the first time in his life, self-involved, greedy in his thinking, when he should be disinterestedly intellectual. Grief seemed to have taken away all his strength. At least he was doing one pure, unmotivated thing, besides working on his project of palingenesis. He was teaching Mary Tree how to read.

Mistress Elizabeth came to Gresham College to deliver a basket of

Kenelm's bedding and sundries. After the dissolution of the Digby household she was expected to go and live with the boys and Mary Mulsho on the Gayhurst estate, but it emerged, to everyone's surprise, that she had a husband in service with another recusant family in the city, and she was setting up house with him instead.

Mary Tree took the opportunity to question Mistress Elizabeth about Venetia's possessions and the contents of her closet when she died. Elizabeth responded with guarded hostility, thinking this wench wanted a garter, or an under-garment, or a scrap of lace or tiffany for a talking point. And so she kept her counsel, and told Mary Tree nothing.

When Mistress Elizabeth had gone, Mary discovered, at the bottom of the basket, a pair of lady's silver slippers, very finely made, with short heels and marks where chopines or pattens had once been attached. Mary sat a little straighter as she held them, as if they had rebuked her for her impropriety, and yet she also wanted to hold on to them, like treasure, as they gleamed. When Sir Kenelm came in he looked at them absently, and took them into his hands with ceremony, as if to say they were now in his safekeeping, and as Mary crept away, she thought she overheard him saying "in case she has need of them again."

"Palingenesis," said Kenelm, over a spoonful of potage, "from the Greek, *palin*, again, and *genesis*, birth, means the re-birth, revival, resuscitation or regeneration of living persons from their ashes or putrefying matter . . ."

"'Tis more effective to make anew," muttered the Professor of Geometry, "which is why Talus the Iron Groom in Spenser's book is germane to the purpose, being composed of an un-compostable ferrous material, which is to say, in a word—"

The Professor of Divinity broke in: "I thought 'palingenesis' referred more usually to the conjuror's impostorous practice of creating a miniature castle, flower or other such vain fancy out of ashes, for the amusement of a vulgar crowd. In my ignorance I was not aware that it had been practised upon persons living, or dead."

Sir Kenelm did not notice the professor's withering tone of voice. "Aye, there's the rub, sir," he replied enthusiastically. "Not yet, not yet! It is not practised, but it exists in the minds of men already, as a word, an idea, an ideal and a dream, and as we know that truth and fiction are so intimately connected that Galileo calls his astronomy a fiction—"

"Iron," continued Geometry. "Iron will, and no discernment, this is what makes an Iron Groom. He is in truth a weapon that walks about upright, composed of armour and clockwork. Armies of Iron Grooms would spare a nation in the wars . . ."

"Then Spenser's verses brings ideas to birth also," said Kenelm. "Make him, sir. Make the Iron Groom. Bring him to being. For as we dream, so we ought to do."

"Now I consider it, the phoenix rises from the ashes," said the Professor of Divinity. "It is no work of man to bring this about, though. It is heresy to attempt it."

"Try, try, try, and let them try me," said Kenelm. "La."

The others ignored him, being busy looking into their own thoughts and pottingers.

Mary Tree having the duty of cleaning Sir Kenelm's belongings, it was natural that she should find among them various relics of Venetia, including a box containing cosmetic pots and other feminine impedimenta, which she dared to suppose were the contents of Venetia's closet. For the first week she respectfully refused to look inside it, and for the second week she left it in a prominent place in his rooms, hoping Sir Kenelm would do that instead of her. By the third week, she decided to take the matter in hand.

Two gallypots of subliming calomel; a beaker of brandy; a few sticky vials stained red; private correspondence with a midwife; a large quantity of bloody face-bandages, hidden in a wash-bag; dried herbs that Mary Tree could not identify, though they made her sneeze; a wrapper bearing the wax seal of a fat viper, and a few words of commendation from an apothecary; an enamel box containing two milk teeth, thought to be young Kenelm's; and a large quantity of millipedes in a jar, presumably waiting to be used in a beauty preparation.

Mary Tree did not know what to do with this intelligence, only that she must keep it in mind. As she fell asleep she ran over the letters and word-sounds Sir Kenelm was teaching her, and she recited this list over and over, laying the letters out in front of her eyes, which started to crawl before her as she fell asleep, and formed into snakes like the fat viper on the apothecary's seal.

All around her, in their lamplit kingdoms, the Gresham professors followed their callings, the Astronomer using his mariner's astrolabe to navigate stormy seas of cloud, and the Professor of Law poring by candlelight over his edicts and assizes. The Professor Without Portfolio, for his part, gazed for hours into the red glow of his furnace at the ashes of a mound of cow-parsley, willing them to revive.

When the night was at its darkest, and the ashes were cool, he put on his black overmantle and took, after the fashion of a Melancholy Man, solemn perambulations about the gardens of Gresham and beyond, walking in the figure of the circle and the square. He smelled the spirits of the earth, rising up as the ground exhaled its night vapours, and he wondered whether the world still turned or if it was all over now.

Moonlight picked out the veined cheeks of ivy leaves, and the willow tree's hair fell finely as it turned its back to him. Sir Kenelm glided beyond the kitchen gardens, and he saw the stock pond wink at him, and the long white arms of the path rise to beckon him. He lay down on the wet grass and rested his face on the breast of the earth, and talked to the soil.

He did not convene with ghosts, but apparitions of men who had not yet been born. Pre-ghosts, proto-ghosts. Widowers with pink eyes and foreign clothes, heavy spectacles misted with tears. He could not understand their customs, or their style, or rank, but he recognised their suffering.

"Have you found no cure for this, three, four hundred years hence?"

"No cure, no cure," sighed the wind.

"Some ease for the mind," drawled the earth. "Talking, talking."

"Shock therapy," lashed the tree.

"But no ease for the soul," sang the wind.

"Pills to take away the pain. Sleeping draughts for wakeful hours," groaned the willow.

"No cure for loss," spat the wind.

"This is love's price," announced the bell of the church of St. Margaret. Four in the morning.

Sir Kenelm lifted himself upon one elbow, into the pose of Melancholy

Thoughtfulness. A pattern of grass-blades was indented on his cheek and he was numbed by cold, as he desired. He resembled the statuary upon his own tomb. He realised why he felt no fear of the darkness, nor of the spirits he encountered. He had become a ghost himself.

But as the dawn came, when he paced lightly back to his rooms across the quadrangle, his feet left prints upon the wet grass.

A Discourse Concerning the Vegetation of Plants

Spoken by Sir Kenelm Digby, knight, at Gresham College

[Sir Kenelm's words are in the following chapter taken verbatim from a transcript of his lecture made at Gresham College in 1665 to the embryonic Royal Society.]

THE LECTURE HALL at Gresham College was full of contained expectation, like a pot before the boil. This being the occasion of Kenelm's first public address since *the accident,* it was the cause of much interest, some salacious, and a large and varied crowd assembled, each trying to wear a casual face. Alongside the usual Gresham lecture-goers, the earnest autodidacts and shrewd men of business, there were more dubious visitors, newsbook writers, and common tongue-wags, as well as idle moochers come in out of the cold. They sat mixed amongst Sir Kenelm's coterie, his correspondents through the Invisible College, Sir John Scudamore, Samuel Hartlib and Endymion Porter, his hair flowing over his collar, and out of breath, coming in at the last. There was also a distinguished divine, sent to gather intelligence by Archbishop Laud, while at the back of the hall glowered a row of half a dozen Puritans with their high hats on and their arms folded.

Chater could not help staring at Endymion. His countenance was too tight about the eyes and jowls, which had been clipped and pinned. His nose seemed to have been worked over as an afterthought, and it was somewhat raw, as if grated. After feasting his curious eyes too long, Chater pretended to look away. Endymion tapped Chater on the shoulder, while Chater shrank like a guilty sea urchin. In a low voice, Endymion told him to keep his eyes to himself.

"Or else take a closer look at what my surgeon has effected," said Endymion, leaning in towards Chater, his vein-shot eyes bulging as he raised his collar to show off a blood-blister, "to put right the ravages of cannon-shot. I've been taken by pirates in the Channel oft enough on my service for the King, and now I'll not be served with timid prying eyes, so look at me and take your fill, sir." Endymion sat down with heavy satisfaction.

Sir Kenelm came in walking slowly, an antic figure.

> "He [Sir Kenelm] lived like an Anchorite in a long grey coat accompanied by an English masty [mastiff] and his beard down to his middle."
>
> Finch Manuscripts, 1691

While Kenelm arranged his papers, his dog Asparagus settled under his chair. Kenelm surveyed the crowd. So many shunned him now. There was no Davenant, no Killigrew, no Cavendish, no Thomas Howard, no, not even James Howell, even though his life was once saved by practice of the Cure of Sympathy.

Kenelm started with a few droll asides, about the longness of the lecture and the shortness of life, to put everyone at their ease. He was thinner, and his hair was scarce, but he still had an easy and natural manner of speaking, a warmth that was almost entirely unforced. He enjoyed his own presence and his voice; he was made for broadcasting.

He started off with simple figures:

"Seeds growing are not a perpetual miracle, though you could be excused for thinking so . . ." He delivered to the audience a reassuring smile.

"An ackhorne grows to a spread, vast oak. A single bean to a tall green tender plant . . . And after, death, which is an essential dissolution of the whole compound, must follow: the perfect calm of death."

The lecture hall's attention tightened like an archer's bowstring.

"Trees look dead during drought, till some rain do fall to cure them

of their sickness," he said. *"And then vegetables take a new green habit. Now, my spagyrick art tells me it is nothing else but a nitrous salt which is diluted in the water . . ."*

"Spagyrick?" said one would-be inkhorn in the front row to another. "Alchemical," scrawled his friend on his parchment.

"Salt," announced Kenelm, *"is the food of the lungs and the nourishment of the spirit."*

He explained that just as the drought-dead tree revives with nitrous salt, so *"if it were made proportionable to mens bodyes there is no doubt but it would work alike effect on them."*

The direction of this lecture was emerging. Its immortal preoccupation was attracting newcomers, and the back of the hall became crowded with more figures: the shadowy form of Sir Francis Bacon, dead seven years ago of a cold caught in the snow at Highgate while investigating the possibility of freezing bodies for their resurrection. Another figure came shuffling in: Old Parr, the Shropshire farm tenant brought to London by Aletheia and Thomas Howard because he was said to be 152 years of age, and who died shortly after his inspection by William Harvey, who declared that the cause of Old Parr's death was his removal to London. Behind him peeped Mary Shelley, a teenager, 161 years unborn, clasping a notebook.

Sir Kenelm continued quietly, controlling his voice. *"In a villa in Rome Cornelius Drebell made an experiment in which salt revived a plant—I saw the wonderful corporifying of it . . . Quercetanus, the famous physician of Henri IV, did the same with flowers—rose, tulip, clove-gilly flower. On first view, they were nothing but a heap of ashes. As soon as he held some gentle heate under any of them, presently there arose out of the ashes, the Idaea of a flower, and it would shoot up and spread abroad to the due height and just dimensions of such a flower."*

"The Idaea of a flower?" asked the autodidact.

"That is," whispered his neighbour, "the Platonic ideal, or archetype. The flower in the mind of God."

"But whenever you withdraw heate from it, so would this flower sink down, little by little, till at length it would bury itself in its bed of ashes."

Kenelm was talking loudly now, with glittering eyes. The urgency of his grief pulled him forwards, and the audience with him, into Dark Territory, where he groped for Science.

"Athanasius Kircherus at Rome promised he had done it," said Sir Kenelm, *"but no industry of mine could effect it."* The audience wilted with disappointment. "Until . . ." said Kenelm, reviving them with the word. "Until . . ." He shuffled his papers, cleared his throat.

"I calcined a good quantity of nettles—roots, stalks, leaves, flowers. In a word, the whole plant. With fair water I made a lye of these Ashes which I filtered from the insipide Earth. I exposed the Lye in the due season to have the frost congeal it. I performed the whole work in this very house where I have now the honour to discourse to you. I calcined them in the fair and large laboratory that I had erected under the lodgings of the Divinity Reader."

The Divinity Reader, who was sitting in the front row, changed his expression so subtly it was almost impossible to discern the displeasure this had caused. Asparagus watched him with one eye.

"And I exposed the Lye to congeale in the windows of my Library, among my lodgings at the end of your Great Gallery."

Most of the audience assumed his library was richly furnished, but Mary Tree, peeping in at the back of the hall, knew how bare he was at heart.

"And it is most true that when the water was congealed into ice, there appeared to be an abundance of Nettles. No greenness accompanied them. They were white. But otherwise, it is impossible for any painter to delineate a throng of Nettles more exactly. As soon as the water was melted, all these Ideall shapes vanished, but as soon as it was congealed again, they presently appeared afresh. And this game I had severall times with them, and brought Doctor Mayerne to see it, who I remember was as much delighted with it as myself. What reason this phoenomenon?"

"He's cracked!" whispered one tongue-wag to another; the hall murmured with awe and disquietude. Sir Kenelm imagined this meant his audience had grasped the eternal repercussions of his experiment: palingenesis, revivification, transgenic cloning.

"Good experimental practice," muttered an autodidact. "But to what infernal end?"

"The essential substance of a plant is contained in his fixed salt. This will admit no change into another Nature; but will always be full of the qualities and vertues of the Plant it is derived from; but for the want of the volatile Armonicall and Sulphureall parts, it is deprived of colour. If all the essential parts could be preserved . . . I see no reason but at the reunion of them, the entire Plant might appear in its complete perfection. Were this not then a true palingenesis of the Originall Plant? I doubt it would not be so.

"Then we come to Real palingenesis—as what I have done more than once upon cray-fishes . . ." He smiled at the cameras, the live link-up with his laboratory.

"Boyle them two hours in faire water. Keep this decoction, and put the crevisses [crayfishes] into a glasse-limbeck, and distill all the Liquor that will arise from them; which keep by itself. Then calcine the fishes in a reverbatory furnace, and extract their salt with your first decoction, which filter and then evaporate the humidity . . . In a few dayes you shall find little animals moving there, about the bigness of millet seeds. These you must feed with the bloud of an Oxe, till they be as big as pretty large buttons. You may bring them on to what bignesse you please."

The back of the hall had become a Sergeant Pepper's gallery of faces, Sir Walter Raleigh and Helen of Troy, Dr. Dee and Marilyn Monroe and Guido Fawkes, and also your face, and the face of every other reader of this chapter, and the present author, wanting to see everything, but caught behind the crowd of long-dead figures, and busy imagining what was going on instead.

Sir Kenelm was in his stride: *"All this leadeth me to speak something of the Resurrection of Humane bodyes—"*

The puritans at the back of the hall took this as their cue to stand up and shout, each in turn:

"Necromancer!"

"Abominable Popist!"

"This meddles in life and death!"

Zealots of many stripes, Ayatollahs and Popes and pro-life campaigners yelled:

"Do ye not respect the sanctity of the grave?"

"Where lies your dead wife?"

Asparagus barked at them, and Sir Kenelm tried to answer their questions one by one, facing down their protests with the bald strength of a man who has already been to his wits' end and back, but Endymion Porter and Sir John Scudamore set about a scuffle with them, restraining one Puritan man and knocking another's hat off. The Puritans continued shouting all the while, proclaiming that Judgement was nigh. Chater made a discreet and hasty exit on his own. The Gresham College porters soon came and bundled the Puritans out of the hall, and the audience of learned men and cavaliers were left in uproar, arguing over the innocence of the widower, and the insupportable nature of Puritans. Sir Kenelm remained in the midst of them, silenced. The cold draft of dissent blew through the hall; all the spirits in attendance were long departed.

Later that evening Mary Tree tended Kenelm like an invalid, so weakened was he by his lecture. As she took away his cups and plates, and watered the sick sunflower that crisped upon his windowshelf, she decided that until Venetia's death was solved, he would never be able to heal himself, and moreover, until he cleared his name, he would never be easy.

> "Credulity mingled with precise observation in his wide-ranging, receptive mind . . . Some of his research made positive contributions to scientific progress."
>
> *The Oxford Dictionary of National Biography*, 2012

> "Sir Kenelm was the very Pliny of his age for lying."
>
> Henry Stubbes (1605–1678)

In the Viper's Nest

MARY TREE RETURNED many times to walk the apothecaries' district. She knew she must look, to the passer-by in the street, like a disfigured woman drawn to the chirugeons' doorsteps but too poor or shy to ring their bells. In fact, she was making keen observations of all the establishments, eavesdropping and talking to friendly matrons about the use of dried millipedes, and if they were ever known to be poisonous (they were not), if milk teeth were ever used in beauty rituals (not so far as anyone could tell her), and meanwhile, she continued to study the plaques and emblems that the apothecaries displayed, and the correspondence they sent, always looking for the seal of the fat viper.

It was thus that one afternoon she presented herself upon the doorstep of Lancelot Choice.

"Come in, dearie," said Margaret, who was in an excellent mood, having just discussed with Choice the viability of putting down a deposit on a middling-size manor they had been to see in Bishop's Stortford, complete with dovecote, granary and knot-garden. Margaret took the opportunity to squint at Mary Tree's complexion as she came in, while Mary shrank instinctively from her, being unduly sensitive to this kind of look, which she had known all her life.

The Choices had become well-versed in not suggesting to their clients what might be the matter, be it ever so obvious, and both of them simply looked at Mary Tree, waiting for her to speak first.

"May I purchase one vial of your favourite red drink?" she said.

"Well," said Choice, putting his feet up and using his ivory letter-opener to emancipate a piece of correspondence, talking all the while, "you must understand, miss, that the efficacy of the Wine is achieved by regular daily consumption. A single draft would be wasted—as good as poured away by moonlight. Moreover, it might prove altogether injurious to a young lady such as yourself, if taken in isolation and without due consultation, analysis of your condition, your blood, water, parentage, and so forth."

"Very well," she said, having decided to submit to whatever games Choice played.

"So let me look at you in the light."

When she was by the window, Choice studied her and sucked his teeth. "This will be no easy work," he said, and crossed to his desk to fetch the visitors' book. Mary reproached herself for coming, Marked as she was, to such a merchant of Beauty. Of course he would find her unfit to practise upon. "I require your name, and your coin, and then the consultation can begin."

"Excuse me, sir, for what is probably my foolishness, but I think I can see a sheriff on the steps outside the house—would you reassure me that we are not about to be interrupted?"

Choice came to the window quickly and went down to check, and, left alone with the book, Mary flipped through its pages as quickly as she could, scanning the clients' names, but she could not find the name she sought, or even the initials, and she began to realise that the patients were listed under pseudonyms. She thought she heard his tread on the stairs, and her hand trembled as she turned the densely covered pages again, which grew more crowded week by week.

"Anastasia" she saw, repeated. Then simply "Anastas." It was enough.

When Choice returned she was signing her own name, unsteadily. She laid out the coin he wanted, which she had earned through her work at Gresham. She did not begrudge it, as she knew she had what she needed. Venetia Anastasia Stanley—what student of glamour, what attentive lady's maid, could fail to recognise that rank, outlandish middle name?

He reassured her with no more than a batsqueak of irritation that there were no sheriffs waiting outside, and proceeded to give her a lecture on the fit and proper use of the Wine for curing plainness, dispelling fits of anxiety, and begetting marriage.

The Feast of the Immaculate Conception of the Virgin

8 December 1635

THE BRIGHT NEW bell of the Queen's Catholic chapel at Somerset House was calling the faithful to attend its inaugural service, a much-reviled mass. Incense seeped from the chapel's every aperture, its bell-tower, its doors, its tiny leaded windows, and the gust of it carried over the walls of Somerset House and into the nostrils of the godly. Ranks of Puritans stood on the Strand holding hands, that they might peacefully protest; to circumvent them, guests came up from the river.

The tall doors of the chapel gave onto a bright, incense-filled interior, pristine white, with a starry ceiling painted Ultramarine; candelabra on the high altar illuminated the Rubens altarpiece that made the Queen faint at its unwrapping. Most marvellous of all, around the altarpiece was built a new "apparato," a holy game that represented a great carved throng of painted angels and arch-angels, seraphim and cherubim—more than two hundred in number—who flew upwards and opened their mouths and wings in staggered unison, like a flock of heavenly gulls. The workings behind it were whispered to be several cranks operated by Inigo Jones's unseen hand.

Olivia Porter, following directly behind the Queen, was one of the stars of the ceremony, having just converted to Rome, under the guidance of Father George Conn. Chater himself had effected the initial introductions, and he was in very good odour for it. The Vatican ambassador sent word to Rome claiming—as he had claimed many times before—that the Counter-Reformation in England was finally stirring. Dame Porter was, he wrote, a prominent person, of Protestant English stock, and mother of six children, whom she swore to raise in the Old Faith.

Olivia was no longer wearing mourning colours for Venetia, although she thought of her as she genuflected upon the black and white flagstones. She missed her as a friend and accomplice, and the Wine she missed too, now Chater forbade her to drink it. With dry lips, she said a prayer for Venetia, who had seen the altar-stone laid, but had not lived to see this glorious chapel rise.

Olive was converted, yet she was not changed. Her heart was still open to the pale-faced apothecary who had sent her so many vials of his rubious best blood. She thought of him with secret fondness, which she guarded from Chater particularly.

Chater's first act of power over her, almost as an exercise of his will, was to put her through the suffering and purgation of giving up the Wine. He swore the pain of this was necessary for her redemption. Olive was always attracted by a new regime, and liked to submit herself to any discipline that promised to change her whole existence, be it prayer or Physick. And so she swapped the Wine for another master: Chater, whose ministrations kept her busy from morning Exercises to evening Devotions. Chater's cool hand was always ready to lay upon her brow, and during her weak and degraded moments, as the Wine left her body, she felt he truly loved her.

And yet she knew, even as he humoured her daily indecisions, and helped her choose colours that suited her, that she could never be what Venetia was to him; that she did not have her strength, nor will, nor elegance, nor other qualities besides, which Olive could not even name, being so lacking.

One morning, when Chater came to take her confession, he arrived with the triumphant news that the apothecary Lancelot Choice was implicated in Venetia's death and that the magistrate was soon to be involved. Olive merely pouted and crossed herself in gratitude for her own salvation.

But in the evening, when the children were abed, she slipped away to Fenchurch Street, alone in her private coach, masked and furtive. She would not risk a letter to Choice, but she wanted to warn him, so he might escape imprisonment. It would be better for him to flee to France than for all his clients to be named, and the cause of her ethereal beauty exposed. Besides, there were her love letters to Choice. These must be reclaimed before they fell into the hands of the magistrate. She should never have stopped signing "Proserpina," but her fond heart had led her to be frank.

With her nerves flaming she stood beneath his emblem, the sign of the star. The shop was shuttered for the night and the house was quiet as she waited on the doorstep. She wondered if this meant the household was already packed up, and the Choices fled, and she was about to leave, half disappointed, half relieved that she could slip away, her conscience discharged. But then Margaret Choice answered the door, shockingly dishevelled with her long grey hair, usually tucked away so neatly, swinging about her shoulders, and a mob cap on the back of her head. She was out of breath, and greeted her as Mistress Venetia, before correcting herself. Olive could see she was in a state of high alarm. Except for some braggarts shouting on Cheapside, the street was still. An owl hooted drunkenly from the churchyard of St. Mary Axe.

Olive's ears were not attuned to the night, or else she might have heard a soft slithering of bodies, tipped out of the Choices' back door into the communal servants' yard, or over the side wall into the neighbours' garden, or into the mouldy back alley. But for each viper that darted into the cool dark rat-scented night, there remained a Medusa's head of vipers in the pits, guilty and convoluted.

Seeing Margaret Choice's disarray, Olive was about to excuse herself and leave, but Margaret seemed to think she should stay, and showed her into the downstairs parlour. As she waited she heard bumps and scrapings of furniture upstairs, and voices raised. Then Choice came to her, and in a scene straight out of her fond imaginings, he went down on bended knee before her, ardently kissing her hand, and resting his head in her lap.

By the candlelight, she stroked his lustrous dark hair, which smelled of woody pomander, and wondered if this was truly a new beginning. When he raised his head he studied her with such affection, that she almost felt he was not looking at the creases on her neck at all, but contemplating her as a finished piece of art, one of his own finest creations. She shut her eyes, expecting him to kiss her, only he did not.

"I know; I know," he said. "We are to leave or be apprehended. It is over. The death of Lady Digby is to be put upon us, unwarranted as this is. We are packing away our properties. But you came; you came to warn us. You are indeed the noblest She alive."

He played a little with the lace on her cuffs, looking fondly at them.

"Would you be the kindest, sweetest dame that ever lived, and take for us two trunks of possessions? Your coach would be the perfect vehicle. Only our best plate and some of my new clothes, and books of mine. I doubt their safeness on the Continent, and you are the most trusted friend I have. The letters you speak of are safely stowed within the trunks; these are yours now. The other contents, I will come to claim from you in a matter of months. And until then, you shall keep for me also this, my heart's kiss"—he put his slightly wet lips upon her palm—"in your safe keeping."

With this he closed up her hand, and the way he spoke was so purposive, so full of warmth and carnal intent, that Olive felt as shocked with herself as if she had already committed adultery. The moment was broken only by an odious scratching sound upstairs, as if someone were trying to take up a floorboard. Olive could have lingered there all night, but the trunks were packed, and waiting in the ante-room, and Choice and Margaret hoist them onto Olive's coach themselves. Margaret disappeared quickly upstairs, while Choice urgently embraced Olive, running his thumb over her cheek as he had done at their first appointment, bringing Olive close to delirium. He was about to kiss her, when a sound from the street seemed to startle him, and he saw her out with all haste, slamming the door behind her.

Choice was arrested at his premises that night. He was detained on grounds that he had not paid his tax computations, pending a claim against him by the Crown for the improper practice of his trade. He was a lapsed member of the College of Physicians, and thus he retained no protection from their offices, and indeed, they pledged to assist with his prosecution.

Choice's confinement meant the freedom of others, namely the women who depended on his Wine. They woke up to its absence, and noticed daily with a deeper pang that it came no more, like the letters of a failing love affair. Next, they began to suffer cramps and deliriums. When they visited his shop, sweating, their nostrils wide as horses', some joined the creditors arguing over the flame drapes, hoarsely demanding their Wine. Other ladies sat in the street crying, while still others, who had not been so badly bitten by the Wine, crept away when they saw the over-sized gilt star from above the door, Choice's proud emblem, which once blazed so high, resting upended in the street-mud.

Without the Wine, Lettice was oppressed with agonies of self-doubt and shyness and would not show her face in public for several weeks, until she began to see that without her potion she was still a countess. Sackville, noticing that his bride had lost her easy chatter, was forsaken, and learned to tolerate her quietness, until her spirits picked up and her old garrulousness returned, and even increased, and because of her new position, people were more inclined to listen to her, and to take her opinions seriously. And so she grew in confidence until her conversation was widely said to be her greatest attribute, though some secretly called her windbag.

Aletheia was vexed and fractious when her darling Wine no longer arrived, until she heard the suggestion that Venetia had died from taking Choice's decoction. She had always assumed Venetia's supplier was Sir Kenelm, and the shock of Choice's arraignment put her off all her complexion-enhancement, even her cheek-stuffers and chest lotions, and she threw away her metheglins and tonics, and took on a new project: the colonisation of Madagascar. The isle was hazardously remote at present, to be sure, but in a few years, once trade routes were established, it would prove a gentle pleasure garden. Its groves were chattering with tame monkeys, stripy-tailed and shiny-eyed, and the tree-leaves grew as big as serving platters, and cloves were as plentiful as corn. Aletheia instructed her lawyer to swiftly acquire the deeds to the island on her behalf.

Her husband went along with her plan, as he felt there was no hope for England, where the King was not honouring his debts, and Parliament was addled, and the Puritans growing ever more incautious. Aletheia was delighted that, for once, the Earl had seen sense, and they began the enterprise with a joint purpose that united them for the first time in years. They were painted by Van Dyck in ceremonial dress, with a globe in front of them, Aletheia holding compasses trained on the Kingdom of Madagascar.

The Madagascar Portrait of the Earl and Countess of Arundel, by Anthony Van Dyck, circa 1639

Dorothy Habington liked this development very ill, and took to her bed, and talked of jumping in the Thames. Aletheia, storming into her room when it was finally unlocked, cast her casements open, and briskly bid her throw herself out and snap her neck—*rompi l'osso del collo*—or make herself useful. Dorothy rose from her torpor and rallied further when Aletheia promised to make her Viscountess of Madagascar, and so the three of them planned their cultivation of the island, with zestful maps and drawings.

Penelope became drawn into the business against the King, as her husband was one of the star chamber who resisted him. Her plainness and her lack of pride came to be a badge of calling, which defined her—such was the deformation that politics, in that unstable time, practised upon character.

News of Lancelot Choice's arrest was on every tongue, published in ballads (where his name half-rhymed usefully with "vice") as well as handbills, corantoes and letters between friends carried by little Mercury boys, running. It spilled into every empty ear, and soon the tired and unkind story of the supposed guilt of Kenelm was exchanged for this new, spicy tale of corrupted commerce. Songs were made up about Choice's trial, and prayers for him to be brought to justice were said in church. The story of the lethal apothecary carried on the flow of opinion and washed down the runnels of the communal mind.

The visionary Lady Eleanor Davies, whom Venetia once watched declaiming in the Bourse, was seized by one of her vatic inspirations when rising from a too-hot bath and composed oracular verses, which she urgently declaimed to her publisher that night, waking him for the purpose:

"Pathmos Isle
Hieroglyphick Demonstrations
Paganism rites celebrated.
That fiction, ravished Europa
True as the rape in maps and tapestries ordinary.
Brace of spaniels, Her Grace's swimming match—"

"Er, what does it signify, my lady?" interrupted her publisher. "It's just that I'd rather not be put in Chancery for my pains, so no libel, I beg you."

"Its meaning? I have no inkling of its meaning. It comes to me. I am the channel only. The meaning is occluded, even to the author. But the significance is plain to all." She resumed:

"A Knight Errand, no small Bull,
Because the good spirit moved upon the water
With his Venetian, with her Cup of Viper Wine, that never Awakened,
Whether drunk or no, etc. The Flood's days not equivalent."

From the PROPHETIC WRITINGS of
Lady Eleanor Davies, 1635

The printer nodded. This was good. The benefit of Eleanor Davies' prophecies was they were too vague to constitute libel. And anything about Lady Digby was selling, these days.

The magistrate's men arrived in the third watch of the night to find Lancelot and Margaret Choice still packing their many belongings, sewing gold into their hems and cramming silver and plate behind the wattle and daub.

Once they were apprehended, a search of their premises revealed a vast quantity of vials, expensive medical compounds—none adulterated, according to the assayer—as well as a great deal of esoteric equipment thought to be used for the preparation of Viper Wine. A harsh smell led the magistrates to a large quantity of decocted horses' stale, presumed to be pregnant mare's urine. But those live, mute and unwilling chorus players in this drama were nowhere to be found. The sheriffs searched Choice's premises with caution, expecting to find a horde of black flickering tongues and seamlessly uncurling bodies under any counter, or in any wash basket, a tangle of tender grey undersides and gold-green backs wriggling.

The premises were turned over from top to bottom, and suspicion fell upon the cellar with its unusual furnace, and its reptilian stink, although there were no twisting scaly bodies to be found there, not even one dead worm behind an old flagon.

Olive, full of blissful, forbidden emotions, shuddering every time her coach bumped and smelling the scent of Choice's pomander on her hands, did not think to peep inside Choice's baggage until she had repaired to her bedroom and the trunks been sent up after her. She looked at them for a while, wondering what male delicacies, what hose, combs and nightshirts might be inside. She did not consider herself the type to pick a lock, but she wanted to touch his things before bed, and she first tried her hairpin, then her letter-knife, and then the heel of her chopine. And so like a too-tempted heroine, she cracked the lock, and, raising the sturdy lid, she also raised the household with her screams.

Noctambulations in the Form of the Quincunx

AROUND MIDNIGHT KENELM woke, gasping, and began his nightly walk through the college gardens, pacing the back meadow back and forth, up and down, in the shape of the quincunx. The mystical sign of five: the arrangement of five dots on a playing card, the formation of the trees planted in the garden of Cyrus: the quincunciall lozenge. He walked slowly between each of its essential points, a solemn revenant, summoning her up.

When he had read, in the ink of a common handbill, that Choice was to be prosecuted for supplying Venetia with deadly Viper Wine, he fell into a long and profound sleep, which lasted the entire day. Now midnight was become his noon, and he walked abroad while everyone else slept.

The trees around him swayed, wind-tossed, and he heard each rustling leaf speaking for a different woman: one purged to death by a quack; another poisoned by pain-relief for botched surgery; a third killed by complications following liposuction.

He called to Venetia gently, across the stock pond of Gresham College. He saw her ripple in reply, moving towards him over the pond's milk-white surface. He wished to tell her only that he was sorry. He should have known she would find an apothecary to do her bidding after he denied her. She was ever blessed with a will. He thought he heard her laughing in the bulrushes around the stock pond. Then she was in the air above him, free as breath. It was fitting that he could not see her now, as he had failed to see her, though he looked at her every day, though he lay beside her, though they were as hand in glove. He had studied more closely his papers and his letters, his Chymical preparations; he had taken more interest in his work than his wife. But she should have been his Great Work.

Geese woken by a fox clattered across the marshes, honking: "Real-life shocker: I had a nose job and my husband didn't even notice."

He did not feel she had betrayed him with her secrecy. He understood that she had taken the Wine as an undertaking of pride, in privacy. She was trying to fill the crack in her nature, the needy flaw that was her secret deformity. He failed: he should have fixed her flaw with love, cherished her so she had no need of Wine. When he was young he thought they were Plato's ideal lovers, that they were the same person, ripped apart at the Fall, and forever searching for one another, till they sealed each other up with congress, in this lifetime and the next. Now he was uncertain. Perhaps men and women could not make one another whole; perhaps love was not sufficient.

He tried to hear her voice over gusting leaves, but the lamenting trees around him spoke like a tragic chorus, each leaf telling of another travesty: gums blackened by painting with lead; breasts operated on seventeen times for a non-existent problem; healthy bodies, cut apart by greedy physicians; women misled, traduced, deluded.

Once, Kenelm felt it was his privilege to see how the world was ensouled, to perceive the anima behind every living thing, to see the sparkling atoms in coal dust dancing on the wind. Tonight, it was maddening to hear every leaf's tale of woe.

"I just wanted to fit my wedding dress better," wept the oak.

"I needed to boost my confidence," whined the ash.

"My husband was never meant to know," thrashed the elm.

Each of the leaves was different, rotted to filigree stems, or curled into brittle cadavers. They rustled in drifts under the trees. He had not realised vanity had undone so many.

Seized by inspiration, he tore off the collar of his gown and blindfolded himself, to represent his lack of insight in their marriage: and he held his arms open and trudged towards her, like a blind beggar, staggering in the direction of the stock pond.

"The surgeon received two hours' training . . ."

"It was a surfeit of leeches, applied every hour . . ."

"The implants contained industrial-grade silicone . . ."

He marched towards reunion with her, ready to drown, longing for the cold seal of water over his head.

The horrors of Hieronymus Bosch's hell wiggled before his eyes, and he saw the special circle reserved for silver-tongued apothecaries, so-called surgeons and shysters of the knife and lancet. They were held down on operating tables, their lips injected by frog-headed beasts, or their skin peeled by giant pincer-fingers, or force-fed Wine in great purple draughts until their guts burst.

He marched towards the black oblivion, until he stopped, because of his boys, who ought not to be orphans. Not at their tender years—two little ones the same ages as he and his brother when they were unfathered. He stood alive on the brink of the stock pond, listening to the electricity twitching along the crossrail track, feeling the nearness of death, the roar of the future far below him. He backed away, slowly, from the edge.

> "Understanding and love are the natural operation of a reasonable creature; and this last, being the only thing that is really in his power to bestow, it is the worthiest and noblest that can be given."
>
> *The Private Memoirs of Sir Kenelm Digby,* 1631

Into the Fleet ditch Olive's house-men tipped the scaly bodies, some dead, some dying, rearing up in anguish, floundering. By the light of a lantern they slipped into the coursing water, like a meadesman's eel-catch reversed and running backwards, so the trunk was disgorged of tell-tale snakes. Some floated on the scum, others swam across the surface, propelling themselves in living ogees, moving with instinctive grace, rippling outwards to colonise the night.

Worms turned up all over town in the months that followed, clogging drains and making nests under downstairs beds. They were found in toolboxes and coffins, cellars and sinkholes across London. One bit a woman as she waited at the Cripplegate pump, another killed a baby in Eastcheap.

Soon after, the world turned upside down. The spirit of Mercurius abandoned the isle of Brittanides, which he had formerly loved so well, and left its groves to rot, as brother killed brother, and mothers turned against their sons. Does that sound too poetic? The facts alone, then.

Lady Eleanor Davies took leave of her senses and stormed the private side of Lichfield cathedral, together with two females. She pronounced herself Metropolitan and Primate, and sat in the Bishop's throne, flanked by her holy handmaids. Her next action was to pour tar over the (new) tapestries and altar-hangings.

Sir Kenelm paid a vulgar necromancer, one John Evans, to summon a spirit for him. The conjurer disappeared in a sulphuric cloud, later claiming that he was propelled upwards out of his dwellings in the Minories in east London, carried bodily over London, and landed in a field in Battersea. Whether Sir Kenelm was satisfied by this display is not recorded.

Van Dyck's mistress, Margaret Lemon, mad for him, and jealous of his canvases, bit his thumb to stop him painting. With a splint and bandage, he painted still, although his cavaliers and courtiers were no longer coiffed and elegant, but wearing armour, and worried countenances, and holding instruments of war.

Fugue of Destruction

"It is strange to note how we have slid insensible into the beginnings of a Civil War by one expected accident after another."

Letter from Parliamentarian Bulstrode Whitelocke to his wife, 1642

IT STARTS WITH flecks of torn-up paper, carried on the wind: the demand for Ship Tax, 1637, shredded with the fingertips and blown to all hell.

It builds with the dipping of white handkerchiefs in the blood shed by William Prynne's ears, their tips cut off at Smithfield for his seditious libel against the masques of the Queen and her ladies.

The rose window of the cathedral shatters with the iconoclast's cry, and so it has begun.

A horse is led in to feed from the altar, and the font's naive traceries of Matthew and Mark are hacked away.

Parliamentarian troops, billeted at Gayhurst, carve their names on the masonry.

The Medieval frescoes in Gayhurst chapel are painted over. Adam and Eve, pink and ineptly drawn and vulnerable—whitewashed and gone.

Venetia's family's estate, Tonge Castle, is burned rather than ceded to Parliamentarians.

The Madonna at Snittlefield that Mary Tree once venerated, smashed.

The farmer turned iconoclast, William Dowsing, prays before he wrecks the icons of 150 churches in Suffolk. He works with a hammer, alone.

Six hundred deer are slaughtered wantonly and left to rot in Corse Lawn, Gloucestershire, by men and women desirous of noble blood.

The King and court having removed to Oxford, the royal gardens are picked over by the populace; the Queen's great avenue of Limes is axed for firewood. The monkey Pug's cage is left behind, forgotten, and kicked between townsfolk.

The Great Cross on Cheapside, erected in 1291, dark with soot and soiled by birds, is identified as ungodly and pagan, and destroyed overnight on 2 May 1642 by the Puritan Committee for the Demolition of Monuments of Superstition and Idolatry. Its stones are cracked and flung in the ditch, its icons melted down to be made into bullets.

Those bullets, aimed at the high windows of Westminster Abbey, make starbursts of rubies and sky-flying sapphires. The broken shards are replaced with clear white glass by a Godly glazier.

Penelope Knollys fires a musket in the face of a drummer boy attacking her estate, which she defends for Parliament in her husband's absence for a seven-week siege, until the Royalist troops are called to worthier battles.

Archbishop Laud, aged seventy-five, is condemned to death and executed on a trumped-up bill of attainder.

The maypole on the Strand, and the maypole at St. Andrews, and all other maypole shafts, are lopped down as sinful recreations.

Young Kenelm, now twenty-two, is shot above the heart and killed, riding for the King's men at St. Neots, Huntingdonshire, and his body fished out of the Ouse, river of his childhood games. The skirmish is remembered in dispatches "only for the death of the young and gallant Lord Francis Villiers, brother of the Duke of Buckingham." The whip-sting of this assertion; the pain of it.

Inigo Jones, his beard as grey as Time, is captured by Parliament at the siege of Basing House. His life is spared, but his clothes taken for plunder, his trembling form carried out naked, wrapped in a blanket.

The King's last words, asked hurriedly of his executioner, "Stay for the sign?"

His death, intended to give the country peace, proves no better than putting a stopper on a broken bottle.

The Rubens altarpiece in Henrietta-Maria's chapel, with its pale Christ ascending and the stricken Mary kneeling beside a peacock, is hacked apart by the Irish iconoclast John Clotworthy, who stands on the altar, pricking the painting with his dagger. He asks his men for a halberd and thrusts it through the canvas at Christ's feet, ripping upwards, splitting His holy body, left, and Her suffering face, right, till the painting is in pieces.

Those scraps of canvas, cast into the Thames, carried away on the tide.

Bletchley Park to Outstation Gayhurst

INTO THIS NEW world, Sir Kenelm went wandering.

He was free from the accusation of murder, and from the riddles of guilt that had for so long oppressed him, although by the time he left Gresham College, Kenelm's mind was as clear as hartshorn jelly, and he was weakly in his legs. But Parliament believed he was still a dangerous man, and issued a warrant for his death. He removed himself to Paris, and from his small laboratory in Saint Germain, he practised alchemy to hasten peace. For his pains, the Protectorate was established, and the King's cause defeated.

He returned to London as soon as his pardon was in place. His estates were mortgaged to pay for the Royal cause, and his blond curls reduced to thin dark strands. As he came up the Thames for the first time, he saw swallows dancing across the water, happy, no doubt, to be free from the mud holes where he—and all other observant Naturalists—believed they had wintered, under the river's bank. He had travelled so much further than they.

To Gayhurst he must go, travelling there by public coach, stopping at Bedford to catch a carriage. From Newport Pagnall he walked the final distance home. As in a dream the long drive curved before him, so familiar he could shut his eyes as he walked and see it still. As he came past the trees to the first proper view of the house, he saw that the window of Venetia's former bedroom had been crudely battened over. He peeped through a window on the lower lawn, like a common Tom, and saw by the dozens of greatcoats hung up inside the hall, and the cigarette butts on the grass, and the noise of techno from an upper window, that the enemy still had possession of his house.

The door was locked, and he had no key. His radio mast was missing, his chapel desecrated, his gardens running green and wild.

He came stealthily back from the local tavern under cover of night, and in the silent moonlight on the lawn in front of Gayhurst, he stood where his obelisk once rose, with his arms stretched out, and he felt an alternating current bleeping through him, like a cardiogram.

The signal was still live.

> "During the Second World War a Bombe Outstation to the Government Code and Cypher School at Bletchley Park (Monument HOB 12222785) was based at Gayhurst House."
>
> English Heritage "PastScape," 2013

As Kenelm stood on the lawn he could hear the signal gently syncopating:

. . . *Repeated changes of the electrical pathway from the keyboard to the lampboard implemented a polyalphabetic substitution cypher* . . .

The lovely word torrents passed through his ears.

Codename OSG, codename OSG?

Sir Kenelm could not know, as he stood there, that in 1942 Gayhurst would become Outstation Gayhurst, housing five of Alan Turing's vast Bombes, rotor drums, plugboards, brass plates connected by infinite umbilical curls: the world's first electronic, programmable computers. Instruments of peace.

This is B.P. to O.S.G., do you have Ultra for us?

Rommel's orders were deciphered on the day he sent them, faster than Rupert of the Rhine decoded Cromwell's cyphers, by Bombes at Gayhurst, operated by WREN officers.

Joan and Cynthia; Grace and Marigold. They slept four Wrens to a stable, and dressed in starchy blue. They worked eight-hour shifts, tending the Bombes with cold and diligent fingers, the machinery clacking over, sieving seas of letters on the spot where Kenelm once performed the Great Work.

The messages were decrypted, translated and teleprinted back to Bletchley; memorised by a liaison officer, and then destroyed. The air was thick with thoughts and signals.

Sir Kenelm could not know this. And yet he knew, as he knew that arrow-showers of neutrinos were racing through the blue moonlit lawn, that the Bombes at Gayhurst were whirring things of beauty.

Group Captain Winterbotham calls them Bronze Goddesses.

The divination of the Bronze Goddess thrummed as fast as her handmaids could work.

In the night watch nothing rested, but the air was full of meaning.

At midnight, the expectant pause when the Enigma changed again.

In the silence, Sir Kenelm could hear the Wrens laughing as they sunbathed in the moonlight on the roof of Gayhurst, wondering if the British airmen in the planes passing overhead could see their bodies.

Sir Kenelm was like a string that vibrated with strange frequencies, but now he had no one to tell his dreams to, he let them go. He was like a viol da gamba played in a shut-up house, unheard.

Peace Through War

IN THOSE DARK days of the Commonwealth, a light: Samuel Hartlib had established a new and extensive library. Sir Kenelm was cheered by this—but then he learned that, in keeping with this new era, it was not to be called a "library" but a "public information service" or "Office of Address."

Hartlib was a Polack working for the Protectorate, and yet Kenelm considered him a worthy correspondent. He had written to Sir Kenelm asking for information about the Cure of Sympathy, the weather in Aleppo, the best means to caulk a ship, and the cultivation of crayfish, all in the name of his attempt at Pansophy: the recovery of our happy, original state of complete knowledge and its expression in the pages of an encyclopaedia. Sir Kenelm applauded this project, believing that the dissemination of knowledge was a duty of man, although the idea that all should have access to a library struck him as novel, bold, foolhardy.

> "Hartlib . . . was responsible for patents, spreading information and fostering learning. He circulated designs for calculators, double-writing instruments, seed machines and siege engines . . . His work has been compared to modern internet search engines."
>
> Wikipedia.org/wiki/samuel_hartlib

Kenelm went from Chelsea to the City by public ferryboat, then walked slowly through the rain, into the new kingdom of the Protectorate. The ghost of Asparagus pulled back to ask if this was strictly necessary. Kenelm was not certain when they had arrived, for at the far end of Threadneedle Street a mortar had gone off in the recent fight, and there were no proper buildings, so far as he could discern, only a long, lowly type of barn, with a sign saying "God with Us" in plain, poorly painted letters, and beneath it, smaller, "*Pax quaeritur bello,*" a Cromwellian casuistry at which Kenelm scoffed. It was the motto of the Protectorate, frequently printed on placards and scrolls. Kenelm believed in the divine power of opposites, which should be put to the service of the Great Work. Not to political ends. This was sophistry, to make untruths true, by their repetition. "Peace through war," indeed.

At the doorway men dressed in the plain starched garb of the Commonwealth were coming and going so that Sir Kenelm recognised this must be the Office of Address.

Inside, the walls were bare apart from one or two crude diagrams (one of a monstrous fruit tree, another a bumblebee as large as a kestrel) and a sign declaring that this building was "A Publick Register of Information on Religion, Learning and Ingenuities, and a Centre and Meeting Place of Advices, Proposalls, Treatise and all manner of Intellectual Rarities." There were few books, as far as Sir Kenelm could see, but plenty of boxes, in which papers were stored. There were plain chairs and tables, at which people in drab uniforms were sitting, some reading their papers, some talking. Not only men, but also women.

By talking to a few of them, he discovered that he must address himself to the Great Intelligencer, whom everyone here spoke of as the Paragon of Wisdom.

"He holds every detail you might wish to know, from what time the bells at Powles ring to how to catch a cony," said one.

"But ask wisely, for one question costs six pennies," said another. Kenelm made a joke about the oracle being cheap at the price, but then he remembered, as he now must needs remember frequently, that he was no longer rich.

The country was degraded by war; some quick jack-a-knaves had profited by switching sides, and they now held power—or the illusion of it. The fleur-de-lis wilted on his escutcheon, the green fields between Chelsea and the City were built over, and silk and lace were replaced by rough calico. Cromwell sat to Sir Peter Lely and bid him paint him "warts and all"; the Royal Society rejected alchemy as charlatanism; the innocent heroism of the cavalier was gone, and no one would again say:

I saw Eternity the other night,
Like a great ring of pure and endless light.

A queue had formed in front of a hatch and, out of curiosity, Kenelm joined it. He heard his fellow queuers asking for intelligence on the keeping of pigeons and the milling of spelt. He heard them asking how to find love, how to write in JavaScript code, and how to tie a noose. He could not decide what question he was going to ask of the Great Intelligencer when he got to the hatch. It seemed important he did not waste that special Being's time. He would ask about the cure of wounds, perhaps, or the practice of Divine Gnosis. But when he came to the front of the queue, he recognised the man behind the hatch as none other than Thomas Clack, one-time foreman of his own building work at Charterhouse, now operating in the guise of Great Intelligencer.

Kenelm felt the past open up under him like a great chasm, and wandered out of the building with a sense of wonder.

Epilogue: Mary Tree

I COULD NOT leave you without telling you of the final mystery of my Mark.

Sir Kenelm having noticed my endeavours to find the Cause of Venetia's Ill-health (and so clear his name) said he would do one thing to thank me. On the full moon he bade me lie with my eyes bandaged—which must have looked a strange matter to any witness—while he brushed a medicament across my stained cheek. He used a feather, I think, and a lily-water paste, which he said was often used for the hot gout. As we waited for the paste to dry, he told me that Venetia was ever like a lily to him.

He bid me go to bed, and in the morning when I came in to lay his fire, he was waiting for me with a mirror ready. I was concerned he had painted my cheek with fucus, as a shallow disguise of my Mark, and I knew that my Respect for him would not endure if he had sought to practise that trick upon me. Unwillingly I took the mirror to my face, and to my sight I was almost entirely free from blemish—only a light smattering of pink, where the strawberry botch was once thickly ranged across my whole cheek. I cried out with fear and delight at what he had effected, and I looked at him like he was a Magus, or practitioner of Angelic arts, to have so changed my countenance overnight.

He said he was of a great mind to let me think it was all his Art, but that Reason must trump wild imaginings. He explained I had been born with a strawberry wine mark which was called with good reason a "birthmark" because it had faded a little every year since I was come to my majority, and he had only finished it off with a dab of lily-water. He said he saw with great clarity how constrained I was by my understanding of myself as Marked, that all these years I had been oppressed by an idea, no more.

"We must all look in the mirror sometimes, Mary," he said. "So we can see ourselves directly and say, like Apollo, 'You must change your life.'"

FINIS

LIST OF ILLUSTRATIONS

PAGE

SELECT BIBLIOGRAPHY

PRIMARY SOURCES

Aubrey, John, *Aubrey's Brief Lives*, ed. O. L. Dick, Penguin, 1972

Browne, Thomas, *Religio Medici, Hydriotaphia, and the Letter to a Friend* (Revised Edition), Echo Library, 2007

Digby, Kenelm, Correspondence and papers, BL Add. MS 38175, 41846

Chemical papers, Wellcome Library, Rare Books, MS 2124

Loose Fantasies, ed. V. Gabrieli, 1968

Journal of a Voyage to the Mediterranean, ed. J. Bruce.

Closet of Sir Kenelm Digby, Knt, Open'd, ed. A. McDonell, 1910

Of Bodies and the Immortality of Reasonable Souls, Paris, 1644

A New Digby Letter-Book, "In Praise of Venetia," ed. V. Gabrieli, National Library of Wales Journal vol.9 no.2, 1955-56

A Late Discourse Touching the Cure of Wounds by the Powder of Sympathie, by Sir Kenelm Digby Made in a Solemne Assembly of Nobles and Learned Men at Montpellier, trans. R. White, British Library, Rare Books, 1664

A Discourse Concerning the Vegetation of Plants. Spoken by Sir Kenelm Digby, at Gresham College, on the 23 of January 1660, at a meeting of the Society for promoting philosophical knowledge by experiments, British Library, Rare Books, 1669

Elegies on Venetia Digby's death, British Library, Rare Books, Add. MS 30259

Evelyn, John, The Diary of John Evelyn, ed. W. Bray, JM Dent and Sons, 1973

Gauden, John, *Discourse of Auxiliary Beauty*, or artificial handsomeness, in point of conscience between two ladies, 1656

Jeamson, Thomas, *Artificiall Embellishments*, 1665

Jonson, Ben, *The Complete Poems* ed. G. Parfitt, Penguin Classics, 1988

Lucretius, *The Nature of Things*, translated and with notes by A. E. Stallings, Penguin Classics, 2007

Parkinson, John, *Paradisi in Sole Paradisus Terrestris—A Garden of Pleasant Flowers*, faithfully reprinted from the edition of 1629, Methuen, 1904

Pepys, Samuel, *The Diary of Samuel Pepys*, selected and edited by Robert Latham, Penguin Books, 2003

Porta, John Baptista, *The Ninth Book of Natural Magick: Of Beautifying Women*, 1658, English edition (www.faculty.umb.edu)

Porter, Endymion, *The Life and Letters of Endymion Porter*, ed. D. Townshend, T. F. Unwin, 1897

Rutter, Joseph, *The shepeards holy-day: a pastorall tragi-comaedie acted before both their majesties at White-Hall, by the queene's servants, with an elegie on the death of that most noble lady, the Lady Venetia Digby, 1635*

Wood, Anthony A., *Athenae Oxoniensis*, ed. P. Bliss, repr. 1969

SECONDARY SOURCES

Blake, Robin, *Anthony Van Dyck: A Life, 1599–1641*, Ivan R. Dee, 2000

Bligh, Eric Walter, *Sir Kenelm Digby and his Venetia*, Sampson Low & Co., 1932

Britland, Karen, *Drama at the Courts of Queen Henrietta-Maria*, Cambridge, 2009

Brotton, Jerry, *The Sale of the Late King's Goods—Charles I and His Art Collection*, Macmillan, 2006

Burgess, Anthony, *A Dead Man in Deptford*, Vintage Classics, 1993

Carey, John, *John Donne: Life, Mind and Art*, Faber, 1990

Clifford, JDH, ed. *The Diaries of Anne Clifford*, The History Press, 1993

Coffey, J., and Lim, P. C. H. (eds), *Cambridge Companion to Puritanism*, Cambridge University Press, 2008

Cope, Esther S., *Prophetic Writings of Lady Eleanor Davies*, Oxford University Press, 1995

Didion, Joan, *The Year of Magical Thinking*, Fourth Estate, 2005

Fraser, Antonia, *The Gunpowder Plot—Terror and Faith in 1605*, Phoenix Press, 1996

French, Peter J., *John Dee—The World of an Elizabethan Magus*, Routledge Kegan Paul, 1984

Glassie, John, *A Man of Misconceptions: the life of an eccentric in an age of change* [Athanasius Kircher], Riverhead Books, 2012

Greenblatt, Stephen, *The Swerve—How The Renaissance Began*, The Bodley Head, 2011

Greer, Germaine, *Shakespeare's Wife*, Bloomsbury, 2007

Griffey, Erin, ed. *Henrietta Maria: piety, politics and patronage*, Ashgate, 2008

Harpur, Patrick, *The Philosopher's Secret Fire: A History of the Imagination*, Squeeze Press, 2011

Hill, Christopher, *The World Turned Upside Down: Radical Ideas During the English Revolution*, Penguin, 1972

Horner, J., *The Index of Middle English Prose Handlist 3 of manuscripts containing Middle English prose in the Digby Collection, Bodleian Library*, Oxford, Cambridge: Brewer, 1986

Huxley, Aldous, *The Devils of Loudun*, Vintage Classics, 2005

Jung, Carl, *Psychology and Alchemy*; first published 1952. Princeton University Press, 1988

Karim-Cooper, Farah, *Cosmetics in Shakespearean and Renaissance Drama*, Edinburgh University Press, 2012

Kassell, Lauren, *Medicine and Magic in Elizabethan London: Simon Forman, Astrologer, Alchemist, and Physician*, Clarendon Press, 2005

Leapman, Michael, *Inigo: The Troubled Life of Inigo Jones, Architect of the English Renaissance*, Headline, 2003

McManus, Clare, *Women and Culture at the Courts of the Stuart Queens*, Palgrave Macmillan, 2003

Mendelson, Sara, *The Mental World of Stuart Women*, University of Massachusetts Press, 1988

Millar, Oliver, *The Age of Charles I*, Tate Gallery publications, 1972

Orgel, Stephen, and Strong, Roy, *Inigo Jones and the Theatre of the Stuart Court, including the complete designs of productions at court*, Vols 1 & 2, London and Berkeley, 1973

Peacock, John, *The Look of Van Dyck*, Ashgate, 2006

Petersson, Robert Torsten, *Sir Kenelm Digby, Ornament of England*, Jonathan Cape, 1956

Pignatelli, Princess Luciana, *The Beautiful People's Beauty Book—How to Achieve the Look and Manner of the World's Most Attractive Women*, McCall / Bantam, 1971

Purkiss, Diane, *The English Civil War: A People's History*, Harper Perennial, 2007

Salgado, Gamini, *Cony Catchers and Bawdy Baskets*, Penguin, 1972

Sarasohn, Lisa T., *The Natural Philosophy of Margaret Cavendish: Reason and Fancy during the Scientific Revolution*, University of Chicago Press, 2011

Sherwood-Taylor, F., *The Alchemists: Founders of Modern Chemistry*, Heinemann, 1951

Smith, Barbara, *The Women of Ben Jonson's Poetry: female representations in non-dramatic poetry*, Scolar, 1995

Strong, Roy, *The English Renaissance Garden in England,* Thames and Hudson, 1998

Strong, Roy, *Henry, Prince of Wales and England's Lost Renaissance*, Thames and Hudson, 2000

Stubbs, John, *Reprobates: The Cavaliers of the English Civil War,* Viking, 2011

Sumner, A., ed. *Death, Passion and Politics: Van Dyck's portraits of Venetia Stanley and George Digby*, Dulwich Picture Gallery exhibition catalogue, 1995

Thomas, Keith, *Religion and the Decline of Magic*, Penguin, 2003

Thomas, Roy Digby, *The Gunpowder Plotter's Legacy*, Janus Publishing, 2001

Trevor-Roper, Hugh, *Archbishop Laud* 1573–1645, Macmillan Press, 1988

Walton, Izaak, *Lives of John Donne and George Herbert*, New York Bartleby.com, 2001

Ward, John, *The Lives of the Professors of Gresham College*, 1740, Johnson Reprint Corpn., 1967

Warhol, Andy, *The Philosophy of Andy Warhol*, first published 1975; published by Penguin Books, 2007

Watson, A. G., and Hunt, R. W., *The Bodleian Library Quarto Catalogues, vol. IX*, Oxford: Bodleian Library, 1999

Wedgewood, CV, *Velvet Studies: Cavalier Poetry and Cavalier Politics*, Jonathan Cape, 1946

White, Michael, *Isaac Newton: The Last Sorcerer,* Fourth Estate, 1997

Wolfe, Jessica, *Humanism, Machinery and Renaissance Literature*, Cambridge, 2004

Worsley, Lucy, *Cavalier: The story of a 17th century playboy [William Cavendish]*, Faber, 2008

Wright, Thomas, *Circulation: William Harvey's Revolutionary Idea*, Chatto and Windus, 2012

Yates, Frances A., *Giordano Bruno and the Hermetic Tradition*, Routledge, 1999; *The Art of Memory*, Pimlico, 1992

ACKNOWLEDGMENTS

p. 73 "I saw Eternity the other night"—from the poem by Henry Vaughan

p. 209 "Whenas in silks my Julia goes"—extracts from the poem by Robert Herrick

p. 217–18 Bourse Boy's words taken from Ben Jonson's *Entertainment on the Opening of the New Exchange*, 1609

p. 345–46 Tom Lubbock, writing in the *Independent*, was the first to compare the painting *Venetia, Lady Digby on Her Deathbed* with "Edge" by Sylvia Plath

Heartfelt thanks to:
Zachary Wagman and Sarah Bedingfield at Hogarth; Dan Franklin and Beth Coates at Jonathan Cape; Laura Hassan, Charlie Campbell, and Ed Victor. Dr. Emma Smith of Hertford College, Oxford, Dr. B. C. Barker-Benfield of the Bodleian library, Dr. Andrew Gregory of UCL, David Cameron of the Institute of Physics, Sheila Knox, Sophie Melzack Robins, Carol Savage, Harry Mount, Theo and Flora Rycroft, Gavanndra Hodge, Ian Irvine, Hannah Mackay, Marianne Blamire, David Emmerson and Eddie, Lord Digby. Without my parents, Sir Reginald Eyre and Lady Anne Clements Eyre, and my husband, Dr. Alex Burghart, this book would not have been written. Many thanks to them for aiding, abetting, and inspiring.

Hermione Eyre, London 2014